Honoré de Balzac, Katharine Prescott Wormeley

A Great Man of the Provinces in Paris

Honoré de Balzac, Katharine Prescott Wormeley

A Great Man of the Provinces in Paris

ISBN/EAN: 9783337428709

Printed in Europe, USA, Canada, Australia, Japan

Cover: Foto ©Andreas Hilbeck / pixelio.de

More available books at **www.hansebooks.com**

HONORÉ DE BALZAC

TRANSLATED BY

KATHARINE PRESCOTT WORMELEY

———

A ·GREAT MAN

OF

THE PROVINCES IN PARIS·

ROBERTS BROTHERS

3 SOMERSET STREET

BOSTON

1893

TO

MONSIEUR VICTOR HUGO.

You, monsieur, who, by the privilege of the Raffaelles and the Pitts, were already a great poet at an age when other men are still immature, — you have known, like Chateaubriand and all other true artists, what it is to struggle against Envy ambushed behind the columns of a newspaper, or lurking in the dark places of journalism. Therefore I desire that your victorious name should help to victory the work I now inscribe to it; a work which is, in the minds of some, an act of courage, inasmuch as it is a history of plain truth. Think you that journalists would not have found their place, like physicians, marquises, financiers, and notaries, on Molière's stage? Why then should the "Comedy of Human Life," which *castigat ridendo mores,* spare such a power when the Parisian press itself spares none?

I am happy, monsieur, in being thus enabled to subscribe myself,

Your sincere admirer and friend,

DE BALZAC.

CONTENTS.

CONTENTS.

A GREAT MAN OF THE PROVINCES IN PARIS.

I.

WHEN Lucien Chardon, otherwise de Rubempré, poet and great man in the provinces, left Angoulême to seek his fame and fortune in Paris under the auspices of Madame de Bargeton and in her company, their journey together was not all that might have been expected. Neither he, nor Louise de Bargeton, nor Gentil, her footman, nor Albertine the waiting-maid, ever spoke of the events of that journey, but it can easily be seen how the perpetual presence of servants made it rather an awkward affair for a lover who regarded the matter in the light of an elopement.

Lucien, who had never travelled post in his life, was aghast at seeing nearly the whole sum on which he counted for a year's support scattered along the road between Angoulême and Paris. Like all those who unite the spontaneity of childhood with vigor of intellect, he committed the blunder of expressing his naïve amazement at the novelty of the things he met. A man should have studied a woman thoroughly before he lets

1

her see his emotions or his thoughts as they arise. A mistress who is tender and also noble, smiles at child-like impulsiveness and understands it; but if vanity underlies her affection, she will not forgive a lover for being childish, vain, or petty. Many women are such extravagant worshippers that they insist on making a god of their idol; while others, who love a man for himself before loving him for their own sakes, adore his littleness as much as they do his greatness. Lucien had not yet discovered that Madame de Bargeton's love was grafted on pride; he made the great mistake of not explaining to himself certain smiles which flickered on her lips during this journey when, instead of repress-ing his gambols, he gave way to them like a young rat escaping from his hole.

The travellers stopped before daybreak at the hôtel du Gaillard-Bois, rue de l'Échelle. They were both so fatigued that Louise went to bed immediately, but not until she had ordered Lucien to take a room on the floor above her. Lucien also went to bed and slept till four o'clock in the afternoon, at which hour Madame de Bargeton sent to have him wakened and called to dinner. He dressed himself hurriedly, seeing how late it was, and found Louise in one of those miserable rooms which are the disgrace of Paris, where, in spite of all the great city's pretensions to elegance, there is not a single hotel in which a traveller can have the comforts of a home. Lucien could scarcely recognize his Louise in that cold, sunless room, with its faded curtains, its miserable tiled floor and shabby vulgar furniture, either old or bought at a bargain. It is a fact that some persons never do have the same aspect or the same value when separated from the forms, things, and places which served to frame them. Living personalities have a sort of atmosphere which is needful to them just as the chiaro-scuro of the Dutch interiors is necessary to give life to the figures which the genius of the painters puts into them. Provincials are nearly all thus.

Moreover, Madame de Bargeton seemed to Lucien more dignified, more thoughtful than she ought to be at a moment when their happiness was about to begin without alloy. But he had no chance to complain; for Gentil and Albertine were both in the room serving dinner. The dinner, too, was far from being the abundant, generous meal of the provinces; the dishes, skimped by careful measurement, came from a neighboring restaurant and were ill-served and meanly portioned. Paris is not liberal in the little things of life to which persons of moderate means are condemned. Lucien awaited the end of the dinner to question Louise, in whom he perceived a change that was to him inexplicable. He was not mistaken. A serious event — for reflections are events in the mental life — had happened while he slept.

About two in the afternoon the Baron Sixte du Châtelet had arrived at the hotel, waked up Albertine, urged his desire to see her mistress, and had waited until Madame de Bargeton had time to dress. Louise, whose curiosity was excited by this unexpected arrival in Paris of her former admirer, believing that she had carefully concealed her traces, received him about three o'clock.

" I have followed you at the risk of a reprimand from the administration," he said, " for I foresaw what would

happen. But even if I lose my place, *you* shall not be
lost, — never ! "

"What can you mean?" cried Madame de Bargeton.

"I see too plainly that you love Lucien," he said,
with a tenderly resigned air ; " for a woman must love
a man deeply when she acts without reflection, when
she forgets the proprieties, — you, who know them so
well. Do you seriously think, my own adored Naïs,
that you will be received by your cousin, Madame
d'Espard, who is at the apex of Parisian social life,
or indeed in any salon in Paris, when it comes to be
known that you have fled from Angoulême with a
young man after a duel fought by your husband on his
account? Monsieur de Bargeton's removal to your
father's house at Escarbas has the look of a separation.
In such cases, the husband always begins by fighting
for his wife's honor and leaving her free afterwards.
Love Monsieur Chardon de Rubempré if you choose,
protect him, make what you will of him, but don't live
together. If any one here knew that you had even
travelled to Paris with him in the same carriage, you
would be put in the index expurgatorius of the society
you have come to seek. Besides, Naïs, don't make
such sacrifices to a young man you have never yet compared with others ; whom you have not subjected to any
test ; who may indeed forget you to-morrow for some
Parisian woman whom he thinks more likely than you
to advance his ambitions. I don't wish to do injustice to the man you love, but you must permit me to
consider your interests before his and say to you:
' Study him ! Know the full bearings of what you
do.' If you find the doors of society shut against

you, if the women refuse to receive you, at any rate
have the satisfaction of being sure that the man for
whom you make such sacrifices will always be worthy
of them and comprehend them.   Madame d'Espard is
all the more prudish and severe because she is herself
separated from her husband, — the world does not know
why; but the Navarreins, the Blamont-Chauvrys, the
Lenoncourts, all stand by her, the most straight-laced
women visit her and treat her with the utmost respect;
in short, the Marquis d'Espard is entirely in the wrong.
You will see the truth of what I am telling you the very
first time that you visit her.   I assure you that I, with
my knowledge of Paris, am able to predict that you will
no sooner enter Madame d'Espard's salon than you will
hope she may not find out you are at the hôtel du Gaillard-Bois with the son of an apothecary, — Monsieur de
Rubempré, as he calls himself.   You will have rivals
here who are far more astute and scheming than those
you had in Angoulême; they will not fail to discover
who you are, where you are, whence you came, and what
you are doing.   I see plainly that you have counted on
being to a certain extent *incognita*.   But you are one
of those persons for whom an *incognito* does not exist.
You will meet Angoulême everywhere; for instance, the
deputies from the Charente who come to the opening
of the Chambers, or the general on furlough, who is now
in Paris, — it needs only one person from Angoulême
to divulge that your life has something peculiar about
it; you will then be rated as nothing more than Lucien's
mistress. If you should have any need of me — for any
purpose, no matter what — you will find me at the Receiver-general's, rue du Faubourg-Saint-Honorè, not far

from Madame d'Espard's house. I know the Maréchale
de Carigliano, Madame de Sérizy, and the President of
the Council sufficiently well to present you to them ;
but you will meet so many persons of the highest rank
at Madame d'Espard's that you will, if you take a judicious course now, have no need of me. Far from seeking
an entrance into salons, you will be sought in them.''

Du Châtelet might have talked on longer and Madame de Bargeton would not have interrupted him.
She was struck by the justice of his remarks. The
queen of Angoulême had really been counting on her
incognito.

''You are right, my dear friend,'' she said, '' but
what am I to do?''

'' Allow me to find you a suitable suite of furnished
apartments,'' replied Châtelet. '' The expense will be
less than living at a hotel, and you will virtually be at
home ; if you will take my advice, you will sleep there
to-night.''

'' How did you find out my address?'' she said.

'' Your carriage was easily recognized ; besides, I was
following you. At Sèvres, the postilion who left you
there told your address to my man. Will you allow me
to be your steward? I will write you a line the moment
I have found you suitable lodgings.''

'' Very good,'' she said ; '' do so.''

The words seemed almost nothing, but they meant
all. The Baron du Châtelet had spoken the language
of the world to a woman of the world. He appeared
before her in all the elegance of a Parisian toilet ; a
well-appointed cabriolet had brought him ; after he left
her, Madame de Bargeton walked to the window acci-

dentally, reflecting on her position, and she saw the old dandy drive away. A few moments later, Lucien, abruptly awakened and hastily dressed, presented himself before her eyes in his nankeen trousers, shrunken by a year's washing, and his shabby little frock-coat. He was handsome, truly, but ridiculously dressed. Cover the Apollo Belvedere or the Antinous with the clothes of a porter — would you then perceive the divine creations of Greek and Roman art? The eyes compare before the heart rectifies their hasty mechanical judgment. The contrast between Lucien and du Châtelet was too violent not to strike Madame de Bargeton forcibly.

When dinner was over, about six o'clock that evening, Louise made a sign to Lucien to come and sit beside her on the paltry little sofa covered with yellow-flowered red calico on which she was seated.

" Dear Lucien," she said, " do you not think that if we have committed a folly which will injure us both it would be wise to undo it? We must not, my dear child, live together in Paris, nor let any one suspect we came here in company. Your future depends a great deal on my position, and I must not spoil it at the outset. So, to-night, I am going to move into lodgings not far from here ; you must stay on in this hotel ; we shall see each other every day, and no one can find fault with that."

Louise then expounded the laws of the great world to Lucien, who opened his eyes very wide. Without as yet knowing that women who get over their follies are getting over their love, he did understand that he was no longer the Lucien of Angoulême. Louise now spoke only of herself, her interests, her reputation in society; though, to excuse this selfishness, she tried to make him believe it was all for his sake. He certainly had no rights over Louise, suddenly transformed back into Madame de Bargeton; and he now felt, what was far more serious, that he had no power. He could not restrain the tears from coming into his eyes.

"If I am, as you have so often declared to me, your glory, you are even more than that to me; you are my only hope and all my future," he said. "I believed that if you shared my success you would also share my struggles, and now you are already separating yourself from me!"

"You are judging me," she said; "that proves you no longer love me." Lucien looked at her with so piteous an expression that she could not refrain from adding: "Dear child, I will stay, if you demand it; we shall lose all and be without social support; but, when we are both equally miserable, both rejected by society, when failure (for we ought to foresee all) has driven us to Escarbas, you must remember, my dear love, that I foresaw the result, and prayed you at the start to master the world by obeying its laws."

"Louise," he answered, clasping her, "it frightens me to see you so wise. Remember that I am but a child in the world's ways, and that I have already given myself up to your dear will in everything. For myself, I desired to triumph over men and things by sheer strength; but if I can reach the same result more rapidly by your assistance than alone, I shall be glad indeed to owe you all. Forgive me! I have trusted my all to you; how therefore can I now help fearing? This separation seems

to me the forerunner of desertion ; and desertion would
be death."

" But, dear Lucien, how little is asked of you," she
answered ; " merely to sleep here ! You can be with
me all day, and no one will object to that."

A few caresses calmed him. In an about an hour
Gentil appeared with a note from du Châtelet, in which
he told Madame de Bargeton he had found her a suite
of rooms in the rue Neuve-de-Luxembourg. She inquired the situation of the street ; finding it was not far
from the rue de l'Échelle, she encouraged Lucien by
whispering, " We are neighbors."

Two hours later Madame de Bargeton got into the
carriage du Châtelet sent for her, and went, accompanied by Lucien, to her new home. This apartment,
one of those which upholsterers furnish and lease to
rich deputies or to persons of importance who come to
Paris for a short time, was sumptuous but inconvenient.
Lucien went back to his little hotel at eleven o'clock
having, so far, seen nothing of Paris but the small section of the rue Saint-Honoré which lies between the rue
Neuve-de-Luxembourg and the rue de l'Échelle. He
went to bed in his miserable little room, comparing it
with the magnificent suite Louise was now occupying.

He had no sooner left the house than the Baron du
Châtelet arrived, on his way from the ministry of Foreign Affairs, in all the splendor of full evening dress.
He came to tell Madame de Bargeton of the agreements
he had made in her name. Louise was rather uneasy
on this point ; the luxury of the rooms frightened her.
Provincial customs had in course of time reacted on her
own habits and she had grown very careful of expenses ;

she was in fact so careful that in Paris her ideas would seem stingy. She had brought nearly twenty thousand francs with her in a draft on the Receiver-general, intending to make that sum cover all her surplus expenses for four years. Already she began to fear it might not be enough and that she would have to run in debt. Du Châtelet told her that the apartment would only cost her six hundred francs a month.

"A mere nothing," he said, observing how she started. "You have a carriage at your command for five hundred francs a month; and besides that you will have only your toilet to think of. I assure you that a woman who goes into the great world, as you will, cannot do differently. If you wish to get Monsieur de Barge-ton made a Receiver-general or obtain a place for him in the King's household, you must not live on a poor scale. Here nothing is ever given except to the rich. It is fortunate for you," he went on, "that you have Gentil to go about with you and Albertine to dress you, for Parisian servants are ruinous; and with such an introduction into society as you have, you will seldom eat a meal at home."

Madame de Bargeton and the baron talked of Paris. He told her all the news of the day; the thousand nothings that persons must know under pain of not being Parisian at all. He gave her much advice as to the shops from which she ought to supply herself with what she wanted; Herbault he named for head-dresses, Juliette for bonnets, and he gave her the name of a dressmaker worthy to take the place of Victorine. In short, he made her feel the necessity of dis-Angoulêm-izing herself as soon as possible. Then he departed with a stroke of policy which occurred to him at the last moment.

" To-morrow," he said carelessly, " I shall no doubt have a box at one of the theatres, and I will come for you and Monsieur de Rubempré, for I hope you will permit me to do the honors of Paris to both of you."

"He has more generosity in his nature than I thought," said Madame de Bargeton to herself on finding Lucien included in the invitation.

In the month of June the ministers never know what to do with their boxes at the theatres; the ministerial deputies and their constituents are busy with their vintage or in getting in their hay; the most exacting acquaintances of the ministers are travelling or living in their country-places; consequently at that time of the year the best boxes at the Parisian theatres are filled with an anomalous crowd of persons whom the regular attendants never see again, and who give the auditorium somewhat the appearance of a shabby carpet. Du Châtelet knew that, thanks to this circumstance, he could procure Madame de Bargeton the pleasure all provincials prefer at small expense.

The next day, Lucien, for the first time since he had known Louise, was told she was out when he went to see her. Madame de Bargeton had gone to make certain indispensable purchases, and take counsel with the solemn and illustrious authorities in female dress whom du Châtelet had named to her; for she had written on her arrival to her cousin, the Marquise d'Espard, and wished to be prepared for what might follow. Though Madame de Bargeton had that confidence in herself which comes of long ascendency, she was, nevertheless, singularly afraid of seeming provincial. She had tact enough to know that first impressions count for much in the relations between women; and though she knew she had sufficient capacity to put herself on the level of superior women like Madame d'Espard very soon, she felt the need of friendly goodwill at the start, and saw the necessity of not missing any element to success. She felt therefore infinitely obliged to du Châtelet for having shown her the means of preparing to enter the great world on equal terms.

It so chanced that the Marquise d'Espard was in a position which made her extremely well pleased to be able to do a service to a member of her husband's family. Without apparent cause, the Marquis d'Espard had retired from the world; he paid no attention to his own affairs, nor to political matters, nor to his family, nor to his wife. Left mistress of herself, the marquise felt the necessity of being supported by the world. She was very glad therefore of an opportunity to take her husband's place in this instance and make herself the protectress of his family. She determined to put some ostentation into her patronage in order to make her husband's neglect the more obvious. No sooner, therefore, did she receive the note Louise addressed to her than she wrote to " Madame de Bargeton, née Nègrepelisse," one of those charming missives the style of which is so fascinating that it takes some time to perceive their want of depth.

" She was delighted," she said, " that circumstances should bring into her family a person of whom she had so often heard and with whom she ardently desired to become acquainted; Parisian friendships were not so exclusive as to prevent her from wishing to love others ; and if that wish were not fulfilled in this instance, it would be only one more illusion to bury with the rest. She placed herself wholly at the disposal of her cousin, and would have gone to see her at once were it not for a slight indisposition which kept her at home ; but she desired to express how much obliged she was that her cousin had thought of her."

During Lucien's first rambling walk along the boulevards and through the rue de la Paix, he was, like all new-comers, far more interested by things than by persons. The first things that strike a mind new to Paris are the great masses, the luxury of the shops, the height of the houses, the multitude of carriages, the violent contradiction between extreme luxury and extreme poverty. Amazed at a crowd of which he had never seen the like, this creature of imagination was conscious of a sense of his own extreme diminution. Persons who receive consideration of any kind in the provinces and meet at every step some proof of their importance, cannot easily accustom themselves to this total and sudden loss of value. To be something in one's own neighborhood and nothing in Paris, are two states of being which need a transition period ; and those who pass too abruptly from one to the other fall into a species of humiliated depression. To a young poet who wanted an echo to all his sentiments, a confident for all his ideas, a soul to share his every emotion, Paris was likely to be a desert.

Lucien, who had sent his humble wardrobe by carrier rather than exhibit to Madame de Bargeton the poverty of his baggage, had not yet fetched the box, marked

" to be called for," which contained his best blue coat;
so that he felt embarrassed by the meanness, not to
say dilapidation, of his clothes when he called to see
Madame de Bargeton at the hour he had been told
she would return; he found with her the Baron du
Châtelet, who carried them both to dine with him at
the Rocher de Cancale. Lucien, bewildered by the
whirl of Paris, could say nothing to his mistress, for
they were all three in the carriage, but he pressed her
hand, and she replied in an amicable manner to the
thoughts he thus expressed.

After dinner du Châtelet took his guests to the
Vaudeville. Lucien felt much secret discontent at
du Châtelet's aspect, and privately cursed the accident
which brought him to Paris at that particular time.
The baron had put his journey to the score of his
ambition; he hoped, he said, to be appointed secretary-general of one of the ministries, and to enter the
Council of State as master of petitions; and he had
come to Paris to remind the government of the promises
made to him, — a man of his pretensions could not remain a director of taxes; he would rather be nothing,
or become a deputy, or return to diplomacy. So saying
he swelled and magnified himself; and Lucien, vaguely
recognizing in the old dandy the superiority of the man
of the world who knows Parisian life, felt especially
mortified in owing him a pleasure. Just where the
young man and poet felt particularly uneasy and embarrassed the man of social life was like a fish in its
element. Du Châtelet smiled at the hesitations, amaze-
ments, questions, all the little mistakes into which want
of knowledge cast his rival, like the old sea-dogs who

laugh at greenhorns before they get what are called
their sea-legs. However, the pleasure Lucien took in
his first glimpse of the sights of Paris compensated for
the annoyance his blunders caused him.

This evening was remarkable for Lucien's secret
repudiation of many of his ideas about provincial life.
The circle of his opinions widened, society took other
proportions. The proximity of several pretty Parisian
women, elegantly dressed with a certain crisp freshness,
led him to notice the old-fashioned look of Madame
de Bargeton's gown, though it was rather pretentious ;
neither the material, nor the cut, nor the color was in
the style of the day. The fashion of her hair, which
had lately so fascinated him in Angoulême, now seemed
to him in shocking taste compared with the charming
arrangement of the heads about him. " Will she always
look like this?" thought he, not knowing that her day
had been spent in preparing for a transformation.

In the provinces there is neither choice nor comparison to be made ; faces that are constantly seen acquire
a conventional beauty. A woman who is thought pretty
in the provinces obtains little or no attention when
translated to Paris, for she has only been beautiful by
the application of the proverb, " In the country of the
blind the one-eyed men are kings." Lucien's eyes
made the comparison which Louise had made the
night before between du Châtelet and himself. Moreover, at this very moment Louise was allowing herself
to make further strange reflections about her lover.
Notwithstanding his great beauty, the poor poet had no
style. His coat, the sleeves of which were too short,
his countrified gloves, his frayed waistcoat, made him

absolutely ridiculous beside the young men about them ;
Madame de Bargeton thought his whole air pitiable.
Du Châtelet, paying her unobtrusive attentions, watching over her with a silent care that betrayed a deep
sentiment, — du Châtelet, elegant and as much at his
ease as an actor who returns to the boards of his own
theatre, now regained in two days all the ground he
had lost in her mind in the last six months. Though
commonplace persons will not admit that feelings can
change abruptly, nothing is more certain than that two
lovers do diverge from each other far more quickly than
they come together. A disillusion was beginning for
Louise and Lucien about each other, the cause of which
was Paris itself. Life was suddenly magnified to the
poet's eyes, just as society took a new aspect in those
of Louise. For the one, as well as for the other,
nothing was needed but some chance accident to snap
the ties that united them. The occasion was not long
in coming. Meantime, on the evening in question
Madame de Bargeton dropped the poet at his hotel and
returned to her own rooms accompanied by du Châtelet ;
a most unpleasant circumstance to the poor lover.

" What will they say about me ? " he was thinking as
he went up the stairs to his dismal chamber.

" That poor lad is certainly extremely dull," said
du Châtelet, smiling, as soon as the carriage door was
closed.

" It is always so with those who have a world of
thought in their heart and brain," said Madame de
Bargeton. " Men who have many things to express in
noble works long meditated despise conversation, — an
employment in which the intellect cheapens itself into

small change," added the proud Nègrepelisse, who still found courage to defend Lucien, — less however for Lucien's sake than for her own.

" I grant you that," said the baron, " but we live with persons, and not with books. My dear Naïs, I see that there is nothing really between you and Lucien as yet, and I am delighted. If you decide to put into your life an interest which you have never had so far, I do entreat you let it not be for a sham man of genius. Suppose you were mistaken! suppose that after a time, when you came to compare him with real talent, with the remarkable men whom you are about to meet, suppose you should then discover, dear, beautiful siren, that you had taken upon your dazzling shoulders and borne to port, not a man with a lyre, but a little rhyme-ster, without manners, without scope, silly, presuming, one who may have intellect enough for l'Houmeau, but shows a very ordinary capacity in Paris! After all, volumes of verse quite as good as Monsieur Chardon's poetry are published weekly in Paris. I implore you to pause, consider, compare. To-morrow, Friday, is an opera night," he added as the carriage turned into the rue Neuve-de-Luxembourg. " Madame d' Espard has the box of the Gentlemen of the Bedchamber and will, no doubt, invite you to go with her. To see you in your glory, I shall go to Madame de Sérizy's box. They give ' Les Danaïdes.' "

" Adieu," she said.

The next day Madame de Bargeton endeavored to arrange a suitable morning dress in which to call upon her cousin Madame d'Espard. The weather was cold and she could find nothing better in her old-fashioned

Angoulême wardrobe than a certain green velvet gown trimmed in a rather excessive manner. Lucien, on his side, had felt the necessity of fetching his famous blue tail-coat (with the rest of his baggage sent from Angoulême by carrier); for he was by this time seized with horror at his shabby surtout, and wished to put himself in proper clothes in case he met Madame d'Espard or was invited to her house unexpectedly. He jumped into a hackney-coach in order to bring his parcels back more expeditiously. In two hours' time he spent four francs, which gave him much to think of as to the financial demands of Parisian life. After arraying himself in the superlatives of his wardrobe, he went to the rue Neuve-de-Luxembourg, where, on the threshold of Madame de Bargeton's apartment, he met Gentil in company with a magnificently plumed chasseur.

"I was going to your house, monsieur; madame sends you this little note," said Gentil, knowing nothing of the formulas of Parisian respect, accustomed as he was to the easy ways of provincial life. The chasseur accordingly took the poet for a servant.

Lucien opened the note, which told him that Madame de Bargeton was spending the day with Madame d'Espard and would go with her to the Opera at night; but Lucien, added Louise, was to go there also, for the marquise offered a seat in her box to the young poet to whom she was delighted to procure that pleasure.

"She loves me! my fears are foolish," thought Lucien; "she wishes to present me to her cousin to-night."

He skipped for joy, and resolved to spend his time gayly till the happy evening came. Rushing to the

Tuileries he determined to walk about and dream until it was time to go and dine at Véry's. Behold him springing, light with happiness and gayety, along the terrace of the Feuillants, examining the promenaders, the pretty women with their admirers, the elegant young men arm in arm in pairs saluting each other with glances as they passed. What a contrast that terrace presented to the Promenade of Angoulême! The birds of this magnificent aviary were very different from those of Beaulieu! Here was a wealth of all the colors of the ornithological families of India and America compared to the gray tones of the birds of Europe.

Lucien passed two agonizing hours in the Tuileries; he had a violent revulsion of feeling, and judged himself and things as they were. In the first place he did not see a single tail-coat on any of these elegant young men. If he did see a coat of that cut it was sure to be worn by some old man of another class or some poor devil, evidently from the suburbs, or perhaps a shopman. As soon as he perceived that there were two styles of dress, one for the morning another for the evening, our poet, with his quick perceptions and keen emotions, saw the ugliness of his own apparel and the defects which made his coat ridiculous, with its old-fashioned cut and eccentric color, and its front flaps, limp with use, flapping together; its buttons, too, were rubbed at the edges, and fatally white lines defined its creases. Then his waistcoat was too short, and the style of it so grotesquely provincial that he hurriedly buttoned his coat in order to hide it. And lastly, as a final blow, he did not see a single pair of nankeen trousers except among the common people; well-bred

persons were all wearing charming fancy materials or
irreproachably fresh white ones. Besides, all trousers
were made with straps and his met the heels of his
boots with difficulty, their bottom edges curling up as
if from a violent antipathy. He wore a white cravat
with embroidered ends, worked by his sister, who, having seen the dandies of Angoulême wearing them, had
made him a supply. Not only did no one, except grave
personages, old financiers, stern magistrates, wear white
cravats in the morning, but poor Lucien beheld, hurrying along the pavement of the rue de Rivoli on the outside of the iron railing, a grocer-boy carrying a basket
on his head, at whose chin the poet of Angoulême
spied two ends of a cravat embroidered by the hand of
some adored grisette. At the sight, Lucien received a
blow on that organ, still very doubtfully defined, where
our sensibilities harbor, and where, ever since emotions
have existed, men lay their hands when excessive joy
or excessive pain overtakes them.

Pray do not call this statement puerile. To the rich
who have never known this sort of suffering there must
be something mean and incredible in it ; but the anguish
of the poor and the unfortunate, from whatever cause it
comes, is not less deserving of attention than the crises
which revolutionize the lives of the powerful and the
privileged of the earth. Besides, is there not as much
real misery on the one side as on the other. Change
the terms : instead of a coat or a costume more or less
desirable, call it the ribbon of an order, a distinction,
a title. Those apparently trifling things have made
the misery of many a brilliant existence. These petty
matters are moreover, of enormous importance to those

who wish to appear to have what they have not; often they are their only means of possessing such things later. Lucien felt a cold sweat run down his back in thinking that he would have to appear that evening in his present clothes before the Marquise d'Espard, a relation of the first Gentleman of the Bedchamber, a woman whose house was frequented by the illustrious men of all careers, — the choicest in France.

" I look like the son of an apothecary, nothing better than a shop-boy," he thought, with rage in his heart as he watched the graceful, elegant young men of the faubourg Saint-Germain, all of whom had a certain air which rendered them alike in the fineness of their lines, the nobility of their carriage and general bearing, while all were individually different by the setting in which they chose to present themselves. Each made the most of his personal advantages by a certain scenic presentation which is quite as well understood and practised among the young men of Paris as among the women. Lucien derived from his mother those precious physical distinctions which now met his eyes; but in him the gold was in the nugget and not minted. His hair was ill-cut. Instead of raising his chin by a supple whale-bone stock, he felt his face buried in a villanous shirt-collar; the cravat, offering no resistance, allowed his head to hang. What woman could have imagined his shapely feet in those ignoble country boots? What young man would have envied that graceful figure hidden by the blue sack he had hitherto believed to be a coat? He saw ravishing studs on dazzling shirts, — his own shirt was grimy! All these elegant gentlemen were exquisitely gloved, — his gloves were those of a gendarme! That youth twirled a cane with a beautiful knob, this other wore a shirt with cuffs held in place by tiny gold buttons! One, who was talking to a woman, played with a charming whip, and the full plaits of his trousers, on which were little splashes of mud, also his clanging spurs and his tightly buttoned overcoat showed that he was about to mount one of two horses held by a little tiger no bigger than his thumb. Another took from his fob a watch as flat as a five-franc piece, and looked at the hour like a man who was either awaiting or had missed an appointment.

Gazing at all these charming externals, the like of which Lucien had never so much as imagined, he became suddenly aware of the world of superfluities, and he trembled to think what an enormous capital was needed to play the part of a man in society. The more he admired the easy, happy air of these young men, the more he was conscious of his own awkward air, the air of one who does not know where the path he is following ends; who cannot find the Palais-Royal when almost in it; and who when he asks a passer-by to tell him where the Louvre is, receives for answer, " Why, this is it."

Lucien felt himself parted from the world about him by a sort of gulf, and he began to consider how he should cross it, for he firmly resolved to be like this delicate, graceful, refined youth of Paris. All these patricians bowed to women divinely dressed and divinely beautiful, — women for whom Lucien would have been hacked in pieces, like the page of Countess Königsmark, as the price of a single kiss. In the twilight of his memory Louise loomed up, compared

with these sovereigns, as an old woman.   He met several women on this occasion of whom the history of the
nineteenth century will one day speak ; whose mind,
beauty, and love-affairs will not be less celebrated than
those of the queens of former days.   He saw a sublime
young woman, Mademoiselle des Touches, better known
under the name of Camille Maupin, a writer of emi-
nence, as distinguished for her beauty as for the loftiness of her mind, whose name was repeated in a low
voice by many persons, men and women, on · the
promenade.

"Ah !" thought Lucien, " this is poesy."

What was Madame de Bargeton beside that angel,
brilliant with youth and hope and promise, smiling
softly, yet with a black eye vast as heaven, burning as
the sun.   She was laughing and talking with Madame
Firmiani, one of the most charming women in Paris.
A voice cried in Lucien's soul: "Intellect is the lever
with which to move the world ;" but another voice
cried as loudly, that the fulcrum of intellect was
money.

He would not stay amid his ruins, on the stage of his
defeat, and he turned to the Palais-Royal, after asking
his way, for he did not yet know the topography of
the neighborhood.   Once there he went to Véry's and
ordered, by way of initiation into the pleasures of Paris,
a dinner which consoled his despair.   A bottle of Bordeaux, Ostend oysters, a fish, a partridge, and some
macaroni, with fruit, formed the *ne plus ultra* of his
desires.   As he regaled himself on this innocent debauch he thought of how he could show his mind
before the Marquise d'Espard that evening, and redeem

the meanness of his clothes by a display of his intellectual wealth. From this dream he was awakened by the total of his bill, which took from him fifty francs, a sum on which he had intended to live for some time. The dinner cost him exactly the price of one month's existence in Angoulême. Consequently, he closed the door of Véry's palace respectfully, reflecting that he might never enter it again.

"Eve was right," he said, thinking of his sister as he made his way back to the hotel to get more money, "Paris prices are not those of l'Houmeau."

As he went along he looked with admiration into the tailors' shops, remembering the well-dressed young men he had seen that day.

"No!" he cried suddenly, "I won't go to Madame d'Espard's in such clothes as these."

He ran with the speed of a deer to the hôtel du Gaillard-Bois, rushed to his room, took three hundred francs, and returned to the Palais-Royal, resolved to reclothe himself from head to foot. He had passed boot-makers, linen-shops, hair-dressers, as well as tailors; in fact, his future elegance was scattered through a dozen shops. The first tailor whose place he entered made him try on as many coats as he would, persuading him that they were all of the very last fashion. Lucien issued from the shop in possession of a green coat, white trousers, and a fancy waistcoat, for the sum of two hundred francs. He soon found a pair of boots, equally elegant, which fitted him exactly; and finally, after buying all that he felt was absolutely necessary, he ordered a hairdresser to come to his hotel, where his various purchases were to be sent at once.

At seven o'clock he got into a hackney-coach to be driven to the opera, frizzed and curled like a little Saint-John in a procession, well waistcoated, well cravatted, but a good deal embarrassed by the sort of sheath into which he had put himself for the first time.

II.

THE GREAT MAN'S ENTRANCE INTO THE GREAT WORLD.

WHEN Lucien reached the Opera-house, he followed Madame de Bargeton's instructions, and asked for the box of the Gentlemen of the Bedchamber. At sight of a man whose spick and span elegance made him look like a waiter at a wedding, the box-keeper requested him to show his ticket.

"I have none."

"Then you cannot enter," was the curt reply.

"But I belong to Madame d'Espard's party."

"We know nothing of that," said the box-keeper, exchanging an imperceptible smile with his colleagues.

Just then a carriage drew up under the peristyle. A chasseur, whom Lucien did not recognize, let down the steps of a coupé, from which two women in evening dress descended. Lucien, who did not wish to receive an insolent request from the box-keeper to stand aside, made way for the two ladies.

"That lady is the Marquise d'Espard whom you pretended to know," said the box-keeper, sarcastically.

Lucien was dumfounded, all the more because Madame de Bargeton seemed not to recognize him in his new plumage. But when he approached her she smiled and said : —

"This is fortunate ; come."

The men in the box-office were sobered. Lucien followed Madame de Bargeton, who, as she went up the broad staircase of the Opera-house, presented her Rubempré to Madame d'Espard. The box of the Gentlemen of the Bedchamber is the one that stands projected at the lower end of the auditorium ; the occupants can see all, and every one present can see them. Lucien placed himself in a chair behind Madame de Bargeton, glad to remain in the shade.

" Monsieur de Rubempré," said the marquise in a flattering tone of voice, " you have come to the Opera-house for the first time, and you ought to have a full view of it. Take this seat ; place yourself in front ; my cousin and I will permit it."

Lucien obeyed ; the first act was just concluding.

" You have employed your time well," said Louise, in a low voice, in her surprise at the change which had taken place in Lucien's appearance.

Louise herself was not changed. The juxtaposition of a woman in the height of the fashion like Madame d'Espard was so great an injury to her, the brilliant Parisian was such a foil to the imperfections of the provincial beauty, that Lucien, doubly enlightened by the brilliant world before him and by the elegant creature beside him, saw, alas ! in poor Louise the real woman, the woman such as the Parisians saw her, — tall, thin, pimpled, faded, angular, stiff, affected, pretentious, provincial in speech, and, above all, ill-dressed. The folds of an old Parisian gown will still show taste ; it can be understood and imagined as it once was ; but an old provincial gown is inexplicable, laughable. The dress and the woman were equally devoid of grace or freshness; the velvet was as dappled and spotted as the complexion. Lucien, ashamed of having loved this bag of bones, reflected that he could take advantage of her next sermon on virtue to leave her.

His excellent sight enabled him to see all the opera-glasses turned to this, the most fashionable and aristo-cratic box in the house. The elegant women present were all examining Madame de Bargeton, and smiling to one another as they did so. If Madame d'Espard observed these gestures and feminine smiles and knew their cause, she was quite indifferent to them. In the first place, she was well aware that every one would know her companion to be a poor relation from the provinces, a class of persons with whom every Parisian family is afflicted. Besides, when her cousin had expressed some fears as to her dress, she had reassured her cordially; per-ceiving that Madame de Bargeton, once properly dressed, would fulfil all the other requirements of manner and conduct. Louise might be wanting in the ways of the world, but she possessed the native dignity of a woman of rank, and that nameless something which is called *race*. The following Monday she would take her revenge and show them Madame de Bargeton in another light. Moreover, after society had learned that this woman was her cousin, the marquise knew it would suspend its satire, and wait for further examination to judge of her.

Lucien had no conception of the change that could be wrought in Madame de Bargeton's appearance by a scarf wound round her throat, a pretty gown, an ele-gant head-dress, and the advice of Madame d'Espard; who had, for instance, as they went up the stairway, told her cousin not to carry her handkerchief displayed in her hand. Good or bad taste is shown by a thousand little trifles of that kind, which a clever woman instantly learns, and many women never comprehend. Madame de Bargeton, already very willing to learn, had even more intelligence than she needed to perceive her mistakes. Madame d'Espard, sure that such a pupil would do her honor, did not hold back from advising her. Between the two women a compact was at once formed and cemented by their mutual interests. Madame de Bargeton felt a sudden worship for the idol of the day, whose manners, wit, and surroundings had seduced, dazzled, and fascinated her. She recognized in Madame d'Espard the occult power of an ambitious *grande dame*, and soon told herself that her best means of success lay in becoming the satellite of such a planet; she therefore unreservedly admired her. The marquise was alive to this ingenuous adoration; she was interested in a cousin who seemed to her dependent and poor; she liked to have a pupil to train, and asked nothing better than to turn Madame de Bargeton into a lady-companion, a slave who would sing her praises, — a treasure as rare among Parisian women as a devoted critic is in the literary tribe.

However, the stir of curiosity became so visible that the new importation could not fail to perceive it; and Madame d'Espard politely endeavored to turn her off the scent of its real meaning.

"If we have any visitors," she said, "we shall perhaps find out to what we owe the honor of the notice those ladies are bestowing upon us."

"I suspect that my old gown and my provincial face amuse them," said Madame de Bargeton, laughing.

" No, it is not you; it is something I cannot quite make out," replied Madame d'Espard, looking directly at the poet for the first time, and seeming to think him singularly dressed.

" There's Monsieur du Châtelet," said Lucien, at this instant raising his finger and pointing to the box (that of Madame de Sérizy) where the old beau, much rejuvenated, was sitting.

Madame de Bargeton bit her lips with vexation at Lucien's gesture, and the marquise did not restrain a look and smile of astonishment which said so disdainfully: "Where does this young man come from?" that Louise was humiliated in her love, — the most galling of all sensations to a Frenchwoman, and one she never forgives a lover for having caused her. In this social world where little things are made of such importance, a gesture, a word may destroy a man. The principal merit of fine manners and the tone of good society is that it offers an harmonious whole in which all things are well-blended and nothing salient shocks. Even those who, either from ignorance or from some impulse of thought, do not observe the laws of the science of society, will nevertheless understand that in this harmonious whole a single discord is, as it is in music, a complete negation of the science itself, in which all the conditions ought to be observed to the smallest particular under pain of its ceasing to exist.

"Who is that gentleman?" asked the marquise. "Do you already know Madame de Sérizy?"

"Ah! is that lady the famous Madame de Sérizy who has had so many adventures and is received everywhere in spite of them?"

"An unheard-of thing, my dear," replied the marquise; "explicable perhaps, but unexplained. The most important men are friends of hers; why? no one has ever solved the mystery. Is that gentleman who is with her now the lion of Angoulême?"

"Monsieur le Baron du Châtelet," said Louise, who gave him in Paris, out of vanity, the title she denied him in Angoulême, "is a man who makes people talk about him. He is a friend and companion of General de Montriveau."

"Ah!" said the marquise, "I never hear that name without thinking of the poor Duchesse de Langeais, who disappeared like a shooting-star. There," she went on, indicating another box, "are Monsieur de Rastignac and Madame de Nucingen, wife of a banker, a business man, a second-hand dealer on a large scale; a man who has hoisted himself into society by his money, and who is said to be little scrupulous in his ways of increasing it. He takes a world of pains to make people believe in his devotion to the Bourbons; he has made several attempts to be received by me. In taking Madame de Langeais' opera-box his wife expected to acquire the poor duchess's grace and wit and vogue, — the fable of the jay in the peacock's feathers!"

"How can Monsieur and Madame de Rastignac, whom we know to have only three thousand francs a year, support their son in Paris?" remarked Lucien to Madame de Bargeton, surprised at the elegance and luxury exhibited in the young man's dress.

"It is easy to see that you have just come from Angoulême," said the marquise, sarcastically, without lowering her opera-glass.

Lucien did not understand her; he was entirely absorbed in gazing at the different boxes, where he felt that opinions were being formed on Madame de Bargeton, and saw the curiosity of which he himself was the object.

On the other hand, Louise was singularly mortified at the little notice the marquise took of Lucien's beauty. "He cannot be as handsome as I thought him," she said to herself. After that, it was but a step to think him less brilliant.

The curtain was now down. Du Châtelet had gone to pay a visit to the Duchesse de Carigliano, whose box adjoined that of Madame d'Espard, and he now bowed to Madame de Bargeton, who replied by an inclination of her head. A woman of the world sees everything, and the marquise noticed the elegance and style of du Châtelet's clothes. Just then four gentlemen came into Madame d'Espard's box, one after the other; all four were celebrities in the gay world of Paris.

The first was Monsieur de Marsay, a man famous for the passions he had inspired, and personally remarkable for a species of girlish beauty, a soft, effeminate beauty, counteracted however by a fixed, calm, clear, and rigid glance like that of a tiger; he was loved, but he terrified those who loved him. Lucien also was handsome; his glance was soft, but his eyes were so blue and limpid that he seemed to lack the force and power by which so many women are attracted. Moreover, nothing as yet had brought the poet into notice and given him confidence, whereas de Marsay had a vigor of mind, a consciousness of pleasing, a style of dress appropriate to his character which crushed all rivals who approached him. Imagine what Lucien, stiff and starched in his new clothes, was in such a presence! De Marsay had conquered the right to say impertinent things by the wit and grace of manner with which he accompanied them. The greeting accorded to him by the marquise instantly revealed to Madame de Bargeton his importance.

The second visitor was a Vandenesse, — the one who had caused the scandal about Lady Dudley; a young man of gentle manners, modest and intelligent, whose success in the world was through the opposite qualities to those on which de Marsay relied; he had been warmly introduced to Madame d'Espard by her cousin Madame de Mortsauf. The third was General de Montriveau, the cause of the flight and death of the Duchesse de Langeais. The fourth was Monsieur de Canalis, one of the most illustrious poets of the day, — a young man still in the dawn of fame, and who, prouder of being a nobleman than a poet, was pretending to " pay attentions " to Madame d'Espard, the better to conceal his passion for her aunt the Duchesse de Chaulieu. In spite of his many affected graces, the vast ambition which cast him later into the whirlpool of politics was already discernible. His beauty, almost finical, and his caressing manners scarcely disguised even now the profound egotism of his nature and the perpetual scheming for a position that was still problematical; but the choice he had made of Madame de Chaulieu, a woman over forty years of age, had lately earned for him certain court benefits, the approval of the faubourg Saint-Germain, and the abuse of the liberal party, who called him the " poet of the sacristy."

Studying the four young men, Madame de Bargeton understood the indifference that the marquise had shown for Lucien. After the conversation began, and each of these clever, acute minds was revealed by remarks which had more sense and more depth than Louise had heard in a month in the provinces, and, above all, after the great poet had uttered a few thrilling words (significant of the materialism of the day gilded by poesy), Louise understood du Châtelet's warning of the previous evening. Lucien was henceforth nothing. Every one regarded the poor unknown young fellow with such cruel indifference, he seemed to be there in their midst so like a stranger who did not know their language, that after a while the marquise took pity on him.

"Allow me," she said to Canalis, "to present to you Monsieur de Rubempré. Your position in the literary world is so high that I am sure you will welcome an aspirant. Monsieur de Rubempré has just arrived from Angoulême ; he needs your introduction to those whose business it is to bring genius to light. He has as yet no enemies who can make his fortune by attacking him. It would certainly be a very original thing to enable him to obtain through friendship that which the rest of you obtain through jealousy."

The four young men all looked at Lucien while the marquise spoke. Though de Marsay was less than six feet from him, he took up his eyeglass to look him over, then his glances went from Lucien to Madame de Bargeton, and from Madame de Bargeton back to Lucien, uniting them in one sarcastic look which mortified them cruelly ; he examined them as though they were curious animals, then he smiled. That smile was like the thrust of a dagger to the great man of the provinces.   Félix de Vandenesse seemed more charitable, and Armand de Montriveau gave Lucien a look which sounded him to the core.

"Madame," said Monsieur de Canalis, bowing, "I will obey you, in spite of the personal interests which prompt us not to do services to rivals, — but you accustom us to miracles."

" Then do me the favor to dine with me on Monday next and meet Monsieur de Rubempré; you can talk at your ease about literary affairs; and I will try to catch a few of the tyrants of literature and the noted persons who patronize them, — the author of 'Ourika,' for instance, and some of the young poets with right opinions."

" Madame la marquise," said de Marsay, "if you favor Monsieur de Rubempré for his intellect, I shall do so for his beauty; I will give him such advice as will make him the happiest dandy in Paris.   After that he can be a poet if he likes."

Madame de Bargeton thanked her cousin by a look full of gratitude.

"I did not know you were jealous of men of intellect," said Montriveau to de Marsay.   "Happiness kills poets, you know."

" Is that why Monsieur de Canalis is proposing to be married?" said de Marsay, wishing to see how Madame d'Espard would receive the idea.

Canalis shrugged his shoulders, and Madame d'Espard, Madame de Chaulieu's niece, began to laugh.

Lucien, who felt in his new clothes like one of the Egyptian hermæ, was ashamed of having nothing to

reply.   At last, however, he managed to say to Madame
d'Espard in his tender voice : " Your goodness, madame, will oblige me to succeed."

Du Châtelet entered the box at this moment, snatch-
ing his opportunity to make his friend Montriveau, one
of the kings of Paris, present him to the marquise.
He bowed to Madame de Bargeton, and begged
Madame d'Espard to pardon the liberty he had taken
in invading her box ; he had been so long separated
from his comrade Montriveau, — they had not seen
each other since they parted in the desert.

" To part in the desert, and meet at the opera ! " said
Lucien.

" Truly theatrical," said Canalis.

Montriveau at once presented the Baron du Châtelet
to the marquise, who granted the former secretary of
the Imperial princess a reception that was all the more
cordial partly because she had seen him well received
in three boxes (Madame de Sérizy especially receiving
only those who were properly admitted), and also because he had the honor of being one of Montriveau's
companions.   This last claim was evidently so strong
that Madame de Bargeton observed in the tone and
looks and manners of the four gentlemen that they
admitted du Châtelet as one of themselves without
discussion.   The dictatorial bearing of du Châtelet in
the provinces was thus explained to her.

Presently the Baron seemed to see Lucien for the
first time, and he made him one of those chilling little
bows by which one man slights another and indicates to
men of the world the inferior position that he holds in
society.   The bow was accompanied by a look which

seemed to say, "How did he get here?" The look
was understood, for de Marsay leaned over to Montriveau and said in his ear, but loud enough for the baron
to hear him: "Ask him who that singular young man
is; he looks like the lay figure in a tailor's window."

Du Châtelet spoke for a moment in a low voice with
his friend Montriveau, as if renewing acquaintance, but
really, no doubt, he was cutting his young rival to
pieces.

Surprised by the readiness of mind and the brilliant
cleverness with which these men answered each other,
Lucien was bewildered by the wit and epigram, and,
especially, the facile flow of their talk and their ease
of manner. The luxury of clothes and surroundings
which had so confounded him in the morning, he now
found in ideas and in words. He asked himself by what
mysterious faculty these men could find at will such
piquant reflections and repartees, which he knew that he
himself could not have imagined without long meditation. Besides, these five men of the world were perfectly at their ease, not only in their talk, but also in
their clothes; they seemed to wear nothing new and
nothing old; there was nothing resplendent about them,
and yet they attracted the eye. Their luxury to-day
was that of yesterday and would be that of to-morrow.
Lucien became suddenly aware that he looked like a
man who was handsomely dressed for the first time in
his life.

"My dear fellow," said de Marsay to Félix de
Vandenesse, "that little de Rastignac is flying himself
like a kite! there he is with the Marquise de Listomère;
he's making progress! I wonder why he keeps his

opera-glass on us, — possibly he knows monsieur?"
added the dandy, addressing Lucien, but without looking at him.

"It would be strange," remarked Madame de Bargeton, "if the name of a man we are all proud of in his
native town had not reached him; his sister lately
heard Monsieur de Rubempré read some fine verses at
my house."

Félix de Vandenesse and de Marsay now took leave
of Madame d'Espard and made their way to Madame
de Listomère, a sister of Félix. The second act was
beginning, and Madame d'Espard, her cousin, and Lucien
were presently left alone, — some of the visitors departing to explain Madame de Bargeton to the women who
were puzzled by her presence; others to tell of the arrival
of a poet and to laugh at his clothes. Canalis returned
to the Duchesse de Chaulieu, and did not leave her box
again. Lucien was thankful for the dispersion caused
by the rising of the curtain.

All Madame de Bargeton's fears concerning Lucien
were increased by the attention her cousin had bestowed
on the Baron du Châtelet, which was totally different
from the protecting politeness she had showed to Lucien.
During the second act Madame de Listomère's box
continued full of visitors, who seemed to be excited
by some conversation relating to Madame de Bargeton
and Lucien. Eugène de Rastignac was evidently the
wit of the party; he gave the cue to that Parisian
laughter which, daily seeking pastures new, hurries to
exhaust the present subject and to leave it, old and
worn-out, for another. Madame d'Espard herself became uneasy; but knowing that spite does not long

leave those it wounds in ignorance of its malice, she awaited the end of the act.

When feelings undergo a revulsion, as was now the case with Lucien, and also with Madame de Bargeton, very strange things can happen in a short space of time ; moral revolutions are produced by laws which work rapidly. Louise had constantly in her memory the wise and politic words which du Châtelet had said to her about Lucien as they drove home from the Vaudeville. Every sentence was a prophecy, and Lucien seemed bent on fulfilling them all. In losing his illusions about Madame de Bargeton, as Madame de Bargeton had lost hers about him, the poor lad, whose fate was something like that of Jean-Jacques Rousseau, imitated the latter in so far as being fascinated by Madame d'Espard and falling in love with her on the spot.

Young men, or men who remember the emotions of their youth, will know that this passion was extremely probable and natural. The charming little manners, the choice language, the delicate tones of the voice of this graceful woman, so high in station and so envied, affected the poet as Madame de Bargeton had affected him in Angoulême. The mobility of his character prompted him to desire her powerful influence, — could he but win her, it was his ! he had succeeded in Angoulême with another woman, why not here ? Involuntarily, and in spite of the magic of the opera, novel as it was to him, his eyes, attracted by this magnificent Célimène, turned to her constantly ; the more he looked at her, the more he longed to look.

Madame de Bargeton intercepted one of these sparkling glances. She began to observe Lucien, and soon saw that he was more intent upon the marquise than upon the play. She would willingly have resigned herself to be deserted for the fifty daughters of Danaus; but no sooner had a glance, more ambitious, ardent, and significant than the rest, explained to her what was passing in Lucien's mind, than she became jealous, though less for the future than for the past.

"He never looked at me like that!" she thought. "Good God! Châtelet was right."

She saw the blunder of her love. When a woman comes to repent of her weakness, she passes, as it were, a sponge over her life and effaces everything. Nevertheless, though every movement of Lucien angered her, she continued calm.

De Marsay returned between the acts accompanied by Monsieur de Listomère, for the purpose of informing the haughty marquise that the over-dressed youth she had admitted to her box was no more named de Rubempré than a Jew was possessed of a Christian name; Lucien, they told her, was the son of an apothecary named Chardon. Monsieur de Rastignac, who was well-informed about Angoulême, had been, they said, amusing two boxes already at the expense of the mummy whom Madame d'Espard called her cousin, and the precaution that lady took to have an apothecary in her train. To this de Marsay added a number of Parisian witticisms, forgotten as soon as said, behind which, however, lurked du Châtelet, the actual worker of this Carthaginian treachery.

"My dear," said Madame d'Espard to Madame de Bargeton, behind her fan, "do pray tell me if your protégé is really Monsieur de Rubempré."

" He has taken his mother's name ! " said Louise, embarrassed.

" But what was his father's name ? "

" Chardon ! "

" What did he do ? "

" He was a chemist ! "

" I felt certain, my dear cousin, that those people could not be laughing at you, a lady whom I accept. But I must say I do not care to have jokes made about my acquaintance with the son of an apothecary. If you are willing, let us leave the theatre together immediately."

Madame d'Espard's look and manner became at once supercilious, though Lucien could not imagine in what way he had caused so great a change of countenance. He first thought that his waistcoat was in bad taste (which was true), that the fashion of his coat was exaggerated (which was also true), and he determined to go the next day to the most celebrated tailor in Paris and obtain the proper clothes in which he might, on the following Monday, rival the men he was to meet at Madame d'Espard's dinner. Lost in reflection, he sat during the third act with his eyes fixed on the stage. While apparently looking at the splendid show before him, he was giving himself up to his dream about Madame d'Espard. The sudden coldness of her manner was a violent rebuff to the intellectual ardor with which he plunged into this new emotion, careless of the difficulties he perceived and resolving to vanquish them. He came out of his meditation at last to look again at his new idol, but, on turning his head, he saw that he was alone ; he heard a slight noise, the door was closing; Madame d'Espard had carried off her cousin. Lucien was amazed to the last degree at this abrupt desertion; but he did not think long about it, for the reason that it was utterly inexplicable.

When the two women were in their carriage and it was rolling along the rue de Richelieu towards the faubourg Saint Honoré the marquise said in a tone of repressed anger : —

"My dear friend, what are you thinking of? Pray wait till the son of an apothecary is really famous before you take him up. The Duchesse de Chaulieu does not yet acknowledge Canalis; though he is already celebrated, and a gentleman too. That youth is neither your son nor your lover — at least I suppose so?" said the haughty woman, casting a sharp inquisitive look at her cousin.

"How lucky for me that I kept him at a distance and granted nothing," thought Madame de Bargeton.

"Well," resumed the marquise, who took the expression of her cousin's eyes for an answer, "let him go now, I entreat you. To dare to assume an illustrious name! — why that's an audacity society ought to punish. Of course I admit it is his mother's name; but pray reflect, my dear, that the king alone has the right to confer, by letters-patent, the name of the family of Rubempré on the son of a daughter of the house. If she made a mésalliance, the favor would be immense, and it would require a fortune, the rendering of great services, and very high influence to obtain it. Those absurdly fine clothes he is wearing prove that he is neither rich nor a gentleman; his face is handsome, but he strikes me as very dull; he does not know how to carry himself, nor how to talk; in short, he has never had any social education. How came you ever to take him up?"

Madame de Bargeton, who now rejected and denied Lucien as Lucien had already rejected and denied her in his own mind, was terribly alarmed lest her cousin should find out the truth of her journey from Angoulême.

" Dear cousin," she said. " I am in despair at having compromised you."

" I cannot be compromised," said Madame d'Espard, smiling. " I am thinking only of you."

" But you invited him to dinner on Monday."

" I shall be ill," said the marquise, quickly; " you can let him know of it; I shall give orders that he is not to be admitted under either of his names."

Lucien took it into his head to walk about the foyer between the two last acts, seeing that everybody did so. None of the persons who had come into Madame d'Espard's box bowed to him or even appeared to see him, which seemed a most extraordinary thing to the poet of the provinces. Also du Châtelet, whom he tried to join, watched him out of the corner of his eye, and evaded him. Growing more and more convinced by the appearance of the men who were walking about the foyer that his clothes were ridiculous, Lucien returned to his box and sat in a corner of it, where he stayed during the rest of the opera, absorbed partly by the splendid spectacle of the ballet in the fifth act, partly by the aspect of the boxes along which his eyes ranged, and partly by his own reflections in presence of this great world of Parisian society.

" So this is my kingdom ! " he said to himself; " this
is the world I have to master ! "

He went back to his hotel on foot, thinking over all
that was said by the persons who had come to Madame
d'Espard's box; over their manners, their gestures,
their way of coming in and going out; all of which came
back into his memory with astonishing accuracy.

III.

ONE LOST ILLUSION.

THE next morning, towards mid-day, Lucien's first act was to go to Staub the great tailor of that period. From him he obtained, by entreaty and the assurance of cash payment, a promise that his coat should be ready for the famous Monday. Staub even went so far as to promise him a waistcoat, a pair of trousers, and a charming overcoat for the decisive day. Lucien ordered shirts, handkerchiefs, in short, a complete little outfit at a linen-maker's, and had himself measured for boots and shoes by a celebrated boot-maker. He bought a handsome cane at Verdier's, gloves and shirt-buttons from Madame Irlande; in a word, he did his best to put himself on the level of the greatest dandies. When he had gratified all his fancies, he made his way to the rue Neuve-de-Luxembourg and found that Louise had already gone out.

"Madame dines with Madame d'Espard," said Albertine, "and will not return till late."

Lucien dined at a restaurant in the Palais-Royal for forty sous and went to bed early. The next day, Sunday, he called to see Louise by eleven o'clock, and was told she was not up. At two o'clock he returned.

"Madame does not receive," said Albertine; "but she gave me a little note for you."

" Does not receive ! " exclaimed Lucien, " why I am nobody."

" I don't know," said Albertine in a very impertinent tone.

Lucien, less surprised at Albertine's behavior than at the fact of receiving a note from Madame de Bargeton, took the missive and read the following disheartening lines as he walked along : —

" Madame d'Espard is indisposed; she cannot receive you on Monday. I myself am not well, but I am just dressing to go to her and keep her company. I am very sorry for this little disappointment; but your talents reassure me. I am certain you will succeed without clap-trap assistance."

" And no signature ! " exclaimed Lucien, who found himself in the Tuileries without knowing he had walked a step. The gift of second sight which some men of talent possess made him suspect the catastrophe of which this chilling note was merely the forerunner. Lost in thought he wandered on, looking at the statues in the place Louis XV. The weather was fine. Handsome carriages passed him in a steady stream, going towards the avenue of the Champs Élysées. He followed the crowd of pedestrians, and watched the three or four thousand carriages which flock along that fine avenue of a Sunday and make it another Longchamps.

Dazzled by the brilliant show of horses, toilets, and liveries, he walked on and on, till he reached the Arc de Triomphe, then unfinished. What were his feelings when, as he turned to retrace his steps, he saw Madame d'Espard and Madame de Bargeton in an elegant calèche, behind which waved the plumes of the chasseur in green and gold ! The stream of carriages went slowly and then stopped on account of an obstruction. Lucien could see the transformation of Louise; her old self was not recognizable; the colors of her toilet were chosen in a way to set off her complexion; her gown was charming, her hair most becomingly arranged, while a dainty bonnet of exquisite taste was remarkable beside even that of Madame d'Espard, who controlled the fashion. There is an indefinable way in which a man must wear a hat; too far back and it gives him a bold look; too far forward and you think him suspicious; over to one side and his air is cavalier; but a well-bred woman may put on her bonnet precisely as she fancies, and she always looks well. Madame de Bargeton had solved that curious problem instantly. A belt defined her slender waist. She had already caught the gestures and ways of her cousin; sitting beside her, she played with an elegant vinaigrette fastened to one of the fingers of her right hand by a little chain, exhibiting thus her slender and well-gloved hand without apparently intending it. In short, she had made herself like Madame d'Espard without imitating her; she was a worthy cousin of the elegant marquise, who seemed to be proud of her pupil.

The men and women on the sidewalk gazed at the brilliant equipage which bore the arms of the d'Espards supported by those of the Blamont-Chauvrys. Lucien was surprised at the great number of persons who seemed to know the two cousins; he was ignorant that the whole of Paris, comprised in twenty salons, already knew of the relationship between Madame d'Espard and Madame de Bargeton. Young men on horseback, among whom Lucien recognized de Marsay and Rastignac, joined the calèche of the two ladies to escort it to the Bois. Lucien could easily perceive by their gestures that they were complimenting Madame de Bargeton on her toilet. Madame d'Espard sparkled with grace and health ; her illness was evidently a pretext to avoid receiving Lucien ; for, as he did not fail to observe, she had not postponed the dinner to another day. The angry poet went towards the calèche, walking slowly, and when he was within full view of the two women he bowed to them. Madame de Bargeton would not see him ; the marquise looked at him through her eyeglass and did not return his bow.

This repudiation by the Parisian aristocracy was by no means the same as that by the sovereigns of Angoulême ; when the latter attempted to wound him they admitted his power and considered him a man ; whereas, to Madame d'Espard he actually had no existence. It was not a judgment ; it was a refusal of justice. A cold chill seized the poor poet when de Marsay took up his eyeglass and looked at him ; that done, the Parisian lion dropped the glass in a manner that seemed to Lucien like the fall of the knife of the guillotine.

The carriage passed on. Anger and a desire for vengeance took possession of the despised man ; if he could have laid hands on Madame de Bargeton then and there, he would have strangled her ; he would have made himself a Fouquier-Tinville for the delight of sending Madame d'Espard to the scaffold ; gladly would he have made de Marsay suffer some of those refined tortures which savages invent. He saw Canalis go by on horseback, elegant as the most winning of poets should be, and bowing right and left to the prettiest women.

"My God! gold at any price!" thought Lucien; "money is the only power before which this world kneels. No," cried his conscience, "not money, fame; and fame is, work! Work? that is David's word. Good God, why I am here? But I will triumph yet! I will drive along this avenue with chasseurs to my carriage; I will win some Marquise d'Espard yet."

Muttering these furious words, he went to dine at Hurbain's for forty sous. The next day, at nine o'clock, he went to see Louise, intending to reproach her for her barbarity. Not only was Madame de Bargeton "not at home" to him, but the porter at the gate refused to allow him to pass up. He then stationed himself in the street and watched till twelve o'clock. At that hour du Châtelet left the house, caught sight of the poet out of the corner of his eye, and endeavored to avoid him. Lucien, stung to the quick, pursued his rival; du Châtelet, feeling himself cornered, turned back and bowed with the evident intention of passing on after showing that civility.

"Monsieur," said Lucien, "grant me a moment; I have two words to say to you. You have shown me some friendship, and I invoke it to ask you a trifling service. You have just left Madame de Bargeton; explain to me the cause of my rejection by her and by Madame d'Espard."

"Monsieur Chardon," replied du Châtelet, with false kindliness, "do you know why those ladies left you at the Opera?"

"No," said the poor poet.

"Well, Monsieur de Rastignac has done you a bad turn at the start. That young dandy, being questioned about you, declared that your name is not de Rubempré, but Chardon, that your mother is a monthly nurse, that your father during his lifetime was apothecary at l'Houmeau, a suburb of Angoulême, and that your sister, a pretty young woman who ironed shirts admirably, was about to marry a printer in Angoulême named Séchard. Such is the world ! If you come before it you must be discussed. Monsieur de Marsay returned to Madame d'Espard's box to laugh over the affair with her, and the two ladies at once disappeared, feeling that they were compromised in being seen there with you. Don't attempt to see either of them again. Madame de Bargeton will not be received by her cousin if she continues to know you. You have genius ; revenge yourself. The world disdains you ; disdain the world. Take refuge in a garret ; write masterpieces ; seize power in some way, and the world will be at your feet ; you can then return the bruises it has given you on the very ground where you received them. The more regard Madame de Bargeton has shown you in the past, the greater the aversion she will now feel to you. That is the way with women's feelings. The question now is not to recover her as a friend, but to avoid making her an enemy. I will show you a means of doing this. She must have written you letters ; send them all back to her ; she will be touched by such an act, which is that of a gentleman ; later, if you should happen to need her, she will not be hostile. As for me, I have so high an opinion of your future career, that I am already defending you everywhere ; and henceforth if I can be of any service to you, you will find me ready."

Lucien was so dejected, pale, and overcome, that he

did not return the frigidly polite salutation which the old beau bestowed upon him. He returned to his hotel, where he found Staub himself, who had come, less to try on the clothes (which he did try on) than to ascertain from the landlady of the " Gaillard-Bois " the financial standing of his customer. Lucien had arrived in a post-chaise ; Madame de Bargeton had brought him back from the theatre in her carriage last Thursday evening. So far so good. Staub called Lucien " Monsieur le comte," and took pains to show him with what talent he had brought out his handsome shape.

" A young man dressed like that," he said, " may walk in the Tuileries and marry a rich Englishwoman in a fortnight."

This joke of the German tailor, the perfection of his clothes, the fineness of the cloth, and the grace he beheld in his person as he turned himself about before the glass, did certainly comfort Lucien and make him less gloomy. He told himself, vaguely, that Paris was the capital of chance, and for the time being he believed in chance. Had n't he a volume of poetry, and a magnificent romance, " The Archer of Charles IX.," in manuscript? Staub promised the overcoat and the rest of the garments for the following day.

The next morning the boot-maker, the shirt-maker, and the tailor arrived, all with their bills. Lucien, ignorant of the usual way of getting rid of them, and still under the influence of provincial customs, paid the bills ; but having paid them, he became aware that only three hundred and sixty francs remained out of the two thousand he had brought with him, — and this at the end of a week ! Nevertheless, he dressed himself and went

to walk on the terrace of Les Feuillants. There he had
some success. He was so well-dressed, so handsome,
so graceful, that several women looked at him ; and
one or two were sufficiently struck by his beauty to
turn round and observe him closely. Lucien studied
the bearing and manners of the young men, and learned
his lesson in deportment, all the while thinking of his
three hundred and sixty francs.

That evening, alone in his room, it occurred to him
that he had better clear up the problem of his life at
the hôtel du Gaillard-Bois, where he always breakfasted
in the plainest manner, thinking to economize. He
now asked for his bill, with the air of a man who
intends moving, and found himself a debtor to the
amount of a hundred francs. The next day he rushed
to the Latin quarter, recommended to him by David as
the least expensive. After a long search he found a
miserable furnished lodging-house in the rue de Cluny,
near the Sorbonne, where he obtained a single room for
the price he was willing to give. He paid his bill at
once at the hôtel du Gaillard-Bois, and installed himself
in the hôtel Cluny in the course of the day.

After taking possession of his miserable chamber he
collected all Madame de Bargeton's letters and made a
package of them ; then he laid it before him on the table
and set himself to think over the events of that fatal
week before beginning to write to her. He did not tell
himself that he had been the first to reject his love in
his own mind, without a thought of what might become
of his Louise in Paris ; he did not see his own faith-
lessness ; he saw only his actual position, and he laid
the blame on Madame de Bargeton ; instead of sup-

porting him, she had ruined him. He worked himself into a rage, turned bitter, and wrote the following letter, in a paroxysm of anger : —

"What think you, madame, of a woman who, having taken a fancy to a poor timid youth full of those noble beliefs which in their later years men call illusions, employs all the charms of her coquetry, the subtleness of her mind, and the glorious semblances of love to lead that youth astray? The flattering promises with which she dazzled him cost her nothing; she drew him to her ; she took possession of him ; she reproached him at times for his want of faith; she cajoled him. When that youth abandoned his family and followed her blindly, she led him to the shore of a boundless sea ; with a smile she bade him enter a fragile skiff, and then — she pushed him forth, alone and helpless, to the storm ; wishing him good-luck, she sat upon a rock above him and laughed.

"That woman is you; that youth is I. In the hands of that youth a proof exists which can betray the crime of your faithless affection and the favors you now repudiate. You may blush when you meet the youth whom you flung into the waves if the proof that you once held him to your bosom remains in his hands. Therefore, when you open this packet the proof I speak of will be in yours. You are free to forget all. After indulging the noble hopes to which you pointed, I fall to the realities of misery in the mud of Paris. While you are passing, brilliant and adored, among the grandeurs of the world to the threshold of which you enticed my steps, I shall shiver in the lonely garret to which your hand has cast me.

"Perhaps remorse may seize you in the midst of your feasts and pleasures ; perhaps you will then think of him whom you drove into the gulf. Well, when that day comes, feel no remorse ! From the depths of his misery that youth offers you the only thing that remains to him, — forgiveness.

."Yes, madame, thanks to you, nothing does remain to me—nothing? do I say nothing? but it is of that the world was made; genius must follow God. I begin by imitating His mercy; you need not tremble unless I turn to evil; then indeed you will be the accomplice of my faults. No! I pity you because you will no longer be a sharer in the fame to which I go, led on by labor."

Having written that emphatic letter, full of the sombre dignity which an artist of twenty-one takes pleasure in exaggerating, Lucien's mind reverted to his own family. He saw once more the pretty rooms David had arranged for him by sacrificing part of his narrow means; a remembrance of the tranquil, modest, middle-class joys he once had tasted came over him; visions of his mother, of his sister, of David, were about him; he saw once more the tears they shed as he left them to seek his fortune, and he wept; for he was now alone in Paris, the city of his hopes, without friends, without protection.

A few days later Lucien wrote as follows to his sister who was married by that time to David Séchard : —

My Dear Eve, — Sisters have the melancholy privilege of sharing more griefs than joys when they are part of the existence of brothers vowed to Art, and I begin to fear I shall continue to be a burden to you. Have I not already worn you out, — all of you who have sacrificed yourselves for me?

But the memory of the past, full of the joys of home, supports me in the solitude of my present. I fly, like an eagle returning to its nest, across the space that parts me from those true affections, after experiencing the first miseries, the first deceptions of the world of Paris.

Have your candles blinked? have the logs on the hearth rolled down? and has my mother said, "There, Lucien is thinking of us"? and did David answer, "He is battling with men and things"?

Eve, I write this letter for no eye but yours. To you alone do I dare to tell the good and the evil which happen to me, blushing for both, for good is as rare here as evil should be. You are now to hear many things in few words. Madame de Bargeton was ashamed of me; she deserted, dismissed, repudiated me on the ninth day after our arrival. When she sees me she turns away her head; and I, to follow her into society, have spent seventeen hundred and fifty of the two thousand francs which you, my dear ones, obtained for me with such difficulty. "Spent them!" I hear you say, "on what?" My poor sister, Paris is a strange whirligig; a dinner can be had for eighteen sous, but the simplest at a fashionable restaurant costs fifty francs; there are waistcoats and trousers for four francs forty sous, but good tailors will make none under a hundred francs. People pay a sou to cross a gutter when it rains; but the slightest distance in a hackney-coach costs thirty-two sous.

After living for a time in the fashionable quarter, I have now come to a house in the rue de Cluny, one of the meanest and gloomiest streets in Paris, squeezed between three churches and the old buildings of the Sorbonne. I occupy a furnished room on the fourth floor of this house, and though it is very dirty and shabby I pay fifteen francs a month for it. I breakfast on a two-sous roll and a sou's worth of milk, but I dine very well at the restaurant of a man named Flicoteaux on the place de la Sorbonne. Until next winter my living will not cost more, at least I hope not, than sixty francs a month, everything included. Therefore my remaining two hundred and forty francs will keep me four months. Between now and then I shall surely have sold my novel, "The Archer of Charles IX." and the poems you know of, which I shall call "Daisies."

Therefore you must not be at all uneasy about me. If the present is mean, and bare, and chilling, the future is blue, and rich, and splendid. Nearly all great men have experienced the vicissitudes which now affect but do not overwhelm me. Plautus, a great comic poet, was a miller's drudge; Machiavelli wrote "The Prince," at night after laboring in a crowd of other workmen by day. The great Cervantes, who lost an arm at the battle of Lepanto, and was called "the old one-armed" by the scribblers of his time, was forced by lack of a publisher to put an interval of ten years between the first and second parts of his sublime "Don Quixote."

We, of our time, are not so badly off as that. Distress and poverty can only touch the unknown men of talent; the moment they make a name, writers become rich, and I shall be rich. I live by thought; I pass the greater part of my day in the library of Sainte-Geneviève, where I am gaining the education I still need, without which I could not go far.

To-day, therefore, I am almost happy. In a few more days I shall be joyously reconciled to my position. I give myself up through all my waking hours to a toil I love; material living is secured to me; I meditate much, I study; I do not see that I can now be wounded, having renounced society, in which my vanity did suffer for a time. Illustrious men in all ages have lived apart from the world. They are like the birds in a grove, they sing, they charm all Nature, but no eye sees them. Thus will I do — and so doing I shall realize the ambitious plans of my soul.

I do not regret Madame de Bargeton. A woman who could act as she has acted does not deserve a thought. Neither do I regret having quitted Angoulême. That woman did well for me when she persuaded me to Paris and cast me upon my own resources. Paris is the home of writers, thinkers, poets. Here, alone, can fame be cultivated; already I feed upon the noble sustenance she garners for the soul in these days. Here writers find, in the museums, in the collections, the living works of all the genius of the past to warm and stimulate their imagination. Here, alone, vast libraries, always open, offer food and information to the mind. In short, there is in Paris, in the air, in every detail of its being, a soul which breathes and impresses itself on all literary creation. We learn more things in half an hour, by merely conversing in a café or by spending one evening at the theatre, than in ten years of provincial life. Here, in truth, all things are a drama to the eye, comparison and instruction to the mind. Extreme cheapness, excessive cost, that is Paris, where every bee can find its honey and every soul may assimilate what it needs. Therefore, though I suffer just now, I repent of nothing. On the contrary, a noble future spreads before me and uplifts my heart, wounded for the moment only.

Adieu, my dear sister; do not expect to hear from me regularly; one of the peculiarities of Paris is that one does not realize how time flies. Life rushes on with frightful rapidity. I kiss my mother, and David, and you, dear Eve, more tenderly than ever.

Your   LUCIEN.

IV.

TWO VARIETIES OF PUBLISHER.

FLICOTEAUX is a name inscribed on many memories. Few students lived in the Latin quarter during the first twelve years of the Restoration who did not frequent that temple of hunger and poverty. The dinner, composed of three dishes, cost eighteen sous, including a decanter of wine or a bottle of beer; twenty-two sous with a whole bottle of wine. The cause that undoubtedly prevented this friend of youth from making a colossal fortune was an item in his prospectus printed in large letters and thus worded: BREAD AT DISCRETION, — in other words, unlimited bread. Many a distinguished fame had Flicoteaux for its foster-father. Certainly the heart of more than one famous man must be conscious of a thousand ineffable memories as he passes that well-known shop window, with its little panes, looking on the place de la Sorbonne and the rue Neuve-de-Richelieu, which Flicoteaux II. and III. have respected, even after the July days. These successors of the first Flicoteaux have had the sense to leave untouched the dingy tints and the respectable elderly air which manifest so deep a disdain for the charlatanism of exteriors, — that novel form of advertisement made to the eyes at the expense of the stomach by nearly all the restaurateurs of these days. Instead

of the stuffed game-birds destined never to be cooked;
instead of those fantastic fishes, such as never swam;
instead of " early vegetables " (which might be called
antediluvial), exposed in specious show to entice the
corporals and their womenfolk, the honest Flicoteaux
exhibited his salad-bowls, patched with many a rivet,
or heaps of stewed prunes, rejoicing the eyes of the
consumer, sure that the word *dessert*, delusive on other
prospectuses, was a reality at Flicoteaux's. Six-pound
loaves cut in four were likewise reassuring as to the
bread ad libitum.

Such was the luxury of an establishment which, had
it existed in his day, Molière would have rendered
famous, so mirth-provoking is the sound of an epigrammatic name. Flicoteaux exists; it will exist so long
as students eat to live. Yes, it was and is where they
eat, — nothing more nor less than that; but they eat
there as they work elsewhere, with a serious or joyous
diligence according to their characters or their circumstances. This celebrated establishment consisted, at
the time of which we speak, of two long, low, narrow
rooms, placed at right angles, and lighted, one from the
place de la Sorbonne, the other from the rue Neuve-de-
Richelieu. Both were furnished with tables, probably
taken from some convent refectory, for their length was
monastic; and the places for the regular customers
were marked by napkins rolled up and thrust into numbered metal rings. Flicoteaux I. changed his table-
linen only once a week, but Flicoteaux II. changed, it is
said, twice a week as soon as he found that competition
was threatening the dynasty.

This restaurant was, in fact, a workshop with suitable

utensils, rather than a hall of festive pleasure; every one ate his food and departed quickly. The waiters came and went without lingering; all were busy; all were needed. The viands were not various; the potato was perpetual. Ireland might not possess a potato; the root might be lacking everywhere else, but at Flicoteaux's never. For the last thirty years it has flourished there, of that beautiful golden color loved of Titian, with minced-up greenery scattered over it; such as you knew it in 1814 you will find it in 1840. The cutlets and the beefsteaks are to the dinner-lists of this establishment what grouse and sturgeon are to those of Véry, — extraordinary dishes, which must be ordered in the morning. The female of the genus ox prevails and her son abounds under the most ingenuous aspects. When the mackerel and the whiting bear down upon the coasts of France they bound thence to Flicoteaux's. There the vicissitudes of agriculture are reflected and the caprices of French seasons. You can learn things there about the phases of nature which the rich and idle and indifferent have no idea of. A student penned in the Latin quarter acquires at Flicoteaux's the most accurate knowledge of times and seasons; he knows when string-beans and peas do ripen, when cabbage will scent the hall, what species of salad abounds, and why the beetroot fails. An old calumny, lasting even to the time when Lucien appeared there, attributed the appearance of beefsteaks to a period of mortality among horses.

Few Parisian restaurants offer a really finer sight. Here you will meet with youth and faith gayly enduring poverty, though grave and ardent, earnest and anxious

faces are not lacking.   Clothes are generally neglected.
Customers who come well-dressed are remarked upon,
for everybody knows what such unwonted apparel sig-
nifies, — a mistress expected, a theatre in prospect, or
a visit to the upper spheres.   Here, it is said, lasting
friendships have been formed among students who,
later in life became celebrated men ; in fact, an instance
of that will be found in this history.   Nevertheless,
excepting the young men of the same country neighborhood who congregate together at an end of the tables,
the diners have, as a general thing, a gravity which
does not easily unbend, perhaps because of the catholi-
city of the wine.   Those who have cultivated Flicoteaux
for any length of time can remember several grave and
mysterious personages wrapped in a fog of chilling
poverty, who have dined there for two or more years
and have then disappeared ; no light on the lives of
such Parisian wraiths being ever given to the eyes of
their inquisitive co-diners.   The friendships started at
Flicoteaux's were clinched in the adjoining cafés to the
fumes of a spirituous punch or the glow of a half-cup
of coffee hallowed by a *gloria* of some sort.

   During the first days of his installation in the rue de
Cluny, Lucien, like other neophytes, was timid and regular in his behavior.   After his disastrous trial of fashionable life which had swept away his capital, he threw
himself into work with that youthful ardor that soon
succumbs to the difficulties and the amusements offered
by Paris to all existences, be they luxurious or poverty-
stricken, — difficulties and temptations which can be
only resisted by the savage force of real talent or the
dogged will of ambition.

Lucien usually betook himself to Flicoteaux's about half-past four in the afternoon, having observed the advantage of arriving among the first; the dishes were then more varied, and there was still enough of whichever he preferred.   Like all poetic natures he liked a particular seat, and his choice in this instance was not without discernment.   From the first day of his attendance at Flicoteaux's he had noticed, near the *comptoir*, a table at which the faces of the diners and the scraps of their conversation which reached his ears indicated literary companionship.   Moreover, a sort of instinct told him that by sitting near the *comptoir* he would be in closer relations with the heads of the restaurant. Accordingly he sat down at a little square table near by, where he saw two covers laid with clean napkins not in metal rings, intended, no doubt, for transient guests. Directly opposite to him sat a pale and thin young man, apparently as poor as himself, whose fine, worn face revealed that hopes relinquished had wearied his mind and left within his soul deep furrows where no seed now could germinate.   Lucien felt himself impelled to this unknown man by these vestiges of poesy lingering about him and by an irresistible impulse of sympathy.

This young man, the first person with whom the poet of Angoulême conversed, after exchanging civilities and observations for about a week, was named Étienne Lousteau.   Like Lucien, Étienne had left his provincial home, a town in Berry, about two years earlier.   His animated gestures, his burning glance, his curt, succinct speech, betrayed at times some bitter knowledge of literary life.   Étienne had come from Sancerre with a tragedy in his pocket, drawn to Paris by the same

desires which enticed Lucien, — fame, power, money.
At first he dined daily at Flicoteaux's, soon only now
and then. Lucien missed him. When young men
have met the night before, the interest of their conversation holds over into that of the next day; but
these intervals of absence obliged Lucien to break the
ice anew each time they met, and retarded an intimacy
which, during these first weeks, had made but little
progress.

By questioning the *dame du comptoir* Lucien learned
that his acquaintance was on the staff of a *petit journal*,
and wrote the dramatic articles on pieces acted at the
Ambigu-Comique, the Gaîté, and the Panorama-Dramatique. This was enough to make him a personage
to Lucien, who determined to begin a conversation and
make some efforts to obtain a friendship which might
be useful to his own career. The journalist was absent
two weeks. Lucien did not as yet know that Étienne
only dined at Flicoteaux's when he had no money,
which fact gave him his morose, disillusioned look, and
the stiffness which Lucien met with courteous smiles and
pleasant words. Nevertheless, such an intimacy required deliberate thought before it was entered upon;
for this unknown journalist was evidently leading a
costly life, mingled with *petit verres*, cups of coffee,
bowls of punch, theatres, and suppers. Now, during
his first weeks in the Latin quarter Lucien's behavior
was that of a child bewildered by his first experience
of Parisian life. After studying the costs of living
and calculating his resources, he dared not follow the
ways of Étienne, fearing to be again drawn into the
blunders he now so deeply regretted. Still under the

influence of his provincial faiths, his guardian angels, Eve and David, rose before his mind at every evil thought, reminding him of the hopes they had placed upon him, of the happiness of his mother, for which he was accountable, and of all the promises of his genius. He continued therefore to spend his mornings in the library of Sainte-Geneviève studying history; where his first researches showed him horrible mistakes in his "Archer of Charles IX." When the library closed he returned to his cold damp bedroom to correct his work, recast it, or reject whole chapters. After dining at Flicoteaux's he walked along the Passage du Commerce to Blosse's "Literary Cabinet," where he spent his evenings reading contemporary literature, newspapers, periodicals, and volumes of poetry, to keep himself in touch with the intellectual movement of the day, and returned to his wretched room at midnight having saved the cost of fuel and lights. These readings changed his ideas so completely that he revised the collection of his sonnets upon flowers, his dear "Daisies," and worked over them until scarcely a hundred lines remained the same.

At first, therefore, Lucien led the pure and innocent life of those guileless young provincials who think the food provided by Flicoteaux luxurious living compared with that of their family home, who refresh themselves by sauntering slowly along the alleys of the Luxembourg, looking obliquely at the pretty women, with swelling hearts, and who never leave the student quarter, where they devote themselves religiously to work for the sake of their future career. But Lucien, born a poet, soon possessed by eager desires, was powerless against the seductions of theatrical posters. The Théâtre-Français the Vaudeville, the Variétés, the Opera-Comique, where he sat in the pit, took some sixty francs out of his pocket. What poet could resist the enjoyment of seeing Talma in the parts which he made so famous? The theatre, that first love of all poetic natures, fascinated Lucien ; the actors and the actresses seemed to him imposing personages. He never dreamed of the possibility of crossing the foot-lights and seeing them familiarly. These givers of his delight were to his mind wonderful beings whom the journals ought to treat as one of the great interests of the State. To be a dramatic author, to see his plays acted, — oh, what a dream to nurse ! That dream a few bold spirits, like Casimir Delavigne, had realized !

Such teeming thoughts, such moments as these of belief in himself, followed by despair, agitated Lucien's being and kept him in the path of toil and economy, notwithstanding the low mutterings of more than one importunate desire. Through excess of virtue he forbade himself to ever enter the Palais-Royal, that place of perdition, where in a single day he had spent fifty francs at Véry's and nearly five hundred francs in clothes. When he yielded to the temptation of seeing Fleury, Talma, the two Baptistes, or Michot, he stood for five hours in the queue to obtain a seat in the dark gallery. Often on such occasions, after waiting two hours, the words "There are no seats left" would echo in the ears of many a disappointed student. After the play Lucien returned home with lowered eyes, looking at nothing in the streets, crowded at that hour with seduction. A few adventures of extreme simplicity

5

may have happened to him, such as take a vast place in timid and youthful imaginations.

Frightened one day when counting his money at the rapid diminution of his capital, Lucien felt cold chills run down him as the necessity of obtaining a publisher and doing some work for pay came over him. The young journalist of whom he would fain have made a friend no longer dined at Flicoteaux's. Lucien waited and hoped that something would turn up, but nothing came. In Paris, lucky accidents happen only to those who are much in the world; the variety of a man's intercourse with life increases his chances of success; luck is always on the side of numbers. Like a true provincial, in whom the sense of prudence long remains, Lucien did not wish to reach a period when a few francs only would remain to him. He resolved to face a publisher.

On a cold morning in the month of September he walked along the rue de la Harpe with his manuscripts under his arm. He went as far as the quai des Augustins, following the sidewalk and looking alternately at the waters of the Seine and the shops of the publishers, as if some guardian angel were advising him to throw himself into the river rather than into literature. After agonizing hesitation, after examining with the deepest attention the faces he could see through the windows or the doors, faces more or less kindly, cheerful, scowling, joyous, or sad, he came upon a house before which the clerks were packing books in haste. Shipments were evidently being made; the walls were covered with advertisements : —

" For sale: The Solitary, by M. le Vicomte d'Arlincourt, third edition. Léonide, by Victor Ducange, 5 vols. 12mo, printed on fine paper, price 12 frs. MORAL INDUCTIONS, by Kératry."

" They are lucky, those fellows ! " thought Lucien.

The advertisement, or rather the poster, a new and original invention of the famous Ladvocat, was then flourishing for the first time on the walls of Paris. The city was soon overrun by the imitators of this novel method of advertising, which brought in quite a revenue to the State. Lucien, his heart swelling with ardor and disquietude, Lucien, so great in Angoulême, so little in Paris, slid along the walls of the houses trying to summon courage to enter that shop, full of clerks, customers, and publishers.

" And perhaps authors," thought Lucien.

" I wish to speak to Monsieur Vidal or to Monsieur Porchon," he said to a clerk.

He had read the sign in large letters : " VIDAL AND PORCHON ; publishing-commissioners for France and foreign countries."

" They are both engaged," said the busy clerk.

" I will wait."

The poet was left to himself in the shop, where he examined the packages. He stayed there two hours looking at the titles of books, opening the volumes and reading a page of them here or there. At last, he found himself leaning against a glass partition covered with small green curtains, behind which he now suspected that either Porchon or Vidal was ensconced, for he overheard the following conversation : —

" Will you take five hundred copies ? If so, I 'll let you have them at five francs and give you a double commission."

"What price does that make them?"

"Sixteen sous less."

"Four francs, four sous?" said Vidal or Porchon, to whoever was, making the offer.

"Yes," replied the seller.

"With time allowance?"

"Old screw! then you'll pay me in eighteen months with notes at a year's sight?"

"No, paid at once," replied Vidal or Porchon.

"What time, nine months?" asked the writer, or, more probably, his publisher, who was doubtless offering a book.

"No, my dear fellow, one year," replied the buyer.

There was silence for a moment.

"You are squeezing the blood out of me!" cried the seller.

"But do you suppose we shall sell five hundred copies of 'Léonide' in a year?" replied the publishing-commissioner to the agent of Victor Ducange. "If books went off as publishers wish, we should be millionnaires, my dear friend; but they go as the public choose. Walter Scott's novels are selling at eighteen sous a volume, three francs twelve sous the set, and you expect me to sell your trash higher! If you want me to push the book, make it worth my while. Vidal!"

A stout man left a desk and came forward, putting his pen behind his ear.

"On your last journey how many Ducange books did you get off?" asked Porchon.

"I sold two hundred of the 'Little Old Man of Calais;' but in order to do that I had to come down on two other books which give less commission, — regular nightingales."

Later, Lucien learned that the nickname " nightingale " is applied by publishers to books which stay perched upon their shelves in the darkest depths of the warehouses.

" Besides, you know," continued Vidal, " Picard is preparing to sell novels. We are promised twenty per cent discount on the trade price in order to make him a success."

" Very good, then ; at one year," said the seller, dolefully, frightened by the last remark made, as it were confidentially, between Vidal and Porchon.

" Is that settled? " asked Porchon.

" Yes."

The selling publisher left the place. Lucien heard Porchon remark to Vidal, " We have three hundred copies already engaged ; payment is delayed a year ; we can sell the whole batch of the 'Léonide' at five francs, payment in six months and — "

" Yes, I see," said Vidal ; " that is fifteen hundred francs clear."

" Oh ! I knew he was pressed."

" He is losing money ; he pays Ducange four thousand francs for two thousand copies."

Here Lucien stopped Vidal short by showing himself at the door of the glass cage.

" Gentlemen," he said to the partners, " I have the honor to wish you good-morning."

The publishers scarcely returned his salutation.

" I am the author of a novel on the history of France, in the style of Walter Scott ; it is called 'The Archer of Charles IX. ;' and I propose to you to publish it."

Porchon cast a frigid look at Lucien, and laid his pen

on his desk. Vidal looked at the author rudely, and replied : —

" We are not publishers ; we sell books on commission. We never undertake books on our own account, unless the writers have made a name. Besides, in any case, we deal only in serious books, histories, compendiums."

" But my book is serious ; its object is to depict in a true light the struggle of the Catholics who stood for absolute government against the Protestants who wanted a republic."

" Monsieur Vidal ! " called a clerk.

Vidal slipped out.

" I don't say, monsieur, that your book may not be a masterpiece," said Porchon, with an uncivil gesture, " but we only concern ourselves with books already printed. Go and see those firms which buy manuscripts ; there 's Père Doguereau, rue du Coq, near the Louvre ; he buys novels. If you had come sooner you might have seen Pollet, Doguereau's rival, one of the publishers in the Galeries de Bois ; he has just gone out."

" Monsieur, I have a collection of poems — "

" Monsieur Porchon ! " called some one.

" Poems ! " cried Porchon, angrily ; " whom do you take me for ? " he added with a sneer, disappearing into a wareroom behind him.

Lucien crossed the Pont-Neuf a prey to many reflections. The facts he had discovered from this commercial lingo showed him plainly enough that to such publishers books were like hats to hatters, — goods to buy cheap and sell dear.

" I made a mistake in going there," thought he ; but he was, all the same, shocked at the brutal and material aspect under which literature had been shown to him.   He presently came to a modest little shop in the rue du Coq, over the door of which was painted, in yellow letters on a green ground, the words : "DOGUEREAU, PUBLISHER."   Lucien remembered having seen that name at the bottom of the titlepages of various novels he had opened in Blosse's reading-room.   He entered, not without that inward trepidation which all men of imagination feel at the prospect of a struggle.   He found a singular old man within, — one of the most original figures of the book-trade under the Empire.

Doguereau wore a black coat with long square skirts, though the fashion of the day required what were called " cod-fish tails."   He had a waistcoat of some common woollen material in squares of divers colors, from the pocket of which depended a steel chain and a brass key, which jingled against a pair of huge black breeches. The watch must have been about the size of an onion. This attire was completed by a pair of thick woollen stockings, iron-gray in color, and shoes with silver buckles.   The old man was bareheaded, and his gray hair hung down rather poetically in straggling locks. Père Doguereau, as Porchon had called him, resembled a professor of belles-lettres as to coat, breeches, and shoes, but his waistcoat, watch, and stockings were those of a shopkeeper.   His countenance did not contradict this curious combination ; he had the magisterial, dogmatic air and the worn face of a professor of rhetoric, and the keen eyes, the suspicious mouth, the vague uneasiness of a bookseller.

" Monsieur Doguereau ? " said Lucien.

" Myself, monsieur."

" I am the author of a novel," continued Lucien.

" You are very young," said the publisher.

" But, monsieur, my age has nothing to do with the matter."

" True," said the old publisher, taking the manuscript. " Ah, the deuce ! 'The Archer of Charles IX.,' — that 's a good title.   Well, young man, tell me your subject in two words."

" Monsieur, it is an historical work in the style of Walter Scott, in which the nature of the struggle between the Catholics and the Protestants is shown to be a contest between two systems of government ; a contest which seriously threatened the throne itself.   I take the Catholic side."

"Hey ! young man ; why, those are really ideas !   Well, I 'll read your book ; I 'll promise you that.   I would rather have a novel in the style of Mrs. Radcliffe ; but if you are really a worker, if you have style, construction, ideas, and the art of dramatically presenting your subject, I am not unwilling to be of use to you.   What we want now are really good manuscripts."

" When may I call again ? "

" I am going into the country this evening, and shall return the day after to-morrow ; by that time I shall have read your work, and if it suits me, we can arrange matters that day."

Lucien, finding his new acquaintance so cordial, had the unlucky idea of pulling out the manuscript of " The Daisies."

" Monsieur, I have also a collection of poems."

" Ah ! you are a poet, are you ? Then I don't want your novel," said the old man, holding out the manuscript. " Rhymesters always fail when they try prose. Prose can't be mere stuff; it must have something to say, and it says it."

" But, monsieur, Walter Scott wrote poems."

" That's true," said Doguereau, relenting somewhat ; he guessed the poverty of the young man, and kept the manuscript. " Where do you live? I'll go and see you."

Lucien gave his address without suspecting the old man of any ulterior meaning ; he did not perceive him to be a publisher of the old school, of the days when publishers liked to keep such men as Voltaire and Montesquieu under lock and key in a garret, dying of hunger.

" I return by way of the Latin quarter," said the old man, after reading the address ; " I will call."

" He's a worthy man," thought Lucien, after leaving old Doguereau. " I have met a friend to youth, — a connoisseur who really knows something. Commend me to that sort of sponsor. I told David that talent would easily make its way in Paris."

Lucien went back to his quarters, light-hearted and dreaming of fame. Without thinking further of the sinister words which had reached his ears in the office of Vidal and Porchon, he imagined himself in possession of at least twelve hundred francs. Twelve hundred francs represented one year's sojourn in Paris, — one year, during which he could prepare new works. How many projects were built upon this hope ! How many brilliant reveries he indulged as he saw his living secured and himself free to labor. He planned a new abode, arranged his mode of life, a little more and he would even have made purchases for it. He whiled away the time and his impatience in Blosse's reading-room. Two days later old Doguereau, greatly surprised at the style Lucien had displayed in a first work, pleased with the exaggeration of the characters which the period of the drama permitted, struck with the ardor of imagination with which the young author had developed his plot (the old man had not lost his power of appreciation), — old Doguereau, we say, came to the house where his embryo Walter Scott was living. He had made up his mind to pay a thousand francs down for the absolute possession of " The Archer of Charles IX." and to bind Lucien in writing to supply him with other works. But when the old fox saw the house he reconsidered his intentions.

" A young man who lives in such a place as this," thought he, " has humble tastes ; he loves study and work ; eight hundred francs will be enough to give him."

The landlady, of whom he asked his way to Monsieur Lucien de Rubempré's apartment, replied, " Fourth floor ! " The publisher looked up, saw that the sky was above that floor, and thought to himself : —

" This young man is a good-looking fellow ; he is in fact a very handsome man ; if he earns much money he will waste it, he won't work any longer. In our mutual interests I shall offer him six hundred francs, — in ready money, not bills."

So thinking, he went upstairs and rapped three knocks on Lucien's door, which the young man opened.

The bareness of the room was depressing. On the table was a bowl of milk and a two-sous roll. This penury of genius struck old Doguereau.

" May he long keep to these simple habits, this frugality, these modest wants," thought he ; then he said aloud : " I am very glad to see you. This is how Jean-Jacques, with whom you have much in common, lived. In such lodgings as these the fire of genius burns and does great works. This is how men of letters ought to live, instead of junketing in cafés and restaurants, losing their time, their talent, and our money." So saying, he sat down. " Young man," he went on, " your novel is not bad. I was once a professor of rhetoric, and I know French history ; there are excellent things in the book ; in short, you have a future before you."

" Ah ! monsieur."

" Well, as I told you, we can do business together. I will buy your novel."

Lucien's heart glowed, he palpitated with joy, he was about to enter the literary world, at last he would see himself in print.

" I will pay you four hundred francs, said Doguereau, in a honied tone and looking at Lucien in a way that seemed to indicate an effort at generosity.

" A volume ? " said Lucien.

" The whole book," replied Doguereau, not heeding Lucien's astonishment. " But," he added, " it will be in ready money. You must bind yourself to give me two such books every year for six years. If the first is sold off within six months I will engage to pay you six hundred for the succeeding books. At the rate of two a year you will earn a hundred francs a month ; that will secure your livelihood and you will be happy. I have authors to whom I pay only three hundred francs a novel. I give two hundred francs for a translation from the English. Formerly, such prices would have been exorbitant."

"Monsieur, we cannot come to any agreement on such terms, and I request you to return my manuscript," said Lucien, cruelly disappointed.

"There it is," said the old man. "You don't understand business, monsieur. In bringing out an author's first work a publisher risks sixteen hundred francs on the printing and the paper. It is easier to make a novel than it is to produce that sum of money. I have a hundred novels now on my hands but I haven't a hundred and sixty thousand francs in my cashbox. Alas, I haven't made that sum during all the twenty years I have been a publisher. No man can make a fortune by bringing out novels. Vidal and Porchon will only sell them for us on terms which are becoming day after day more extortionate. Where you risk your time I am forced to spend two thousand francs. If I make a mistake, for *habent sua fata libelli,* I lose my two thousand francs ; while as for you, you have only to launch an ode against public stupidity. After thinking over what I have had the honor to say to you, you will come and see me, — yes, you will come back to me," repeated the publisher, authoritatively, in reply to a gesture of superb disdain from Lucien. "Far from finding other publishers willing to risk two thousand francs on an unknown author, you will not find even a clerk who would give himself the trouble to read your manuscript. I, who have read it, can show you a good many faults of grammar in it." Lucien looked mortified. "When I see you again you will have lost a hundred francs," added the old man; "for I shall then give you only three hundred for that novel." He rose, bowed, and turned to go; but on the sill of the door he stopped and said: " If you had no talent, no future before you, if I did not take an interest in studious young men, I should never have proposed to you such liberal terms. A hundred francs a month! think of it! However, a novel in a drawer is not a horse in a stable; it won't eat oats — but then, it does n't provide any! "

Lucien took his manuscript and flung it on the floor crying out, " I 'd rather burn it! "

" You have the head of a poet," said the old man.

Lucien devoured his bread and gulped down his milk and went out. The room was not big enough to contain him; he would have turned and doubled upon himself like the lion in his cage at the Jardin des Plantes.

V.

THE FIRST FRIEND.

AT the library of Sainte-Geneviève, to which Lucien now made his way, he had long noticed, and always in the same corner, a young man about twenty-five years of age, who seemed to work with a steady application which nothing disturbed, — the test of true literary toilers. This young man had evidently been in the habit of coming to the library for some time ; the clerks and the librarian himself showed him attentions ; he was allowed to take out books which, as Lucien noticed, he brought back punctually the next day. The poet recognized in this unknown student a brother in penury and hope.

Small, thin, and pale, this toiler hid a noble brow beneath a thick black mane of hair, somewhat ill-kept ; his hands were beautiful ; he attracted the eye of even non-observing persons by a vague resemblance to the portrait of Bonaparte engraved after Robert Lefebvre. That engraving is a poem of passionate melancholy, repressed ambition, subdued activity. Examine it well. You will find there genius and discretion, shrewdness and grandeur. The eyes have a soul like the eyes of a woman. Their glance is eager into space, desirous of difficulties to vanquish. Were the name " Bonaparte "

not written beneath it you still would pause to gaze
upon that portrait and contemplate it. The young man
who seemed to embody this engraving usually wore
trousers *à pied* in thick-soled shoes ; a frock-coat of
common cloth, a black cravat, a waistcoat of gray and
white cloth, buttoned to the neck, and a cheap hat. His
contempt for all unnecessary care in dress was obvious.

This noticeable person, marked with the seal which
genius stamps upon the forehead of her slaves, Lucien
had seen at Flicoteaux's. He was, in fact, the most
regular of the customers ; he ate to live, paying no
attention to the food, with which he seemed familiar ; he
drank water only. Whether in the library or at
Flicoteaux's, he manifested in all things a sort of dignity which came no doubt from the consciousness that
his life was occupied with great things ; this made
him, in some degree, inapproachable. His glance was
thoughtful. Meditation inhabited that noble brow,
which was finely cut. Lucien felt an involuntary
respect for him. Several times they had mutually
glanced at each other as if to speak, when entering or
leaving the library or the restaurant, and then refrained
as if neither dared to take the step. This silent guest
always took his place in a retired corner of the dining-
room looking on the place de la Sorbonne. Lucien had,
therefore, no opportunity of joining him, though he felt
strongly drawn to the young worker who showed so
many unspoken signs of superiority. The natures of
both, as they knew later, were timid and virgin, and
subject to those fears which are pleasurable emotions to
solitary minds. Without a sudden meeting between
them at the moment of Lucien's present disaster per-

haps they would never have come into personal communication. But now, as Lucien entered the rue des Grès, he saw the unknown worker returning from Sainte-Geneviève, at an unusual hour.

"The library is closed, I do not know why, monsieur," he said.

Tears were in Lucien's eyes at the moment. He thanked the student with a gesture more eloquent than words, — one of those gestures which, from youth to youth, open instantly all hearts. They walked on side by side along the rue des Grès towards the rue de la Harpe.

"Then I shall go and walk in the Luxembourg," said Lucien. "When we have once come out it is hard to turn back to work."

"Yes, we are no longer in the current of our ideas," said the other. "You seem distressed, monsieur."

"A strange thing has just happened to me," said Lucien.

He related his visit to Vidal and Porchon and that to the old publisher, and told of the proposals the latter had made to him; he gave his name and added a few words as to his situation. For the last month he had spent sixty francs on food, thirty francs for lodging, twenty at the theatre, ten for the reading-room, — in all a hundred and twenty francs; and only a hundred and twenty now remained to him.

"Monsieur," said his companion, "your history is mine and that of the thousand or twelve hundred other young men who annually come to Paris from the provinces. But we are not among the most unfortunate. Do you see that theatre?" he said, pointing to the roofs of the Odéon. "One day a man of talent came to live in the garret of one of those houses near the theatre. He was sunk in the depths of poverty; he was married, — an aggravation of misery which has not yet come to you or me, — married to a woman he loved; additionally poor (or rich if you choose) in possessing two children; overwhelmed with debt, but confident in his pen. He offered the Odéon a comedy in five acts. It was accepted; the comedians favored it; the manager pressed on the rehearsals. The poor author, living in a garret which you can see from here, exhausted his last resources in living through the period required to bring out his play; his wife took her clothes to the pawnshop; the family ate nothing but bread. The day of the last rehearsal, the evening before the first representation, that starving household owed fifty francs to the baker, the milkman, the porter. The author had kept his necessary clothes from the pawn-shop, a coat, shirt, trousers, waistcoat and boots. Certain of success, he clasped his wife to his breast, telling her they had seen the last of their troubles. 'There is nothing now against us,' he cried. 'There is fire,' said his wife. 'Look, the theatre is burning!' Monsieur, the Odéon was burned. Do not complain, therefore; you have neither wife nor children; you have a hundred and twenty francs in your pocket, and you owe no man anything. That play had a run of a hundred and twenty nights at the Théâtre Louvois. The king gave a pension to its author. As Buffon said, Genius is Patience. Patience is that which most resembles, in man, the process which Nature employs in her creations. What is Art, monsieur? It is Nature concentrated."

6

The two young men were walking about the Luxembourg. Lucien soon learned the name, afterwards famous, of the man who was trying to console him. He was Daniel d'Arthèz, now among the most illustrious writers of our day, and one of those rare beings who, in the beautiful words of the poet, present "the harmony of a noble talent with a noble soul."

"No one can be a great man cheaply," said d'Arthèz in his gentle voice. "Genius waters her work with tears. Talent is a moral being which, like all other beings, is subject to the maladies of childhood. Society rejects undeveloped talent just as nature removes her feeble or deformed creations. Whoever wishes to rise above his fellows must be prepared to struggle, and not recoil at difficulty. A great writer is a martyr who does not die, — that's the whole of it! You have upon your brow the stamp of genius," continued d'Arthèz, casting a look upon his companion which seemed to envelop him, "but, if you have not will within your soul, if you have not angelic patience, if — at whatever distance from attainment the caprices of your fate may fling you — you cannot, like the tortoise, return along the path towards your Infinite as the tortoise returns to its Ocean, then renounce, renounce to-day this career."

"Are you, yourself, expecting tortures?" said Lucien.

"Yes, trials of all sorts, — calumny, betrayal, injustice of rivals, the trickery, harshness, insolence of publishers. If your work is a fine one, what matters a first loss?"

"Will you read and judge my work?" said Lucien.

" Yes," replied d'Arthèz. "I live in the rue des Quatre-Vents, in a house where one of the most illustrious men and one of the greatest geniuses of our time, a phenomenon of science, Desplein, the great surgeon, endured his martyrdom in struggling with the first difficulties of life and fame in Paris. The thought of Desplein gives me every night the dose of courage which I need every morning. I live in the very room where he ate, like Rousseau, bread and cherries,—but without Thérèse. Come there in an hour and I shall be at home."

The two poets parted, pressing each other's hand with an unspeakable effusion of melancholy tenderness. Lucien went to fetch his manuscript, Daniel d'Arthèz to pawn his watch and buy two bundles of wood that his new friend might find a fire in his cold room. Lucien was punctual; he found a house even less decent than the one he lived in, entered through a dark alley, at the end of which was the staircase. D'Arthèz' room, on the fifth floor, had two wretched windows, between which stood a bookcase in blackened wood, full of ticketed paper boxes. A poor bedstead of painted wood, like those of schoolboys, a bedside table, and two armchairs covered with horsehair stood at the farther end of the room, the walls of which were covered with checked paper stained by time and smoke. A long table piled with papers was placed between the fireplace and one of the windows. Opposite the fireplace was a miserable mahogany bureau. A shabby carpet covered the whole floor; this necessary luxury lessened the need of fuel. Before the table stood a common office-chair covered with red sheep's-skin, whitened by wear; six other shabby chairs completed the furniture.

On the fireplace Lucien saw an old card-table candle-stick, with four wax candles, covered with a shade. Later, when he one day asked the meaning of such luxury in the midst of all other symptoms of direst poverty, d'Arthèz answered that it was impossible for him to endure the smell of a tallow candle. This little circumstance shows the delicacy of his senses, — a sure indication of an exquisite sensibility.

The reading lasted seven hours. Daniel listened attentively, without saying a word or making an observation, — one of the rarest proofs of good taste an author can give.

" Well? " said Lucien, laying the manuscript on the fireplace.

" You are in a good and noble path," answered the young man, soberly, but your work should be done over again. If you do not wish to be a mere imitator of Walter Scott you must make for yourself another style, — for you have imitated him. You begin, like him, with a long conversation to introduce your characters; when they have talked, you bring in description and action. This juxtaposition, which is necessary to all dramatic art, you employ last. Reverse the order of things. Substitute for those diffuse conversations, which are fine in Scott but colorless with you, descriptions, to which our language vividly lends itself. Let dialogue be an expected consequence which crowns your preparation of description and action. Enter at once upon the action. Handle your subject first one way, then another; grasp it by the head or the tail; in short, vary your methods, don't be always the same. Walter Scott is without passion; either he is ignorant of it, or the hypocritical morals of his nation forbid him the use of it. To him woman is duty incarnate. With rare exceptions his heroines are absolutely the same; he has the matter-of-fact formula for all of them. They proceed from Clarissa Harlowe; reducing them to one idea he could not help making them of one type, varied of course, by a more or less vivid coloring. Woman has brought disorder into society through passion. Passion has an infinitude of aspects. Depict passions and you have immense resources, of which this great genius deprived himself that he might be read by the families of prudish England. In France, you find the charming faults and brilliant manners of Catholicism contrasting with the severe and gloomy figures of Calvinism during the most passionate period of our history. But each authentic reign, from Charlemagne down, demands at least one work, — sometimes four or five; especially those of Louis XIV., Henri IV., and François I. You might thus write the picturesque history or drama of all France, in which you could paint the costumes, furniture, houses, homes, private life itself, presenting at the same time the spirit of the age, instead of laboriously narrating well-known facts. You have a means of being original by correcting the popular errors which disfigure the memory of so many of our kings. Dare, for instance, in this first work of yours, to portray the grand and magnificent figure of Catherine, which you have sacrificed to the prejudices which still hover round her. Paint Charles IX. as he was, and not as Protestant writers have made him. At the end of ten years' toil and persistence you will have fame and fortune."

It was now nine o'clock.   Lucien imitated the secret generosity of his new friend by asking him to dine at Édon's, where he spent twelve francs.   During this dinner d'Arthèz revealed the secret of his hopes and studies.   He believed in no great, incomparable talent without a deep, a profound metaphysical knowledge. At the present moment he was culling the philosophic riches of ancient and modern times to assimilate them. He wished, like Molière, to be a deep philosopher before making comedies.   He studied the written world and the living world ; the thought and the fact.   His friends were naturalists, young physicians, political writers, and artists, — serious men and studious, all of them full of promise.   He lived by writing conscientious articles, poorly paid, for dictionaries, either biographic, encyclopedic, or of natural sciences.   He wrote neither more nor less than was necessary for his livelihood while following his real purpose.   D'Arthèz was also writing a work of imagination, undertaken solely to study the resources of the French language.   This book, still unfinished, he took up and laid aside capriciously, reserving it for days of great distress.   It was a psychological study of deep import in the form of a novel.

Though Daniel unfolded himself modestly he seemed gigantic to Lucien.   By the time they left the restaurant, at eleven o'clock, Lucien was possessed by an ardent friendship for that virtue without vainglory, that noble nature so unconsciously sublime.   He did not discuss Daniel's advice, he followed it to the letter.   His fine talent, already ripened by thought, accepted this criti-

cism, made for him and not for others, which opened
to him the gates of a glorious palace of the imagination. The lips of the provincial were touched with a
live coal; the words of the Parisian toiler found fruit-
ful ground in the brain of the Angoulême poet. Lucien
recast his work.

Joyful in having met in the desert of Paris a heart
which overflowed with generous sentiments in harmony
with his own, the great man of the provinces did as all
other young fellows who are hungry for affection do;
he fastened like a chronic malady on d'Arthèz; he
called for him on his way to the library; he walked
with him in the Luxembourg if the weather were fine;
he accompanied him home in the evening after dining
beside him at Flicoteaux's; in short, he hugged to him
as closely as the soldiers of the Grand Army hugged
each other on the frozen plains of Russia. During the
first days of his acquaintance with Daniel, Lucien noticed
with some mortification that his presence caused a certain constraint among the friends who surrounded
d'Arthèz. The talk of these superior men, of whom
Daniel spoke to him with suppressed enthusiasm, often
seemed restrained within the limits of a reserve which
was not in keeping with their evidently ardent friendship; at such times Lucien would take his leave dis-
creetly, feeling pained by the ostracism of which he
was the object, and also goaded by the curiosity he felt
as to these unknown persons, who were called by none
but their baptismal names. All of them bore upon
their foreheads, like d'Arthèz, the stamp of some special
genius.

After certain secret oppositions, privately overcome

by Daniel, Lucien was at last deemed worthy of admission into this brotherhood of great minds.   Henceforth he knew these men, united by the warmest sympathies and by the serious purposes of their intellectual lives, who met nearly every evening at d'Arthèz's lodging. They all foresaw in Daniel a great writer; they considered him their leader ever since the loss of their first head, one of the most extraordinary geniuses of modern times, who, for reasons unnecessary to mention here, had returned to his life in the provinces, — a man whom Lucien often heard the others mention under the name of Louis.   The reader will easily understand the interest and curiosity these various persons roused in the young poet's mind when we mention those who have since, like d'Arthèz, achieved fame; some others failed.

VI.

THE BROTHERHOOD OF HEARTS AND MINDS.

Among those who are still living was Horace Bianchon, then a pupil at the Hôtel-Dieu, since one of the
lights of the École de Paris, and too well known now
to make it necessary to describe his person or explain
his character and the nature of his mind. Next to him
came Léon Giraud, the profound philosopher, the bold
theorist, who has probed all systems, expounded them,
formulated them, judged them, and laid them at the feet
of his idol, HUMANITY, — always grand, even in his errors, ennobled by sincerity. Intrepid toiler, conscientious scholar, he is now the leader of a school of social
and moral philosophy on which time alone can pronounce
judgment. If his convictions have turned his destiny
into regions foreign to those of his comrades, he is none
the less their faithful friend.

Art was represented by Joseph Bridau, one of the
best painters of the New School. Were it not for
private troubles, to which his too impressionable nature
condemned him, Joseph (whose final word is not yet
said) might have continued the traditions of the old
Italian Masters; for his drawing is that of Rome and
his coloring of Venice. But love has killed him; it fills
not his heart only, but his brain; it upsets his life and
leads him to describe strange zigzags. If his mistress

makes him too happy or too miserable Joseph sends to
the Exposition either sketches in which the color
smothers the design, or pictures, finished under the distress of some imaginary grief, in which the drawing has
so absorbed him that the color, which he handles at will,
is not distinguishable.   He constantly disappoints both
the public and his friends.   Hoffmann would have
adored him for his bold innovations on the field of Art,
for his whims, for his fancy.   When he is quite himself
he rouses admiration ; he enjoys it ; and is angry when
he receives no praise for his failures, in which the eyes
of his own soul see that which is absent for the eyes of
the public.   Capricious to the last degree, his friends
have often seen him destroy a finished picture because
he thought it too carefully worked up.   " Too fiddling,"
he would say, " mere pupil work."   Original, and sometimes sublime, he has all the troubles and all the enjoyments of nervous temperaments in whom a desire for
perfection often turns to disease.   His spirit is companion to that of Sterne, — not, of course, in literary
achievement.   His sayings, his flashes of thought have
unspeakable savor.   He is eloquent and knows how to
love his friends, though always with the natural caprice
which he puts into his feelings as he does into his work.
He was dear to the brotherhood for precisely that which
the commonplace world would have called his defects.

Next we have Fulgence Ridal, one of the few writers
of our day who are highly gifted with the comic view ;
a poet indifferent to fame, tossing to the theatres his
commonest productions, and keeping in the harem of
his own mind, for himself and for his friends, his choicest scenes ; asking nothing from the public but the

necessary money to maintain his independence, and doing no more work when that was attained. Lazy, yet
prolific as Rossini, compelled, like all the great comic
poets, like Molière and Rabelais, to consider everything on the side of the *pro* and against the *contra*,
he was sceptical, he could laugh and he did laugh at
everything. Fulgence Ridal is a great practical philosopher; but his science of society, his genius of observation, his contempt for fame have by no means
withered his heart. As active for others as he is in-
dolent for himself, when he does make a move it is
always for a friend. Not to give the lie to his outward
man which is truly Rabelaisian, he neither dislikes good
living nor does he seek it; he is both grave and mirth-
ful. His friends used to call him " the dog of the
regiment," and the name suits him well.

Three others, quite as remarkable as the four now
sketched in profile, were fated to succumb in the battle
of life: Meyraux first, who died after exciting the
famous dispute between Cuvier and Geoffroy-Sainte-
Hilaire on the great question which divided the scientific world between those rival geniuses some months
before the death of the one who held to close analytic
science, against the pantheism of the other, who still
lives and whom Germany reveres. Meyraux was the
special friend of Louis Lambert, who was soon to be
torn from the world of intellect by a premature death.

To these two men, each marked for untimely death,
both to-day obscure in spite of the vast reachings of
their knowledge and of their genius, we must add
Michel Chrestien, a republican of broad views, who
dreamed of a reconstructed Europe, and who in 1830

counted for much in the moral movement of the Saint-
Simonians.   A politician of the stripe of Saint-Just and
Danton, but simple and gentle as a girl, full of illusions,
full of love, gifted with a melodious voice that would
have ravished Mozart, Weber, or Rossini, and singing certain songs of Béranger in a way to intoxicate
a heart of poesy, love, and hope, — Michel Chrestien,
poor as Lucien, as Daniel, as all his friends, earned his
living with the indifference of a Diogenes.   He made
tables of contents for great works, prospectuses for publishers, keeping silence about his real opinions, as the
grave is silent on the secrets of death.   This gay
bohemian of intellect, this great mute statesman, who
might perhaps have changed the face of the world, died,
a simple soldier, in the cloister of Saint-Merri.   The
ball of a shopkeeper sent out of life one of the noblest
creatures that ever trod the soil of France.   Michel
Chrestien perished for other doctrines than his own.
His ideal federation threatened European aristocracy
far more than the republican propaganda ever did ; it
was more rational, less wild, than the shocking ideas
of indefinite liberty proclaimed by those young madmen
who thought themselves the heirs of the Convention.
This noble plebeian was mourned by all who knew him ;
none have ceased to think, and think often, of this
great and hidden statesman.

   These nine men formed a brotherhood in which esteem and friendship caused peace and good-will to reign
among ideas and doctrines that were utterly opposed to
each other.   Daniel d'Arthèz, a man of rank from
Picardy, held to monarchy with a conviction equal to
that of Michel Chrestien for his European federalism.

Fulgence Ridal laughed at the philosophical doctrines of Léon Giraud, who himself predicted to d'Arthèz the end of Christianity and also of the Family. Michel Chrestien, who believed in the religion of Christ, the divine law-giver of Equality, defended the immortality of the soul against the scalpel of Bianchon the analyst. They all argued and discussed, but never disputed. They had no vanity, being their own audience. They talked of their work and consulted each other with the adorable sincerity of youth. Was it a matter of serious moment? then the opposer abandoned his own views to enter into the thoughts of his friend, — all the more qualified to help because he was impartial in a cause, or in a work, which was foreign to his own ideas. Nearly all these brethren were gentle and tolerant in spirit; two qualities which proved their superiority. Envy, that horrible record-office of hopes deceived, talents miscarried, successes foiled, pretensions wounded, was unknown to them. All, moreover, were following different paths.

Thus it was that those who were admitted, like Lucien, to this brotherhood felt at their ease. True talent is always frank, hearty, open, never stiff; its wit and epigram delight the mind, and are not directed against self-esteem. When the first emotion of respectful diffidence passed off, nothing remained but infinite pleasure in the companionship of these fine young men. Familiarity did not exclude the sense that each had his own value; every man felt a deep respect for his neighbor; therefore each, feeling the power within him to be either the benefactor or the one benefited, accepted kindnesses from his neighbor without demur. Their conversations, full of charm and never flagging, covered the most varied subjects. Winged like arrows, their words flew to their point, and flew fast. Great external poverty and the splendor of intellectual wealth produces a singular contrast. Among these friends, none thought of the hard realities of life unless to make amicable jokes upon them. One day when the cold had set in unexpectedly, five of d'Arthèz' friends, each prompted by the same thought, arrived with an armful of wood under their cloaks, as often happens at picnics, where each guest is asked to bring a dish, and they all bring pâtés.

Gifted with that moral beauty which reacts upon form, and which, not less than toil and midnight study, gilds young faces with a tint divine, each of these friends had marked and rather haggard features, which the purity of their lives and the fire of thought composed and sanctified. Their foreheads were noticeable for poetic breadth. Their eager, brilliant eyes revealed a life unstained. The sufferings of poverty, when felt, were so gayly borne, so heartily accepted, that they did not change the serenity characteristic of the faces of young men who are still guiltless of grave wrong, who have not belittled themselves by any of those base compromises to which poverty, ill-endured, tempts youth — the longing for success through any means whatever, fair or foul, or the facile compliance with which so many literary men either welcome or pardon treachery. That which makes such friendships among men indissoluble, and doubles their charm, is a sentiment which can never belong to love, — namely, security. These young men were sure of themselves; the enemy of one was the enemy of all; they would have ruined their own

most urgent interests to obey the sacred solidarity of
their souls.   Incapable of baseness, each could pronounce a formidable " No ! " to every accusation against
the others ; he knew he might securely defend them.
Equals in nobility of heart, equals in strength of feeling, they could think all and say all to each other on
the common ground of science and of intellect ; hence
the candor of their intercourse, the gayety of their
speech.   Certain of understanding each other, their
minds could ramble as they pleased ; they kept nothing
back, neither their hopes and fears, nor their griefs and
joys ; they thought and suffered with open hearts.   The
precious delicacy which makes the well-known fable of
the " Two Friends " a treasure to fine souls, was habitual with them.   Their reluctance to admit an untried
new-comer into their sphere can be readily understood.
They were too well aware of the happiness and loftiness of their intercourse to risk its being troubled by
new and unknown elements.

 This federation of feelings and interests lasted without jar or disappointment for twenty years.   Death,
which first took Louis Lambert, Meyraux, and Michel
Chrestien, alone had power to disperse this noble
pleiades.   When, in 1832, Michel Chrestien fell, Horace
Bianchon, Daniel d'Arthèz, Léon Giraud, Joseph Bridau,
and Fulgence Ridal went, in spite of the danger of such
a step, and recovered his body at Saint-Merri, to pay it
their last honor in the face of burning Politics.   They
took the dear remains to Père-Lachaise by night.   Horace
Bianchon faced all difficulties and yielded to none ; he im-
plored the sanction of the ministers, telling them of his
long friendship for the dead Federalist.   That burial was

a scene deep-graven in the memory of the friends, and they were few in number, who surrounded the five already celebrated men who prepared it. As you walk through that beautiful cemetery, you may see a spot, bought *à perpétuité*, where a grassed grave lies, and at its head a black wooden cross on which is marked a name in scarlet letters, MICHEL CHRESTIEN. It is the only monument of its kind. The five friends thought they could best do homage to that simple man by such simplicity.

Here, then, in this cold attic-room, the noblest aspirations of feeling were realized. There these brothers in love, all equally strong in their different departments of knowledge, all tested as by fire in the crucible of poverty, enlightened each other mutually in simple good faith, telling their every thought, even their worst. Once admitted to the friendship of these choice souls and accepted as an equal, Lucien stood among them for poesy and beauty. He read them his sonnets, and they admired them. They would ask him for a sonnet as he would ask Michel Chrestien to sing a song. In the desert of Paris Lucien found an oasis in the rue des Quatre-Vents.

At the beginning of October, Lucien, having spent his last penny in buying a small supply of wood, was without resources in the midst of his most ardent toil, that of remodelling his book. Daniel d'Arthèz burned peat, and bore his poverty heroically; he never complained; he was careful as an old maid and methodical as a miser. Such courage excited that of Lucien, who, lately admitted to the brotherhood, felt an invincible repugnance to speak of his distress. One morning he went as far as the rue du Coq to sell "The Archer of Charles IX." to Doguereau, but did not find him. Lucien did not yet understand the comprehension of great minds. Each of his new friends was fully able to conceive the weakness of the poetic nature, the depression that must follow the efforts of a soul over-excited by the topics it was his mission to reproduce. These men, so strong to bear their own troubles, were tender to those of Lucien. They discovered his want of means. After a restful evening of talk, and meditation, and poesy, of flights with outspread wings through the regions of intellect, the future of nations, the domain of history, the brotherhood crowned their day by an act which will show in its sequel how little Lucien had really understood his new friends.

"Lucien, my friend," said Daniel, "you did not come to dinner at Flicoteaux's, and we all know why."

Lucien could not restrain the tears which came into his eyes.

"You've lacked confidence in us," said Michel Chrestien, "we shall score that up, and — "

"We have all," said Bianchon, "found some extra work: I have been taking care of a rich patient for Desplein, d'Arthèz got an article to write for the 'Encyclopédie;' Chrestien was starting one evening to sing in the Champs Élysées with a handkerchief and four candles, when he got a pamphlet to write for a man who pretends to be a statesman, and wanted six hundred francs' worth of Machiavelli; Léon Giraud has borrowed fifty francs of his publisher; Joseph sold some sketches; and Fulgence got his play acted Sunday to a full house."

7

"And here are two hundred francs," said Daniel; "accept them, and don't let us have to scold you again!"

"I do believe he wants to hug us," said Chrestien, "as if we had done something extraordinary!"

To fully understand Lucien's feelings in the midst of this living encyclopedia of young minds, all of diverse originality and all equally generous, we must here give the answers which Lucien received the following day from his brother-in-law, his sister, and his mother, in reply to a letter written by him to his family, — a masterpiece of sensibility and good intentions, but a dreadful cry drawn from him by his pecuniary distress.

My dear Lucien (wrote David Séchard), — You will find inclosed a draft at ninety days to your order for two hundred francs. You can negotiate it with Monsieur Métivier, paper-maker, rue Serpente, who is our correspondent in Paris.

My dear brother, we have absolutely nothing. My wife has taken charge of the printing-office, and does her task with a devotion, a patience, a business activity which make me bless heaven daily for having given me such an angel. She said it was impossible to send you the help you need. But, my dear friend, I think you are in so right a road, and have chosen such noble companions, that you cannot fail of your destiny. Therefore, unknown to Eve, I send you this draft, which I will find means of paying when it falls due. Do not abandon the path you are in; it is hard, but it will be glorious. I would rather suffer a hundred evils than have you fall into any of those Parisian mud-holes I have known of. Have the courage to avoid, as you have already done, bad places and bad friends, also heedless minds and a certain class of literary men whom I learned to estimate at their true value during my stay in Paris. Be the worthy emulator of the noble souls of whom you tell me, — d'Arthèz, Chrestien, Giraud, who, for the future, will be dear to me also. Such a course cannot fail to be soon rewarded.

Adieu, my dearly-beloved brother. Your letter delights my heart, for I did not expect of you such courage.

DAVID.

MY DEAR LUCIEN (wrote his sister, less cheerfully), — Your letter made us weep. Tell those noble friends towards whom your guardian angel led you that a mother and a sister pray for them. Yes, their names are engraved upon my heart; I hope I may some day see them. Here, my dear brother, we are working like laborers. My husband, that great unrecognized soul, whom I love daily more and more as I hourly discover new riches in his heart, has neglected the printing-office, and I know why. Your poverty, and mine, and the mother's cut him to the heart. Our dear David is like Prometheus gnawed by the vulture, a bitter grief with a sharp beak. As for himself, the noble man ! he never thinks of self, and yet he aspires to a fortune — for our sakes ! He spends his whole time in experiments for making paper ; and he has asked me to take his place in managing the printing-office, where he helps me as much as his absorbing occupations will allow. But alas ! I am pregnant. That event, which might have crowned me with joy, fills me with dread in the situation in which we now are. My mother has renewed her youth, and found strength for the fatiguing duties of monthly nursing.

If it were not for the anxieties of money, we should be so happy. Old Monsieur Séchard will not give a farthing to his son. David went to see him and tried to borrow a small sum to help you in your present necessity, for your letter distressed him greatly, but the old man said: "I know Lucien ; he'll have his head turned, and commit follies."

My mother and I, without David's knowledge, have pawned a few things, which my mother will redeem as soon as she earns the money. We have thus collected a hundred francs, which I send you by coach.

If I did not answer your first letter do not be vexed with me, dear friend. We were then sitting up all night, and I was working like a man; I did not know I had such strength. Madame de Bargeton is a woman without heart or soul; she owed it to herself, even if she loved you no longer, to protect and help you after tearing you from us and flinging you into that horrible Parisian ocean, where it is only by the mercy of God that you have found true friends amid the flood of men and selfish interests. She is not to be regretted. I have wished you had some devoted woman near you, — another myself; but now that I know you have such friends, I am satisfied. Spread your wings, my beautiful loved genius! you will yet be our glory as you are our love.

Your   EVE.

MY DARLING CHILD, — After all that your sister has said I have only to add my blessing, and tell you that my thoughts and prayers are filled with you, — alas! to the detriment, I fear, of those about me; in some hearts the absent are always present, — it is so with mine.

Your   MOTHER.

Thus it happened that Lucien was able, two days later, to return the loan his friends had so gracefully made him. Never, perhaps, had he felt more inward pride; and the elation of his self-satisfaction did not escape the searching eyes of his friends and their delicate sensibilities.

" One would think you had a horror of owing us anything," cried Fulgence.

"The satisfaction he shows is very serious to my eyes," said Michel Chrestien; "it confirms an observation I have already made; Lucien has a great deal of vanity."

"He is a poet," said d'Arthèz.

"Why are you vexed that I should have such a natural feeling?" asked Lucien.

"We ought to give him credit for not hiding it," said Léon Giraud; "he is still frank, but I am afraid he will some day avoid us."

"Why?" asked Lucien.

"Because we read your heart," replied Joseph Bridau.

"You have a diabolical spirit," said Michel Chrestien, "which makes you justify to your own mind a thing quite contrary to our principles; instead of being a sophist in ideas, you are a sophist in action."

"On what do you base that charge?" said Lucien.

"Your vanity, my dear poet, which is so great that you bring it into your friendships," said Fulgence. "All vanity of that kind is shocking egotism, and egotism poisons friendship."

"Good heavens!" cried Lucien, "you don't understand how truly I love you."

"If you loved us as we love each other, would you have made such haste and shown such eagerness in paying back the money we had so much pleasure in giving you?"

"We never lend here, we give things outright," said Joseph Bridau, brusquely.

"Don't think us very brutal, dear boy," said Michel Chrestien, "we are only far-seeing. We are afraid the day may come when you will prefer to shake us off rather than owe anything to pure friendship. Read Goethe's Tasso, — the finest work of his fine genius; there you will see how the poet loved brilliant stuffs and festivals, and triumphs, and all that dazzled him. Well, do you be Tasso without his folly. If the world and its pleasures call to you, stay here with us. Put into the region of ideas the emotions you would spend upon the vanities of life. Make your actions virtuous; keep the evil of life for your thoughts; and beware, as d'Arthèz told you, of thinking right and doing ill."

Lucien bowed his head; he knew his friends were right.

" I admit I am not as strong as you all are," he said, with an adorable look. "I have neither the shoulders nor the loins to wrestle with Paris or bear up bravely. Nature has given us different temperaments and different faculties; you can see as I cannot both sides of vice and virtue. For my part, I am already tired out; and I tell you so frankly."

" We will support you," said d'Arthèz; " that is exactly what faithful friends are made for."

" The help I have just received is accidental," continued Lucien; " we are all poor together. I shall soon be in want again. Chrestien has no influence with publishers; Bianchon, too, is outside of the business. D'Arthèz knows only the scientific houses, or the specialists who have nothing to do with the publication of light literature. Léon, Fulgence and Bridau work in a line of ideas which are leagues away from publishers. No; I must decide upon a course, — I must find some career."

" Keep to ours and suffer," said Bianchon; " suffer bravely and trust to toil."

" What is suffering to you is death to me," said Lucien, hastily.

" Before the cock crows thrice," said Léon Giraud, smiling, " he will betray the cause of toil and take to indolence and vice."

" What has toil done for you?" asked Lucien, laughing.

" Rome is not half-way between Paris and Italy," said Joseph Bridau. " You expect your spring peas to ripen ready cooked."

" They only do that for the sons of peers of France," said Michel Chrestien. " As for us, we have to sow them, and water them, but they taste all the better for that."

The conversation now turned pleasantly to other subjects. These delicate hearts and keen minds tried to make Lucien forget the little quarrel; he had learned, however, that it would be difficult indeed to mislead them.

Before long an inward despair took possession of him, but he carefully hid it from the brethren, implacable mentors as they now seemed to him. His Southern nature, which played so easily upon the keyboard of sentiments, led him to make various contradictory resolutions. Several times he dropped hints of entering journalism, but when he did so his friends would all cry out: " Beware of that!"

" It would be the grave of the beautiful, poetic Lucien whom we know and love," said d'Arthèz.

" You are not strong enough to resist the alternations of work and pleasure in the life of journalists; such resistance comes from the very depths of virtue. You would be so delighted to exercise such power, a power of life and death over the works of thought, that you could make yourself an accomplished journalist in a couple of months. Once a journalist, and you are proconsul in the republic of letters. He who can say all will do all, — that was Napoleon's own maxim ; and it is easily interpreted."

"But I shall always be near you," said Lucien.

"No, indeed," cried Fulgence ; "we shall count for nothing then. When you are a journalist you will think no more of us than a brilliant, idolized opera-girl in her silk-lined carriage thinks of her village, her cows, and her wooden shoes. As it is, you have too many of a journalist's requirements ; you have all his brilliancy and suddenness of thought ; you would never repress a witty saying, however much it might cut a friend. I know what journalists are ; I see them at the theatre and they shock me. Journalism is hell, — a pit of iniquity, falsehood, treachery, which no one can cross and no one can leave with a pure soul, — unless it be Dante under protection of Virgil's laurel."

The more the brotherhood warned him against this course, the more Lucien's desire to know its perils tempted him to risk them ; and he began to discuss the question seriously with himself : Was it not ridiculous to allow distress to overtake him without attempting in this way to avoid it? His unsuccessful efforts in behalf of his first book made him reluctant to begin another. Besides, how could he live during the time it would take to write it? One month's privation had exhausted his supply of patience. Why could not he do nobly what journalists did ignobly, without conscience or dignity? His friends insulted him by their want of trust; he would prove to them his strength of character. Besides, he might soon be able to help them and be the herald of their fame.

"What is friendship worth if it shrinks from a man under any circumstances?" he said one night to Michel Chrestien, having walked home with him in company with Léon Giraud.

"Our friendship would shrink from nothing," replied Chrestien. "If you were so unfortunate as to kill your mistress I would help you to hide the crime, and I might perhaps esteem you the more for it; but if you made yourself a spy I would avoid you with horror, for you would then be deliberately base and infamous, — and that is journalism described in two words. Friendship pardons error, the unreflecting act of passion; but it ought to be implacable to those who deliberately traffic on their souls, their minds, their thought."

"Why cannot I make myself a journalist merely to sell my own novels and poems, and give up journalism when I have once made myself a name?"

"Machiavelli could do that, but not Lucien de Rubempré," said Léon Giraud.

"Ha!" cried Lucien, "I'll prove to you that I am better than Machiavelli!"

"There!" exclaimed Michel, seizing Léon by the shoulder, "you have driven him into it! Lucien," he went on, "you have three hundred francs now; that is enough to live on comfortably for three months; well, then, go to work; write a second novel; d'Arthèz and

Fulgence will help you with the plot; you will improve, you have the makings of a novelist in you. While you do that I will go myself into one of those *lupanars* of thought; I'll make myself a journalist for six months and sell your next book to a publisher by attacking his publications; I'll write articles and get them written for you; we'll organize a success; you shall be a great man and still remain our Lucien."

"Then you despise me so much that you think I should fail where you would succeed?" said the poet.

"Good God, forgive him! what a child he is!" cried Chrestien.

VII.

EXTERNALS OF JOURNALISM.

LUCIEN had, meanwhile, studied the wit and the character of the articles in the *petits journaux*. Satis-fied that he was fully the equal of the cleverest of their writers, he practised their gymnastics of thought in secret until, at last, he set out one fine morning with the full determination of taking service under some colonel of what we may call the Light Brigade of the Press. He dressed himself in his best, and reflected, as he crossed the bridges, that authors, journalists, writers, in short, his brethren of the pen, would certainly be more disinterested and would show him more considera-tion than the two species of publisher who had hitherto crushed his hopes. He could not, he thought, fail to meet with sympathy, perhaps affection, such as the fraternity in the rue Quatre-Vents had already given him.

Filled with such thoughts and the emotions of pre-sentiment not yet distrusted, — a species of emotion dear to all men of imagination, — he reached the rue Saint-Fiacre, near the boulevard Montmartre, and stood at last before a house in which were the offices of a *petit journal*, with as much trepidation as a young man feels on entering a place of ill-repute. Nevertheless, he went up the stairs to the *entresol*, where the offices were. In the first room, divided into two equal parts by a partition partly of wood and partly of wire grating which reached to the ceiling, he found a one-armed soldier, who was holding several reams of paper on his head with his one hand, and the certificate required by the Stamp office between his teeth. This poor man, whose face was yellow and mottled with red spots (which earned him the name of Coloquinte), motioned Lucien to the cerberus of the newspaper, who was behind the partition. This personage was an old officer wearing a decoration, his nose enveloped in a gray moustache, a black silk cap on his head, and he himself buried in an ample blue overcoat, like a tortoise within its shell.

"On what day does monsieur wish his subscription to begin?" asked the officer.

"I have not come to subscribe," replied Lucien. The poet looked at the door opposite to the one by which he had entered and read the words: "EDITORIAL OFFICE," and underneath them the further legend, "*The public not admitted.*"

"A remonstrance, no doubt," resumed the soldier of Napoleon. "Well, yes, we certainly were rather hard on Mariette,—I don't even know why as yet; but if you want satisfaction I am ready," he added, glancing at a row of foils and pistols,—a warlike array set up, like a stand of arms, in a corner.

"Nothing of the kind, monsieur," said Lucien. "I came to speak to the editor-in-chief."

"No one is ever here till four o'clock."

"I say, old Giroudeau, I've done eleven columns; a hundred sous apiece makes fifty-five francs; and you've only given me forty; therefore, as I was saying, you still owe me fifteen."

These words came from a pinched little face, transparent as the half-boiled white of an egg, lighted by a pair of blue eyes that were terrifying in their malignancy, — a face belonging to a thin young man hidden behind the opaque body of the old officer. The voice rasped Lucien; it was something between the mewing of cats and the asthmatic strangulation of hyenas.

" Yes, yes, my little man," said the officer, " but you are counting titles and blank spaces, and I have Finot's orders to add up the total of the lines and divide them by the number required for each column. Having performed that constricting operation on your copy I make you out three columns short."

" Does n't pay for blanks! the Jew! — but he counts them to his partner in the price of the whole edition. I shall go and see Étienne Lousteau, Vernou — "

" I can't disobey orders, my boy," said the officer. " What nonsense to cry out against your wetnurse for fifteen francs, — you who can write articles as easily as I can smoke a cigar. Treat your friends to one less bowl of punch, or win an extra game of billiards, and that will square you."

" Finot is making savings which shall cost him dear," said the journalist, departing.

" Monsieur," said Lucien, " I will return at four o'clock."

" Bless me," thought the cashier, looking at Lucien; " one might think him Rousseau or Voltaire."

During the discussion, Lucien, standing by, had noticed on the walls portraits of Benjamin Constant, General Foy, and the seventeen illustrious orators of the Liberal party, mingled with various caricatures against the government. He had looked with special interest at the door of the sanctuary, where the witty sheet that amused him daily and enjoyed the right of ridiculing kings and solemn events and of turning things upside down with a clever saying, was elaborated.

He now departed to saunter along the boulevards, — a novel pleasure, but so attractive that the hands of the clocks in the watch-makers' windows pointed to four before he remembered that he had not been to breakfast. Then he rapidly retraced his steps to the rue Saint-Fiacre, ran upstairs, opened the door, and found no one but the one-armed soldier, sitting on the stamped paper and eating a crust of bread; evidently on sentry-duty for the newspaper, as in former days in barracks. Seeing him thus employed, the bold thought occurred to Lucien to pass this wary sentinel. He therefore pulled his hat over his eyes and opened the door of the sanctuary as though he had the run of the house. The sacred precincts presented to his eager eyes a round table covered with a green cloth, and six cherry-wood chairs with straw seats that were still good. The brick floor had been colored but not yet polished; still it was clean, a proof that the public did not frequent the place. On the fireplace was a mirror, a common shop-clock covered with dust, two candlesticks with two tallow candles crookedly stuck into them, and a few scattered visiting-cards. On the table lay a heap of old newspapers round an inkstand adorned with crowquills, on which dried inkspots looked like lacquer. There, too, he saw a number of articles written in an illegible almost hieroglyphic hand, torn across the top by the compositors in the printing-room, a sign by which to know the pages already set up. Here and there Lucien saw and admired certain clever caricatures drawn on wrapping-paper, no doubt by persons who were trying to kill time by killing anything else that came to hand. On a sheet of pale-green paper were pinned nine pen-and-ink drawings ridiculing "The Solitary," — a book then much in vogue throughout Europe. On the margin of a newspaper Lucien perceived a drawing signed by a name that was afterwards to become famous but never illustrious, representing a journalist holding out his hat, and underneath was written: "Finot, my hundred francs?" Between the fireplace and the window was a tall desk, a mahogany arm-chair, a waste-paper basket, and a long rug, all covered with a thick layer of dust. The windows had small curtains. On the top of the desk lay about twenty books, engravings, sheets of music, snuff-boxes à la Charte, the ninth edition of "The Solitary," (the current joke of the day) and a dozen sealed letters.

When Lucien had taken an inventory of this queer furniture and made his reflections upon it, he went back to the one-armed soldier, intending to question him. Coloquinte had finished his crust and was waiting with the patience of a sentinel for the return of the old officer, who was perhaps taking a walk on the boulevard. Just then a woman appeared in the doorway, having announced her coming by the rustle of a dress on the stairway and the light feminine footfall so easily recognized. She was rather pretty.

"Monsieur," she said to Lucien, "I know why you praise those bonnets of Mademoiselle Virginie, and I have come to subscribe for a year; but tell me first what conditions she makes."

"Madame," replied Lucien, "I do not belong to this newspaper."

"Ah!"

"Do you subscribe from this date?" inquired the one-armed man.

"What may madame want?" said the old officer reappearing.

The handsome milliner turned to him and they had a conference. When Lucien, growing impatient, re-entered the front room he heard their final words: —

"I shall be delighted, monsieur; Mademoiselle Florentine may come to my shop and choose what she likes. I keep ribbons. So it is all understood, is n't it? You are not to say anything more about Mademoiselle Virginie, — a bungler! incapable of producing a shape! whereas I am really an inventor."

Here Lucien heard the jingle of coins as they fell into a drawer; then the officer sat down to make up his daily accounts.

"Monsieur, I have been here over an hour," said the poet, somewhat displeased.

"*They* have n't come," said the Napoleonic veteran, manifesting a polite regret. "I am not surprised. It is some time since I have seen *them*. It is the middle of the month, and they only come, those fellows, about pay-day, — the 29th or 30th."

"But Monsieur Finot?" said Lucien, who now knew the name of the editor-in-chief.

" He is at home, rue Feydeau. Coloquinte, old man, take him all that has come in to-day when you carry the paper to the printing-office."

" Where is the work of the newspaper really done? " said Lucien, as if speaking to himself.

" The newspaper? " said the officer, " the newspaper? — broum! broum! Look here, old man, be at the printing-office to-morrow at six, and keep some order among the newsboys, will you? The work of the newspaper, monsieur, is done in the streets, in the writers' houses, in the printing-room between eleven and twelve o'clock at night. In the old days of the Emperor, monsieur, these shops for wasting paper didn't exist. Ha! he'd have cleared them out with a corporal's guard; he'd never have let 'em gibe him, like *ceux-ci*. Ah, well, no use talking! If my nephew finds it profitable to write for the son of *l'autre* — broum! broum! what matter? where's the harm? However, to-day subscribers don't seem to be coming in a solid phalanx, so I shall shut up and depart."

" Monsieur," said Lucien, " you seem to me to be well-informed as to the editing of a newspaper?"

" Under its financial aspect, broum! broum! " said the old officer, disposing of the phlegm that was in his throat. " According to talent, five or three francs a column, fifty lines of forty letters, no blanks, — that's what I know. As for the editors and reporters, they are queer scamps, fellows I would n't have kept in my troop; young fools who because they can dabble ink over paper affect to despise an old captain of the Imperial guard, a brevet major, who entered every capital of Europe with Napoleon."

8

Lucien, feeling himself elbowed towards the door by the soldier of Napoleon, who was all the while brushing his blue coat with the manifest intention of leaving the place, had the courage to make a stand.

"I have come to be a writer on the paper," he said, "and I assure you I have the deepest respect for the captains of the Imperial guard, those men of iron."

"Well said, my little civilian," cried the officer, poking Lucien in the ribs. "But what class of writer do you want to be?" continued the old veteran, slipping past Lucien and down the stairs to the porter's lodge, where he stopped to light his cigar. "If any subscribers come, Mère Chollet, take the money and make a note of it. Subscriptions! always subscriptions; I know nothing else," he said, turning to Lucien who had followed him. "Finot is my nephew,—the only one of my family who has done anything to help me. Therefore, whoever quarrels with Finot will have to do with old Giroudeau, captain of the dragoons of the Guard, once a plain trooper in the army of the Sambre-et-Meuse, five years fencing-master to the First Huzzars, Army of Italy. One—two—and the grumbler is in Hades!" he added, making a pass. "Now, my little man, we have different sorts of editors and reporters: there's the editor who edits and gets his pay; and the editor who edits and does n't get any pay,—we call him the volunteer; and besides these, there's the editor who does n't edit (lucky for him, for he can't make blunders); this kind writes, he's a journalist, he invites us to dinner, he hangs about the theatres, keeps an actress, and makes himself happy. Which kind do you want to be?"

"Why, the writer who is well paid."

" Yes, you are like all recruits, who want to be marshals of France. Now, you take the advice of old Giroudeau, — to the right about, march! better pick rags in the gutter for a living. There's that young fellow you saw this morning; he has earned only forty francs this month, and Finot thinks him the wittiest man on the staff; will you do any better?"

" When you enlisted in the Sambre-et-Meuse did no one warn you of danger?"

"Of course they did."

" Well, I am not afraid."

" Very good; then go and see my nephew Finot, a good fellow, the best of fellows if you can catch him, but slippery as an eel; always on the go. His business, you see, is not to write, but to make others write, and it seems to me his troopers would rather be dangling after actresses than blotting paper. Oh, yes, as I say, they are a queer lot! I have the honor to wish you good-day."

So saying the veteran twirled a formidable leaded cane, a weapon worthy of Germanicus, and left Lucien standing on the boulevard as stupefied by this presentation of journalism as he had been by the definite results of literature brought to his knowledge at Vidal and Porchon's.

Ten times did Lucien call on Andoche Finot, editor-in-chief, at his house in the rue Feydeau, without finding him. If it was early morning Finot had not come home; at mid-day Finot was out, breakfasting, it was said, at a certain café. At the café, whither Lucien betook himself to inquire for the editor with extreme reluctance, Finot had just departed. Finally, worn-out and disheartened, Lucien began to regard Finot as an apocryphal, even fabulous personage; and he thought his best chance lay in watching for Étienne Lousteau at Flicoteaux's. That young journalist might be able to explain to him the mystery which seemed to hang about the paper on which he was employed.

Since the day, the blessed day, when Lucien had made the acquaintance of Daniel d'Arthèz he had changed his seat at Flicoteaux's; the two friends dined together side by side, talking in a low voice of literature, of subjects to take up, of methods of treatment and development. At this particular time Daniel d'Arthèz was correcting the revised manuscript of "The Archer of Charles IX.;" he had even written some of the finest pages, and a noble preface, which does in fact excel the book, and throws a strong light on the dawning literature of the day.

One afternoon, just as Lucien was about to sit down in his usual place by Daniel, who had waited for him, he saw Étienne Lousteau in the doorway. Instantly he let go Daniel's hand which he had taken, and told the waiter he would dine in his former place near the *comptoir*. D'Arthèz gave Lucien one of those angelic looks in which forgiveness mingled with reproach, and so touched the poet's heart that he caught up Daniel's hand once more and pressed it.

"It is on a matter of great importance to me; I will tell you about it later," he said.

Lucien had taken his old place by the time Lousteau was in his. He was the first to bow and open the conversation, which made such rapid strides that before Lousteau finished his dinner Lucien had gone to his lodgings to fetch the manuscript of the "Daisies." The journalist had consented to listen to the sonnets, and Lucien relied upon that outward show of cordiality to obtain a footing on the newspaper, and perhaps a publisher. As he returned, he noticed the sad look which Daniel, sitting with his head in his hand, gave him ; but, weary of poverty and lashed by ambition, he pretended not to see his true friend, and followed Lousteau.

It was towards evening, and the pair, the journalist and the neophyte, seated themselves under the trees in that part of the Luxembourg which lies between the avenue of the Observatoire and the rue de l'Ouest. The latter was then a long, muddy road beside a marsh, and so little frequented that during the Parisian dinner-hour two lovers might safely quarrel there and kiss and make up without fear of being seen. The only person likely to see them was the veteran on guard at the gate of the gardens on the rue de l'Ouest, if he took it into his head to lengthen his monotonous beat by a few rods.

Here it was that the two young men established themselves on a wooden bench between two lindens, and Étienne listened to certain sonnets which Lucien selected as specimens of his "Daisies."

VIII.

THE SONNETS.

ÉTIENNE Lousteau, who now had, after two years' apprenticeship, his foot in the stirrup of journalism, and who counted among his friends several of the celebrities of the day, was an imposing personage in Lucien's eyes. Consequently, as he unrolled the precious manuscript of his " Daisies," he deemed it wise to make a sort of preamble to the reading of them.

" The sonnet, monsieur," he said " is one of the most difficult forms of poesy ; in fact, it has been generally abandoned. No one in France has ever rivalled Petrarch, whose language, infinitely more supple than ours, admits of a play of thought which our positivism (forgive the word) rejects. I have therefore thought it original to make my début by a collection of sonnets. Victor Hugo chose the ode ; Canalis prefers more fugitive verse ; Béranger has monopolized song ; Casimir Delavigne, tragedy ; and Lamartine, meditation."

" Are you a classicist or a romanticist?" asked Lousteau.

Lucien's puzzled expression denoted such absolute ignorance of the then state of things in the republic of letters that Lousteau thought it best to enlighten him.

" My dear fellow, you have come into the thick of a

desperate fight, and you must immediately choose your side.   Literature is, of course, separated into several zones ; but our great men are divided into two hostile camps.   The Royalists are the romanticists ; the Liberals are the classicists.   This divergence of literary opinions is connected in a way with the divergences of political opinion ; consequently, there is war to the death with all weapons, ink in torrents, wit with sharpened blade, calumny ground to a point, nicknames flying between the rising lights and the setting ones, — coming fame, and dead glory.   By a singular oddity the Royalist romanticists demand literary liberty and the revocation of the laws which give conventional forms to literature ; whereas the Liberals want to maintain the unities, the swing of the alexandrine, and the classic tradition.   Literary opinions are therefore out of harmony in each camp with the political opinions of its own side.   If you are eclectic you will have no one with you.   Which side will you take ? "

" Which side is the stronger ? "

" The liberal journals have many more subscribers than the royalist and ministerial journals ; nevertheless, Canalis succeeds, though he is monarchical and religious and protected by court and clergy.   But sonnets ! pooh, that 's literature before the days of Boileau," said Etienne, seeing that Lucien was frightened at the idea of having to choose between two banners.   " Be a romanticist.   The romanticists are young men, the classicists old fogies ; the romanticists are certain to carry the day.   Now, read on."

" EASTER DAISIES ! " read Lucien, choosing the first of the two sonnets which gave the title to the book.

O Easter-daisy, your harmonious tints
Are not contrived to dazzle wearied eyes,
But to our souls they speak, in half-veiled hints,
That sound the depths of human sympathies.
Do not your gold and silver symbolize
The treasures that we strive so hard to gain?
Is not our life-blood, given to win the prize,
Shown in your petals with the crimson stain?
Is it because your tiny flowers were born
When Christ, arisen, on that Easter morn
Cast love and blessing o'er the sleeping earth,
That now, when autumn days are chill and drear,
You still recall the season of your birth,
With happy hours long past, yet doubly dear?

Lucien was piqued by Lousteau's absolute immovability as he listened to the reading; he knew nothing as yet of the disconcerting impassibility which comes of the habit of criticism, — a distinguishing mark of journalists wearied with prose and verse and drama. The poet, accustomed to applause, swallowed his disappointment, and read the sonnet preferred by Madame de Bargeton and by some of his friends among the brotherhood.

"Perhaps this will force some expression from him," thought he.

The Daisy.

My name is Margarita, fairest flower
That star-like shines on many a verdant lawn;
And once, in peace and joy, each rosy dawn
Beheld me opening to the sun or shower.
But now, alas! a strange and unknown power
Consumes my life. Love questions, I reply.
Unsought, to me was given a mortal dower:

I read the book of Fate, and reading, die.
No more for me are silence and repose ;
My heart is plucked by lovers in despair,
To find if, haply, love itself be there ;
And as the deep-hid secret I disclose
I die, robbed of my white-rayed coronet, —
The only flower flung down without regret!

When he had finished reading the poet looked at his Aristarchus. Étienne Lousteau was attentively observing the trees of the adjoining nursery.

" Well ? " said Lucien.

" Well, my dear fellow, go on ! I 'm listening. Listening without saying a word is praise in Paris."

" Have you had enough ? " asked Lucien.

" Go on," said the journalist, rather roughly.

Lucien read the following sonnet ; but he did it with death in his heart, for Lousteau's impenetrable coolness froze him. Had he been a little farther advanced in his literary career he would have known that the silence or roughness of authors under such circumstances betrays their jealousy at a fine work ; just as their admiration proves the pleasure they feel at a commonplace thing which reassures their vanity.

THE CAMELLIA.

In Nature's poem flowers have each their word :
The rose of love and beauty sings alone ;
The violet's soul exhales in tenderest tone ;
The lily's one pure simple note is heard.
The cold Camellia only, stiff and white,
Rose without perfume, lily without grace,
When chilling winter shows his icy face,

Blooms for a world that vainly seeks delight.
Yet, in a theatre, or ball-room light,
With alabaster petals opening fair,
I gladly see Camellias shining bright
Above some stately wman's raven hair,
Whose noble form fulfils the heart's desire,
Like Grecian marbles warmed by Phidian fire.

"What do you think of my poor sonnets?" asked Lucien, resolutely.

"Do you wish the truth?" said Lousteau.

"I am young enough to love it, and I am so anxious to succeed that I can hear it without anger — but not, perhaps, without despair," replied Lucien.

"Well, my dear fellow, the involved style of the first shows work done in Angoulême, which no doubt cost you so much trouble that you can't bear to give it up; the second and the third certainly have a Parisian tone; but read me another," added Lousteau, with a gesture which seemed perfectly charming to the great man of the provinces.

Encouraged by the invitation, Lucien proceeded to read, with more confidence than he had yet felt, the sonnet which d'Arthèz and Joseph Bridau preferred, perhaps on account of its color: —

THE TULIP.

I am the Tulip; from the Hague I came;
So fair am I that e'en the thrifty Dutch
Esteem this precious bulb of mine as much
As costly diamonds; such is beauty's fame!
I have a feudal air; like some proud dame
In ample kirtle stiff and farthingale,
I bear, emblazoned, gules on argent pale

Upon my robes, or purple barred with flame,
Woven of sun-rays and the royal dye ;
The colors of heaven tell my Maker's name.
No garden flower with me can hope to vie
In splendid vesture or in gorgeous bloom;
But in my vase-like chalice broad and high,
Ungenerous Nature poured no rich perfume.

" Well ? " said Lucien, after a moment's silence, which seemed to him of interminable length.

" My dear fellow," said Étienne Lousteau, gravely, looking down at the boots which Lucien had brought from Angoulême, and which were now pretty nearly worn-out, " I advise you to black your boots with your ink and save your blacking ; make tooth-picks of your pens to look as if you had been dining, and find some situation where you can earn a living. Be a sheriff's clerk if you have the nerve, or a shop-boy if there's strength enough in your loins, or a soldier if you love a bass-drum. You have got the stuff of three poets, but before you succeed you'll die six times of hunger if you intend to live on the proceeds of your poems. I gather from your rather juvenile discourse that you expect to coin money out of your inkstand. Now mark, I'm not judging your sonnets, which are far superior to the poetry which is choking up the shops of the book-sellers. Those elegant nightingales (which sell for more than other people's poems because of the superfine paper on which they are printed) all come to an end over here on the banks of the Seine, where you can study their song if you choose to make an instructive pilgrimage along the quays from old Jerome's booth to the Pont Notre-Dame and the Pont-Royal. You'll

encounter on that short trip the Poetical Essays, Inspi-
rations, Exaltations, Hymns, Songs, Ballads, Odes, —
in short, all the coveys hatched for the last seven years;
muses thick with dust, splashed by the hackney-coaches,
and rudely fingered by the quay loungers who look for
the illustrations.   You say you don't know any one in
Paris; you have no access to a newspaper.   Your
' Daisies ' will stay chastely folded as they are ; they 'll
never blossom to the world in the glory of broad mar-
gins and adorned with arabesques and tail-pieces such
as the great Dauriat, that publisher of celebrities, that
king of the Galeries de Bois, lavishes.   My poor boy,
I came to Paris like you with my soul full of illusions,
prompted by the love of Art, led by an unconquerable
impulse to seek fame.   I learned the realities of that
career, the struggles for publication, the practical side
of poverty.   My ardor, long since repressed, my first
enthusiasm, concealed the mechanism of the world ; I
had to discover it for myself; I had to butt against its
machinery, to be nipped in its hinges, to be greased
with its oil, and to hear the clanking of its chains and
fly-wheels.   You are going to see, as I saw, under all
the beautiful things of which we dreamed, how men
behave from passions and necessities.   You will be
forced to share in dreadful struggles, man against man,
work against work, party against party, in which you
must fight systematically or you will go under.   Such
unworthy struggles disenchant the soul, deprave the
heart, and wear it out to its own loss ; for your efforts
will often end in crowning your rival whom you hate,
some commonplace talent called, in spite of you, a genius.
Literary life is like the stage.   Success, snatched or

merited, is applauded by the audience ; the ugliness behind the scenes, the supernumeraries, the *claqueurs*, the
scene-shifters, they make the play. My dear fellow, you
are now among the audience. There is still time ; give
up the career before you put your foot on the first step
of the throne for which so many ambitions are fighting,
and don't dishonor yourself, as I am doing, to live"
(a tear moistened Étienne Lousteau's eyes). "Do you
know how I live?" he continued, in a savage tone.
"The little money my family could give me was soon
spent. I was utterly without resources when I got a
play accepted at the Théâtre-Français. At the Théâtre-
Français the protection of a prince or the first Gentleman of the Bedchamber is not sufficient to secure the
playing of an accepted piece ; the comedians will only
play the plays of those who have some means of
injuring their self-love. If you have power to get it
said that the leading gentleman wheezes, or the leading
lady has an ulcer, no matter where, or that the sou-
brette's breath is vile, your play will be acted to-morrow.
I don't know whether in two years from now I shall
have that power, — it takes too many friends. Meantime, how and where was I to earn my bread? that was
the question I had to answer when hunger seized me.
After many attempts, such as writing a novel which
Doguereau bought for two hundred francs (and he did
not make much out of it either), I made up my mind
that journalism alone would support me. But how
could I get into it? I won't tell you now all my useless
efforts and entreaties, nor the six dreadful months I
spent, working like a galley-slave only to be told that I
frightened off subscribers, when in fact I was really

educating them, — I pass over such affronts. At the present time I am writing the dramatic articles on the boulevard theatres, almost for nothing, in a journal which belongs to Finot, that fat fellow who breakfasts once or twice a month at the Café Voltaire — but you don't go there ! Finot is the editor-in-chief. I live by selling the tickets which the managers of the theatres give me to pay for my good word, and the books the publishers send me, which I review. Besides this I traffic, after satisfying Finot, in a variety of tributes made to me by tradesmen for or against whom he lets me write articles. 'Paste of Sultans,' 'Cephalic Oil,' 'Brazilian Mixture' will all pay twenty or thirty francs for a puff. I am obliged to bark at publishers who don't send copies enough to the paper ; Finot keeps two and sells them, and I want two to sell. If a book is likely to sell well and the publisher is stingy he gets pommelled. I know it is base ; but I live by it, and so do a hundred others. Don't think, either, that the political world is a bit better than the literary world ; it is all corruption in both ; every man is either corrupted or corrupting. When a publisher has some new and rather important enterprise on hand he pays me for fear I shall attack him. My revenues are always in proportion to the prospectuses. When there are fine lists going among the trade my pocket jingles, and I invite my friends to dinner ; when trade is dull I dine at Flicoteaux's. Actresses pay for puffs, but the cleverest of them want criticism ; silence is what they are most afraid of. Consequently a criticism, so written that you can revoke it later, pays better than mere praise, which is forgotten the next day. Controversy, my dear fellow, controversy is the pedestal of celebrity. By this fine trade, as hired assassin of ideas and reputations, industrial, literary, and dramatic, I make, say, a hundred and fifty francs a month; I can manage to sell a novel for five hundred francs, and I am beginning to be thought a dangerous man, a man to propitiate. When, instead of living with Florine at the cost of a druggist who gives himself the airs of a lord, I live in my own house and get upon one of the great papers and have a *feuilleton*, — on that day, my good fellow, Florine will become a great actress. As for me, I don't know what I'll then become: minister or honest man, all is still possible." (He raised his humiliated face and cast a terrible look of despairing reproach towards the trees.) "And yet I have a tragedy accepted at the Français! I have among my papers a noble poem that will die there! I once was good! my heart was pure! and now I live with an actress of the Panorama-Dramatique, — I, who dreamed of noble loves among the best of women! But, worst of all, if a publisher refuses a book to my paper, I say harm of a work I think beautiful!"

Lucien, moved to tears, seized Étienne's hand.

"Outside of the literary world," continued the journalist, rising and going towards the Avenue de l'Observatoire, where the two poets walked up and down as if to get more air into their lungs, "there is not a single person who even suspects the horrible odyssey through which we must pass to reach what is called, according to merit, vogue, fashion, reputation, distinction, celebrity, public favor, — the rounds of the ladder which lead to fame, but can never take its place. Fame, that bril-

liant moral phenomenon, is made up of a thousand
incidents which vary with such rapidity that no two
men ever reached it by the same path. Canalis and
Nathan, two men who are now attaining it, are two
dissimilar facts, neither of whom can be reproduced.
D'Arthèz, who is wearing himself out with toil, will
come to fame through some mere accident. A long-de-
sired reputation is almost always like a prostitute. Yes,
literature in its low estate is like some wretched girl
shivering in the street ; its secondary phase, as it issues
from the baser regions of journalism, in which I now
am, is that of a kept mistress ; but literature successful, fortunate, is a brilliant, insolent courtesan, pays
taxes to the state, receives the great lords, treats, or
ill-treats them, has its livery, its equipage, and can
keep its hungry creditors waiting its convenience. Ah !
those to whom it seemed — to me formerly, to you now,
— an angel with radiant wings, draped in a spotless tunic,
a palm in one hand, a flaming sword in the other, partly
a mythical abstraction living at the bottom of a well,
partly a noble being attaining riches only through the
lights of virtue and the efforts of a glorious courage, —
what becomes of us when we find it soiled, trampled,
violated, thrust into the mud? There are men of iron
brains whose hearts are still warm under the snows of
experience, but they are rare, rare in that Paris you see
before you," he cried, pointing to the great city as it lay
seething in the sunset.

A vision of the brotherhood passed rapidly through
Lucien's mind and stirred it ; but a moment more, and
Lousteau, continuing his dreadful lamentation, forced
him away from all such thoughts.

" Yes, they are rare and far between in that great
vat fermenting there; rare as true lovers in the world
of love; rare as honest fortunes in the world of money;
rare as pure and decent men in journalism. The experience of the man who once told me what I am telling
you was wasted, as mine no doubt is wasted now on
you. The provinces send us yearly the same if not a
growing number of beardless ambitions filled with the
same enthusiasms. Their heads high, their hearts
elate, they rush to the assault of fame, that princess of
the Arabian Nights for whom every man considers himself the prince! Ah! few indeed have guessed the
enigma. They all drop into the ditch, — into the mud
of journalism, into the bog of book-making. Poor
beggars, they glean, glean, facts for biographical arti-
les, or items for the columns of a newspaper, or they
write books for prudent publishers who would rather
have trash written in a fortnight than masterpieces
which take time to place and sell. Poor caterpillars,
crushed before they can be butterflies; living in shame
and infamy, forced to rend or praise a dawning talent
as some pacha of the ' Constitutionnel' or the ' Quotidienne' or the ' Debats' orders him; to throttle a
good book at a signal from a publisher, at a threat
from a jealous comrade, or, worse still, for a dinner!
Those who surmount all obstacles forget the misery of
their beginning. I who speak to you, I did, for six
months, write articles, in which I put the very flower
of my mind, for a wretch who called them his, and
who on those specimens of *his* powers became the
editor of a *feuilleton.* He did not take me as an
associate, he did not so much as give me five francs,

but I am forced still to give him my hand and to
shake his."

" Why ?" exclaimed Lucien, haughtily.

" Because I may want some day to put a few
lines into his paper," replied Lousteau, coldly. " Believe me, my friend, work is not the secret of success
in literature ; that secret is, mark my words, to live by
the work of others. The owners of newspapers are
contractors, we are masons and journeymen. The
more commonplace or second-rate a man may be, the
sooner he will advance himself; he can swallow toads,
he can resign himself to anything, and gratify the low
and petty passions of the literary sultans, — like a late-
comer from Limoges, Hector Merlin, who used to do
politics on a paper of the Right Centre, but now works
on ours ; I have seen that fellow pick up the hat of the
editor-in-chief. By affronting no one he will manage
to pass between and beyond rival ambitions while they
are fighting each other. But you, I feel a pity for you.
I see myself in you, just as I once was ; and I feel sure
that in a year or two you will be what I am now. Perhaps you will think there is some secret jealousy, some
personal interest in the bitter advice I'm giving you ;
no, it is that of a lost soul who cannot leave the hell
he is in. No one else will dare say to you as I say,
like Job on his dunghill, with despair in my heart:
Behold my sores ! "

" I must fight to live," said Lucien, " on this field or
elsewhere."

" Remember," said Lousteau, " it is a fight without
truce if you have talent; your best chance would be
to have none. Your conscience, pure to-day, will yield

to the will of others when you see your success or
failure in their power, — the power of men who with a
word could give you life, and will not say it! For, believe me, the successful writer of the day is harder,
more insolent, to a new-comer than the most brutal of
publishers. Where the publisher fears only loss the
author dreads a rival; one cheats you, the other crushes
you. In your ardor to do fine work, my poor boy, you
will turn all the tenderness, sap, and energy of your
heart into ink and display them in passions, sentiments,
fine phrases. Yes, you'll write rather than act; you'll
sing instead of fighting; you will love and hate and live
in your books; and when you have spent all your riches
on your style, all your gold and purple on your characters, when you are walking the streets of Paris in
rags, happy in the production of personages called
Adolphe, Corinne, René or Manon, when you have
ruined your own life and your stomach in giving life
to your creation, you will see it vilified, betrayed,
thrust into oblivion by journalists, buried by your best
friends. Can you await the day when your creations
shall rise from such oblivion? and at whose call? how?
and when? There is at this moment a noble book, the
pianto of unbelief, ' Obermann,' which is wandering
desolate in the dark corners of the shops; publishers
ironically call it a nightingale; when will the Easter-
morn arise for that book? Ah! no one knows. Well,
since you are determined to follow literature, try to
find a publisher bold enough to print your ' Daisies.'
It doesn't matter whether he pays you or not; only
get them printed. You will then see curious things."

This harsh tirade, delivered in the diverse tones of

the various passions it expressed, fell like an avalanche of snow upon Lucien's heart and turned it cold as ice. He stood motionless and silent for a moment. At last, however, his courage, as if stimulated by the horrible picture of these difficulties, burst forth; he wrung Lousteau's hand and cried out: "I will triumph!"

"Ah!" said the journalist, "another Christian who goes down into the arena to fight the beasts. My dear fellow, there's a first representation to-night at the Panorama-Dramatique; it does not begin till eight o'clock; it is now six. Go home and put on your best clothes; make yourself the thing. Then come and fetch me. I live in the rue de la Harpe, over the café Servel, fourth floor. We will go and see Dauriat first, — for you do persist, don't you? Well, then, I'll make you known to-night to the king of publishers and several journalists. After the theatre we'll sup together at Florine's, — that's my mistress, — for our dinner didn't amount to much. You'll meet Finot, the editor-in-chief and proprietor of the newspaper I am on."

"I shall never forget this day," said Lucien.

"Bring your manuscript and wear your best clothes, — less for Florine than for the publisher."

The good-nature of the invitation, following so closely on the bitter cry of the poet describing the warfare of literature, touched Lucien as keenly as d'Arthèz' earnest and sacred words had touched him almost in the same place. Excited by the prospect of an immediate encounter with literary men, the youth, inexperienced as he was, had no conception of the reality of the moral evils of which the journalist had warned him. He did not know that he stood at the angle of two distinct paths, two systems, represented by the Brotherhood and by Journalism; of which one was long and honorable and sure, and the other strewn with rocks and perilous, crossed by foul gutters in which his conscience must be soiled. Lucien's nature led him to take the shortest way, apparently the most agreeable way, and to snatch at decisive and rapid methods. He could see at this moment no difference between the noble friendship of d'Arthèz and the ready fellowship of Lousteau. His lively mind saw a weapon to his hand in journalism; he felt himself able to handle it, and he resolved to take it. Dazzled by the proposals of his new friend, whose hand grasped his with easy cordiality, how could he know that in the great Press army every man needs friends, as generals need soldiers? Lousteau, seeing his determination, was merely enlisting him with the intention of using him. The journalist was making his first friend, and Lucien, as he thought, his first protector; the one wanted to rise from the ranks, the other to enter them.

IX.

A THIRD VARIETY OF PUBLISHER.

THE would-be recruit ran joyously back to his poor lodging, where he dressed himself as carefully as on the fatal day when he sought to produce an effect in Madame d'Espard's box; but by this time his clothes sat better on him; he knew better how to wear them. He now put on his handsome, light-colored, tight-fitting trousers, a pair of boots with tassels (which had cost him forty francs), and his evening coat. A barber was called in to curl and perfume and friz his fine and abundant blond hair. His forehead assumed a confidence derived from a sense of his value and his coming future. His delicate feminine hands were carefully attended to, and the rosy almond nails were polished. The rounded whiteness of his throat and chin were well set off by the black satin stock. No handsomer young man ever ran down the hill of the Latin regions. Beautiful as a Grecian god, Lucien jumped into a coach and was set down at seven oclock before the door of the house in which was the café Servel. The porter invited him to climb four stories, giving him rather complicated topographical directions. Thus instructed he found, not without difficulty, an open door at the end of a long dark passage which gave entrance into a classic garret of the Latin quarter. Poverty was there, as it was with himself in the rue de Cluny, with d'Arthèz, with Chrestien, everywhere! everywhere, too, it bore the imprint of the character of the occupant. Here, it was malign. A miserable bedstead without curtains, and a strip of carpet beside it, window-curtains yellow with smoke from a chimney that would not draw, a Carcel lamp, given by Florine and still escaping the pawn-shop, a tarnished mahogany bureau, a table covered with papers and two or three quill-pens, no books but those brought in the night before, — such were the contents of this room (in which there was nothing of value), to which must be added a shabby collection of broken boots and dilapidated slippers in one corner, in another, cigar-ends, dirty handkerchiefs, shirts in two editions and cravats in three. In short, it was a literary bivouac, supplied with little or nothing, of a bareness the mind can scarcely imagine. On the night-table, piled with books read during the morning, shone the scarlet roll of "Fumade;" on the mantel-shelf lay a razor, a pair of pistols, and a cigar-case; crossed foils and a mask were fastened to the wall; three chairs and two armchairs, unworthy of even the poorest lodging-house in this poor street, completed the outfit. This gloomy, dirty room was typical of a life without peace or dignity; a man slept there, a man worked there in haste, but only of necessity and eager to get away. What a difference between that cynical disorder and the neat and decent poverty of d'Arthèz! This silent counsel wrapped in a memory Lucien did not heed, for Lousteau was ready with a joke to cover the nudity of his squalor.

"This is my kennel," he said; "my grand appearance

is in the rue de Bondy, in a new apartment which a certain druggist has furnished for Florine; we are going to inaugurate it to-night."

Étienne himself was wearing black trousers and well-polished boots, his coat was buttoned to the chin, and his shirt (Florine probably had another ready for him) was hidden under its velvet collar; he brushed his hat carefully to make it look like new.

"Shall we start?" said Lucien.

"No, not yet; I am waiting for a publisher, for I must have money; they'll play, perhaps, and I haven't a farthing; besides, I want some gloves."

Just then a man's step was heard in the passage.

"There he is," said Lousteau. "Now you'll see, my dear fellow, the form and fashion which providence puts on when it appears to poets. Before contemplating Dauriat, the fashionable publisher, in all his glory, you shall see the publisher of the Quai des Augustins, the turn-a-penny publisher, the dealer in literary old-iron, a Norman ex-vendor of green-stuffs. Come in, old Tartar!"

"Here am I," said a voice as jangling as a cracked bell.

"With money?"

"Money! there's no money now in the trade," replied a young man who entered the room, and looked inquisitively at Lucien.

"Well, in the first place, you owe me fifty francs," said Lousteau. "Besides that, here are two copies of 'A Voyage in Egypt,' which they say is fine; it swarms with engravings, and is sure to sell. Finot has been paid for two articles which I am going to write

about it. Next, the last two novels of Victor Ducange,
illustrious in the Marais ; also, two copies of the second
work of a rising young man, Paul de Kock, who writes
in the same style ; also, two copies of ' Yseult de Dôle,'
a very pretty provincial tale, — one hundred francs
retail price for the books, call it fifty. Therefore, my
little Barbet, pay me one hundred francs."

Barbet looked the books over, examining the edges
of the leaves and the bindings carefully.

"Oh ! they are all in a perfect state of preservation,"
cried Lousteau. " The ' Voyage,' is n't cut, nor the
Paul de Kock, nor the Ducange, nor that other book
on the chimney-piece, ' Observations on Symbolism,' —
I 'll throw that in ; mystical things are such a bore, I'll
give it away sooner than see the mites run out of it."

" But," said Lucien, " if you don't read the books,
how will you write your articles ? "

Barbet cast a look of unfeigned astonishment at
Lucien ; then he turned his eyes on Lousteau and
remarked, with a sneer, "It is plain that monsieur
has n't the misfortune to be a literary man."

" No, Barbet, he is n't ; he 's a poet, — a great poet,
who will put Canalis, and Delavigne, and Béranger into
the shade. He is bound to make his way, unless he
flings himself into the Seine, — and even then, he'll go
to Saint-Cloud."

" If I might give monsieur a bit of advice," said
Barbet, " it would be to let poetry alone and stick to
prose. They won't take verses any more on the quai."

Barbet wore a shabby frock-coat, fastened by one
button ; the collar was greasy ; he kept his hat on his
head, wore shoes, and under his half-opened waistcoat

a good shirt of coarse linen was visible. His round
face, enlivened with two eager eyes, was not without a
certain good-humor; but his glance had the vague
uneasiness of a man accustomed to be asked for money,
and who has it. He had the appearance, however, of
being frank and good-natured, for his shrewdness was
well wadded with fat. After being for some years a
clerk, he now had a miserable little shop of his own
on the quai, whence he darted on journalists, authors,
printers, and bought at a low price the books they
obtained as perquisites, gaining in this way as much,
perhaps, as fifteen or twenty francs a day. Rich by
saving, he scented the needs of all with whom he had
dealings; he watched their necessities for a good
stroke of business, and often discounted for authors
the notes they received from publishers, charging them
fifteen per cent. The next day he would purchase from
the same publishers, after haggling over the price, certain good books that he needed for his trade, paying
back to them their own notes instead of ready money.
He had some education, just enough to make him carefully avoid poetry and modern novels. He liked small
enterprises, useful books, the copyright of which did
not cost him more than a thousand francs, and which
he could put on the market in his own way; such, for
instance, as the " History of France adapted for Children," " Book-keeping in twenty lessons," " Botany for
Young Ladies." Once or twice he had allowed good
books to slip through his fingers from his inability to
make up his mind to buy the manuscripts, after making
the authors come twenty times or more to his shop.
When reproached for his cowardice he would show the

history of a certain celebrated lawsuit culled from the public prints, the copy for which had of course cost him nothing, out of which he had made some two or three thousand francs. Barbet was the trembling publisher, living, so to speak, on bread and nuts, who makes few notes, shaves all he can off a bill, hawks his own books about, no one knows where, but manages to place them and get the money for them. He was a terror to printers, who never knew how to manage him; he would pay them under discount and shave their bills, especially if he knew they needed money, and then when he had fleeced them to the last penny he never employed them again, fearing reprisals.

" Well, well ! " said Lousteau, " let us go back to our business — about these books."

" Hey, my boy ! " said Barbet, familiarly. " I 've at least six thousand volumes now in my shop to sell; and you know very well books are not francs ; the trade is bad just now."

" My dear Lucien," said Étienne, " if you were to go into his shop you would find on his counter — a shabby oak thing that came from some auction in a wine-shop — one tallow candle, unsnuffed because that makes it burn longer. By the light of that anomalous gleam you would see empty shelves. A small boy in a blue jacket keeps watch over this nothingness, blowing his fingers, stamping his feet or beating his arms like a frozen coachman on his box. Look about you, and you won't see more books than there are in this room at this moment. No one would ever guess the business that is done there."

" Here's a note for a hundred francs at three

months," interposed Barbet, who could not help smiling as he pulled a stamped paper from his pocket, " and I'll carry off your trash. You see, I can't possibly pay any more ready money ; sales are so slow. I thought you wanted something out of me, and as I had n't a sou, I signed this note to oblige you ; for you know I don't like to give my signature."

" And do you expect my esteem and gratitude for that? " said Lousteau.

" Well, feelings won't go far in paying notes, but I'll accept your esteem all the same," replied Barbet.

" But I must have gloves, and the perfumer will certainly be base enough to refuse your paper," said Lousteau. " Look here ! I've a splendid engraving — there, in the top drawer of that bureau ; it is worth eighty francs before lettering and after the article I've written on it, which is mighty droll, all about Hippocrates refusing Artaxerxes' gift. I tell you, it is a fine plate, which will please all the doctors who refuse the extravagant fees of the Parisian satraps. You'll find a lot more novels under the engraving. Take the whole and give me forty francs cash."

" Forty francs ! " exclaimed the publisher, with the screech of a frightened hen. " Twenty at the utmost ! and I may lose those," added Barbet.

" Let me see the twenty francs," said Lousteau.

" Faith ! I don't know if I've got them," said Barbet, rummaging his pockets. " There they are. You are robbing me ; you get the better of me — "

" Come, let us be off," said Lousteau, picking up Lucien's manuscript and making a stroke of ink just beneath the twine that fastened it.

" Have you anything more?" asked Barbet.

" Nothing, my little Shylock. I 'll put you in the way of an excellent bit of business before long (in which you shall lose a thousand crowns to teach you to rob me in this way)," added Étienne in a low voice to Lucien.

" But your articles? how can you write them without the books?" said Lucien as they drove to the Palais-Royal.

" Pooh! you don't understand how easily that sort of thing is done. As for the ' Voyage in Egypt,' I did open the book and read here and there without cutting the leaves; I found eleven mistakes in grammar; I can make a column out of that by saying that though the author may have learned the hieroglyphic language of those Egyptian milestones called obelisks, he does n't know his own, and I 'll give the blunders, for I wrote them down. I shall then tell him that instead of writing about the natural history and antiquity, he had better have concerned himself with the future of Egypt, the progress of civilization, the means of uniting it to France which, having once conquered Egypt and then lost it, could still obtain a moral ascendency over it. That gives a chance for a fine patriotic flourish interlarded with tirades about Marseilles and the Levant and our present commercial interests."

" But suppose the author had said all that himself, what would you do?"

" Oh, then I should say that instead of boring us with politics, he had better have written about Art and described the country under its picturesque and territorial aspects. There's a chance for a lament. We

are overrun with politics, politics here, there, and
everywhere. I regret those charming books of travel
which explained the difficulties of navigation and the
delights of crossing the Line, in short, what persons
who never travel want to know, — all the while laughing, of course, at travellers who make great events of
gulls, porpoises, whales, first sight of land, and shoals
avoided. Subscribers laugh, and that is all that's
wanted. As for novels, Florine is the greatest reader
of novels there is in the world. She tells me what they
are about, and I knock off an article accordingly.
When she is bored by what she calls ' author's
phrases,' I give the book a respectful notice, and ask
the publisher for another copy, which he sends me out
of gratitude for the puff."

" Good God! and criticism, sacred criticism?" cried
Lucien, still imbued with the principles of the brotherhood.

"My dear fellow," said Lousteau, "criticism is a
brush which you can't use on thin material, or it tears
it to rags. Well, don't let us talk of the business any
more. Do you see that mark?" he went on, pointing
to the line he had made on the outside sheet of the
"Daisies." "It is exactly under the twine. If Dauriat
reads your manuscript, he will certainly not be able to
tie the string in exactly the same place. Your manuscript is as good as sealed, and you will know whether
he opens it, — not at all a useless experience for you.
Now, take notice of another thing; you are not making
your entrance into the trade alone and without a
sponsor, like other young fellows who go the round of a
dozen publishers none of whom will offer them a chair."

Lucien already felt the truth of this assertion. Lousteau had paid the cabman three francs, to the poet's utter amazement; such prodigality on the heels of penury seeming incredible to him.

The new friends now entered the Galeries de Bois, where Dauriat's great publishing concern called "The Novelty" reigned supreme. At the period of which we speak the Galeries de Bois of the Palais-Royal were among the most noted of the sights of Paris. It is by no means useless to draw a picture of that ignoble bazaar, which for thirty-six years played so great a rôle in Parisian life that there are few men of forty to whom the following description, incredible to younger men, will not be of interest.

In place of the present cold, lofty, and broad Galerie d'Orléans, a sort of green-house without flowers, there stood in those days a line of wooden barracks, or, to be more exact, plank huts, small, poorly roofed and ill-lighted from the court and garden and also from the roof by small sashes, called casements, which were more like the dirty openings of the dance-halls beyond the barriers than actual windows. A triple line of booths made two galleries about twelve feet high; those down the centre faced to each side, and the fetid air which rose from the crowded passage-ways had little chance to escape through the roof, which admitted only a dim light through its dirty casements. These centre booths or cells were thought so valuable, because of the crowds who passed them, that in spite of their narrow space (some being scarcely six feet wide and eight or ten feet long) they brought enormous prices, — some as much as three thousand francs. The side booths, which were lighted from the court and from the garden, were protected by small, green trellises, possibly to prevent the crowd outside from demolishing by pressure the lath-and-plaster walls which formed the sides of the sheds. Here, therefore, was a space of some two or three feet in width where the most amazing products of a botany unknown to science vegetated, mingled with the cast-off scraps of industries that were not less flourishing. Rose-trees and waste-paper, flowers of rhetoric and flowers of nature, ribbons of all colors, remnants of the fashions, in short, the refuse of the interior commerce was there collected. The outer walls of this fantastic palace, towards the court and towards the garden, presented the lowest aspect of Parisian shabbiness; the coloring of the stucco was washed off, the plaster itself was falling, or patched, or scribbled over with grotesque writings. On both sides a nauseous and disgusting approach seemed to warn delicate persons from entering these galleries; and yet delicate and refined persons were no more kept away by these horrible things than princes in fairy-tales recoil from dragons and other obstacles interposed by evil genii between them and the princesses.

These galleries were, as the Galerie d'Orléans is to-day, divided by passage-ways, from which they were entered by the present porticos, which were begun before the Revolution and left unfinished for want of money. The handsome stone gallery which now leads to the Théâtre-Français was in those days a narrow passage-way of excessive height and so ill-covered that the rain wet it. It was called the Galerie Vitrée, to distinguish it from the Galeries de Bois. The roofs of all these miserable

sheds were in such a bad state that the House of Orléans
had a lawsuit with a famous shopkeeper who found his
cashmeres and other goods injured during a single night
to a large amount of money. The man won his case.
A double thickness of tarred cloth served for a covering
in some places. The floor of the Galerie Vitrée (where
Chevet's fortune began), also that of the Galeries de
Bois was the soil of Paris, with such other soil added
as the boots and shoes of a myriad of pedestrians had
imported there. In all weather the feet were forced to
stumble among mountains and valleys of hardened mud,
constantly swept by the shopkeepers, but, even so, re-
quiring all new-comers to learn a method of management in order to walk with safety.

This disgusting mass of mud, these dirty panes of
glass thickened by rain and dust, these flat-roofed huts
covered outside with ragged cloth, the filth of the outside walls, in short, this whole assemblage of things,
which was like a camp of gypsies, or the barracks at a
fair, or the provisional boardings put up in Paris round
houses that are building, all this grinning vulgarity was
wonderfully in keeping with the different trades which
swarmed beneath these nasty sheds, — bold, shameless,
voluble, and wildly gay; for an incalculable business
was done here from the Revolution of 1789 to that of
1830. For twenty years the Bourse was directly opposite, on the ground-floor of the palace. Rendezvous
were given before and after the opening of the exchange
in these galleries. Consequently, public opinion and
reputations were made and unmade here, and political
and financial affairs incessantly discussed. The Paris
world of bankers and merchants congregated in the

square of the Palais-Royal, and swarmed into the galleries when it rained. The construction of these wooden buildings, which had sprung up heaven knows how, made them singularly resonant. Bursts of laughter echoed through them; not a quarrel could take place at one end that the other end did not know what it was about. The place was occupied solely by the shops of booksellers and publishers (poetry, politics, and prose) and by those of milliners. At night the women of the town appeared there. Novels and books of all kinds, new and old reputations, political plots and counterplots, the lies of publishers and booksellers all flourished there. There, too, novelties were sold to a public that persisted in not buying them elsewhere. In the course of a single evening thousands of copies have been sold of a pamphlet by Paul-Louis Courier or the " Adventures of the Daughter of a King," which, by the by, was the first shot fired by the House of Orléans at the Charter of Louis XVIII.

At the particular period when Lucien first appeared there, a few of the booths had windows with rather elegant panes of glass; these were, of course, on the side booths looking either to the court or the garden. Up to the time when this strange colony disappeared under the wand of Fontaine the architect, the booths in the centre were entirely open, supported by pillars, like booths at a country fair, and the eye could look across and through them to the gallery on the other side. As it was impossible to make fires, the merchants used foot-warmers, which they took care of themselves; for one piece of carelessness would instantly have wrapped in flames that whole republic of planks dried in the sun, with all its inflammable contents of paper, gauze, and muslin. The shops of the milliners were full of wonderful bonnets, which seemed to be there less for sale than for show, hanging by hundreds on iron trees and enlivening the galleries with a thousand colors. For twenty years the loungers in the galleries had wondered on what heads those dusty bonnets would end their days. Saleswomen, for the most part ugly, but brisk, hooked the female sex adroitly in the style and language of marketwomen. One grisette, whose tongue was as free as her eyes were active, stood on a stool and attacked the passers: " Buy a pretty bonnet, madame ! " " Let me sell you something, monsieur." Their rich and picturesque vocabulary was varied by inflections of the voice, and interspersed with knowing looks and criticisms on those who passed them. The publishers and the milliners lived on good terms with each other.

In the passage called so gorgeously the Galerie Vitrée, the most extraordinary enterprises were carried on. There ventriloquists and charlatans of all kinds had settled themselves, and shows were offered where it was a lottery whether you saw nothing or the whole world. It was there that a man first established himself who afterwards made seven or eight hundred thousand francs in fairs all over France. His sign was a sun revolving in a black frame, round which were the following words in scarlet letters: " Here man may see what God can never see. Entrance two sous." The door-keeper never allowed one person to go in alone, nor more than two at a time. Once in, you found yourself confronted with a huge mirror. Then a voice, which might have startled even Hoffmann of Berlin himself, went off like a mechanism when the spring is touched, and said: "There, gentlemen, you see that which throughout all eternity God can never see; namely, your like, — God has no like." You went away ashamed and silent, unwilling to acknowledge your stupidity.

From all the little doors issued voices of the same nature, inviting you to visit cosmoramas, views of Constantinople, puppet-shows, automatons playing chess, dogs who could pick out the handsomest woman in society. The ventriloquist Fitz-James flourished in the café Borel, before he went to die at Montmartre among the pupils of the École Polytechnique. Here were fruiterers and bouquet-makers, and a celebrated tailor whose military gold lace shone at night like suns. In the mornings up to half-past two o'clock these galleries were dismal and deserted. The shopkeepers talked among themselves as if at home. The appointments which the Parisian population gave themselves did not begin till about three o'clock, the hour for the Bourse. As soon as the crowd poured in, the gratuitous readings at the booksellers' counters by penniless young men hungry for literature began. The shopmen whose business it was to watch the books thus exposed for sale charitably allowed these poor fellows to turn the leaves. If the book happened to be a 12mo of two hundred pages, like "Smarra," "Peter Schlemil," "Jean Sbogar," "Jocko," two visits would enable the reader to devour it. In those days circulating-libraries did not exist; it was necessary to buy a book in order to read it; and this was why novels were sold in numbers that now seem fabulous. There was something indescribably French in these mental alms bestowed on youthful, eager, poverty-stricken intellect.

The tragic aspect of this terrible bazaar began to show itself towards evening. Through all the adjacent streets women poured in, who were allowed to walk there unmolested; from every section of Paris came prostitutes to " do the Palais." The stone galleries belonged to privileged establishments, who paid for the right to expose their creatures, dressed like princesses, between such and such an arch with a corresponding right to the same distance in the garden; but the Galeries de Bois were the common ground of women of the town, " the Palais," *par excellence*, a word which signified in those days the temple of prostitution. Any woman might come there and go away, accompanied by her prey, wheresoever it pleased her. They drew such crowds to the Galeries de Bois that every one was compelled to walk at a snail's pace as they do in the procession at a masked ball. But this slowness, which annoyed no one, enabled persons to examine each other. The women were all dressed in a style and manner that no longer exists; their gowns were made low to the very middle of their backs, and also very low in front; their heads were dressed fantastically to attract notice; some were Norman in style, others Spanish; the hair of one was curled like a poodle, that of another in smooth, straight bands; their legs, covered with white stockings, were shown, it would be difficult to say how, but always à propos. All this picturesque infamy is now done away with. The license of solicitation and answer, that public cynicism so in keeping with the place itself, is no longer to be seen, either there or at masked balls, nor in the celebrated public balls which are given in the present day. The scene was horrible and gay. The white flesh of the shoulders and throats shone and sparkled against the clothing of the men which was usually dark, producing magnificent contrasts. The roll of voices and the noise of steps sent a murmuring sound to the middle of the garden, like the breaking of the waves upon a sandbank. Well-dressed persons and striking-looking men were cheek by jowl with evident gallows-birds. There was something impossible to define, something piquant, about these infamous assemblages; even the most insensible men were stirred by them, — so much so that all Paris came there until the last moment, and walked the wooden planks with which the architect covered the cellars of the new Galerie d'Orléans as he built it. Deep and unanimous regret was felt at the demolition of those disgraceful wooden galleries.

X.

A FOURTH VARIETY OF PUBLISHER.

LADVOCAT, the publisher, had lately established himself at the corner of the passage which divided the two galleries, opposite to the establishment of Dauriat, a young man now forgotten, but a daring fellow, who cleared the way along which his rival subsequently advanced to fortune. Dauriat's shop was at the angle of the passage and gallery looking towards the garden; that of Ladvocat was towards the court. Dauriat's place was divided into two unequal parts; one a ware-room for his publications, the other a sort of office.

Lucien who was in this scene for the first time at night, was bewildered by its strange aspects, which provincials and indeed all young men are unable to resist. He soon lost his companion in the crowd.

" If you were as handsome as that fellow, I'd give you something in return," said one of the women to an old man, pointing to Lucien.

Lucien turned as shamefaced as a blind man's dog, and he followed the torrent in a state of excitement and bewilderment impossible to describe. Harassed by the glances of the women, dazzled by their white shoulders and their bold throats, he clasped his manuscript and held it close, fearing, poor innocent, that some of them would steal it.

"What is it, monsieur?" he cried, feeling himself seized by the arm, and fancying that his poems might have attracted some author. Turning round, he saw Lousteau, who laughed and said: —

"I knew you would end by coming this way."

The poet was in front of Dauriat's wareroom, into which Lousteau now took him. The place was full of persons, all waiting their turn to speak with the sultan of publishers. Printers, paper-makers, designers, were clustering about the clerks and questioning them as to the business they had in hand or were meditating.

"There 's Finot, the editor of my paper," said Lousteau; "he is talking with a young man who has talent, Félicien Vernou; a little scoundrel as dangerous as a secret disease."

"Well, you 've got a first representation, old man," said Finot, coming up to Lousteau, with Vernou; "but I 've disposed of the box."

"You 've sold it to Braulard?"

"Suppose I have? You can easily get a place. What have you come to see Dauriat about? I have agreed that we will push Paul de Kock; Dauriat has taken five hundred copies. Victor Ducange refused him a novel; so Dauriat wants, he says, to set up a new author in the same style. You are to write up Paul de Kock over Ducange."

"But Ducange and I have a play together at the Gaîté," said Lousteau.

"Then tell him I wrote the article, — let him suppose I made it savage and you softened it; he 'll owe you thanks for that."

"Can't you manage to get Dauriat's clerk to cash

me this little note for a hundred francs?" said Étienne to Finot; "you know! we are to sup together to-night to inaugurate Florine's new apartment."

"Ah, yes, true; you treat us," said Finot, as if he were making an effort of memory. "Look here, Gabusson," said the editor, taking Barbet's note and handing it to the cashier, "give monsieur ninety francs for me. Endorse the note, old man."

Lousteau took the cashier's pen while the latter counted out the money, and endorsed the note. Lucien, all eyes and ears, lost not a syllable of the conversation.

"But that's not all, my dear friend," continued Étienne, "and I shall not say 'thank you' either, for there's friendship to the death between you and me of course. I want to present this gentleman to Dauriat, and you must make him willing to listen to us."

"What's in the wind?" asked Finot.

"A collection of poems," replied Lucien.

"Oh!" exclaimed Finot, shrugging his shoulders.

"I take it that monsieur has not had much to do with publishers as yet," remarked Vernou, looking at Lucien, "or he would hide his manuscript in the deepest recesses of his own room."

At this moment a handsome young man, named Émile Blondet, who had just made his mark by articles of great public import in the "Journal des Débats," entered the place, shook hands with Finot and Lousteau, and bowed slightly to Vernou.

"Come and sup with us to-night at Florine's," Lousteau said to him.

"So be it," said Blondet; "who's to be there?"

" Well, Florine and Matifat," said Lousteau, " and Du Bruel, who gives Florine the rôle for her first appearance to-night, and a little old fellow named Cardot, and his son-in-law Camusot; also Finot."

" Does the druggist do things in style? "

" He won't drug us I hope," remarked Lucien.

" Monsieur is witty," said Blondet looking gravely at Lucien ; " will he be there, too, Lousteau? "

" Yes."

" Then we shall have some fun."

Lucien reddened to the tips of his ears.

" How long before I can see you, Dauriat? " said Blondet, rapping on the window, which was high up in the partition between the office and the shop.

" I 'll be with you directly," said a voice.

" Good," said Lousteau to his protégé ; " that young man, almost as young as you are, is on the ' Débats.' He 's among the princes of criticism ; everybody fears him ; Dauriat will come and fawn upon him, and we shall have a good chance to speak to the pacha of vignettes and printers. If it had n't been for this we might have waited till eleven o'clock before our turn came to see him ; see how the crowd increases."

Lucien and Lousteau followed Blondet, Finot, and Vernou, and together they made a little group at the farther end of the shop.

" What is Dauriat about? " said Blondet to Gabusson, the head-clerk, who came forward to speak to him.

" He is buying a broken-down weekly paper, which he wants to revive in order to check the influence of the ' Minerve,' which is too exclusively for Eymery, and the ' Conservateur,' which is blindly romanticist."

" Does he pay a good price for it? "

" As usual, — more than it is worth," replied the cashier.

Just then a young man who had lately published a fine novel, which had sold rapidly and won immediate success (the second edition being now under way), entered the place. The appearance of this young man, endowed with that peculiar, fantastic air and manner which characterizes the artistic nature, struck Lucien powerfully.

" Here 's Nathan," said Lousteau in Lucien's ear.

In spite of the almost savage pride expressed in his countenance, then in its first youth, Nathan approached the journalists hat in hand, and placed himself humbly before Blondet, whom he as yet knew only by sight. Blondet and Finot kept their hats on their heads.

" Monsieur," began Nathan, addressing Blondet, " I am most happy in the opportunity which chance affords me — "

" He is so agitated he talks pleonasms," whispered Vernou to Lousteau.

" — to express my gratitude for the fine review you were so good as to give me in the ' Journal des Débats.' More than half of the success of my book is owing to you."

" No, no, my dear friend, no ! " said Blondet, with a protecting manner only slightly masked by kindliness. " You have talent, and I 'm delighted, the devil take me, to make your acquaintance."

" As your article has already appeared I shall not be thought to curry favor ; I may feel at my ease with you. Will you do me the honor and the pleasure of dining with me to-morrow? Finot will be there; Lousteau, old man, you won't refuse me?" added Nathan, grasping Lousteau's hand. "Ah! you have chosen a noble course, monsieur," he continued, addressing Blondet; "you are following the Dussaults, Fiévées, Geoffroys. Hoffmann spoke of you to Claude Vignon, his pupil, a friend of mine, to whom he said that the 'Journal des Débats' would live long with such articles as yours. They must pay you enormously for them."

"A hundred francs a column," replied Blondet, "and that's a small price when one has to read so many books in order to find one, like yours, that is worth reviewing. Your work gave me great pleasure, on my word of honor."

"And it helped him to earn fifteen hundred francs," said Lousteau to Lucien.

"But you write chiefly on political subjects, don't you?" said Nathan.

"As occasion offers," replied Blondet.

Lucien had admired Nathan's book, he revered the writer as a demi-god, and was therefore, fledgling that he was, stupefied at the man's abasement before this critic, whose name and influence were unknown to him. "Shall I ever come to that? must a man abdicate his own self-respect?" thought he. "Put on your hat, Nathan! you have written a fine book, and that critic has only made an article on it." Such thoughts lashed the blood in his veins. As he stood there he saw numberless timid young men, needy authors, all anxious to speak to Dauriat, but who, seeing the shop full and despairing of getting an audience, turned and went out, remarking sadly, "I will call again."

Two or three public men were talking of the convocation of the Chambers and of politics among a knot of celebrities in national affairs. The weekly journal for which Dauriat was now negotiating had the right to discuss politics. In those days this was rare ; a newspaper was a privilege as much run after as a theatre. One of the influential stockholders of the " Constitutionnel" happened to form one of this group. Lousteau had certainly acquitted himself well in his office of cicerone, for, at every word, Dauriat was magnified in Lucien's mind as politics and literature were seen to converge upon him. But the sight of a fine writer prostrating his talent before a journalist, humiliating Art, as woman was humiliated and prostituted beneath those shameless galleries, was a terrible education to the provincial poet. Money ! yes, money was the key to the whole enigma. Lucien felt himself alone, helpless, clinging only by the weak thread of an uncertain friendship to success and fortune. He accused his true and far-seeing friends in the brotherhood of having painted this world in false colors ; he blamed them for having dissuaded him from flinging himself into the arena, pen in hand.

" I might by this time have been another Blondet ! " thought he.

Lousteau himself, who had lately cried in his ears in the gardens like a wounded eagle, Lousteau, whom he had thought so great, was now dwarfed ; one man alone seemed to him important, — this fashionable publisher, who was literally the means by which all these lives existed. The poet, as he stood there, manuscript in hand, was conscious of a trepidation that resembled fear. In the centre of the shop our poet noticed several busts on wooden pedestals painted to resemble marble, — one of Byron, one of Goethe, and one of Canalis, from whom Dauriat was desirous of obtaining a volume. Gradually he began to lose the sense of his own value; his courage weakened. He foresaw the influence that this Dauriat was to exercise over his destiny, and he nervously awaited his appearance.

"Well, my friends," said a fat and oily little man, with a face like that of a Roman pro-consul, softened, however, by a good-humored expression which beguiled superficial minds, "behold me the proprietor of the only weekly paper that could be purchased, with a list of two thousand subscribers."

"Nonsense! the Stamp-Office rates them at seven hundred; and that's over the mark," said Blondet.

"On my sacred word of honor there are twelve hundred. I make it two thousand," added Dauriat, lowering his voice, "because of those printers and paper-makers over there. — I thought you knew better than that," he said aloud.

"Do you want partners?" asked Finot.

"That depends," replied Dauriat. "Will you take a third at forty thousand francs?"

"All right, if you'll agree to put the men I want on the staff, — Émile Blondet here present, Claude Vignon, Scribe, Théodore Leclercq, Félicien Vernou, Jay, Jouy, Lousteau —"

"And why not Lucien de Rubempré?" said the poet of the provinces, boldly.

"— and Nathan," concluded Finot.

"Yes, and why not everybody who is walking about?"

said the publisher, frowning, and addressing the author of the "Daisies." "To whom have I the honor of speaking?" he said, with an impertinent air.

"One moment, Dauriat," interposed Lousteau. "I brought monsieur to see you. While Finot is thinking over your proposal, let me have a word with you."

Lucien's shirt felt wet upon his back as he saw the cold, displeased look of this formidable padishah of publishers, who had greeted all the writers present with an air of familiar contempt.

"Is it some new affair, my boy?" asked Dauriat; "you know very well I have got eleven hundred manuscripts now on hand. Yes, gentlemen," he cried, "positively eleven hundred, — ask Gabusson. I shall soon need a staff of clerks to register them, and another staff of readers to examine them; there 'll be meetings to vote on their merits, with ballots, and a secretary to report results; a sort of annex to the Académie Française, in which the academicians shall be better paid in the Galeries de Bois than they are at the Institute."

"A good idea," said Blondet.

"A bad idea," retorted Dauriat. "I have no intention of examining the lucubrations of such of you as start in literature because you can't be anything else, — neither bootmakers, nor corporals, nor servants, nor sheriffs, nor magistrates, nor capitalists of any kind. No one is admitted here unless his reputation is made. If you are celebrated you shall have floods of gold, not otherwise. I have made three men famous during the last two years and they are all three ungrateful. There 's Nathan, who wants six thousand francs for the second edition of his book, which has cost me three

thousand francs in reviews, and hasn't yet brought
me in a thousand. I paid for Blondet's two articles
one thousand francs and a dinner which cost five
hundred — "

"But, monsieur, if all publishers said that, how
would a first book ever get published?" asked Lucien,
in whose eyes Blondet had a sudden fall in value when
he learned the price Dauriat had paid for the articles in
the " Débats."

" That doesn't concern me," replied Dauriat with
a murderous glance at the handsome youth, who was
smiling at him agreeably. " For my part, I don't publish books on which I risk two thousand francs to make
two thousand. I speculate in literature. I publish
forty volumes of ten thousand copies each, as Panc-
kouke and the Beaudouins do. My name and the reviews I procure make it a matter of hundreds of
thousands of francs, instead of merely two thousand for
a single volume. It would give me more trouble to
push a new author and his book than it does to bring
out the 'Théâtres Etrangers,' 'Victoires et Conquêtes,'
or the ' Mémoires sur la Révolution,' all of which
brought in a fortune. I'm not here to be made a stepping-stone to future fame, but to make money and pay
money to celebrated men. The manuscript that I buy
for a hundred thousand francs is less dear than that an
unknown author asks six hundred for. Though I'm
not altogether a Mecænas I have a right to the gratitude of literature. I have already more than doubled
the price of manuscripts. I give you this information
because you are a friend of Lousteau, my little man,"
said Dauriat slapping the poet on the shoulder with an

odious gesture of familiarity. "If I were to talk with all the authors who want me to be their publisher I should have to shut up shop, for my whole time would be spent in conversation, agreeable perhaps, but much too costly. I'm not rich enough to listen to the monologues of vanity. No one ever does that except on the stage in the classic tragedies."

The luxury of this terrible Dauriat's apparel enforced, to the eyes of a provincial poet, the cruel logic of his words.

"What has he got there to publish?" said Dauriat to Lousteau.

"A volume of fine verses."

Hearing this reply Dauriat turned to Gabusson with a gesture worthy of Talma.

"Gabusson, my friend, from this day forth if any one comes here to offer me manuscripts — Now listen to this, all the rest of you," he said, addressing three clerks who appeared from behind the piles of books on hearing the choleric voice of their master, who was looking at his nails and well-shaped hands, — "remember, when any one brings a manuscript you are to ask if it is prose or verse. If it is verse, send him away, get rid of him; verses are the ruin of the trade."

"Bravo! well said, Dauriat!" cried all the journalists.

"It is true," said the publisher, walking up and down the shop with Lucien's manuscript in his hand. "You don't know, gentlemen, what evils Lord Byron's success and Victor Hugo's, Lamartine's, Casimir Delavigne's, and Béranger's have produced. Their fame has brought down upon us a horde of barbarians. I

11

am positive there are thousands of poems in the hands of publishers at this very moment beginning in the middle, and without head or tail, like 'The Corsair' and 'Lara.' Young men rush into incomprehensible strophes and call it originality, and dash off descriptive poems, and think they are making a new school, when they are only reviving Delille. For the last two years poets have swarmed like cockchafers; I lost twenty thousand francs on them last year! — ask Gabusson. There may be immortal poets in the world; I know some fresh and rosy ones that don't yet shave; but to the publishing trade, young man," he said turning to Lucien, " there are but four poets : Béranger, Casimir Delavigne, Lamartine, and Victor Hugo; as for Canalis ! — he's a poet made by reviewers."

Lucien had not the nerve to pull himself up and show pride before those men of influence who were all laughing heartily, — he felt he should only cover himself with ridicule; but all the same a violent longing seized him to spring at the throat of that publisher and destroy the insulting perfection of his cravat, and break the chain that glittered on his waistcoat. His infuriated self-love opened a door in his mind to vengeance, and he swore a deadly enmity to that man on whom he smiled.

"Poetry is like the sun, which starts the growth of primeval forests and begets flies and gnats," said Blondet. "There is no virtue that isn't lined with a vice. Literature begets publishers."

"And journalists," said Lousteau.

Dauriat burst out laughing.

"What is this anyhow?" he said tapping the manuscript.

" A collection of sonnets that would make Petrarch ashamed," replied Lousteau.

" How do you intend that remark?" asked Dauriat.

" As most persons would," answered Lousteau, seeing a sly smile on the lips of those present.

Lucien could not be angry, but he sweated under his harness.

"Well, I'll read it," said Dauriat, with a royal gesture, meant to show the full importance of this concession. " If your sonnets are up to the level of the nineteenth century, I'll make a great poet of you, my little man."

" If his talent is equal to his beauty you won't run great risks," said one of the most famous orators of the Chamber, who was standing near, conversing with a reporter for the " Constitutionnel" and the editor of the " Minerve."

" General," said Dauriat, " fame is only made by twelve thousand francs' worth of newspaper articles and three thousand francs' worth of dinners ; ask the author of ' Le Solitaire,' whether that's not so. If Monsieur Benjamin Constant will consent to write an article on this young poet, I will not hesitate to come to terms with him."

As the great man of the provinces heard the title " General" and the name of the illustrious Benjamin Constant, the shabby shop took on the proportions of Olympus.

" Lousteau, I want to speak to you," said Finot ; " but we shall meet at the theatre. Dauriat, I'll take your offer on certain conditions. Come into your office."

"Very good, come on, my boy," said Dauriat, motioning Finot to precede him, and making the gesture of a busy man to a dozen others who were trying to speak to him ; he was just disappearing when Lucien, losing patience, stopped him.

"You have my manuscript," he said ; "when am I to have an answer?"

"Well, my little poet, you may come back in three or four days, and I'll see about it."

Lucien was dragged away by Lousteau, who would not give him time to bow to Vernou, or Blondet, or Raoul Nathan, or General Foy, or Benjamin Constant, whose work on the Hundred Days had just appeared. Lucien had scarcely time to see that refined fair head, with its oval face and spiritual eyes and charming mouth, — the face of the man who for twenty years was the Potemkin of Madame de Staël, who made war upon the Bourbons after making it on Napoleon, and was destined to die horrified at his victory.

"What a place that is!" cried Lucien as he took his place in a cab beside Lousteau.

"Panorama-Dramatique, — and as fast as you can ; thirty sous for your fare!" called Étienne to the cabman. "Yes ; Dauriat is a rascal who sells from fifteen to sixteen hundred thousand francs' worth of books yearly ; you might call him the minister of literature," said Lousteau, whose vanity was pleasantly tickled, and who now posed as instructor to Lucien. "His cupidity, quite equal to that of Barbet, is on a grand scale. Dauriat has his own ways, however ; he can be generous, but he is always vain. As for his mind, that's made up of what he hears around him ; his shop is a very good place to frequent ; you can get into conversation there with the leading men of the day. A young man can learn more there, my dear fellow, in one hour than he can in hanging over books for a year. There they discuss articles and start new topics, and a man can attach himself to celebrated or influential persons who may be very useful to him. It is most important in these days to make connections. All is mere chance, as you can see by this time. The most dangerous thing is to have an intellect kept hidden in a corner."

" But that fellow is so impertinent," said Lucien.

" Pooh ! we all laugh at Dauriat," replied Étienne. " If you have need of him he 'll trample you underfoot ; but he needs the 'Journal des Débats,' and Émile Blondet twirls him like a top. Oh ! if you are determined to enter literature you 'll see many such things. What did I tell you? "

" Yes, you were right," answered Lucien, " but I suffered in that shop more cruelly than I expected, even after what you said."

" Then why do you put yourself in the way of such suffering? I tell you that the things that cost us our life, the subjects which tear our brains through studious nights, the fields of thought we toil among, the work we build and cement with our blood, are to publishers merely a paying or a non-paying venture. They sell or they don't sell your work, — that 's the whole problem to them. A book to them is only a risk of capital. The finer the book, the less chance it has of selling. All superior minds are above the masses ; their success depends therefore on the necessary time it takes for their work to be appreciated. No publisher is willing to wait for that. The book of to-day must be sold to-morrow. Publishers will refuse books of real substance which advance slowly to high appreciation."

" D'Arthèz was right !" cried Lucien.

"Do you know d'Arthèz?" said Lousteau. "There is nothing more dangerous than solitary minds that expect, as that poor fellow does, to bring the world to their feet. By fanaticizing their young imaginations with a belief that merely flatters their inward sense of power, such foolish awaiters of posthumous glory are prevented from bestirring themselves at an age when movement is possible and profitable. I 'm for Mohammed's system : after ordering the mountain to come to him he cried out, ' If you don't come to me, I 'll go to you.' "

This sally, in which reason was the incisive force, made Lucien hesitate in mind between the system of laborious and submissive poverty inculcated by the brotherhood and the doctrine of aggression which Lousteau expounded to him. The poet of Angoulême kept silence after that until they reached the boulevard du Temple.

XI.

BEHIND THE SCENES.

THE Panorama-Dramatique, the site of which is now occupied by a private house, was then a charming theatre standing opposite to the rue Charlot on the boulevard du Temple, which failed of success under two managements, although Bouffé, an actor who inherited Potier's fame, made his first appearance there; also Florine, who, five years later, became a noted actress. Theatres, like men, are doomed sometimes to fatality. The Panorama-Dramatique was forced into competition with the Ambigu, the Gaîté, the Porte-Saint-Martin, and the vaudeville theatres; it was unable to withstand their intrigues, the restrictions placed upon its privileges, and the lack of good plays. Authors are afraid of displeasing successful theatres by working for a new establishment the future of which is doubtful. However, at the present moment the management was counting on a new piece, a sort of comic melodrama by a young author, the collaborator of several celebrities, named Du Bruel, who claimed that he had written this play alone. It was brought out for the first appearance of Florine, until then a subordinate actress at the Gaîté, where for the last year she had played insignificant rôles successfully, without, however, obtaining a good engagement. The Panorama had therefore abducted her from its rival. Another actress, named Coralie, was also to make her first appearance on this occasion.

When the two young men arrived Lucien was astonished by a new example of the power of the press.

"Monsieur is with me," said Étienne to a doorkeeper, who bowed low.

"You will find it hard to get a seat," said the head-doorkeeper; "there is nothing available but the manager's box."

Étienne and Lousteau lost some time in wandering through the corridors and negotiating with the box-openers.

"Let us go into the green-room and speak to the manager," said Lousteau; "he will take us into his box. I'll present you to Florine, the heroine of the evening."

At a sign from Lousteau the porter of the stalls took a small key and opened a hidden door made in a wall. Lucien followed his friend and passed instantly from the brilliantly lighted corridor to a dark hole, which, in nearly every theatre, is the means of communication between the auditorium and the part called in general terms, "behind the scenes." After mounting a few damp stairs the provincial poet entered the latter region, where the strangest sight awaited him. The narrowness of the passage-ways, the enormous height of the roof, the lamplighters' ladders, the various decorations horrible to behold near-by, the whitened actors, their singular garments made of the commonest materials, the scene-shifters with greasy jackets, the hanging ropes, the stage manager walking about with his hat on his head, the waiting supernumeraries, the scenery suspended over-head, the fire-buckets and the firemen, — in short, the whole assemblage of things absurd, dismal, dirty, hideous, and tawdry was so little like what Lucien had seen from his seat in the theatre that his amazement was uncontrollable.

A good, old-fashioned melodrama, called "Bertram," was just ending, — a play adapted from a tragedy by Maturin, greatly admired by Nodier, Lord Byron, and Walter Scott, but wholly without success on the French stage.

"Don't let go my arm unless you wish to fall through some trap, or receive a forest on your head, or knock over a palace, or carry off a cottage," said Lousteau. "Is Florine in her dressing-room, my beauty?" he said to an actress who was waiting her cue to go upon the stage.

"Yes, my love; and thank you for what you said about me; you are so much nicer since Florine joined us."

"Take care! don't miss your entrance effect, my dear," said Lousteau. "Rush on, hands up! say it well: 'Pause, wretched man!' The house is full, receipts immense."

Lucien was amazed to see the actress collect herself and then rush on, exclaiming: "Pause, wretched man!" in tones of horror. She was no longer the same woman.

"So this is the theatre!" he said to Lousteau.

"Just the same thing as the publishing concern in the Galeries de Bois, or literature in a newspaper office, — a regular cook-shop," responded his new friend.

Nathan appeared.

"Whom have you come to see?" asked Lousteau.

"I'm doing the lesser theatres for the 'Gazette,' till I get something better," replied Nathan.

"Then come to supper to-night, and say good things for Florine in return," said Lousteau.

"At your service," answered Nathan.

"You know she lives now in the rue de Bondy."

"Who is that handsome young man, my little Lousteau?" said the actress, coming off the stage.

"Ah, my dear, a great poet! a man who is going to be celebrated. Monsieur Nathan, as you are to sup together allow me to present Monsieur Lucien de Rubempré."

"You bear a distinguished name, monsieur," said Nathan to Lucien.

"Lucien, Monsieur Raoul Nathan," added Lousteau.

"Ah, monsieur," said Lucien, "I was reading you only two days ago, and I cannot understand how, having written such a novel and such poems, you could be so humble to that journalist."

"I shall wait till you have published your first book before answering you," said Nathan, with a meaning smile.

"Bless me! ultras and liberals shaking hands!" cried Félicien Vernou, coming upon the trio.

"In the morning my opinions are those of my journal," said Nathan; "but at night I think as I please."

"Étienne," said Vernou, "Finot came with me, and he wants you — ah! here he is."

"Look here! there isn't a seat left," said Finot.

"There's always one in our hearts for you," said the actress, giving the editor-in-chief an agreeable smile.

"So, so, my little Florville, you have got over your

love-affair, have you? I thought you were carried off by a Russian prince."

"Nobody carries off women now-a-days," said la Florville, the actress who had just declaimed, "Pause, wretched man!" "We stayed ten days at Saint-Mandé, and the prince paid a proper indemnity to the management. And the management," she added, laughing, "is now praying God for more Russian princes; indemnities are receipts without costs."

"And you, little one," said Finot to a pretty peasant-girl who was listening to them, "where did you get those diamond earrings? Have you captured an Indian rajah?"

"No, only a man who sells blacking, an Englishman; and he is gone already! It is not so easy to get hold, like Florine and Coralie, of millionnaire shop-keepers tired of their homes; are n't they lucky, those two?"

"You 'll miss your entrance, Florville," cried Lousteau.

"If you want to make a stroke," said Nathan, "instead of screaming like a fury, 'He is saved!' go on calmly and walk to the footlights and say in a chest voice, 'He is saved,' — just as Talma says, 'O patria,' in Tancredi. Come, go along," he added, pushing her.

"It is too late," said Vernou; "she lost her chance."

"What did she do? just hear the applause!" said Lousteau.

"She went down on her knees and showed her bosom; that's her great resource," said the widow of the blacking.

"The manager has given us his box; you 'll find me there," said Finot to Étienne.

Lousteau then took Lucien behind the stage and through a labyrinth of corridors and stairways until, accompanied by Nathan and Vernou, they reached a small room on the third floor.

"Good-evening, gentlemen," said Florine. "Monsieur," she added, turning to a short, stout man, who stood in a corner, "these are the arbiters of my fate; my future is in their hands; nevertheless, I hope they will be under our table to-morrow morning, — if Monsieur Lousteau has forgotten nothing."

"Forgotten! no! you will have Blondet of the 'Débats,'" said Étienne, — "Blondet himself, the true Blondet, — Blondet, I tell you!"

"Oh, my little Lousteau, I'll kiss you for that," cried the actress, throwing her arms round the journalist's neck.

At this demonstration, Matifat, the stout man in the corner, looked serious. At sixteen, Florine was thin. Her beauty, like a flower-bud full of promise, could only please artists who prefer sketches to pictures. This charming actress had a delicacy of feature which characterized her and gave her a likeness to Goethe's Mignon. Matifat, a rich druggist in the rue des Lombards, had supposed that a little actress of a boulevard theatre would not be expensive. Instead of that she had cost him in eleven months over sixty thousand francs. Nothing had, as yet, seemed more extraordinary to Lucien than the spectacle of that respectable shopkeeper planted like a Hermes in this ten-foot dressing-room; which was hung with a pretty paper, furnished with a psyche-glass, a sofa, two chairs, a carpet, a fireplace, and full of closets. A waiting-maid was putting the last touches to the actress's dress, which was Spanish. The piece was a complicated drama, in which Florine played the part of a countess.

"In five years that girl will be the handsomest actress in Paris," said Nathan to Vernou.

"Ah, my dear loves," said Florine to the three journalists, "be good to me to-morrow. In the first place, I have engaged carriages to-night, for you will all go home as drunk as Cæsar. Matifat has wines, — oh! such wines! worthy of Louis XVIII., and he has hired the cook of the Prussian minister."

"We expect enormous things in meeting monsieur," said Nathan.

"He knows he is entertaining the most dangerous men in Paris," replied Florine.

Matifat looked at Lucien uneasily, for the young man's beauty roused his jealousy.

"But here is some one I don't know," said Florine, looking at the poet. "Which of you has brought the Apollo Belvedere from Florence? Monsieur is as charming as a figure of Girodet."

"Mademoiselle," said Lousteau, "Monsieur Lucien de Rubempré is a poet from the provinces. Forgive me for not presenting him, but you are so beautiful this evening that you have made me forget matter-of-fact and empty civility."

"Is he rich enough to write poetry?" asked Florine.

"Poor as Job," replied Lucien.

"How tempting for us!" exclaimed the actress.

Du Bruel, the author of the piece in which Florine was about to make her début, now came hastily into the room. He was a short, slender young man, wearing a frock-coat; and his general air was something between a government official, a broker, and a property owner.

"My dear little Florine, are you sure you know your part, hey? No break-down of memory, you know. Be careful about that scene in the second act; it needs to be incisive, sarcastic. Mind you say, 'I do not love you,' in the way we agreed on."

"Why do you take parts in which there are sentences like that?" said Matifat.

A general laugh followed this inquiry of the worthy druggist.

"What does that matter to you if I don't say it to you, old stupid?" said the actress. "Oh! he's the joy of my life with his stupidities," she added, turning to the others. "On the word of an honest girl I would pay him in kind if it would n't ruin me."

"Yes, but you will look at me when you say it, just as you have been doing when you learned your part, and I don't like it," persisted Matifat.

"Very good, then I 'll look at my little Lousteau," said the actress.

A bell rang in the corridors.

"There, go away all of you," said Florine, "and let me read over my part and try to understand it."

Lucien and Lousteau were the last to leave the room. Lousteau kissed Florine's shoulders, and Lucien heard her say, —

"Impossible to-night; that old stupid has told his wife he was going into the country."

"Is n't she pretty?" said Étienne to Lucien.

"Yes, my dear fellow; but — Matifat?" cried Lucien.

"Hey, my dear boy, you don't know anything as yet of Parisian life," replied Lousteau. "There are things one is forced to put up with. It is the same as being the lover of a married woman, that's all."

Étienne and Lucien now went to one of the proscenium boxes on the ground-floor, where they found the manager of the theatre and Finot. Matifat was in the box directly opposite, with a friend of his, — a silk mercer named Camusot, who " protected " Coralie, and a sturdy, little old man, his father-in-law. The three tradesmen polished their opera glasses and looked at the pit, the tumultuous excitement of which seemed to make them uneasy. The boxes presented the usual queer society which appears at a first representation, — journalists and their mistresses ; old habitués who never miss a first night ; persons of good society who like such emotions. In a box on the first tier with his family was the minister of finance, who had given Du Bruel a place in his bureau, where the maker of plays received the salary and perquisites of a sinecure. Lucien, in the short period since his dinner, had gone from one astonishment to another. Literary life, which for the last two months had seemed to him so poverty-stricken in his own experience, — so barren, so horrible in Lousteau's room ; so humble and yet so insolent in the Galeries du Bois, — now took on a strange magnificence under divers singular aspects. This jumble of things noble and base ; these compromises with conscience ; this mingling of superiority and meanness, treachery and pleasure, grandeur and servitude, bewildered him as though he were gazing at some unnatural, unheard-of show.

"Do you think this play of Du Bruel's will stand you in money?" asked Finot of the manager.

"Well, it is a play with a plot in which Du Bruel has tried to be Beaumarchais. The boulevard public does n't like that style; it wants to be convulsed with emotions. Intellect is never appreciated here. Everything depends to-night on Florine and Coralie, who are really ravishing in grace and beauty. They are wearing very short skirts, and they do a Spanish dance which may carry the public off its feet. This representation is about the same as a game of chance. If the newspapers give me a few lively articles and make it a success, I may get two or three hundred thousand francs out of the piece."

"Ah! I see; it will only be a *succès d'estime* in any case," said Finot.

"There's an organized cabal from the three other boulevard theatres, who will hiss the play anyhow; but I have taken measures to balk it. I have paid the *claqueurs* who are sent against me, and they'll hiss stupidly. Those two shopkeepers over there have each, in order to secure a triumph to Coralie and Florine, taken a hundred tickets and given them to acquaintances who will applaud enough to silence the cabal. The *claqueurs*, paid twice over, will let themselves be drowned; and that always has a good effect on the public."

"Two hundred tickets! — what precious men!" exclaimed Finot.

"Yes; if I had two other actresses as handsomely kept as Florine and Coralie I should feel secure."

For the last two hours everything to Lucien's ears

had turned on money. At the theatre as with the publishers, with the publishers as with the newspapers, there was no thought of art or fame. These blows of the great pendulum of Money striking on his head and on his heart tortured him. While the orchestra played the overture he could not help contrasting the applause and hisses of the excited audience with the calm, pure scenes of poesy and aspiration he had known in David's printing-room, where together the two poets had visions of the marvels of art, the noble triumphs of genius, the white wings of Fame. Then he remembered his evenings with the brotherhood, and tears filled his eyes.

"What is the matter?" said Lousteau, noticing them.

"I see poesy in the gutter," he answered.

"Hey, my dear fellow, full of illusions still!"

"But must a man crawl on his belly and submit to those fat Matifats and Camusots, as actresses submit to journalists, and we submit to publishers?"

"Look here, young one," whispered Lousteau, with a motion towards Finot. "You see that clumsy fellow, without mind or talent, but grasping; resolved on making money by any means, and clever at that. You saw him in Dauriat's shop cut me off ten per cent on that note of Barbet's, with an air as if he were doing me a favor? Well, that fellow has letters from several dawning men of genius who go down on their knees to him to get a hundred francs."

Disgust choked Lucien's heart as he remembered the drawing he had seen on the green table of the newspaper office, and its legend, "Finot, my hundred francs!"

" I 'd rather die ! " he said.

" You 'd better live," replied Lousteau.

When the curtain rose the manager left the box to give certain orders behind the scenes.

"My dear Étienne," said Finot, as soon as the manager was out of hearing, " I 've arranged with Dauriat, and I 'm to have a third in the weekly paper. The agreement is thirty thousand francs down on condition that I am made editor-in-chief and director. It is a splendid affair. Blondet tells me the government are preparing restrictive laws against the press, and none but existing newspapers will escape them. Six months hence it will cost a million to start a new paper. I have therefore clinched the bargain, though I don't own at the present moment more than ten thousand francs. Now, listen to me. If you can get Matifat to buy half my share — that is, one sixth — for thirty thousand francs, I 'll make over to you the whole management as editor-in-chief of my '*petit journal*,' and two hundred and fifty francs a month. You shall be my *locum-tenens*. Of course I shall still direct the paper and keep all my interests in it, but without appearing to do so. All articles will be paid to you at the rate of a hundred sous a column ; therefore you can make yourself a bonus of fifteen francs by paying only three francs, and profiting by the gratuitous editing. That will be at least four hundred and fifty francs a month. I must be master, and free to attack or defend men or matters as I choose ; but you may satisfy all your friendships and hatreds, as long as you don't interfere with my policy. I may be ministerial or *ultra ;* I am not sure as yet : but I mean to keep in hand all my liberal connections. I tell you this frankly because you're a good fellow and I can trust you. Perhaps I'll let you do the Chambers for that other paper I am on, for I doubt if I can keep them. Now, set Florine on this bit of jockeying; tell her to press the button hard on her druggist; I am allowed only forty-eight hours to give up the arrangement if I find I can't possibly raise the money. Dauriat has sold the other third to his printer and paper-maker. He gets his own third for nothing, and ten thousand francs to boot, for the whole concern cost him only fifty thousand. In a year from now it will be worth two hundred thousand to the court to buy us out, if the king has, as they say he has, the good sense to intend to buy up the press."

"You are a lucky fellow!" cried Lousteau.

"If you had gone through the wretchedness that I have you wouldn't say that," replied Finot. "And even now I'm the victim of a misfortune that can't be remedied. I am the son of a hat-maker who still sells hats in the rue du Coq. Nothing but a revolution can ever put me socially where I ought to be. One of two things I must have, — either a general social upset, or a way to make millions. Of the two I don't know but what a revolution is easiest. If I had a name like that of your friend here my career would be made. Hush! here's the manager. Adieu!" added Finot, rising; "I must go to the opera; and I may, perhaps, have a duel on hand to-morrow. I have written and signed with an 'F.' a thundering article against two *danseuses* who each has a general for her friend. I have attacked and raided the opera."

"Oh, nonsense!" said the manager.

"Yes, the theatres are all getting so stingy," replied Finot. "One tries to cut me down in boxes; another refuses to subscribe for the usual fifty copies. I have given my ultimatum to the opera: I insist on a hundred subscriptions and four boxes for myself. If they accept, my paper will have eight hundred subscribers to supply and one thousand who pay; and I know where I can get two hundred more subscriptions. We shall be twelve hundred by January —"

"You'll end by ruining all of us," said the manager.

"You! you need n't complain, with your ten subscriptions. Did n't I get two good articles for you into the 'Constitutionnel'?"

"Oh, I'm not finding fault!" cried the manager.

"Well, good-night!" said Finot. "Lousteau, let me have an answer to-morrow at the Français, where there's a first representation; I can't write the article myself, so you may do it and have my box. I give you the preference; you've worked yourself to death for me, and I'm grateful. Félicien Vernou offers to pay twenty thousand francs, and give up all salary and emoluments for one year, for a third of the paper; but I have refused; I want to remain sole master of it. Adieu!"

"Knave!" muttered Lucien to Lousteau.

"Yes, a gallows-bird, who'll make his way all the same," replied Étienne, indifferent as to whether he were heard or not by the shrewd fellow who was closing the door of the box.

"He?" said the manager; "he'll be a millionnaire, and win general respect, and probably friends."

"Good God!" cried Lucien; "what a cave of

iniquity! Lousteau," he continued, dropping his voice and looking at Florine, who was casting her glances at them, "you are surely not going to defile that charming girl with such a negotiation?"

"She'll succeed. You don't know the cleverness and devotion of those dear creatures," replied Lousteau.

"They redeem their faults and wipe out all their wrong-doings by the intensity of their love when they do love," said the manager. "The genuine love of an actress is all the finer from the contrast it makes to her surroundings."

"It is like finding in the mud a diamond worthy of the proudest crown on earth," added Lousteau.

"But," said the director presently, "do you notice Coralie? She isn't thinking of what she's about. Your handsome friend here has turned her head. She's missing her effects. There, that's the second time she has failed to hear the prompter. Monsieur, I do beg of you, sit out of sight in this corner. I shall go and tell Coralie you have gone."

"No, no!" said Lousteau; "tell her that monsieur will be at the supper to-night, and she can do what she likes with him. If you tell her that, she'll play like Mademoiselle Mars."

The manager departed.

"My dear friend," said Lucien, "is it possible that you have no scruple in asking Mademoiselle Florine to get thirty thousand francs out of that druggist for a half share of a whole which Finot has just bought at that price? —"

Lousteau would not leave Lucien the time to finish his sentence.

"Where do you come from, my lad? That druggist is n't a man, he is only a purse."

"But your own conscience?"

"Conscience, my dear fellow, is a stick we take to beat our neighbor with; nobody ever uses it on himself. What the devil are you quarrelling with? Chance has done for you in one day a miracle you might have waited years for; and here you are finding fault with its methods! You! who seem to me to have a mind, and the independence of ideas which all intellectual adventurers must have in the world we live in, — you, to dabble in scruples like a nun who confesses to eating an egg with concupiscence! If Florine succeeds I shall be editor-in-chief; I shall earn a fixed sum of two hundred and fifty francs a month; I shall take the great theatres and leave the vaudevilles to Vernou; and you shall put your foot in the stirrup by taking my present place in the Boulevard theatres. You will earn three francs a column and write one a day; thirty a month will give you ninety francs; you will have sixty francs' worth of books to sell to Barbet; and you can get ten tickets monthly, forty in all, from each of the theatres, which you will sell to a theatrical Barbet (I'll introduce him to you). All this will give you two hundred francs a month. Besides which, if you'll make yourself useful to Finot he will put a hundred-franc article of yours into his weekly paper, — always supposing you display talent, for there the articles have to be signed; no dashing off things anyhow as in the little papers. That will give you, at the least, three hundred francs a month. My dear fellow, there are men of genius in Paris, like that poor d'Arthèz who dines every day at

Flicoteaux's, who can't earn three hundred francs a month at the end of ten years. You will make at least four thousand francs a year with your pen, not counting what you may get from publishers. Now a subprefect gets a salary of only three thousand francs, and his life is as dull as ditch-water in its petty round. I won't say anything about the pleasure of going to the theatre without paying for it, because that soon gets to be a bore; but you will have a footing behind the scenes of four theatres. Be severe and witty for a couple of months and you'll be overrun with attentions of all kinds from the actresses; their lovers will court you, and you'll never have to dine at Flicoteaux's, — except on days when you happen to be low in cash and nobody has asked you to dinner. At five o'clock this afternoon in the Luxembourg, you did n't know where to lay your head, and you are now on the eve of becoming one of the hundred privileged persons who give opinions to France. In three days, provided we succeed, you will be able with thirty sarcasms, printed at the rate of three a day, to make a man curse his life and wish he was never born; you can get mortgages of pleasure on all the actresses of the four theatres; you can break down a good play and send all Paris to applaud a bad one. If Dauriat refuses to publish your 'Daisies,' you can bring him cringing to your feet and make him buy them for two thousand francs. Use your talent and get two or three articles in two or three journals which threaten some of Dauriat's speculations, a book for instance on which he counts, and you'll have him climbing the stairs to your garret and hanging round there like a clematis. As for your novel, the publishers, who now turn you out of doors more or less civilly, will stand in line to catch you, and that very manuscript old Doguereau cheapened to four hundred francs they'll be glad enough to get at four thousand. Such are the benefits of journalism. For this reason it behooves us to keep new-comers out; it needs not only great talent but also great luck to get within its precincts. You've had that luck in one afternoon, and now you are quarrelling with it! Just see! if you and I had not happened to meet to-day at Flicoteaux's you might have cooled your heels for years, or died of hunger, like d'Arthèz, in a garret. By the time d'Arthèz is as learned as Bayle and as fine a writer as Rousseau we shall have made our fortunes and shall be masters of him and his fame; Finot will be a deputy, and the proprietor of one of the great newspapers; and we shall be that which we have made ourselves, — either peers of France or prisoners for debt in Sainte-Pélagie."

"And Finot will sell his great newspaper to whichever political party will give him most money, just as he sells puffs to Madame Bastienne and disparages Mademoiselle Virginie, declaring that the bonnets of the former are better than those of the latter, whom he cried up last week!" cried Lucien, remembering the scene he had witnessed in Finot's office.

"You're a simpleton, my dear fellow," said Lousteau, sharply. "Three years ago Finot was utterly down at heel, dined at Tabar's for eighteen sous, wrote prospectuses for ten francs, and how his coat held on his back was a mystery as impenetrable as the Immaculate Conception. Finot now has in his sole right a newspaper worth a hundred thousand francs. Counting subscriptions paid without copies, and real subscriptions, and indirect taxes (as you may call them) levied by his uncle, he makes twenty thousand francs a year; he dines sumptuously every day; for the last month he has set up a cabriolet; and now here he is at the head of a weekly paper, getting one sixth of the property for nothing, with five hundred francs a month salary, to which he'll add a thousand more for work he'll get done gratis and make his partners pay him for. You'll be one of the first; for if Finot consents to pay you fifty francs a page you'll be only too glad to write him three articles for nothing. When you are in a like position you will be able to judge of Finot, and not till then; a man can't be judged except by his equals in condition. You have at this moment a fine opening, provided you blindly obey orders and attack when Finot says, "Attack!" and praise when he says, "Praise!" When you have a vengeance of your own against any one all you have to do is to say to me, 'Lousteau, I want that man smashed,' and we can put into our own little paper any day and every day something that will kill your enemy. And if the matter is of real importance to you, Finot would get an article into one of the great journals which have ten or twelve thousand subscribers."

"Do you think that Florine will be able to make her druggist accept the scheme?" asked Lucien, dazzled.

"Of course I do. Here's the interlude, and I'll go round and see her now and try to get the thing done to-night. When I have once explained the matter to Florine, she'll act with my intelligence and her own to boot."

"And that respectable old shopkeeper sitting over

there with his mouth wide open admiring Florine is to have thirty thousand francs extracted from him!"

"That's another piece of nonsense. One would suppose we were robbing him," cried Lousteau. "My dear friend, if the administration buys that journal, as it will, in six months the druggist will have fifty thousand francs for his thirty thousand. Besides, Matifat does n't care for the journal; what he is thinking of is Florine's interests. When it is known that Matifat and Camusot (for they will share the venture) are part proprietors of a weekly review, all the other journals will have friendly articles about Florine and Coralie. Florine is certain to become celebrated; she may get an engagement for twelve thousand francs at one of the other theatres, and Matifat can save the money he now spends in gifts and dinners to journalists. You don't yet know men or business."

"Poor man!" said Lucien; "and he thinks himself happy."

"He'll be sawn in two with arguments," said Lousteau, laughing, "till he shows Florine the signed agreement for the purchase of Finot's sixth. The very next day I shall be editor-in-chief, and earning a thousand francs a month. That's the end of all my miseries!" cried Florine's lover joyously.

He went off leaving Lucien stupefied, swept onward by a whirlwind of thought, lost in a vision of life as it really is. He had seen in the Galeries de Bois the secrets of publishers, and the methods by which literary fame was cooked; he had passed behind the scenes of a theatre and learned on what foundations dramatic glory rested; and he perceived with a poet's insight

the hidden side of consciences, — the wheels within
wheels, the material mechanism of all things in this
Parisian life. He envied Lousteau's happiness as he
watched his mistress on the stage ; already he had
half forgotten Matifat. He sat there alone for an imperceptible time, — possibly not more than five minutes, and yet it was an eternity ! Ardent thoughts
inflamed his soul, while his senses were kindled by the
sight of those actresses with wanton eyes and rouged
cheeks and dazzling shoulders, dressed voluptuously
with shortened skirts, showing their legs in red stockings with green clocks in a way to put the whole pit in
a ferment. Two corruptions marched side by side on
parallel lines, like two sheets of water striving, after an
inundation, to meet again. They threatened to overwhelm the poet sitting in the corner of the box, his
arms on the red velvet cushion before him, his hands
hanging down, his eyes fixed on the curtain now lowered, and he himself all the more accessible to the en-
chantments of this life before him, because it shone
like the dazzle of fireworks upon the dark and gloomy
background of his toilsome, obscure, and monotonous
life.

Suddenly through an aperture in the folds of the
curtain an eye met his with a flood of loving light.
Waking from his torpor, he recognized Coralie ; then
he lowered his head and looked at Camusot, who was
sitting directly opposite. The latter was a stout, thick
man, — a silk mercer in the rue des Bourdonnais ; one
of the judges of the Courts of Commerce ; the father
of four children ; married to a second wife ; and worth
about eighty thousand francs a year ; but with it all fifty-

six years of age, a mop of gray hair on his head, and
the unctuous look of a man who means to make the most
of the time that remains to him, and lose no chance of
enjoyment after a long life spent in submitting to the
indignities of shopkeeping. That forehead, the color
of fresh butter, those rosy, monastic cheeks, seemed
scarcely broad enough to contain the expansion of his
superlative delight. Camusot was alone, without his
wife, and he listened with undisguised satisfaction while
Coralie was applauded to the echo. Coralie represented
the united vanities of this rich tradesman ; with her he
could fancy himself one of the lords of the olden time.
At this particular moment he felt he counted for more
than half in the actress's success, and he had all the
more reason for thinking so because he had paid for
it. His conduct was sanctioned by the presence of his
father-in-law, Cardot,—a little old man with white hair
and lively eyes, but respectable in appearance. Lucien
felt a violent repugnance come over him. He remembered the pure and exalted love he had felt for Madame
de Bargeton ; the love of poets wrapped its white wings
round him ; a thousand memories, with their blue hori-
zons, surrounded the once great man of Angoulême,
who now sank back into a state of dreamy thought.
The curtain rose ; Florine and Coralie were on the
stage together.

"My dear, he does n't care a straw for you !" said
Florine, in a low voice, while Coralie was making one
of her speeches.

Lucien could not help laughing, and looked at Coralie. That young woman — one of the most charming
and delightful actresses in Paris ; the rival of Madame

Perrin and Mademoiselle Fleuriet, whom she resembled, and whose fate ought to have been hers — belonged to the class of women who possess the faculty of fascinating men at will. Her face was of the noblest Jewish type, — that long, oval face of pure, fair ivory, with lips as scarlet as a pomegranate, and a chin as delicate as the edge of a cup. Beneath the eyelids, with their curving lashes, burned eyes of jet, from which could come languishing or sparkling glances as occasion offered. Those eyes, sunken in an olive circle, were surmounted by arched black brows. On the ivory forehead, crowned by bands of ebony on which the lights were glancing, sat enthroned a wealth of thought which seemed to be that of genius. And yet, like many other actresses, Coralie, without wit, in spite of her green-room repartee, without education beyond her boudoir experience, had no talent except the intelligence of the senses and the perceptions of an affectionate woman. But who could think of her mental qualities when she dazzled the eye with her round and polished arms, her tapering, slender fingers, her beautiful shoulders, and that bosom sung by the Song of Songs, with the mobile, curving throat, and those adorably graceful legs encased in red silk stockings? These beauties, all of them truly Oriental, were placed in still higher relief by the conventional Spanish costume of our theatres. Coralie was the delight of the audience, who clasped in fancy that pretty waist so trigly tightened in her basque, or followed with their eyes the undulations of the skirt as it betrayed every movement of the hips. There came a moment when Lucien, observing how this creature played for him alone, — thinking no more of Camusot

than the boys in the gallery thought of a bit of apple-
peel, — placed sensual love above pure love, enjoyment
above emotion, and the demon of lust whispered in his
soul atrocious thoughts. "I do not know what love,
and luxury, and wine, and the joys of matter are," he
said to himself. "I have lived by thought and not by
act. A man who describes all should know all. This
is my first grand supper, my first debauch in a strange,
new world; why should I not taste for once those
celebrated pleasures in which the seigneurs lived with
wantons in the olden time? If it were only to compare
them with the true, pure love of nobler regions, ought I
not to understand the joys, the perfections, the trans-
ports, the resources, the delicacies of the love of courtesans and actresses? And is there not, after all, a
poesy of the senses? Two months ago such women
seemed to me enchantresses guarded by dragons; yet
here is one whose beauty far surpasses that of Florine,
for which I envied Lousteau. Why not profit by her
fancy when the greatest lords would spend a treasure
to buy her? Ambassadors themselves, when they once
put foot into these gulfs, think neither of the past nor
of the future. I should be a fool to have more delicacy than princes, especially now when I love no other
woman."

Lucien had forgotten Camusot. After manifesting
to Lousteau the utmost disgust for the odious partnership, he fell into the same ditch; he floated on a desire,
impelled by the jesuitism of passion.

XII.

HOW JOURNALISM IS DONE.

" Coralie is crazy about you," said Lousteau re-entering the box. " Your beauty, worthy of Greek marble, is turning all heads behind the scenes. You are lucky, my dear fellow. At eighteen, and after to-night's success, Coralie could make sixty thousand francs a year out of her beauty. She is still well-behaved. Her mother sold her three years ago for sixty thousand francs; the girl has never had anything but annoyance out of it, and she longs for happiness. She took to the stage in despair; she hated de Marsay, her first lover, and when she got rid of him, for the king of the dandies soon let her go, she took that solid old Camusot, whom she does n't love; but he is like a father to her; she puts up with him and lets him love her. She has already refused very rich proposals, and keeps to Camusot, who never worries her. You will really be her first love. It seems she was shot through the heart at the first sight of you. Florine has gone to her dressing-room to reason with her, for she has taken what she calls your coldness so to heart. The play will fail if she forgets her part, and then, good-by to the engagement at the Gymnase which Camusot has almost obtained for her."

" You don't say so? — poor girl!" said Lucien, whose every vanity was tickled by the words and who felt his heart expanding with self-conceit. " More events have happened to me, my dear Lousteau, within the last two months than in all the previous years of my life put together."

And he thereupon related to his new friend the betrayal of his love for Madame de Bargeton, and his hatred against the Baron Sixte du Châtelet.

" Bless me! the paper wants a *bête-noire*, and he'll just do for us. That baron is an old beau of the Empire who has made himself a ministerialist; I know all about him, he'll suit us to a *t*. I have often seen your great lady, too, in Madame d'Espard's box at the Opera; the baron is usually there, making love to your ex-mistress, who is as dry as a cuttle-fish. I have just got a message from Finot to say that one of the staff, that little scamp Hector Merlin, has left the paper in the lurch because his blanks were not paid for, and they want copy. Finot is hurrying to write an article against the opera, and he wants more. Look here, my dear fellow, get something ready on the play here; look, listen, and think it up. As for me, I'll go into the director's room and see what I can cook up into three columns."

" So this is how newspapers are made, is it?" said Lucien.

" Yes, invariably," replied Lousteau. " For the ten months I've been in journalism they are always short of copy by eight in the evening."

That slang typographical word, " copy," means the manuscript from which the type is set up; perhaps because authors are supposed to send only a copy of their writing; or it may be an ironical use of the Latin word *copia* (abundance), for copy is always lacking.

"The grand plan which is never realized is to have several issues ready in advance," said Lousteau. "It is ten o'clock now, and there's hardly a column written. I'll find Vernou and Nathan, and get them to lend us a dozen or so of epigrams on the deputies, or Chancellor *Crusoe*, — any one, friends or foes; for at such times one has to murder one's father if necessary; we are like pirates who load their guns with doubloons rather than surrender. Make your article witty and it may advance you a good stride in Finot's opinion; he is grateful on speculation. That's the best and most solid form of acknowledgment, — except, of course, a pawn-broker's receipt."

"Good heavens! what sort of men are journalists?" cried Lucien, "how can they sit down at any minute and write off witty things?"

"Precisely as you light a lamp — till the oil gives out."

As Lousteau opened the door to leave the box the manager and Du Bruel entered it.

"Monsieur," said the author of the play to Lucien, "can I say to Coralie that you will go with her to supper? if not, my play will fail. The poor girl really does not know what she is about; she is likely to cry where she ought to laugh, and laugh where she ought to cry. You can save my piece; and it is not anything unpleasant that is asked of you."

"Monsieur, I am not in the habit of putting up with rivals," answered Lucien.

"Don't say that to Coralie," interposed the manager;

" she is just the sort of girl to turn Camusot out of doors and ruin herself for you.. That worthy old silk-mercer, who owns the ' Cocon-d'Or,' gives her two thousand francs a month, and pays for all her dresses and her *claqueurs.*"

" As your promise does not commit me to anything, go, and save your piece," said Lucien, with the air of a sultan.

" Yes, but don't look as if you wished to rebuff that charming girl," said Du Bruel, deprecatingly.

" Well, so be it!" cried the poet. " I see that I am destined to write the article on your play and to smile on your young actress."

The author disappeared, and Coralie was soon after seen to be acting delightfully. Bouffé, who was playing the part of an old alcalde, in which he showed for the first time his wonderful talent for making up and imitating old age, came forward amid thunders of applause to say: " Gentlemen, the play we have the honor to present to you this evening is by Messieurs Raoul and de Cursy."

" Well, well, so Nathan is in it!" exclaimed Lousteau. " I wondered why he was here."

" Coralie! Coralie!" cried the house; while from the box where the three shopkeepers were sitting came a thundering voice calling, "Florine, too!"

" Florine and Coralie!" cried a number of voices. The curtain rose and Bouffé appeared leading the two actresses, to whom Matifat and Camusot flung wreaths. Coralie picked up hers and held it out to Lucien.

As for Lucien, the two hours spent in the theatre were like a dream. The work of fascination had begun behind the scenes, odious as those surroundings were. The poet, still innocent, had breathed the air of license and of lust. Among those dirty passages, choked with machinery and hung with smoking lamps, lurks a pestilence which kills the soul. Life cannot continue real or saintly there. Serious things are laughed at, impossible things seem true. The whole scene acted like a narcotic on Lucien, and Coralie completed its effect by plunging him into a species of joyous intoxication. The great chandelier was extinguished. No one remained in the auditorium but the door-openers, who were making a curious noise by moving the little benches and closing the box-doors. The footlights, blown out like candles, were exhaling a nasty smell. The curtain was drawn up ; a lantern hung from the roof. The firemen began their rounds with the watchmen. The fairy-land of the stage, the gorgeous spectacle of the boxes filled with beautiful women, the dazzling lights, and the splendid magic of decorations and brilliant costumes were now succeeded by cold obscurity, noisomeness, vacancy. It was horrible.

"Are you coming ?" called Lousteau from the stage.

Lucien was in a state of indescribable bewilderment.

"Jump down here !" cried the journalist.

With one bound Lucien was on the stage. He scarcely recognized Florine and Coralie without their gay clothes, wrapped in cloaks and wadded mantles, their heads covered with bonnets tied on by black veils, and resembling butterflies returning to the condition of larvæ.

"Will you do me the honor to give me your arm," said Coralie, trembling.

"Willingly," said Lucien, who now felt the girl's heart beating beside him like that of a bird when caught in the hand. The actress, pressing against him, was like a cat rubbing against her master's leg with soft satisfaction.

"We are to sup together," she said.

All four, Florine and Lousteau, Coralie and Lucien, left the theatre and found two hackney-coaches before the actors' entrance, which opened on the rue des Fossés-du-Temple. Coralie made Lucien get into one in which Camusot and his father-in-law Cardot were already seated. She offered a place to Du Bruel. The manager had departed in the other coach with Florine, Matifat and Lousteau.

"These hackney-coaches are odious," said Coralie.

"Why don't you have a carriage of your own?" remarked Du Bruel.

"Why, indeed?" she cried in a pet. "I don't want to say why before Monsieur Cardot, who rules his son-in-law. Would you believe that Monsieur Cardot, such a little old man! only gives Florentine five hundred francs a month, to pay her rent and her living and her finery. That old Marquis de Rochegude, who has six hundred thousand francs a year, has been offering me a coupé for the last two months. But I'm an artist, not a *cocotte.*"

"You shall have a carriage the day after to-morrow, mademoiselle," said Camusot graciously; "you never asked me for it before."

"Ask? is it likely I should ask for it? When a man loves a woman he should n't let her paddle through the mud and risk breaking her ankles in the gutters."

As she said the words, in a sharp tone which cut Camusot to the heart, Coralie slipped her hand into that of Lucien and pressed it. She was silent after that, and seemed absorbed in one of those dreams of enjoyment which compensate these poor creatures for past troubles and all their many griefs, and develop in their souls a poesy of which other women, who are happily protected from these violent extremes, know nothing.

" You ended by playing as well as Mademoiselle Mars," said Du Bruel.

" Yes," said Camusot, " mademoiselle seemed upset in the beginning; but after the middle of the second act she was magnificent. She made half your success."

" And I half hers," said Du Bruel.

" You don't either of you know what you are talking about," she said in a high voice.

The actress profited by a moment's darkness to carry Lucien's hand to her lips, moistening it with tears as she kissed it. Lucien was moved to the very marrow of his bones. The human feeling of the courtesan who loves has a greatness in it which brings her back among the angels.

" Monsieur is to write the article," said Du Bruel to Camusot, alluding to Lucien. " He will make a charming paragraph on our dear Coralie."

" Oh, yes, do us that service, monsieur," cried Camusot, in the tone of a man on his knees before Lucien; " you will find me at your service now and always."

" Do leave him his independence," cried the actress, " he shall write what he chooses. Papa Camusot, buy me carriages, but not flattery."

" You shall have that without price," replied Lucien, politely. "I have never yet written for the newspapers, and I don't know their customs; you will inspire the virgin effort of my pen."

"That's odd," said Du Bruel.

"Here we are at the rue de Bondy," said Cardot, who had been silenced and cast down by Coralie's attack.

"If I have the first fruits of your pen, you have those of my heart," said Coralie, during the brief moment when Lucien and she were alone together in the carriage.

Coralie went to join Florine in her bedroom, and put on the dress she had already sent there. Lucien was unprepared for the luxury which rich merchants who are determined to enjoy life heap upon their mistresses. Though Matifat, whose fortune was nothing like as large as that of his friend Camusot, was said to do things in a rather skimping way, Lucien found a dining-room artistically decorated, furnished in green cloth studded with gold nails, lighted by handsome lamps, and full of flowering plants; also a salon, hung in yellow silk with brown trimmings, in which the furniture was of the newest fashion; there was also a chandelier by Thomire, a carpet of Persian pattern, and a clock, candelabra, and a fireplace all in the best taste. Matifat had left these arrangements to Grindot, a young architect who had built him a house, and who, knowing the destination of these rooms, had bestowed some special care upon them. Matifat, always the shopkeeper, was cautious in touching certain articles; he seemed to have the total of the bill before his eyes, and looked around at these magnificences as if they were jewels imprudently taken out of their cases.

"This is what I shall have to do for Florentine," was the thought that could be read in Père Cardot's little eyes.

Lucien suddenly understood why it was that the squalor of Lousteau's garret did not disturb that journalist. Secretly king of these revels, Étienne enjoyed the fine things as his own. He stood before the fireplace talking with Du Bruel and the manager as though he were master of the house.

"Copy! copy!" cried Finot, suddenly rushing in upon them. "There's nothing in the box. The compositors have got my article on the Opera, but they'll soon have finished it."

"We'll be ready," said Étienne. "There's a table and a fire in Florine's boudoir. If Monsieur Matifat will kindly give us ink and paper we can write the articles while Florine and Coralie are dressing."

Cardot, Camusot, and Matifat disappeared, eager to find all the writers wanted. Just then one of the prettiest *danseuses* of the day, named Tullia, darted into the room.

"My dear child!" she said to Finot, "your hundred subscriptions are granted. They are not to cost the management anything; they are saddled on the singers and the orchestra and the *corps de ballet.* Your paper is so witty we none of us complain. You are to have your four boxes. I have come to tell you instantly. And here's the money for the first three months," she added, holding out a couple of bank-bills. "Now, don't attack me."

"Good heavens!" cried Finot, "I must suppress that article, and I haven't anything to take its place."

"What an exquisite *pas* that was, my divine Laïs!" cried Blondet, who followed the *danseuse* with Nathan, Vernou, and Claude Vignon, whom he had brought with him. "Stay to supper with us, dear love, or I'll crush you like the butterfly that you are! Being a *danseuse*, you can't excite any jealousies here; and as for beauty, you and Florine and Coralie have too much sense to be rivals."

"My dear fellows," cried Finot, "save me! You, Du Bruel, Nathan, Blondet, I implore you to save me! I must have five columns!"

"I can do two with the play," said Lucien.

"And I one," said Lousteau.

"Well, then, Nathan, Vernou, Du Bruel, fill up the rest with witticisms. This good Blondet I know will grant me the two little half-columns on the first page. I must go straight to the printing office and stop my Opera article. How lucky, Tullia, you kept the carriage!"

"Yes, but the duke is in it with the German minister."

"Let's invite the duke and the minister to supper," said Nathan.

"A German always drinks well and listens well. We'll tell him a lot of queer stories and he'll write them to his court!" cried Blondet.

"Who is the most dignified among us? for that person must go down and invite them up. Come, Du Bruel, you are a bureaucrat; give your arm to Tullia and go and fetch the Duc de Rhétoré and the German minister. Good gracious, Tullia, how handsome you are to-night!"

"That will make us thirteen!" said Matifat, turning pale.

"No, fourteen!" said Florentine, overhearing him as she entered the room. "I have come to look after Milord Cardot."

"Besides," said Lousteau, "Blondet has brought Claude Vignon."

"I brought him here to drink!" said Blondet, picking up an inkstand. "Come, all of you, have wit enough to pay for the fifty-six bottles of wine we are going to absorb. Above all, stir up Du Bruel; he's a vaudevillist, and he's capable of spicy things when driven to a point."

Lucien, inspired with a desire to show off his faculties before such a remarkable set of men, wrote his first newspaper article on a round table in Florine's boudoir, by the light of the crimson wax-candles which were lighted for him by Matifat.

PANORAMA–DRAMATIQUE.

First Representation of " The Alcalde in Difficulties;" Imbroglio in three Acts. First Appearance of Mademoiselle Florine. Mademoiselle Coralie. Bouffé.

They enter, leave the stage, talk, walk, search for something, find nothing; all is uproar. The Alcalde has lost his daughter, but finds his night-cap. But, lo! the night-cap does not fit him; it must be the night-cap of a thief! Where is the thief? Again they enter, pass in and out, talk, walk, and search more than ever. The Alcalde ends by finding a man without his daughter, and his daughter without a man, which is satisfying to the magistrate, but not at all so to the public.

Quiet is restored. The Alcalde wishes to interrogate the man. He seats himself in a chair of state and arranges his sleeves, — the sleeves of an Alcalde. Spain is the only country where they have alcaldes appended to enormous sleeves, and wearing ruffs about their necks which, on the stage of Paris, are more than half their functions. This Alcalde, who trots about with the short steps of a wheezy old fellow, is Bouffé, — Bouffé, the successor of Potier, a young actor who plays old men so well that he makes the oldest old men laugh. There's a future of a hundred old fellows in that bald head, that quivering voice, those trembling, spindling legs which bear the body of a Géronte. He is so old, this young actor, that he frightens you; you are afraid you'll catch his oldness like a contagious disease. But what an admirable Alcalde! what a capital uneasy smile! what important silliness! what stupid dignity! what judicial irresolution! How able he is to perceive that all things are alternately false and true! how fitted to be the minister of a constitutional king! In reply to each question of the Alcalde the mysterious man interrogates the Alcalde. Bouffé replies, and the result is that, questioned by answers, the Alcalde ends by clearing up everything himself. This eminently comic scene, redolent of Molière, delighted the audience. Everybody on the stage appeared to be perfectly satisfied, but I myself am wholly unable to tell you what was true or what was false, what was clear or what was cloudy. And why?

The daughter of the Alcalde was there, — a true Andalusian, a Spaniard with Spanish eyes, Spanish complexion, Spanish waist and walk; a Spaniard from head to foot, her dagger in her garter. her love in her eyes, her cross on a ribbon at her throat. At the close of the first act some one asked me how the piece was going, and I answered: "She has red stockings with green clocks, a tiny foot in varnished shoes, and the handsomest leg in Andalusia!" Ah! that daughter of the Alcalde! she makes one's mouth water; she fills a man with insane desires; you want to spring upon the stage and offer her your heart and a cottage, or thirty thousand francs a year and your pen. This Andalusian girl is the handsomest actress in Paris. Coralie, since we have to name her, — Coralie is fitted to be either countess or grisette; it is difficult to know in which character she would please us best. She can be what she chooses to be; she is born capable of doing all things. What more can be said of an actress of the Boulevards?

In the second act a Spanish lady arrives from Paris, with chiselled features and murderous eyes. I asked some one near me who she was and whence she came, and I was told she was Mademoiselle Florine, who had come from the wings. But no; impossible to believe it! There was too much fire in her movements, too much fury in her love. This rival of the daughter of the Alcalde was the wife of a grandee wrapped in the mantle of Almaviva, in which, by the bye, there was stuff enough to furnish a hundred of our great boulevard seigneurs. Though Florine did not wear red stockings with green clocks, or varnished shoes, she wore a mantilla, and a veil which she manœuvred charmingly, like the great lady that she is. The tigress became a cat. At the first incisive words the two beauties said to each other, I saw a whole drama of jealousy. But in spite of that, matters were nearly arranged, when the stupidity of the Alcalde again embroiled everything. The whole crowd of torch-bearers and valets, and figaros and grandees, alcaldes, and girls and women, set out once more to search, and go and come, and turn and twist about. The plot thickens, and I let it thicken; for the two women — the jealous Florine and the happy Coralie — have caught me again in the folds of their basques and their mantillas; the points of their pretty little feet are in my eyes.

However, the third act came and I had not disgraced myself; the commissary of police had not interfered; the audience were not scandalized ; and I consequently shall believe henceforth in the strength of those public and religious morals about which the Chamber of Deputies is just now so much concerned that you might suppose there was no morality in France. I began to perceive that the play was about a man who loved two women without being loved by either ; or it may be that they both loved him and he did not love them ; neither did he like the Alcalde, or else the Alcalde did not like him ; but, whichever way it all was, he was a noble grandee who loved some one, himself or God for want of a better, and he made himself a monk. That is all I can tell you about the piece, and if you want to know more, you must go to the Panorama-Dramatique. I have told you enough to show that you must go there once to make acquaintance with those adorable red stockings and green clocks, those tiny feet so full of promises, those eyes that filter sun-rays, once to learn the coquetry of the Parisian disguised as an Andalusian, and of the Andalusian disguised as a Parisian ; and you must go a second time to really enjoy the play, which will make you die of laughing over a slobbering old man in the guise of a lover.

The play has had a double success. The author, whose collaborator is one of our distinguished poets, has aimed at success with a beauty in each hand ; he kept his audience in a tumult of pleasure throughout ; in fact, the legs of those beauties seemed as witty as the author ; and yet when they left the stage the audience thought the dialogue not a whit less witty, — a triumphant proof of the excellence of the play. The author's name was announced amid applause which must have made the architect of the building anxious ; but the author, accustomed to the upheaval of that Vesuvius which sits beneath the chandelier, did not tremble ; it was Monsieur de Cursy. As for the two actresses, they danced the famous bolero of Séville which found favor with the fathers of the faith in the olden time, and is still permitted by the censor in spite of the indecency of the attitudes.

While Lucien was writing these columns, which produced a revolution in journalism by introducing a new and perfectly original style of comment, Lousteau was making use of the poet's confidences in an article under the general head of Manners and Customs, entitled " The Ex-Beau." It began as follows : —·

" The Beau of the Empire is always a long, slender man, well preserved, who wears corsets and the cross of the Legion of honor. His name is, let us say, Potelet, and in order to curry favor with the court of to-day the baron of the Empire bestows upon himself a *du*, — du Potelet, — ready, however, to be once more Potelet in case of a revolution. He is a man of two careers (like his name) ; he now pays court to the faubourg Saint-Germain, after holding office as the glorious, useful, and fascinating train-bearer of the sister of the man whom propriety forbids me to name. Though du Potelet is now anxious to deny his service to the Imperial Highness, he still sings the songs of his former benefactress."

The article was a tissue of the silly personalities which were in vogue in those days, — a style improved upon later, more especially by the " Figaro." Lousteau invented a fable in which a great lady to whom the baron was paying court was compared to a cuttle-fish. The ex-beau was likened to a heron ; and the loves of the heron, who vainly endeavored to swallow the cuttle-fish, which broke in three when he let it drop, was provocative of laughter even to those who did not know the two persons held up to ridicule. The joke, which was carried on subsequently through several numbers, made a great commotion in the faubourg Saint-Germain, and was one of the thousand and one causes of the restrictions laid soon after on the Press.

In about an hour Blondet, Lousteau, and Lucien returned to the salon, where they found the other guests: the duke, the minister, the four women, the three merchants, the manager of the theatre, Finot (who had returned), and the three authors. A printer's boy, wearing a paper cap, had come to fetch copy for the paper.

"Here, go back and give the compositors these ten francs, and tell them to wait," said Finot.

"If you send them that money, monsieur, they'll get drunk, and then good-bye to the paper."

"The common-sense of that boy actually frightens me," remarked Finot.

Just then the three writers returned with their articles Blondet's was an extremely clever diatribe against the romanticists; Lousteau's made every one laugh, though the Duc de Rhétoré advised him to slip in a compliment to the Marquise d'Espard, in order not to antagonize the faubourg Saint-Germain.

"And you," said Finot, addressing Lucien, "let us hear what you have written."

When Lucien, trembling with fear, had finished reading, the salon rang with applause, the actresses kissed him, the tradesmen in their delight almost squeezed the breath out of him; Du Bruel seized his hand with a tear in his eye, and the manager asked him to dinner.

"As Monsieur de Chateaubriand has already called Victor Hugo ' the sublime child,' " said Blondet, " I can only say of you that you were born a man of wit, heart, and style."

"Monsieur is on our paper," said Finot, with a gratified nod at Lousteau, and the shrewd glance of one who makes the most of an advantage. " Here, carry off all this copy," he said to the apprentice. "That's all they need. The paper may be a little veneered, but it will be a fine number," added Finot, turning to the group of writers, who were taking Lucien's measure covertly.

"He seems to have talent," said Blondet.

"That article was good," responded Claude Vignon.

"Come! to supper!" cried Matifat.

The duke gave his arm to Florine, Coralie took Lucien's, and Tullia sat between Blondet and the German minister.

"I don't understand why you attack Madame de Bargeton and the Baron du Châtelet," said the duke. "I hear the baron is just made Prefect of the Charente and Master of petitions."

"Madame de Bargeton abandoned Lucien as if he were of no account," said Lousteau.

"Such a fine young man!" exclaimed the minister.

XIII.

THE SUPPER.

THE supper, served on new plate and Sèvres china and double damask, exhaled an atmosphere of substantial magnificence. Chevet supplied the viands; the wines were chosen by the famous dealer on the Quai Saint-Bernard, an intimate friend of Camusot, Matifat, and Cardot. Lucien, who saw the details of Parisian luxury for the first time, went from one surprise to another; but he had now learned to conceal his amazement, like the man of wit, heart, and style that Blondet had proclaimed him.

As they crossed the salon Coralie whispered to Florine, "Do please make Camusot so drunk that he will be forced to stay and sleep here to-night."

"Then you have captured your journalist?" said Florine.

"No, my dear, but I love him," replied Coralie with a pretty little motion of her shoulders.

The words echoed in Lucien's ear, brought there by the fifth capital sin. Coralie was charmingly well-dressed; her toilet brought into relief her special beauties; for all beautiful women have certain points which particularly belong to them. Her gown, like that of Florine, was of a new material not yet placed upon the market, called "mousseline de soie;" the

first specimens of which had been sent to Camusot, one
of the largest buyers from the Lyons manufacturers.
Love and dress, the decoration and fragrance of women-
kind, were added to the seductions of the happy Coralie.
Pure, sincere love, a first love in short, albeit in the
form of one of those fantastic frenzies which seize
upon these poor creatures, added to the admiration
caused by Lucien's extreme beauty, gave intelligence to
Coralie's heart.

" I would love you ill and ugly ! " she said in his ear
as they sat down to table.

What words to a poet! Camusot disappeared from
Lucien's ken, and he saw only Coralie. Lives there a
man, all enjoyment, all sensation, sickened of provincial
monotony, allured by the vortex of Paris, weary of
poverty, galled by his enforced continence, hating his
monkish life in the rue de Cluny, his toil without result,
who could have turned his back on this gay festival?
Lucien had one foot in the net of Coralie's beauty, the
other in the bird-lime of journalism. After long and
fruitless waiting about the rue du Sentier, he was here,
in the heart of the Press, as it supped and drank and
joked like the hearty good fellow that he found it.
Moreover he had just been avenged for his rankling
wound by an article that on the morrow would stab two
hearts he had longed, ineffectually, to fill with the
pain and wrath they had made him suffer. Looking at
Lousteau he thought to himself: " There, indeed, is a
true friend ; " not imagining that even then Lousteau was
dreading him as a rival. Lucien had made the mistake
of putting forth all his cleverness. A commonplace
article would have answered the purpose. Blondet

counteracted any effect of the jealousy Lousteau was beginning to feel by telling Finot he must make terms with a talent as good as that. This advice influenced Lousteau's conduct; he resolved to remain Lucien's friend, and arrange with Finot to secure the services of the dangerous new-comer by keeping him dependent and needy. It was a plan rapidly laid and understood to its fullest extent between the two men, and expressed in whispered sentences: " He has talent; he 'll be exacting." — " Let him try it ! "

" I am always afraid of supping with French journalists," said the German minister, with calm and dignified *bonhomie*, looking at Blondet, whom he had already met in the salon of the Comtesse de Montcornet. " There is a saying of Blucher's which it seems your mission to justify."

" What saying ? " asked Nathan.

" When Blucher reached the heights of Montmartre with Saacken in 1814, — pardon me, gentlemen, for reminding you of so fatal a day, — Saacken, who was a boor, exclaimed, ' Now we shall burn Paris ! ' ' Mind you don't,' said Blucher, ' France is to die of that cancer,' — pointing to the city, sweltering and smoking at their feet in the valley of the Seine. I thank God that there are no newspapers in my country," continued the minister after a pause. " I have not yet recovered from my fright at that little printer's devil who was here just now in his paper-cap, and the abnormal common-sense of his ten years. I fancy I am now to sup with lions and panthers, who will do me the favor to cushion their claws."

" It is quite certain," said Blondet, " that we are in a

position to say and prove to all Europe that your Excellency has vomited a serpent this evening, with which you have almost poisoned Mademoiselle Tullia, the prettiest of our *danseuses.* Various comments on Eve and the first and the last sin might be made on that; but don't be uneasy, you are here as our guest."

"It would make a funny article," said Finot.

"It might contain scientific dissertations on all the serpents found in the human heart and body, including those of the diplomatic body," said Lousteau.

"Preserved in this flask of cherry-brandy," said Vernou.

"So that you may see and believe in them yourself," said Claude Vignon to the diplomatist.

"Gentlemen, don't show your claws so soon," said the Duc de Rhétoré.

"The power and influence of journalism is still in its dawn," said Finot. "The newspaper is now a babe, but it will grow. Ten years hence everything will be subjected to publicity. Thought will illumine everything and —"

"— blast everything," said Blondet, interrupting him.

"A witty saying, that's all," remarked Vignon parenthetically.

"It will make kings," continued Lousteau.

"And unmake kingdoms," said the diplomatist.

"Consequently," said Blondet, "if the press did not exist, it ought never to be invented; but here it is, — we live by it."

"And you will die of it," said the minister. "Do you not see that the enlightenment of the masses, supposing that you do enlighten them, will make the grandeur of the individual more difficult, and that if you sow the power of reasoning in the minds of the lower classes you will reap revolt, and be yourselves its first victims? What is it they smash in Paris when there's a riot?"

"The street-lamps," said Nathan; "but we are too humble a prey; at the worst they'll only crack us."

"You are too witty a people to allow any form of government, no matter what it is, the time to develop," said the minister. "Otherwise, your pens would attempt to reconquer the Europe your swords could not retain."

"Newspapers are an evil, undoubtedly," said Claude Vignon; "an evil that might be utilized, but governments insist on fighting it. A struggle must come. Who will get the worst of it?—that's the question."

"The government," said Blondet; "I am tired of shouting that. Intellect is the ruling power in France, and journalism has not only all the intelligence of the best minds, but it has the hypocrisy of Tartufe as well."

"Blondet, Blondet," said Finot, "that's going too far; remember there are subscribers present."

"Yes, you are owner of one of those venom reservoirs, and you ought to be afraid; as for me I scorn the trade, though I live by it."

"Blondet is right," said Claude Vignon. "Journalism, instead of being, as it ought to be, a priesthood, has become an engine of parties; being an engine, it is now an article of commerce, and, like all other forms of commerce, it regards neither law nor gospel. All journalism is, as Blondet says, a trade, where they sell to the public the words of the color and stripe the public want. If there were a newspaper for hunchbacks it would declare night and morning the beauty, goodness, and necessity of hunchbacks. A newspaper is no longer written to enlighten public opinion, but to cajole it. Within a given time all papers will end by being base, hypocritical liars, — murderers if you please ; for they will kill ideas, theories, men, and live by that alone. And they'll have every apparent reason on their side ; the evil will be done and no one will be guilty. I, Vignon, you, Lousteau, Blondet, Finot, will be Platos, Aristides, Catos, Plutarch's men, — all of us innocent, and able to wash our hands of infamy. Napoleon gave the reason of that phenomenon, moral or immoral as you choose to call it, in a wonderful saying which his studies of the Convention taught him : ' Collective crimes involve no one.' A newspaper may be guilty of the most atrocious conduct, but no journalist considers that he is personally soiled by it."

" The authorities will make repressive laws," said Du Bruel. " They are preparing them already."

" Pooh ! what can laws do against French wit, the most subtle of all dissolvents," said Nathan.

" Ideas can only be neutralized by ideas," continued Vignon. " Terror, despotism alone can stifle French genius ; and even so, our language is well-fitted for allusion and double-meaning. The more repressive the laws may be, the more vehemently French wit will burst forth, like steam from the throttle of an engine. Journalism will have a thousand methods of evasion. If the king has done well and the paper is anti-royalist, it gives all praise to the ministry, and *vice versâ.* If the paper invents an infamous calumny, it has been told it by others. If the individual complains, the paper will get off on the score of public privilege. If dragged before the courts, it will complain that no one had asked for retraction; ask, and it will turn the whole matter into a scoff and call it a trifle. It will scout at a victim that gets the better of it. It will contrive to say that Monsieur Such-a-one is a thief, while professedly proving him the most honest man in the kingdom; and in course of time it will make its daily readers believe whatever it may choose to put into their minds. It is never wrong. Nothing that displeases it can possibly be patriotic. It will use religion to rap religion, the Charter to rap the king; it will scoff at the law if the law annoys it, and praise it when it serves any popular passion. To gain subscribers, a newspaper will do anything, — serve up its own father raw with the salt of its atticisms rather than not amuse and interest the public. It is like the actor putting the ashes of his son in the urn that he may cry more naturally — ”

“ In short, it is the People in daily print,” cried Blondet, interrupting Vignon.

“ Yes, the hypocritical people, devoid of all generous ideas,” replied Vignon, — “ a people that will banish greatness from its bosom as Athens banished Aristides. Mark my words, we shall see newspapers, managed at first by men of honor, falling later under the control of inferior men who will have the elasticity and resistance of india-rubber, which great souls lack, or into the hands of tradesmen who have the money to support the pens. Why, you can see it already. Ten years hence every youngster out of college will think himself a great man; he'll jump into the columns of the newspaper and knock out his predecessors and take their places. Napoleon was right enough in wishing to muzzle the press! And I will bet that if the opposition papers were to make a government themselves they would attack it with the same reasons and the same articles they now fulminate against the king, the very moment that their own government refused them anything, no matter what. The more concessions are made to newspapers, the more exacting those papers will become. Successful journalists will be constantly succeeded by poor and hungry journalists. The evil is incurable; it is getting more and more malignant, more and more dangerous; and the greater the evil, the more it will be tolerated, until the day when confusion shall overtake journalism as it did Babylon. We all know, such as we are, that the press practises a baser ingratitude than that of kings, a dirtier business in schemes and speculations than the vilest commerce, and sucks our brains out to brew its daily alcohol every morning; and yet we all write for it, like laborers who work a mine of quicksilver and know they'll die of it. Look at that man over there, by Coralie — what's his name? Lucien! — he is handsome, he is a poet, and what is better, for him at least, he has wit; well, he'll enter one of those places of ill-fame called newspapers, he'll fling his finest ideas into it, he'll dry up his brain, he'll corrupt his soul, he'll commit those anonymous infamies which take the place, in the war of minds, of plots, pillage, incendiarism, and the way-laying of guerrilla warfare. When he has, like a thousand

others, spent a fine talent in the service of the proprietors, those sellers of poison will let him die of hunger if thirsty, or of thirst if hungry."

" Thank you," said Finot.

" But, my God ! " added Vignon, " I knew all that ;
I'm in the galleys myself, and the arrival of a new
prisoner gives me pleasure.   Blondet and I are much
abler than Messrs. So-and-so who are speculating on
our talents, but we shall always be worsted by them.
We have a heart within our intellect, and we lack the
ferocious selfishness of the men who are getting the
best of us.   We are lazy, contemplative, meditative,
judicial ; they   suck   our   brains   and   accuse   us   of
idleness — "

" I expected you to be much more amusing," cried
Florine.

" Florine is right," said Blondet ; " let us leave the
cure of public evils to those humbugs the statesmen.
As Charlet says : ' Don't spit into the vintage.' "

" Do you know how Vignon strikes me ? " said Lousteau, with a sign towards Lucien ; " like one of those
stout women in the rue du Pélican who say to the
schoolboys, ' My little fellows, you are too young to
come here.' "

This sally made everybody laugh ; but Coralie liked
it.   The three tradesmen were eating and drinking as
they listened.

" In what nation can you find such a mixture of so
much good and so much evil ? " said the minister to
the Duc de Rhétoré.   " Ah, gentlemen ! you are prodigals who somehow don't ruin yourselves."

Thus, by the blessing of chance, no warning was lack-

ing to Lucien as he stood on the brink of the precipice
down which he was about to fall. D'Arthèz had set the
poet's feet in the noble path of toil by awakening those
emotions before which all obstacles disappear. Lousteau himself had tried to warn him from the gulf, for a
selfish reason, by revealing journalism and literature in
their practical aspects. Lucien had not been willing
to believe in such corruption ; but he now heard journalists themselves proclaiming their own vice ; he saw
them ripping up their own foster-mother to predict the
future. During this evening he was made to see things
as they are. Instead of being filled with horror at this
sight of the very core of the Parisian corruption Blucher
had so well defined, he enjoyed the brilliant scene to
intoxication. These remarkable men, in the polished
armor of their vice and the shining helmets of their
analyses, he thought far superior to the grave and
sober members of the brotherhood. Besides, he was
tasting the first delights of wealth ; he was under the
spell of luxury, the influence of choice food ; his volatile instincts were all awakened ; he drank for the first
time the rarest wine ; he made acquaintance with the
delicacies of Parisian cookery ; he saw a diplomatist,
with a duke and his mistress, mingling with journalists
and admiring their dangerous power ; he felt a horrible
craving to rule this society of kings, and he felt within
him the power of mastering it. Besides all this,
there was Coralie, whom he had made happy with a
few words ; he examined her in the dazzling light of
that festive table, through the fumes of the viands and
the mists of drunkenness, and she seemed to him sublime ; love had made her beautiful ! She was, in fact,

the prettiest, even the handsomest, actress of her day. The brotherhood — that assemblage of noble intellects — was rejected under a temptation so complete on all sides. Lucien's vanity as an author had been flattered by able judges; he had been praised by future rivals. The success of his article and the conquest of Coralie were triumphs which might have turned a head less young than his.

During this discussion the whole company had eaten well and drunk enormously. Lousteau, who was sitting next to Camusot, filled up his neighbor's glass from time to time with kirsch, mingling it with the wine, and inciting the old tradesman to drink. This manœuvre was so adroitly done that Camusot did not notice it; he thought himself, in his own way, as clever as the journalists. As the wine circulated more freely, the speeches and jests became sharper and more malicious. The diplomatist — a man of great good sense — made a sign to the duke and Tullia as soon as he heard the first warnings of the grotesque condition in which these men of wit and intellect ended their orgies, and they all three quietly disappeared. As soon as Camusot had completely lost his head, Coralie and Lucien, who had made love to each other during supper like children of fifteen, slipped down the stairs and jumped into a hackney-coach. As Camusot was under the table, Matifat supposed that he had gone too, and he therefore left the rest of his guests smoking, drinking, laughing, arguing, and followed Florine. Daylight overtook the disputants, or rather Blondet alone, a hardened drinker, who proposed the health of the rosy-fingered Dawn to the sleepers round him.

Lucien had never before been present at an orgy; he was still in full possession of his senses as he went downstairs, but the air overcame him; his intoxication was hideous. Coralie and her maid were obliged to almost carry him up the stairs of the handsome house in which the actress lived, — rue de Vendôme. On the staircase, Lucien, almost insensible, was ignobly ill.

"Quick, Bérénice!" cried Coralie; "some tea! make some tea!"

"It is nothing; it is the air," said Lucien; "and besides, I never drank so much."

"Poor boy! he's as innocent as a lamb," said Bérénice, a stout and very ugly Norman peasant-woman.

Finally Lucien was put half-unconscious into Coralie's bed, — the actress, aided by Bérénice, having undressed him with the care and tenderness of a mother, while he still kept saying: "It is nothing; it is the air. Thank you, mamma!"

"He calls me mamma!" cried Coralie, kissing his hair.

"What pleasure to love such an angel! Where did you find him? I never thought a man could be as handsome as a girl," said Bérénice.

"Did the porter see us, or anybody?" said Coralie.

"No," said Bérénice; "I let you in myself."

"Victoire knows nothing?"

"No, nothing," replied Bérénice.

At five o'clock in the following afternoon Lucien opened his eyes in that chamber of luxury, — all pink and white; a world full of marvellous and coquettish charm, which surpassed anything the poet had imagined. Coralie was dressing. She was to play her Andalusian part again that evening, and was obliged to be at the theatre at seven o'clock. She had contemplated her poet as he slept, feeding upon this new-born love, which united the senses with the heart, and the heart with the senses, exalting both. This exaltation, making them two in sense, one in love, was to her an absolution. Kneeling thus beside the bed, happy in the consciousness of love within her, the actress felt herself sanctified.

This delight was broken in upon by Bérénice.

"Camusot is coming in; he knows you are at home!" she cried.

Lucien sprang up, anxious with natural generosity not to injure Coralie. Bérénice drew aside a curtain and showed him into a dressing-room, where she and her mistress hastily put his clothes. As Camusot entered, Lucien's boots caught Coralie's eye. Bérénice had put them before the fire to warm, after privately polishing them. Both maid and mistress had overlooked their accusing presence. Coralie flung herself into a low chair, and told Camusot to take the armchair opposite. The old man, who adored her, looked at the boots, and dared not raise his eyes to his mistress.

"Ought I to take offence at those boots and let her go?" he thought. "It is a small thing to be angry about. Boots may be anywhere. These had better be at the bootmaker's, or walking the boulevards on a man's legs. But here, even without legs, they throw doubts on fidelity. I am fifty years old, — yes, that is true; better be blind, like love itself."

That weak and cowardly monologue had no excuse. The boots were not like the boots of the present day, which a preoccupied man might easily overlook; they were such as the fashion of the period required, — high boots, very elegant with tassels, and highly polished, which reflected the articles about them like a mirror. They could not but strike the eyes of the worthy shopkeeper; and, let us own, they struck his heart.

" What is the matter? " said Coralie.

" Nothing," he answered,

" Ring the bell," she said, smiling at his cowardice. " Bérénice," she added as the woman entered, " don't forget to take those boots to my dressing-room to-night, and bring a button-hook ; for I suppose I shall have to wear the cursed things."

" Your boots? are those your boots? " said Camusot, who breathed again.

" Whose did you suppose they were? " she asked with a haughty look. " Old fool! I hope you don't suppose — Oh! he did suppose it! " she added to Bérénice. " I play the part of a man in that piece of Berthier's, and I never wore a man's dress before. The bootmaker of the theatre brought me those things to learn to walk in boots while he makes me a pair to measure. He put them on, but they hurt me so I had to take them off."

" Don't put them on again if they hurt you," said Camusot, who had himself suffered more from the boots than his mistress.

" Mademoiselle cried, they hurt her so," said Bérénice ; " and I tell her she ought to have them made of soft morocco. But the management is so mean ! Monsieur, you might order her a pair."

" Yes, of course," said Camusot. " Are you only just up, mademoiselle? "

"Just this minute; I did n't get home till six o'clock, after hunting everywhere for you. You made me keep my hackney-coach seven whole hours! That's what you call tender attentions!—forgetting me for the bottles! I ought to take care of myself, now that I have to play in the Alcalde every night; I don't want to fall behind that young man's article."

"He is handsome, that young fellow, is n't he?" said Camusot.

"Do you think so? I don't like men of that kind,—they are too much like women; they don't know how to make love like you old business men. You are so bored without it."

"Does monsieur dine with madame?" asked Bérénice.

"No, my mouth is parched."

"Ha! you were finely fuddled last night, papa Camusot; I don't like men who get drunk—"

"Do you want to give that young man a present?" said Camusot.

"Yes, I prefer to pay them in money rather than do as Florine does. Come, go away, bad old soul that one can't help loving, or else give me a carriage; for I can't afford to lose my time."

"You shall have the carriage to-morrow in time for the manager's dinner at the Rocher de Cancale. They don't play the new piece Sunday."

"Come, I am going to get some dinner," said Coralie, carrying him off.

Soon after, Lucien was let out of the dressing-room by Bérénice.

"Stay here," she said "Coralie will return alone.

She is ready to give up Camusot and send him off, if
you wish it; but, dear child of her heart, you are too
kind, I'm sure, to ruin her. She told me she was quite
decided to give up everything and leave this paradise
to live in your garret. Ah! that envious lot about her,
they told her you had neither bite nor sup, and lived in
a garret in the Latin quarter! I should follow, that's
certain, and do your cooking. But, monsieur, you have
too much sense to let her commit such a folly. Don't
you see? — the old one has only the shell, but you are the
darling of her heart, the god she gives her soul to. If
you only knew how good and sweet my Coralie is when
I make her learn her parts! a dear darling of a child!
She deserved that God should send her an angel, for
she is disgusted with life. Her mother was so bad to
her, and beat her, and sold her! Yes, monsieur, her
mother, her own mother sold her! If I had had a child
she could n't be more to me than my little Coralie; and
this is the first time I ever saw her happy, — the first
time, too, she has ever been really applauded. It seems
you 've written something, and they have set on a great
force of *claqueurs* for to-night; Braulardcame while you
were asleep and arranged it with her — "

" Braulard! who is he?" asked Lucien, who thought
he remembered the name.

" The head of the *claqueurs*; he arranged with her
all the places where the clapping is to come in. Although
she calls herself her friend, Florine is quite capable of
playing her some ugly trick and getting all the applause
for herself. Your article has made a commotion, I can
tell you."

So saying, she lighted the wax-candles; and by their

light, Lucien, dazzled, began to think himself in the palace of the Queen of the Fairies. Camusot had selected the richest stuffs in the " Cocon d'Or " for the hangings on the walls, and the window curtains. The poet's feet sank in a regal carpet. The carvings of the choice woodwork caught shimmerings of light from the tapers. The chimney-piece of white marble glittered with costly ornaments. A lamp hung from the ceiling, which was fluted with silk. Jardinieres were everywhere, filled with choice plants, beautiful white heath, and camellias without fragrance, tokens of innocence! How was it possible to imagine that the life of an actress and the morals of a theatre were here? Bérénice noticed Lucien's astonishment.

"Isn't it pretty?" she said, in a wheedling voice. "Won't you both be much happier here than in a garret? Don't let her do such a desperate thing," she continued, placing a tray before him, with dishes taken surreptitiously from her mistress's dinner, that the cook might not suspect the presence of a lover.

Lucien dined well, — served by Bérénice on plates painted at a cost of a louis apiece, with silver of the last fashion of engraving. At half-past ten o'clock Coralie returned.

The next day, by two in the afternoon, the actress and her lover were dressed and sitting together as though the new journalist had simply called to pay a visit to his protégée. Coralie had bathed and combed and brushed and dressed Lucien; she had sent Bérénice to buy him a dozen of the finest shirts, a dozen cravats, a dozen handkerchiefs from Colleau, and a dozen pair of gloves in a sandal-wood box. When she heard the sound of a carriage stopping before the door she rushed to the window, followed by Lucien, and together they saw Camusot getting out of a handsome coupé.

"I never believed," she said, "that I should come to hate a man and his luxury."

"I am too poor to consent to your relinquishing them," said Lucien, putting the halter of degradation about his neck.

"Poor dear!" she said, pressing him to her heart; "then indeed you love me well! I asked monsieur," she said to Camusot, with a motion towards Lucien, "to come here this morning, thinking we might drive in the Champ Elysées and try the new carriage."

"You must go without me," said Camusot, ruefully. "I can't dine with you; this is my wife's fête day, and I had forgotten it."

"Poor Musot! what a dismal day you will have!" she said, throwing her arms round his neck.

She was wild with happiness at the thought that she could drive alone with Lucien in the beautiful coupé, and in the rush of her joy she seemed actually to love Camusot, whom she petted and caressed.

"I should like to be able to give you a carriage every day," said the poor man.

"Come, monsieur, it is getting late," said the actress, seeing the look of shame on Lucien's face, and trying to console him with a pretty gesture.

She ran rapidly down the stairs, followed by Lucien, who heard the silk mercer following like a walrus, but unable to overtake them. The poet was intoxicated with delight; Coralie, made beautiful by happiness, wore an elegant toilet in charming taste. The Paris

15

of the Champ Élysées admired these lovers.   In an
avenue of the Bois de Boulogne their coupé met the
calèche of Mesdames d'Espard and de Bargeton, who
looked at Lucien with an amazed air; the poet returned the glance with the scornful eye of one who
feels his coming power and means to use it.   That
moment, when with a glance he cast back to the two
women the thoughts of vengeance they had put into his
heart to corrode it, was one of the sweetest of his life,
and may perhaps have decided his destiny.   Lucien
was once more seized by the demons of pride: he
longed to reappear in society; to take some startling
revenge; and all the social pettinesses which, as a toiler
and a member of the brotherhood he had put behind
him, returned to his soul.   He understood the full value
of the attack Lousteau had made for him.   Lousteau
had served his passions, whereas the brotherhood,
that collective mentor, had sought to curb them in
the interests of the wearisome toil and virtue which
Lucien was beginning to consider useless.   Toil! what
was that but the death of souls eager for enjoyment?
How readily do writers slip into the *dolce far niente*
of good living and the luxurious delights of actresses
and easy women.   Lucien was now possessed by an
irresistible desire to continue the life of the last two
intoxicating days.

The dinner at the Rocher de Cancale was exquisite.
All Florine's guests were there except the German
minister, the duke, and the *danseuse;* except also
Camusot.   In their places were two distinguished actors and Hector Merlin, accompanied by his mistress,
a fascinating creature who called herself Madame du

Val-Noble, the handsomest and most elegant of the
women who formed at that time the questionable class
who in these days are called *lorettes*. Lucien, who had
lived retired for the last forty-eight hours in paradise,
now heard of the success of his article. Beholding
himself sought after, flattered, and envied, the poet
gained assurance; his wit sparkled, and he was for
the first time the Lucien de Rubempré who shone for
many months in the literary and artistic society of
Paris. Finot, a man of undeniable ability in discovering talent, scenting it as an ogre scents blood, cajoled
Lucien for the purpose of committing him to the squad-
ron of journalists whom he himself commanded. Lucien
was readily taken by such flatteries; but Coralie, observing the game of that absorber of intellects, tried to
put Lucien on his guard against him.

"Don't commit yourself, dear!" she said to her poet;
"wait awhile; they want to use you for their own ends;
we'll talk about it to-night."

"Pooh!" answered Lucien; "I am strong enough
to be as shrewd and as clever as they."

Finot, who had evidently not quarrelled perma-
nently with Hector Merlin about the blank lines, presented Merlin to Lucien, and Lucien to Merlin. Coralie
and Madame du Val-Noble fraternized, and the latter
invited Lucien and Coralie to dinner. Hector Merlin,
the most dangerous of all the journalists present, was a
small, spare man with pinched lips, who nursed an un-
bounded ambition and an uncontrollable jealousy of all
talent; he rejoiced in the harm he did to others, and
profited by the quarrels he fomented. His mind was
good, his will weak; but in place of will he possessed

the instinct which leads a self-made man to the most available regions of wealth and power. Lucien and he disliked each other at once. It is not difficult to explain why. Merlin said aloud what Lucien thought in his heart. By the time dessert was served, the closest bonds of friendship seemed to unite all these men, each of them meanwhile thinking himself superior to the rest. Lucien, the new-comer, was the centre of their attentions. They all welcomed him with the utmost heartiness except Hector Merlin, who alone was serious. Lucien asked him the reason of such reserve.

" I see you entering this literary and journalistic life with illusions. You believe you are making friends. We are all friends or enemies according to circumstances. We strike ourselves with the weapons we ought to use only to strike others. You will find out before long that you will gain nothing by fine sentiments. If you are kindly, make yourself ill-natured ; be surly on principle. If no one else has told you this first law, I give it to you now ; and it is a gift that is worth the having. If you wish to be loved, never leave your mistress without having made her weep ; if you wish to make your fortune in literature, wound every one, even your friends ; make the self-loves suffer ; and all the world will court you."

Hector Merlin was gratified when he saw by Lucien's manner that the blade of that dagger had gone to his heart. They played ; Lucien lost all his money. He was carried off by Coralie, and the delights of love made him forget the terrible emotions of gambling, to which he afterwards became a victim. The next day, on leaving his mistress and returning to the Latin quarter, he found in his purse the money he had lost. This kindness at first distressed him; he thought of going back and returning a gift which humiliated him; but he had reached the rue de la Harpe, and after a moment's hesitation he continued on his way to the rue de Cluny. As he went along, his mind was full of this kindness of Coralie; it was one proof the more of that maternal tenderness which women of her sort mingle with their passions. Going from thought to thought, Lucien ended by finding a reason for accepting the bounty. "I love her," he thought; " we will live together as man and wife, and I will never leave her."

XIV.

A LAST VISIT TO THE BROTHERHOOD.

UNLESS we are Diogenes, we shall surely be able to
enter into Lucien's sensations as he ran up the muddy
and evil-smelling stairway of his house, and turned his
key in the creaking lock of the door, and saw the dirty
floor and miserable fireplace of his bare and wretched
room.   On the table lay the manuscript of his novel,
and the following note from Daniel d'Arthèz : —

Our friends are almost satisfied with your work, dear
poet.   You can offer it, they think, to friends and enemies
with confidence.   We have read your charming article on
the Panorama-Dramatique, and think you will rouse as
much envy in journalism as you have caused regrets in us.

DANIEL.

" Regrets ! what does he mean ? " cried Lucien, surprised at the tone of politeness which pervaded the
note.   Did the brotherhood now regard him as an alien ?
After devouring the delicious fruit the Eve of the
coulisses had put to his lips, he still wanted the respect
and friendship of his friends in the rue des Quatre-
Vents.   He remained a few moments lost in meditation
on his present existence in that wretched room and his
future life in that of Coralie.   Harassed by doubts and
a hesitation alternately honorable and depraved, he sat
down and began to examine the condition in which his

friends had returned his work. What was his astonishment to find that in chapter after chapter the able and devoted pens of these great minds, still unknown, had changed his poverty to riches. A teeming, concise, and nervous dialogue took the place of conversations which he now could see were merely wordy compared with this brilliant talk which breathed the spirit of the age. His portraits, rather tame in outline, had been vigorously touched-up and colored; some were connected with the phenomena of human life by physiological observations due no doubt to Bianchon, and given with a delicate shrewdness which made them living. His descriptions, too, also wordy, now had substance and vigor. He had given an ill-made, ill-clothed child, and his friends had returned to him a charming young girl in a white robe. Night found him, with tears in his eyes, subdued by such wisdom, feeling the value of such a lesson, admiring the corrections, which taught him more of literature and art than all his four years of reading, study, and comparison put together. The correction of a sketch ill-drawn, a masterly stroke at the heart of the matter, will often teach far more than theories and observations.

"What friends! what hearts! ah, how fortunate I am!" he cried, as he folded the manuscript.

Carried away by the emotion of his poetic and volatile nature, he rushed to Daniel's room. As he went up the staircase, it came into his mind that he was now less worthy of these hearts, none of which could be swayed from the path of honor. A voice told him that if Daniel had loved Coralie he would never have accepted her with Camusot. He knew the horror the brethren all felt for journalists, and now he was one.

He found his friends, except Meyraux, all assembled ; anguish was on every face.

" What has happened, friends ? " exclaimed Lucien.

" We have just heard of a dreadful catastrophe. The greatest mind of our epoch, our dearest friend, he who for two years has been our light — "

" Louis Lambert ? " asked Lucien.

" Yes, he has fallen into a state of catalepsy which leaves no hope," said Bianchon.

" He is dead in a senseless body, with his mind in the skies," added Michel Chrestien, solemnly.

" He will die as he lived," said d'Arthèz.

" Love was like a fire in the vast empire of his brain ; it became a conflagration," said Léon Giraud.

" Yes," said Joseph Bridau, " he exalted it out of sight of men."

" It is we who must be pitied," said Fulgence Ridal.

" Perhaps he may recover," said Lucien.

" If what Meyraux told us is true, recovery is impossible," replied Bianchon. " His head is the theatre of phenomena over which the medical art has no power."

" But there are agents — " began d'Arthèz.

" Yes," said Bianchon, " he is now only cataleptic ; we might make him imbecile."

" Ah ! if we could but offer a head to the Genius of Evil in exchange for his, I would gladly give mine," cried Michel Chrestien.

" What would become of European federation ? "

" True," replied Chrestien ; " before serving individual man we must serve humanity."

" I came here to-night with my heart full of gratitude to you all," said Lucien. " You have changed my coppers into louis d'or."

" Why thanks? You do not yet understand us," said Bianchon.

"The pleasure is all on our side," said Fulgence.

"Well, so here you are, a journalist!" said Léon Giraud. "The fame of your first appearance has reached even the Latin quarter."

"I am not yet a journalist," said Lucien.

"Ah! so much the better!" cried Michel Chrestien.

"I told you so," said d'Arthèz. "Lucien has a heart that knows the value of a pure conscience; he feels what a strengthening viaticum it is to lay one's head upon the pillow and say: 'I have judged no one, I have made no one suffer, my wit is not a dagger thrust into harmless souls; it has immolated no happiness, it has not even troubled contented folly; above all, I have never unjustly dealt with genius, I have despised the easy triumphs of satire, I have not played false to my convictions — '"

"But," said Lucien, "I think it possible to keep to that standard and yet work at journalism. If I find no other way of living I shall have to come to it."

"Oh, oh, oh!" cried Fulgence, going up one note at each exclamation; "you are capitulating."

"He will be a journalist," said Léon Giraud, gravely. "Ah! Lucien, if you would only stay with us! for we mean some day to publish a paper in which neither truth nor justice shall be violated, — a paper in which to spread the doctrines useful to humanity — "

"You won't get a single subscriber," said Lucien, interrupting Léon with a Machiavelian air.

"They will have five hundred, worth five thousand of the world's kind," said Michel Chrestien.

"You need capital," returned Lucien.

"No," said d'Arthèz, "devotion."

"Ah! Lucien, you are like a perfumer's shop," cried Michel Chrestien, with a comic sniff at the poet's head. "I'm told you've been seen in a gorgeous carriage drawn by blood horses, and seated beside the mistress of a prince!"

"Well," said Lucien, "where's the harm of that?"

"You say that as if there were some harm," cried Bianchon.

"I wish Lucien had a Beatrice," said d'Arthèz, "some noble woman to sustain him in life —"

"But, Daniel, is not love the same wherever we find it?" asked the poet.

"Ah!" said Chrestien the republican, "in that I am an aristocrat. I could not love a woman whom actors kiss on the stage, who bows and smiles to a public crowd, and holds up her petticoats in dancing, or dresses as a man to show that which ought not to be seen; or, if I did love such a woman, she should leave the stage; I would purify her by my love."

"But suppose she could n't leave the stage?"

"I should die of grief, of jealousy, of a thousand miseries. You can't tear a love from the heart like a tooth from the gum."

Lucien grew thoughtful and gloomy. "If they were to know that I submit to Camusot," he said to himself, "they would despise me."

"Look here, Lucien," said the stern republican, with grim good-humor, "you can be a great writer if you will, but I greatly fear you will never be anything more than a paltry wit."

So saying, he took his hat and went out.

"He is merciless," said the poet.

"Merciless and salutary as a dentist's forceps," said Bianchon. "Michel looks to your future, and perhaps at this moment he is weeping over you as he walks along."

D'Arthèz was gentle and consoling; he tried to raise Lucien's courage; but it was hopeless. At the end of an hour Lucien left the brotherhood, tortured by his conscience, which cried to him, like the witches to Macbeth, "Thou shalt be journalist!" From the street he looked up at the dimly lighted window of the patient d'Arthèz; then he returned to his own poor room with a saddened heart and a fearsome mind. A presentiment told him he had been taken to the hearts of those true friends for the last time. As he entered the rue de Cluny from the place de la Sorbonne he recognized Coralie's new carriage. To see her poet for a moment, to wish him good-night, she had come the long distance from the Boulevard du Temple to the Sorbonne. Lucien found her in tears at the mere sight of his garret; she wanted, she said, to be as miserable as he, and she wept as she laid the shirts and gloves and handkerchiefs she had brought with her in the worthless old bureau of the garret. Her grief was so true, so great, that Lucien, who had just heard actresses condemned, thought her a saint eager, out of love, to wear the hair-cloth of poverty. Her pretext for coming was to tell Lucien that the Camusot household was about to return the Matifat supper, and to ask her friend if there were any invitations it would be to his interest to give. Lucien replied that he would ask Lousteau, and

Coralie hastened away, not telling Lucien that Camusot was waiting for her in the carriage.

The next day, by eight o'clock, Lucien went to see Étienne at his lodgings; the editor was not there, and he followed him to Florine's. There he found them breakfasting together in conjugal fashion, and they invited Lucien to join them.

"My dear fellow," said Lousteau, when they were all three at table, and Lucien had told of the supper to be given by Coralie, "I advise you to come with me and invite Félicien Vernou, and to get as intimate with him as you can be with such an utter scoundrel. Félicien may be able to get you a footing on the political paper for which he cooks the feuilleton; and there you could flourish at your ease in the highest styles of journalism and write fine articles. His paper, like ours, belongs to the Liberals, — that's the popular party; besides, if you wanted later to be on the ministerial side you would have all the advantages of being feared. Hector Merlin and his Madame du Val-Noble have asked you and Coralie to dinner, have n't they? You'll meet several great people there, dandies, millionnaires."

"Yes," said Lucien, "and you are to be asked too, with Florine."

"Well, Merlin will be at the office; the rascal is always after Finot; you had better make much of him and ask him to Coralie's supper. Very likely he'll do you some service; spiteful men want everybody's help, and he'd pay well for your pen in an emergency."

"Your article has made sensation enough to open the way for you," said Florine. "Take advantage of it instantly, otherwise you'll soon be forgotten."

"The great affair is settled," said Lousteau. "Finot, that fellow without any talent whatever, is manager and editor-in-chief of Dauriat's weekly journal, with a salary of six hundred francs a month. I am, from this day forth, editor-in-chief of the little journal. Everything happened as I predicted the other evening. Floine has been superb; she might give points to Talleyrand."

"We women hold men by their pleasures," said Florine, "diplomatists hold them only by their interests ;—diplomatists watch their manœuvres, we watch their follies, —that's why we are so powerful."

"The upshot of it is, my dear fellow, that it puts your foot in the stirrup," said Lousteau.

"You were born with a lucky spoon in your mouth," said Florine. "Look at the crowd of poor young fellows who hang about Paris for years and can't get even a single article into a newspaper. It will be with you just as it was with Émile Blondet. Six months hence I shall see you carrying matters with a high hand and lording it over everybody," she added with a satirical smile.

"Have n't I been in Paris for three years?" said Lousteau; "and it was only yesterday that I secured from Finot three hundred francs a month for the editorship, and a hundred francs a column, and another hundred for an article in his weekly."

"Well," said Florine, looking at Lucien, "have n't you anything to say?"

"I 'll wait and see," replied Lucien.

"My dear fellow," said Lousteau, evidently annoyed, "I have done for you as I would for my own

brother ; but I won't answer for Finot.   Finot will be
pursued and badgered during the next two days by a
hundred other writers who will offer to do the work at
a discount.   I have engaged it for you ; of course you
can refuse it if you choose.   You surely don't distrust
your luck ? " continued the journalist, after a pause.
" It brings you into a clique of writers who attack
each other's enemies in various journals and do mutual
service."

   " Well, in the first place, let us go and see Félicien
Vernou," said Lucien, who was really eager to ally
himself with these dangerous birds of prey.

XV.

THE ARCANA OF JOURNALISM.

LOUSTEAU sent for a cabriolet, and the two friends drove to the rue Mandar, where Vernou lived in a house that was up a court, where he occupied an apartment on the second floor. Lucien was much astonished to find this bitter, disdainful, hypercritical critic breakfasting in a dining-room of the utmost vulgarity, hung with an imitation tile-paper and lithographs in gilt frames, in company with a woman too ugly to be anything but legitimate, and two small children perched on high chairs with bars to hold them in. Caught in a dressing-gown constructed of an old cotton gown of his wife's, Vernou looked none too pleased.

" Have you breakfasted, Lousteau?" he said, offering a chair to Lucien.

" Yes, with Florine," said Étienne.

Lucien was still examining Madame Vernou, who was like a comfortable fat cook; quite fair, but superlatively common. She wore a foulard handkerchief over a nightcap tied on with strings which her cheeks overhung. Her breakfast gown, which had no belt and was fastened at the throat by a single button, fell in thick folds, and muffled her so clumsily that she looked like a milestone. Bursting with health, her cheeks were crimson and her fingers like sausages. This woman suddenly explained to Lucien Vernou's embarrassed manner in company. Sick of his marriage, not evil enough to abandon wife and children, but refined enough to suffer from them always, the author could not forgive the success of others; he was dissatisfied with all things because so dissatisfied within. Lucien understood the sour expression of that envious face, the acrid repartees on the journalist's tongue, the bitterness of each sentence sharpened and polished like a stiletto.

"Let us go into my study," said Vernou, rising; "you have come to talk of literary matters, I suppose?"

"Yes and no," replied Lousteau. "In the first place, old man, about a supper."

"I have come," said Lucien, "to invite you, in Coralie's name —"

Madame Vernou looked up.

"— to a supper this day week," continued Lucien. "You will find the same company we had at Florine's, with Madame de Val-Noble and Merlin added, and a few others. We shall play."

"But, my friend, that is the day we are engaged to Madame Mahoudeau," said the wife.

"What does that signify?" said Vernou.

"If we don't go she will be angry, and you know she is very useful in discounting your publishers' notes."

"My dear Lousteau, here's a woman who never can be made to understand that a supper which begins at midnight doesn't prevent a man from going to a party which is over by eleven. I have to work beside her."

" But you have so much imagination!" said Lucien, —a speech which made Félicien Vernou his mortal enemy.

" Well," said Lousteau, " then you can come. But that's not all. Monsieur de Rubempré is now one of us, consequently give him a push with your editor; say he is a fellow capable of the upper walks of literature, and that ought to get him two articles a month on the paper."

" Yes, if he is really one of us; if he is ready to attack our enemies as we attack them, and defend our friends, I'll mention him to the editor to-night at the Opera," replied Vernou.

" Ah! very kind, my dear fellow!" cried Lousteau, pressing Vernou's hand with every appearance of the warmest friendship. " When is your book coming out?"

" That depends on Dauriat," said the father of the family. " I have finished it."

" Are you satisfied?"

" Yes and no."

" Well, we'll organize a success," said Lousteau, rising and bowing to the wife of his co-journalist.

This sudden departure was rendered necessary by the squeals of the children, who were quarrelling and fighting with their spoons, and throwing porridge in each other's faces.

" You have just seen," said Étienne when they had fairly escaped, " a woman who, without being aware of it, is making actual devastation in literature. That poor Vernou cannot forgive the world for his wife. He ought to be relieved of her for the good of the public. We should escape a deluge of infamous articles, — diatribes against our successes and our luck. What won't a man become with such a wife and those intolerable brats? Have you seen Rigaudin in Picard's play, 'The Lottery Shop'? Well, like Rigaudin, Vernou never fights duels, but he makes others fight them. He is capable of putting out one of his own eyes in order to put out both eyes of his best friend. You'll see him, with a foot on the fallen, smiling at everybody's ill luck; attacking princes, dukes, and nobles because his own birth was low; attacking more especially the fame of unmarried men because of his wife; but always preaching morality, pleading for domestic joys and devotion to the duties of the citizen. That highly moral critic is considerate of no one, not even his own children. He lives there in that wretched place with a wife who might be the *mamamouchi* of the 'Bourgeois gentilhomme' and two little Vernous as ugly as toads, and he writes scoffing articles on the faubourg Saint-Germain, where he can't put a foot, and makes the duchesses talk like his wife. That's the man who howls at the Jesuits, insults the court, declares that the king is aiming to re-establish feudal rights and primogeniture, and preaches a crusade in favor of equality, because he feels he is not on an equality with any one. If he were a bachelor he would go into society; he would take the style of the royalist poets, wear the cross of the Legion of honor, and be an optimist. Journalism is full of such motives. It is a great catapult put in motion by little hatreds. How should you like to be married? Vernou has no heart left; it is gall and nothing else. He is a specimen of the journalist *par excellence*, — a tiger with two hands tearing everything to bits, as if his pens were literally insane."

" He's a destructive," said Lucien. " What talent has he?"

" Wit; he is what you may call an article writer. His stock in trade is articles, and nothing but articles. Félicien is incapable of conceiving a work as a whole, of marshalling forces, and leading his personages through a plot which begins, tangles, and finally ends in some climax. He has ideas, but he does n't know how to deal with facts; his heroes are either philosophical or liberal utopians; his style is labored, his inflated sentences collapse if a critic sticks a pin into them. For that reason he is dreadfully afraid of the newspapers, like all those who need the puff and humbug of praise to keep them floating."

" You are talking articles yourself," said Lucien, laughing.

" Yes, but this is the kind we think, my dear fellow; we don't write them."

" Ah! you are getting to be editor-in-chief," said Lucien.

" Where shall I set you down?" asked Lousteau.

" At Coralie's."

" Ha! so we are in love?" said Lousteau. " A great mistake! Make Coralie what I make Florine, a provider, but keep foot-loose yourself and take your swing."

" You'd damn a saint," said Lucien, laughing.

" Well, you can't damn devils," replied Lousteau.

The brilliant, flippant tone of his new friend, the way

in which he looked at life, mingling paradox with the practical maxims of a Parisian Machiavelli, influenced Lucien unconsciously. In theory, the poet saw the danger of such thoughts, but he knew them to be useful in practice. When they reached the Boulevard du Temple the two friends agreed to meet again between four and five o'clock at the newspaper office, where, no doubt, Hector Merlin would appear.

Lucien was, in truth, caught by the pleasures of this love of courtesans who fasten their grapnels to all the most sensitive regions of a man's nature; he was thirsty for Parisian enjoyments; he loved the opulent, magnificent, easy life the actress now made him feel was to be his own in her house. He found her with Camusot, both wild with joy. The offer of an engagement after Easter had been made by the Gymnase, the conditions of which, succinctly drawn up, much surpassed their hopes.

"We owe this triumph to you," said Camusot as Lucien entered.

"Yes, indeed!" cried Coralie, "if it had n't been for him the 'Alcalde' would have fallen flat. Without that article I should have stayed on the Boulevards for six years."

And she flung her arms round Lucien's neck in presence of Camusot. The effusion of her action had something indescribably soft in its rapidity and abandonment. She loved! Like all men in moments of great pain, Camusot lowered his eyes to the ground, and as he did so he noticed on the seam of Lucien's boots the thread of color used by the best bootmakers, — a dark yellow, shining against the polished black of the leather. The peculiar color of this thread had caught his attention during his monologue on the inexplicable appearance of boots in front of Coralie's fireplace. He had read in black letters printed on the white kid lining the name of a famous bootmaker of the period, — Gay, rue de la Michodière.

"Monsieur," he said to Lucien, "your boots are very handsome."

" Everything is handsome about him," said Coralie.

" I should be glad to employ your bootmaker," continued Camusot.

" Oh ! " said Coralie, " how vulgar it is to ask the addresses of a man's trades-people ! Are you going to wear young men's boots and make yourself a dandy? No, no, keep to your own style, which suits a steady man with a wife and children and a mistress."

" Still, if monsieur would be good enough to take off one of his boots he would do me a service," said Camusot, obstinately.

" I could not put it on again without a button-hook," said Lucien, flushing.

" Bérénice can fetch one ; there are plenty here," said Camusot, with jeering eyes.

" Papa Camusot," said Coralie, giving him a glance of the bitterest contempt ; " have the courage of your suspicions. Come, say all you think. Monsieur's boots are just like mine, are not they? — I forbid you to take off your boots," she said to Lucien. " Yes, Monsieur Camusot, yes, those boots are precisely those which you saw before my fire the other day and Monsieur de Rubempré was hidden in my dressing-room and waiting for them, having passed the night here. That's what you're thinking, hey? Well, think it! It is the truth I have deceived you. What of that? I choose to do so."

She sat down without anger or embarrassment and looked at Camusot and Lucien, who dared not look at each other.

"I do not believe what you tell me to believe," said Camusot at last. "Do not jest; I was wrong to be so suspicious."

"Either I am an infamous strumpet who has taken a momentary fancy to monsieur, or I am a poor miserable creature who feels, for the first time, the true love every woman longs for. In either case you must leave me, or take me as I am," she said, with a masterful gesture which crushed the old man.

"Is it true?" said Camusot, who saw by their faces that neither Lucien nor Coralie felt it was a joke, and who longed to be deceived.

"I love mademoiselle," said Lucien.

Hearing those words said with emotion, Coralie again flung her arms round her poet's neck, pressed him to her heart, and turned to Camusot as if to call his attention to her attitude.

"Poor Musot!" she said; "take back what you have given me. I want nothing more from you. I love this one madly, — not for his mind but for his beauty. I prefer poverty with him to millions with you."

Camusot fell into an armchair, put his head in his hands, and was silent.

"Shall we go away?" she asked fiercely.

Cold chills ran down Lucien's back as he saw himself saddled with a woman, an actress, a household.

"Stay here and keep all, Coralie," said Camusot in

a trembling, sorrowful voice, which came from his soul.
" I do not wish to take anything back, though there
is over sixty thousand francs' worth of furniture in these
rooms; but no, I could never bear the thought of
my Coralie in poverty. Whatever monsieur's talents
may be he cannot support you. Ah! this is what we
old men must expect! Coralie, leave me the right to
come and see you sometimes; I may be useful to you.
Beside, it will be impossible to live without you."

The gentleness of the unfortunate man, dispossessed
of all at the very moment he felt himself most happy,
touched Lucien keenly, but not Coralie.

" Yes, come as often as you like, my poor Musot,"
she said. " I shall love you all the more if I don't deceive you."

Camusot seemed satisfied in not being driven from
his terrestrial paradise, where, no doubt, he was now
to suffer much; but already he looked forward to a return into all his rights, relying on the chances of Parisian life and the seductions it would offer to Lucien.
The shrewd old merchant felt that sooner or later so
handsome a youth would allow himself infidelities, and
he resolved to remain on good terms with the pair in
order to watch Lucien and help to destroy him in
Coralie's estimation. Such baseness of passion alarmed
Lucien. Camusot invited them to dinner at Véry's in
the Palais-Royal and they accepted.

" Oh, what happiness!" cried Coralie as soon as
Camusot had departed. " No more garret in the *quar-
tier Latin;* you 'll live here with me; we shall never be
parted. To save appearances, you can take a room in
the rue Charlot, and ' vogue la galère!' "

She began to dance her Spanish fandango with a vim which showed the ardor of her passion.

"I can earn five hundred francs a month by working hard," said Lucien.

"And I get as much as that at the Panorama, without counting extras. Camusot will always pay for my clothes, he is so fond of me. With fifteen hundred francs a month we shall live like Crœsuses."

"But the horses and carriage, and the coachman?" said Bérénice.

"Oh, I'll run in debt," cried Coralie; and she began to dance a jig with Lucien.

"Well, I shall have to accept Finot's proposals," said Lucien.

"Very good," replied Coralie. "I'll dress, and drive you to the office, and wait in the carriage for you on the boulevard."

Lucien sat down on the sofa, watched the actress as she dressed herself, and gave himself up to serious reflections. He would much rather have given up Coralie than be saddled with the obligations of such a marriage; but as he looked at her, so handsome, so well-made, so attractive, he was carried away by the picturesque aspects of this bohemian life and cast his glove in the face of Fortune. Bérénice was ordered to see to the removal of all his things from the rue de Cluny; and then the triumphant and happy Coralie carried off her beloved poet and drove across all Paris to the rue Saint-Fiacre. Lucien climbed the staircase and entered with authority the dingy office in which he had so lately stood as a petitioner. Coloquinte was still staggering under the weight of the stamped paper, and old Giroudeau again began to tell him hypocritically that no one had yet come.

"But the editors must be somewhere to do the work of the paper," said Lucien.

"Probably, but the editing is none of my business," said the late captain of the Imperial Guard, resuming the verification of his vouchers with his everlasting "Broum — broum."

Just then, as luck, whether for good or evil, would have it, Finot came in to tell Giroudeau of his pretended abdication as editor-in-chief, and to caution him to watch over his interests just the same.

"No diplomacy with monsieur, he is on the paper," said Finot to his uncle, taking Lucien's hand and shaking it cordially.

"Ha! monsieur is on the paper, is he?" cried Giroudeau, surprised at his nephew's friendliness. "Well, monsieur, you had n't much trouble in getting there."

"I want to see that you get your rights, and prevent your being fooled by Lousteau," said Finot, giving Lucien a knowing look. "Monsieur is to have three francs a column," he continued, addressing his uncle, "for everything he brings in, including his theatre reports."

"You never gave such terms to any one before," said Giroudeau, looking at Lucien with an air of astonishment.

"He is to have the four Boulevard theatres, and you 'll see that his boxes are not *filched*, and that his tickets are punctually given to him. I advise you, however, to have them sent to your own house," he added, turning to Lucien. "Monsieur agrees to do, outside of his critical work, ten variety articles of about two columns for fifty francs a month for one year. Does that suit you?"

"Yes," said Lucien, now forced by circumstances to accept all terms.

"Uncle," said Finot to the cashier, "write out a memorandum of this agreement, and we'll sign it as we come downstairs."

"Who is the gentleman?" asked Giroudeau, rising and pulling off his black silk cap.

"Monsieur Lucien de Rubempré, writer of the article on the 'Alcalde,'" said Finot.

"Young man," cried the old soldier, tapping Lucien's forehead, "you've a mine of gold there. I'm not literary, but I've read your article with pleasure. I said at once. 'Ha, ha! there's gayety for you! That will bring us subscribers!' and I was right; fifty came in that day."

"Is my agreement with Étienne Lousteau copied in duplicate and ready for signature?" asked Finot.

"Yes," said Giroudeau.

"Then date the one I now make with Monsieur de Rubempré yesterday, so that Lousteau will be held under both." Finot took the arm of his new associate with an air of comradeship which completely beguiled the poet, and led him up the staircase, saying: "Now, your position is defined. I'll present you myself to *my* editorial staff. To-night Lousteau shall introduce you at the different theatres. You can earn a hundred and fifty francs a month on the little paper Lousteau now edits; so I advise you to keep well with him. The rascal won't like it that I have tied his hands in regard to you, but you 've got talent, and I don't want you to be at the mercy of his caprices. Between ourselves, you may bring me two sheets a month for my weekly paper, and I 'll pay you two hundred francs for them. Don't speak of this arrangement to any one; I should be made the victim of a hundred vanities wounded by your advent. Make four articles of your two sheets; sign two with your own name, and two with a pseudonym, so as not to seem to take the bread out of other people's mouths. You owe your position to Blondet and Vignon, who think you have a future. Therefore don't spoil your prospects. Above all, distrust your friends. Serve me well, and I will serve you. You will have forty francs' worth of boxes and tickets to sell, and sixty francs' worth of books to *realize*. That and the paper will give you four hundred and fifty a month. With your capacity you can easily get two hundred more from publishers, who will gladly pay for articles and prospectuses. But you belong to me, remember that. I shall rely on you."

Lucien pressed Finot's hand in a transport of joy.

" We had better not seem to be intimate," said Finot, as they reached the door of a garret room at the end of a long passage on the fifth floor of the house.

Lucien now saw Lousteau, Félicien Vernou, Hector Merlin, and two others whom he did not know, sitting round a table covered with green cloth before a good fire, smoking and laughing. The table was heaped with papers, an inkstand was there for use full of ink, and several rather bad pens, which the writers used nevertheless. It dawned on the new journalist's mind that here was the place where the newspaper was fabricated.

" Gentlemen," said Finot, " the object of this meeting is to install our dear Lousteau in my place as editor-
in-chief, a place I am obliged to give up. But though
my outward opinions must undergo a transformation in
order to become editor-in-chief of the weekly journal,
the principles of which are known to you, yet my convictions are the same, and we shall always remain
friends. I am wholly yours, as you are wholly mine.
Circumstances vary, principles are fixed. Principles
are the pivot on which revolve the hands of the political barometer."

The staff roared with laughter.

" Who taught you that sentence?" asked Lousteau.

" Blondet," replied Finot.

" Wind, rain, tempest, set fair," said Merlin ; " we'll
go through them all together."

" Well," said Finot, " there's no need to flounder in
metaphor. All those who have articles to bring me
will find Finot. Monsieur here," he added, presenting
Lucien, " is one of you. I have made an agreement
with him, Lousteau."

Every one present complimented Finot on his rise
and prospects.

" Here you are astride of us all and of others," said
one of the two men unknown to Lucien. " You'll be
Janus."

" Not Janot, I hope," said Vernou.

" You'll let us stab our *bêtes-noires?*"

" As much as you like," said Finot.

" Ah! by the bye," said Lousteau, " Monsieur Châtelet is savage. We mustn't let him off for a week."

" What has happened?" asked Lucien.

"He came here and demanded satisfaction," replied Vernou. "The ex-imperial beau fell into the hands of old Giroudeau, who, with superior coolness, pointed out Philippe Bridau as the writer of the article. Philippe told the baron to name time and weapons, and there the matter rested. We are now engaged in composing excuses to the baron for to-morrow's issue. Every sentence is a stab."

"Bite him hard, and he'll come and see me," said Finot. "I'll then do him a service by softening you off. He is on terms with the government, and we may hook something there, — a sub-professorship or a tobacco license. We are lucky to have touched him on the raw. Which of you will write me a solid article on Nathan for my new paper?"

"Give it to Lucien," said Lousteau. "Hector and Vernou can do others in their respective journals."

"Adieu, gentlemen! We shall meet again at Barbin's," said Finot, laughing.

Lucien received many compliments on his admission into the formidable ranks of journalism, and Lousteau assured those present that he was a man on whom they might depend.

"Lucien invites you *en masse*," he said, "to sup with his mistress, Coralie."

"Coralie has an engagement at the Gymnase," said Lucien.

"Good! Then it is understood, gentlemen, that we shall all push Coralie, hey? Put a few lines about her in your different papers, and speak of her talent; say the managers of the Gymnase have shown tact and judgment, — will it do to say they are intelligent?"

"Yes, say intelligent," said Merlin. "Frédéric has a play with Scribe there."

"Very good! Then the manager of the Gymnase is the most intelligent, perspicacious, and far-seeing of directors," said Vernou.

"Look here, don't write your articles about Nathan until we have agreed on what is to be said. I'll tell you why," said Lousteau, hastily. "We must be useful to our new comrade. He has two books to publish, — a novel, and a volume of sonnets. By dint of reviews, he ought to be a great poet in three months' time. Let us use his sonnets (he calls them 'Daisies') to smash the Odes, Ballads, Meditations, and all the rest of the romantic poems."

"It would be queer, though, if the sonnets were poor stuff," said Vernou. "What do you think of your sonnets, Lucien?"

"Yes, what do you really think of them?" said one of the writers whom Lucien did not know.

"Gentlemen," said Lousteau, "they are good, — on my word of honor."

"Then I'm satisfied," said Vernou. "I'll be only too glad to trip up those sacristy poets; they bore me to death."

"Well, if Dauriat refuses the 'Daisies,' we'll all hit him with article after article against Nathan."

"But how will Nathan like that?" asked Lucien.

The five journalists burst out laughing.

"He will be delighted," said Vernou. "You'll soon see how we manage matters."

"So monsieur is really one of us?" remarked the second journalist whom Lucien did not know.

"Yes, yes, Frédéric; come, no pranks! You see, Lucien," said Étienne to the new recruit, "how frankly we treat you, and you are not to shrink back when occasion comes. We all love Nathan, but we are going to attack him; you'll understand it all before long. Now, let's divide up the theatres. Frédéric, do you want the Français and the Odéon?"

"If these gentlemen consent," replied Frédéric.

They all nodded; but Lucien saw the envy in their eyes.

"I keep the Opera, les Italiens and the Opéra-Comique," said Vernou.

"Very good! and Hector takes the vaudeville theatres," said Lousteau.

"And I, am I to have none?" said the other man whom Lucien did not know.

"Hector will let you have the Variétés, and Lucien the Porte-Saint-Martin," replied Étienne. "Give him the Porte-Saint-Martin, Lucien; he is crazy about Fanny Beaupré; and you can take the Cirque-Olympique in exchange. As for me, I have Bobino, the Funambules, and Madame Saqui. What is ready for to-morrow's issue?"

"Nothing."

"Nothing!"

"Nothing."

"Gentlemen, you must be brilliant for my first number. You must devise something. The Baron du Châtelet and his cuttlefish can't last much longer; the author of 'The Solitary' is worn to rags."

"The fact is, we want more victims," said Frédéric.

"Suppose we take the virtuous men of the Right,"

cried Lousteau ; " it is easy enough to turn them into ridicule."

" Let us begin with a series of portraits of the ministerial orators," said Hector Merlin.

" Do it yourself," said Lousteau ; " you know them ; they belong to your side, and you can satisfy some intestine hatreds. Stick your claws into Beugnot, Syrieys de Mayrinhac, and others. The articles may as well be ready in advance ; we sha'n't be so harrassed at the last moment."

" We might invent a few cases of refusals to bury, with more or less aggravating circumstances," said Merlin.

" No, don't let us tread in the tracks of the great constitutional papers ; they have their church pigeonholes full of *canards.*"

" Canards ? " said Lucien.

" We call a fact that seems true, but is invented for an item when times are dull, a *canard,*" said Hector. " The *canard* was a discovery of Benjamin Franklin, the man who invented lightning-rods, canards, and republics. That journalist hoaxed the Encyclopedists so famously that Raynal, in his ' Philosophical History of the West Indies,' mentions two of his *canards* as authentic facts."

" I never heard of that," said Vernou. " What were they ? "

" The story of the Englishman who sold a negress who had saved his life, after making her a mother to increase her value ; and the noble pleading of the girl by which she won her cause. When Franklin came to Paris he acknowledged these *canards* to Monsieur

Necker, to the great confusion of the French philoso-
phers, — that's how the new world has twice corrupted
the old."

"Newspapers regard all things as true which are in
any way probable," said Lousteau; "that's our start-
ing-point."

"Criminal justice does the same," said Vernou.

"Well, adieu till to-night, at nine o'clock, here,"
said Merlin.

They all rose, shook hands, and the session ended
with every sign of the most friendly regard.

"What did you say or do to Finot to make him have
an agreement with you himself," said Étienne to Lucien
as they went downstairs. "You are the only one he
has bound to him in that way."

"I? nothing; he proposed it," said Lucien.

"Well, have any arrangements with him you like, I
am willing; we shall only be the stronger, you and I."

On the ground-floor they encountered Finot, who took
Lousteau aside into the inner office.

"Sign the agreement now so that the new editor
may think it was done yesterday," said Giroudeau,
presenting to the new journalist a stamped paper.

As Lucien read over the agreement he heard a rather
sharp discussion going on between Étienne and Finot
as to the proceeds of the journal. Étienne wanted his
full share of the percentages imposed by Finot. There
must have been a satisfactory compromise, however,
for they both came out soon after on cordial terms.

"Meet me at eight o'clock, Galeries de Bois, at
Dauriat's," said Étienne to Lucien as they parted.

A young man had meantime come in with the timid,

anxious air Lucien himself had worn in that office but a short while ago. The fledged journalist now felt a secret pleasure in observing how Giroudeau practised the same little tricks on the new-comer with which the old campaigner had fooled him ; his new interests made him thoroughly understand the necessity of this performance, which placed an insurmountable barrier between all new-comers and the garret of the elect.

"There is not money enough as it is to pay all the writers," he remarked to Giroudeau.

"And if there were more of you, there would be still less for each," replied the veteran ; "and what then?"

The old soldier twirled his loaded cane and marched off, clearing his throat, "Broum—broum," and seeming not a little astonished when he saw Lucien jump into the elegant equipagē which was waiting for him at the corner of the boulevard.

"You are the military in these days, we are the civilians," he said to him.

"I declare to you," said Lucien to Coralie, "those young men seem to me the best fellows in the world. Here I am, a journalist, with the certainty of earning six hundred francs a month if I work like a horse ; but I shall sell my two books and write others, and these friends are going to organize me a success ! So I say with you, Coralie, *vogue la galère !*"

"You'll succeed, my own ; but don't be as good and kind as you are handsome, or you'll come to grief. Be *bad* with men ; that's the best way."

Coralie and Lucien went to drive in the Bois de Boulogne, where they again met the Marquise d'Espard, Madame de Bargeton, and the Baron du Châtelet.

Madame de Bargeton looked at Lucien with a courteous air which might have passed for a bow.

Camusot had ordered the best of dinners at Véry's. Coralie, knowing that she was rid of him, was so charming to the poor shopkeeper that he could not remember when he had ever seen her, during the fourteen months of their connection, so gracious and so attractive.

"Yes, yes," he said to himself, "I'll stay by her *anyhow.*"

He offered her secretly an investment in the Funds to the amount of six thousand francs a year if she would consent to remain his mistress, agreeing to shut his eyes to her relations with Lucien.

"Betray that angel! why, look at him, you poor old fellow, and think what you are!" cried Coralie, motioning towards the poet, whom Camusot had persuaded to drink till he was slightly light-headed.

Camusot looked, and resolved to await the moment when poverty would again give him the woman it had once before delivered to him.

"I will be your friend only," he said, kissing her forehead.

XVI.

RE DAURIAT.

Lucien left Coralie and Camusot to go to the Galeries de Bois. What a change his initiation into the mysteries of journalism had produced in his mind! He now mingled without timidity among the crowd that was flowing through the galleries; he assumed a look of insolence because he had a mistress, and he entered Dauriat's shop with a free and easy air because he was a journalist. There he found a distinguished company. He offered his hand to Blondet, Nathan, Finot, in fact to all the men of literature with whom he had fraternized for the last week; he thought himself a personage, and hugged the belief that he was able to surpass his comrades; the slight exhilaration of the wine he had taken helped him wonderfully; he was witty and brilliant, and showed that he could swim with the current.

Nevertheless, Lucien did not gather in all the spoken or unspoken approbation on which he counted. He observed signs of jealousy among these men, — less uneasy, perhaps, than curious to know what exact place this newly imported talent would hold, and how large a share of the profits of the press it would swallow up. Finot, who thought Lucien a mine to work, and Lousteau, who considered he had rights over him, were the only ones who cordially smiled upon the poet.

Lousteau, having already assumed the bearing of an editor-in-chief, rapped sharply on the glass partition between the wareroom and the office.

" In a moment, my friend," answered the publisher, putting his head over the green curtains and recognizing the new editor.

The moment lasted an hour, after which Lucien and his friend were admitted to the sanctuary.

" Well, have you thought about our friend's poems? " said Lousteau.

" Of course I have," replied Dauriat, leaning majestically back in his armchair. " I have looked them over, and I made a man of great taste, a good judge, read them, for I myself do not pretend to understand poetry. My good friend, I buy fame ready-made, as the Englishman buys love. You are as great a poet as you are handsome. On the word of an honest man, — remark, I don't say on the word of a publisher, — your sonnets are magnificent; they are not labored, which is rare when a writer has imagination and fancy both. Moreover, you know how to rhyme, one of the gifts of the new school. Your ' Daisies,' are a fine collection; but the matter would be a small one for me; I have time for none but great enterprises. My conscience won't let me publish your sonnets, for I could not do them justice; there is not money enough in them to pay the costs of a great success. Besides, you won't keep to poetry; the book, in any case, would be an isolated one. You are young, young man! you have brought me the everlasting collection of first verses such as all men of letters write when they leave college; they all think an immense deal of their poems then, and laugh at them afterwards. Your friend Lousteau must have plenty of his early poems put away among his old socks. Have n't you some you once believed in, Lousteau?" asked Dauriat, with a sly look at Étienne.

"If not, how could I write prose?" replied the editor.

"Well, you see it is so, though he never mentioned it to me; but he knows the difficulties of publishing. For me," he went on in a flattering tone, "the question is not whether these sonnets show poetic talent; you have merit, and a great deal of merit; if I were beginning my career as a publisher I should doubtless commit the mistake of publishing you. But I now know better; I have sleeping-partners and associates who would not hear of it; I lost more than twenty thousand francs last year on poems, and they would n't listen to my printing any more. But the real question to my mind is not that. I admit that you are a true poet, but will you be a prolific one; will you hatch out sonnets regularly? Can I have ten volumes; will you make it an enterprise? Of course not; you are a delightful prose-writer; you have too much sense to spoil your prose style with verse; you will soon be earning thirty thousand francs a year in journalism, and you would n't be such a fool as to barter that for the three thousand francs that you will scarcely make anyhow out of your strophes and cantos and dithyrambs —"

"You know, Dauriat, that Monsieur de Rubempré is now on the paper," said Lousteau.

"Yes," answered Dauriat. "I've read his article; and it is for his own sake that I refuse to publish his 'Daisies.' Yes, monsieur, I shall give you more money during the next six months for the articles I shall ask you to write' for me than you could ever earn by unsalable poems."

" But fame?" cried Lucien.

Dauriat and Lousteau laughed.

" Good heavens!" said Lousteau, " he still keeps to illusions!"

" Fame," replied Dauriat, " means ten years of persistent toil and waiting with an equal chance of a hundred thousand francs loss or gain to the publisher. If you find fools who are willing to print your poems you will respect me a year from now, when you have seen what the result will be."

"Have you the manuscript here?" said Lucien, coldly.

" Yes, here it is, my young friend," replied Dauriat, whose manners to Lucien were singularly softened.

Lucien took the parcel without noticing the condition of the string, so convinced was he that Dauriat had read the sonnets. He left the office without seeming either disappointed or displeased. Dauriat accompanied the two friends into the outer room, talking of his own weekly journal and Lousteau's daily. Lucien held the bundle of manuscript carelessly in his hand.

" Do you think Dauriat has read, or got any one to read your sonnets?" whispered Lousteau.

" Yes," said Lucien.

" Look at the fastening."

Lucien then perceived that the string and the ink line were exactly together.

" Which of my sonnets did you particularly like?" he said, pale with anger, to the publisher.

"They are all remarkable, my friend," replied Dauriat, "but the one to the 'Daisy,' is delightful; the closing thought is so delicate, so refined; it was that which convinced me that your prose writings will have great success. I at once recommended you to Finot for the paper. Write us articles, and we will pay handsomely for them. You see, it is all very well to dream of fame, but don't neglect the solid thing; take the bird in hand. When you are rich you can write poems."

The poet darted out into the gallery to avoid an explosion; he was furious.

"Come, come," said Lousteau, who followed him, "be calm; accept men for what they are, — means to your hand. Do you want to revenge yourself?"

"At any cost," replied the poet.

"Here's a copy of Nathan's book which Dauriat has just given me; the second edition comes out to-morrow. Read the book and dash off an article that will demolish it. Félicien Vernou can't endure Nathan, whose success injures, he thinks, the chances of his forth-coming novel. One of the manias of a little mind like his is that there's no room under the sun for two successes. He'll get your article into the great daily he is on."

"But what can I say against the book? It is fine," cried Lucien.

"Ah, ça! my dear fellow, do learn your business," said Lousteau, laughing. "The book, whether a masterpiece or not, is to become under your pen a piece of stupidity, or a dangerous, unhealthy work."

"But how?"

"Change its merits into defects."

"I am not capable of such a performance."

"My dear friend, a journalist is an acrobat; you must get accustomed to the inconveniences of the profession. Now I'm a kind-hearted fellow myself, and this is the way I manage under similar circumstances. Pay attention to what I say, young one! Begin by calling it a fine work, and you can amuse yourself by saying just what you think about that. The readers will say, 'Come, this critic has no jealousy, he'll be impartial.' After that they'll regard what you say as conscientious. Having thus obtained the readers' respect, you go on to regret the necessity of blaming the new school into which such books are about to lead French literature.. France, you will say, should guide the intelligence of the whole world; until to-day French writers have, from age to age, maintained that ascendency, and have held Europe to the path of analysis and philosophical research by the power of their style and the originality of form they have given to ideas. Here you stick in, to please the bourgeoisie, a panegyric on Voltaire and Rousseau, or Diderot, Montesquieu, and Buffon. You explain how relentless the French language is; how it spreads like a varnish over thought. You set up axioms, such as: 'A great French writer is always a great man; he is compelled by his language to be perpetually thinking; it is not so with other countries,' etc. You prove that proposition by comparing Rabener, a satirical German moralist, with la Bruyère. There is nothing which gives a more solid base to criticism than a few remarks about an unknown foreign author. Kant, for instance, is Cousin's pedestal. Once on that ground you get off a saying which sums up and explains to fools the system of our men of genius of the last century; you call their literature the 'literature of ideas.' Armed with that saying, you can fling the illustrious dead at the heads of all living authors. You explain how in these days there is growing up a literature which abuses the use of dialogue (the easiest form of writing), and of description, which relieves both author and reader of the necessity of thinking. You compare the novels of Voltaire, Diderot Sterne, Lesage, so solid, so incisive, with the modern novel, where everything is presented in scenes and images, and which has been *over-dramatized* by Walter Scott. In a style of that kind, you say, there is no room for creative talent. The Walter Scott romance is, you remark, a style, not a system. You attack the fatal modern style in which ideas are diluted and run to a thread, — a style attainable by the commonest intellect, and with which any one can be an author at the smallest cost; a style on which you fasten the name of 'imaginary literature.' At this point you turn the argument against Nathan and show that he is a mere imitator, and has only the external appearance of genius. The fine, compact form of the eighteenth century is lacking in his work, he substitutes events for sentiments. His action is not life; his scenes offer no ideas. Throw out a lot of sentences like that, and the public will catch them up. In spite of the great merits of this book, it seems to you dangerous, even fatal. It opens the Temple of Fame to the million; you see in the distance an army of petty writers who will hasten to imitate this novel style. Here you can launch out into bitter lamentations on the decadence of taste, and you can slip in praise of Messrs. Étienne, Jouy,

Tissot, Gosse, Duval, Jay, Benjamin Constant, Aignan, Baour-Lormian, Villemain, the ballet-dancers of the Napoleonic liberals, under whose protection Vernou's paper lives. You point to that glorious phalanx, resisting the invasion of the romanticists, holding firmly to ideas and rules of language, against mere images and gabble, maintaining the great Voltairean school against the English and German innovations, just as the seventeen orators of the Left struggle for the nation against the ultras of the Right. Under cover of those names, revered by the majority of Frenchmen (who will always be for the Opposition party) you can crush Nathan, whose work, in many respects so fine, opens the way to a rush of literature without ideas. From that point, you see, it is no question of Nathan and his book, but of France and her glory. The duty of all honest and courageous pens is to firmly oppose such foreign importations. There, you flatter and please subscribers. The French reader is too intelligent to be misled. If publishers, by means to which you will not allude, juggle a success, the real public soon judges for itself and corrects the mistakes of the five hundred fools who compose the literary vanguard. You then say that having had the good fortune to sell off the first edition of this book, the publisher is very audacious in producing a second, and you regret that so able a man understands the instincts of the French people so little. There's your outline : salt it with a little wit, season it with a touch of vinegar, and Dauriat is fried brown on the gridiron. But don't forget to pity Nathan for a passing mistake, and say that if he abandons this style he may become one of the greatest lights of modern literature."

Lucien listened in stupefaction. As Lousteau spoke the scales fell from his eyes; he beheld literary truths he had never once suspected.

"What you say," he cried, "is true; it is just!"

"If it were not, you couldn't batter down Nathan's book," replied Lousteau. "Now you've learnt, my boy, the first style of article we employ to demolish a work. That's the pick-axe style. But there are plenty of others; you'll learn them in time. When you are obliged to speak well of a man you don't like, — for proprietors and editors-in-chief are sometimes under compulsion, — you string out a lot of negations; that's what we call the 'article de fonds.' You put the title of the book at the head of the article; then you begin with general reflections, in which you hark back to the Greeks and Romans if you like, after which you end up by saying, 'These considerations bring us to the book of Monsieur Such-a-one, which will form the subject of a second article.' Of course the second article is never written. It is smothered between two promises. In this case you are not writing against Nathan, but against Dauriat; therefore you want the pick-axe style. If a work is really good the pick doesn't do it any harm, but if the book is bad it goes to the core of it: in the first case it only harms the publisher; in the second it does good service to the public. These styles of literary criticism are used also for political criticism."

Étienne's cruel lesson opened many cells in Lucien's imagination; he began to understand the trade thoroughly.

"Let us go to the office," said Lousteau; "we shall find our friends there, and we can agree on a cavalry charge against Nathan. It will make them laugh, you'll see."

When they reached the rue Saint-Fiacre they went straight to the garret where the paper was concocted, and Lucien was much surprised and gratified to see the alacrity with which his comrades agreed to demolish Nathan's book. Hector Merlin took a slip of paper and wrote the following notice, which he immediately carried off to his newspaper : —

"A second edition of Monsieur Nathan's book is announced. We intended to say nothing of that work ; but this appearance of success will oblige us to publish an article, less upon the book itself than upon the tendencies of our rising literature."

At the head of the witticisms for the next day's issue, Lousteau put the following item in his own paper : —

" Dauriat is about to publish a second edition of Monsieur Nathan's book. He apparently forgets the legal proverb, ' Non bis in idem.' All honor to rash courage."

Étienne's lesson was like a torch to Lucien, whose desire to avenge himself on Dauriat took the place in his soul of conscience and inspiration. Three days later, during which time he did not leave Coralie's chamber, where he worked beside the fire, waited on by Bérénice, and caressed in his moments of weariness by the attentive and silent Coralie, Lucien produced a fair copy of a three-columned criticism, in which he had really risen to a surprising height. It was nine o'clock at night. He ran to the office, found his associates, and read them his article. They listened attentively.

Félicien said not a word, but he took the copy and rushed downstairs.

"What's the matter with him?" cried Lucien.

"He has carried your article to his printing room," said Hector Merlin. "It is fine; there's not a word to take out nor a line to add."

"It was only necessary to show you the way," said Lousteau.

"I'd like to see Nathan's face when he reads that to-morrow," said one of the journalists, on whose face beamed a gentle satisfaction.

"One had better be your friend," remarked Merlin.

"Then you really think it good?" asked Lucien, eagerly.

"Blondet and Vignon won't like it," said Lousteau.

"Here's a little article," said Lucien, addressing his editor-in-chief, "which I have written for you; if you approve it I can supply a series in the same style."

"Read it," said Lousteau.

Lucien thereupon read them one of those delightful articles which subsequently made a fortune for the "petit journal," — articles in two columns sketching the minor details of Parisian life, — a face, a type, an ordinary event, or some salient singularity. This first specimen, entitled "Les Passants de Paris," was written in the new and original method by which thought is struck out from the clash of words, while the chiming of adverbs and adjectives awakens attention. This article was as different from the sober and earnest article on Nathan as "Les Lettres Persanes" differ from "L'Esprit des Lois."

"You are a born journalist," said Lousteau. "That

shall go in to-morrow: write as many more as you like."

"Ah, ça!" said Merlin. "Do you know Dauriat is furious at the two bombs we showed him in his shop. I've just come from there. He fulminated oaths and cursed Finot for having sold you the journal. As for me, I took him aside and whispered in his ear: 'These "Daisies" will cost you dear. Why did you give the cold shoulder to a man of talent whom the newspapers have snapped up?'"

"Dauriat will be annihilated by your article when he reads it in to-morrow's paper," said Lousteau to Lucien. "Now you see what journalism is. Don't you? And, by the bye, your other vengeance is on the way. The Baron du Châtelet came here this morning and asked for your address. The ex-beau hasn't any nerve; he is in despair. Haven't you seen to-day's paper? There was another article about him, very funny, headed, 'Funeral of the Heron wept by the Cuttlefish.' Madame de Bargeton goes by the name of the 'Cuttlefish' in society, and Châtelet is called 'Baron Heron.'"

Lucien took the paper and could not help laughing as he read the article which was written by Vernou.

"They'll soon capitulate," said Hector Merlin.

Lucien did his share joyously of the jokes and lesser articles required for the morrow's paper, the company meanwhile smoking and talking, relating the adventures of the day, the foibles of comrades, or some new detail of their lives. This conversation, which was eminently sarcastic, witty, and ill-natured, gave Lucien a key to the inner life and morals of literature.

"Come, Lucien," said Lousteau, "while they are

setting up the paper I'll take a turn with you and present you to the managers, and usher you behind the scenes of your four theatres; after that we'll go and frolic with Florine and Coralie at the Panorama-Dramatique."

Arm in arm they went from theatre to theatre, at each of which Lucien was enthroned as critic, complimented by the managers, and ogled by the actresses, who all knew by this time that a single article of his had given Coralie and Florine such importance that one was engaged at the Gymnase for twelve thousand francs a year, and the other at the Panorama for eight thousand. It was, in fact, a series of small ovations, which magnified Lucien in his own eyes and gave him the measure of his new power. By eleven o'clock the two friends reached the Panorama-Dramatique, where Lucien assumed an air of easy superiority which did marvels. Nathan was there; he held out his hand to Lucien, who took it and pressed it.

"Ah ça! my masters!" said Nathan, looking at the pair, "I hear you are trying to bury me!"

"Wait till to-morrow, my dear fellow, and you'll see then how Lucien has laid hold of you! I give you my word of honor you'll be satisfied. When a criticism is as deep and serious as that is it does a book great service."

Lucien was scarlet with shame.

"Is it very severe?" asked Nathan.

"It is serious," replied Lousteau.

"Oh, then, there's no harm done," said Nathan. "Hector Merlin said at the Vaudeville that I was unmercifully cut up."

"Let him say so, but wait," said Lucien, escaping to Coralie's dressing-room in the wake of the actress as she left the stage in her bewitching Spanish costume.

The next morning as Lucien and Coralie were breakfasting they heard a cabriolet in the somewhat solitary street, the horse of which had the step of a thoroughbred as he was pulled up before the door. Lucien saw from the window a fine English horse, and Dauriat in the act of throwing the reins to his groom before getting out.

" It is the publisher," said Lucien to his mistress.

" Let him wait," said Coralie to Bérénice.

Lucien smiled at the quiet assurance of the young girl, who so instantly identified herself with his interests, and he rushed to kiss her with true effusion ; her native wit had explained to her the whole matter.

This prompt appearance of the overbearing publisher, the sudden humility of the prince of charlatans, was caused by circumstances which are now almost entirely forgotten, so completely has the business of publishing been transformed within the last fifteen years. From 1816 to 1827, the period at which reading-rooms (established in the first instance for the reading of newspapers) undertook to provide their subscribers with new books, and the pressure of the fiscal laws on the press led to the invention of advertisements, publishers had no other means of announcing their publications than by articles inserted in the *feuilletons* or other parts of the daily papers. Up to 1822 French newspapers were printed on such very small sheets that the great journals were hardly larger than what are called the " little journals," now. To resist the

tyranny and exactions of the journalists, Dauriat and
Ladvocat had invented a system of posters, with which
to catch the attention of all Paris, and on which were
displayed, in fantastic type and coloring, vignettes and
even lithographs, which made the poster a poem to the
eye and often a deception to the purse of the amateur.
These posters finally became so original that one of
those maniacs called " collectors " possesses an un-
broken series of them. This method of advertising,
confined at first to shop windows and the booths along
the boulevards, though it afterwards spread elsewhere,
was partly abandoned after the introduction of advertisements. Nevertheless, the old poster will always
continue to exist, especially since they have found a way
to plaster the walls with them. The advertisement,
within the reach of moderate finances, which has now
converted the fourth page of all newspapers into a fer-
tile field for speculators, was born of the severity of
the stamp duty, the post-office, and the bonds for the
license. These exactions were first imposed during the
ministry of Monsieur de Villèle, who might at that time
have killed the newspapers by cheapening and vulgariz-
ing them ; instead of which he created a privileged class
among them by rendering the foundation of others almost impossible. In 1821, therefore, newspapers had
really a power of life and death over the conceptions of
thought and the enterprises of publishers. An article
inserted among the " Paris Items " announcing a new
book was horribly expensive. Intrigues were so complicated in the newspaper offices, and at night on the battle-
field of the press-rooms about the hour when the clicker
decided the admission or rejection of such or such an

article, that the powerful publishers kept a literary man in their pay to write the little items they needed, in which it was essential to put many ideas into few words. These obscure journalists (who were not paid unless the items were inserted) were often obliged to remain all night in the press-room to make sure of the insertion of either some fine article (obtained heaven knows how!) or those little items contained in a few lines, which were called in after years " réclames." In the present day all the habits and ways of literature and of publishing-houses are so much changed that many persons will regard as fabulous this statement of the immense efforts, solicitations, meannesses, and intrigues which the necessity of obtaining these " réclames," forced on publishers, authors, and other seekers after fame. Dinners, cajoleries, gifts, were all employed in the seduction of journalists.

Here is an anecdote which will show the power of these articles. A book by Monsieur de Chateaubriand on the last of the Stuarts was perched on a publisher's shelves in the condition of a " nightingale." A single article written by a young man in the "Journal des Débats" sold the whole edition in a week! At a period when, in order to read a book it was necessary to buy it, ten thousand copies were often put forth in one edition of certain liberal works much praised by the journals of the Opposition; but then, it is true, Belgian piracy did not exist. The preparatory shots of Lucien's friends and Lucien's own article would have the effect of stopping the sale of the second edition of Nathan's book. Nathan could suffer only in his pride; he had nothing to lose for he had already been paid for his work; but

Dauriat was likely to lose thirty thousand francs. In fact, the whole business of his publishing-house may be summed up in the following commercial estimate : one ream of blank paper is worth fifteen francs ; printed, it is worth, according to success, five francs or three hundred francs. A single article, for or against, often decided, in those days, this financial question. Dauriat, who had five hundred reams at this instant for sale, rushed to propitiate Lucien. The late sultan became a slave. After waiting some time restlessly and making as much noise as he could while parleying with Bérénice, he at last obtained an audience with Lucien. The arrogant publisher assumed the smiling air of courtiers as they enter the royal presence, mingled however with a certain self-sufficiency and jollity.

" Don't disturb yourselves, my dear loves ! " he said. " Ah, how charming ! you make me think of a pair of turtle-doves. Who would suppose, mademoiselle, that this man who has the look of a young girl could be a tiger with steel claws, ready to tear our reputations to pieces? My dear fellow," he continued, sitting down beside Lucien, — " Mademoiselle, I am Dauriat," he said, interrupting himself.

The publisher thought best to fire his name as a pistol-shot, finding Coralie not cordial.

" Monsieur, have you breakfasted? will you keep us company ?" said the actress.

" Why, yes ; we shall talk better at table," replied Dauriat. " Besides, by accepting your breakfast I shall have the right to ask you to dinner with my friend Lucien, — for we must be friends now, close friends, as the hand to the glove."

"Bérénice! bring oysters, lemons, fresh butter, and champagne," said Coralie.

"You are too clever a man not to know what brings me here," said Dauriat, looking at Lucien.

"You have come to buy my sonnets?"

"Precisely," replied Dauriat. "First of all, let us lay down our arms on both sides."

He pulled an elegant portfolio from his pocket, took out three bank-bills of a thousand francs each, laid them on a plate, and offered them to Lucien, with a courtier-like air, saying as he did so: —

"Is that satisfactory to monsieur?"

"Yes," said the poet, who felt suddenly plunged into a nameless beatitude at the sight of such an unhoped-for sum. He contained himself, but he was sorely tempted to sing and dance; he believed in Aladdin's lamp, in wizards, — in short, he believed in his own genius.

"So, then, the 'Daisies,' are mine;" said the publisher; "but you will never attack any of my publications?"

"The 'Daisies,' are yours, but I cannot pledge my pen; that belongs to my friends, as theirs to me."

"But you are now one of my authors. All my authors are my friends. You certainly will agree not to injure my business without giving me due notice so that I may evade the attack."

"Yes, certainly, I will promise that."

"To your coming fame!" said Dauriat, raising his glass.

"I see you have read the 'Daisies,'" said Lucien.

Dauriat was not disconcerted.

"My young friend," he said, "to buy your poems without knowing them is the finest flattery a publisher can offer you. In six months you will be a great poet; you will have articles written upon you; every one will fear you; I shall have no difficulty in selling your book. It is not I who have changed, it is you; last week your poems were no more to me than cabbage-leaves, to-day your position makes them daughters of Pieria."

"At any rate," said Lucien, made adorably impertinent and satirical by the sultanic pleasure of possessing a beautiful mistress and the certainty of success, "if you have not read my sonnets you have certainly read my article."

"Yes, my friend; otherwise do you suppose I should be here? It is, unfortunately, very fine, that dreadful article. Ah! you have immense talent, young one. Take my advice, make the most of your vogue," he said, hiding under an appearance of friendliness the extreme impertinence of his words. "But have you seen the paper? have you read your own article?"

"Not yet," said Lucien, "though it is the first time I ever printed a serious bit of prose; Hector has probably sent the paper to my rooms in the rue Charlot."

"Here, read it!" said Dauriat, imitating Talma in "Manlius."

Lucien took the sheet, but Coralie snatched it from him.

"To me the first-fruits of your pen!" she cried, laughing.

Dauriat was throughout extremely flattering and courtier-like; he feared Lucien, and he therefore invited him with Coralie to a grand dinner he was giving to journalists at the close of the week. Then he carried off the manuscript of the "Daisies," telling *his* poet as he did so to come whenever he liked to the Galeries de Bois and sign the agreement which he would have ready. Faithful to the regal airs by which he endeavored to impose on shallow minds and to pass for a Mecænas rather than a publisher, he left the three thousand francs without taking a receipt, refusing Lucien's offer of one with a careless gesture, and kissing Coralie's hand gallantly as he departed.

"Well, dear love, how many of those little rags would you have had if you'd stayed in a hole in the rue de Cluny, plodding in that old library of Sainte-Geneviève?" said Coralie, to whom Lucien had related his whole previous existence. "Those little friends of yours in the rue des Quatre-Vents strike me as simpletons."

The brotherhood were simpletons! and Lucien laughed as he heard this judgment pronounced! He had read his printed article; he had tasted the ineffable joy of authors, that first enjoyment of self-love which never but once bewitches the soul. Reading and re-reading his article he himself saw more clearly the drift and bearing of it. Print is to manuscript what the theatre is to women; it brings into a strong light both beauties and defects; it injures as much as it embellishes; a defect catches the eye even more vividly than a fine thought. Lucien, quite intoxicated with success, gave no thought to Nathan, — Nathan was only a stepping-stone. Lucien swam in joy; he was rich, success was his! For a lad who had lately gone humbly down the steps of Beaulieu, returning to l'Houmeau and the

Postel garret, where he and his whole family had lived on twelve hundred francs a year, the sum which Dauriat had given him was like the mines of Potosi. Memory, still vivid though the perpetual enjoyments of his Parisian life were soon to efface it, recalled to his mind his beautiful, noble sister Eve, her husband David, and his own poor mother. Under this influence he sent Bérénice at once to the coach office with a package of five hundred francs addressed to his mother. To him and to Coralie this repayment seemed a fine action. The actress kissed her Lucien, calling him a model son and brother, and loading him with caresses; for it is noticeable that acts which they consider generous delight these kind creatures, who carry their own hearts in their hands.

"Now that we have got our dinners secured for a time," she cried, "we'll make a bit of a carnival, — you've worked hard enough."

XVII.

A STUDY IN THE ART OF WRITING PALINODES.

CORALIE, who was bent, womanlike, on exhibiting the beauty of a man whom every other woman would envy her, took Lucien to Staub's, for she did not think him sufficiently well dressed. From there the lovers drove to the Bois, returning to dine with Madame du Val-Noble, where Lucien found Rastignac, Bixiou, des Lupeaulx, Finot, Blondet, Vignon, the Baron de Nucingen, Beaudenord, Philippe Bridau, Conti, the great musician, — all artists or speculators ; men who seek to balance great labor by great emotions. They received Lucien cordially. Lucien, confident in himself, displayed his wit as if it were not his stock in trade, and was at once proclaimed " un homme fort," — the favorite praise of the day among these semi-comrades.

" We ought to wait and see what there really is in him," remarked Théodore Gaillard, a poet patronized by the court, who was just now considering the establishment of a little royalist journal called later " Le Réveil."

After dinner the two journalists accompanied their mistresses to the Opera, where Merlin had a box, and the whole company followed them. Lucien thus reappeared triumphantly on the very ground where some months earlier he had fallen so heavily. He walked about the foyer arm in arm with Merlin and Blondet, and stared at the dandies who had formerly ignored him. Châtelet was under his feet! De Marsay, Vandenesse, Manerville, the lions of society, exchanged a few insolent looks with him. Undoubtedly the handsome and now elegant Lucien had been discussed in Madame d'Espard's box, where Rastignac paid a long visit, for Madame de Bargeton and the marquise turned their opera glasses on Coralie. Did Lucien's presence rouse regrets in the heart of Madame de Bargeton? That thought absorbed the poet's mind. Beholding once more the Corinne of Angoulême, a desire for revenge again shook his soul, as it did on the day he was forced to endure the contempt of that woman and her cousin in the Champs Élysées.

"Did you bring a talisman with you from your province?" said Blondet to Lucien some days later, coming in about eleven o'clock, before the latter was up. "His beauty," went on Blondet, turning to Coralie and kissing her on the forehead, "is making ravages from garret to cellar, from the highest to the lowest. I have come with a request, my dear fellow!" pressing the poet's hand. "Madame la Comtesse de Montcornet wishes that I should present you to her. You won't, I am sure, refuse such a charming young woman, at whose house you will meet the pick of the great world"

"If Lucien is nice," said Coralie, "he won't go and see your countess. Why should he run after the great world? He'd be bored to death."

"Do you want to keep him locked up? Are you jealous of well-bred women?" asked Blondet.

" Yes," cried Coralie ; " they are worse than we
are."

" How do you know that, my little pet ? " said
Blondet.

" By their husbands," she answered. " You forget
I once had de Marsay for six months."

" Do you think, my dear," said Blondet, " that I
am particularly anxious to present so handsome a man
as yours to Madame de Montcornet? If you are opposed to it, let us consider that nothing has been said.
But the matter, as I take it, is less about women than
to make truce with Lucien on account of a poor devil
his paper is tormenting. The Baron du Châtelet is fool
enough to take those articles to heart. The Marquise
d'Espard, Madame de Bargeton, and the friends of
Madame de Montcornet feel for ' The Heron,' and I
have promised to reconcile Laura and Petrarch."

" Ah ! " cried Lucien, whose veins glowed with fresh
blood as he felt the intoxicating delight of gratified
vengeance ; " so, then, I really have them under foot?
You make me reverence my pen, adore my friends,
worship the mighty power of the Press. I myself have
not written an article on ' The Heron ' and his loves ;
but I will, — yes ! " he cried, seizing Blondet round the
waist, " I will go to your Madame de Montcornet as
soon as that couple have felt the weight of this flimsy
little thing." He seized the pen with which he had
written the article on Nathan, and flourished it. " To-
morrow I'll launch two columns at their heads ; and
after that we'll see about it ! Don't be uneasy, Coralie ; it is not love, but vengeance, and I mean it shall
be complete ! "

"There's a man for you!" exclaimed Blondet. "If you only knew, Lucien, how rare it is to meet with an outburst like that in this blasé Paris, you would appreciate yourself. You are a daring scamp," he said (or rather he used a still stronger expression); "you are in the path that leads to power."

"And he'll get there," said Coralie.

"He has already gone a good distance in six weeks."

"Yes; and when there's only a step between him and some great success he may stand on my body," said Coralie.

"You love as in the Golden Age," said Blondet. "Lucien, I compliment you on your great article. It is full of new things. You are a past master already."

Lousteau now came in with Hector Merlin and Vernou. Lucien was immensely flattered at being the object of such attentions. Félicien brought him a hundred francs for his article. The journal felt the necessity of at once rewarding such a piece of work and securing the writer to its interests.

Coralie, seeing this procession of journalists, had sent to the Cadran-Bleu, the nearest restaurant, and ordered breakfast; and she presently invited them into the dining-room. In the middle of the repast, when the champagne was mounting to all heads, the true reason of the visit of these comrades was made apparent.

"Lucien, you don't want to make an enemy of Nathan," said Lousteau. "Nathan is a journalist; he has friends; he'll play you some ugly trick when your first book is published. We saw him this morning, and he is much cut up. You'll have to write another article and squirt a lot of praise in his face."

"What! after my article against his book?" cried Lucien.

Blondet, Merlin, Vernou, and Lousteau all interrupted Lucien with a burst of laughter.

"You have invited him to supper here for the day after to-morrow!" said Blondet.

"Your article," said Lousteau, "was n't signed. Félicien, who is n't as green as you, took good care to put a C. to it; and you can in future sign all your letters so in his paper, which you know is pure Left. Félicien had the delicacy not to compromise your future opinions. At Hector's shop, where it is all Right Centre, you can sign with an L. These precautions are only for attacks; we sign our own names to praises."

"The signatures don't trouble me," said Lucien, "but I don't see anything to say in favor of the book."

"Did you really think what you wrote?" asked Hector.

"Yes," replied Lucien.

"Ah! my dear boy, I thought you stronger than that," said Blondet. "On my word of honor, looking at that forehead of yours, I endowed you with the omnipotence of great minds, all strongly enough constituted to judge of everything under its double aspect. In literature, as you 'll find out, every idea has its obverse and its inverse; no one can take upon himself to say which is the wrong side. All is bilateral in the domain of thought. Ideas are dual. Janus is the myth of criticism, and the symbol of genius. There's nothing triangular but God. That which makes Molière and Corneille so incomparably great is the faculty of making Alceste say, ' Yes,' and Philinte, Octave,

and Cinna, 'No.' Rousseau, in his 'Nouvelle Hé-
loïse,' has written a letter for and a letter against
duelling, and I'll defy any one to say what was his real
opinion. Which of us can judge between Clarissa and
Lovelace, Hector and Achilles? Who is Homer's hero?
What did Richardson really mean? Criticism ought to
consider works under all aspects. We are, in fact,
reporters."

"Do you care so very much for what you have written?" said Vernou, with a satirical air. "We salesmen
of phrases live by our trade. When you want to do
fine work and make a book that will last, you can put
your thoughts and your soul into it, cling to it and fight
for it; but as for these little articles, read to-day and
forgotten to-morrow, they are worth nothing but the
money they bring. If you attach importance to such
trash you might as well make the sign of the cross
and pray to the Holy Spirit to help you write a
prospectus."

They all seemed astonished to find that Lucien had
scruples, and they set about reducing them to rags,
under pretence of investing him with the *toga virilis* of
journalism.

"Do you know how Nathan consoles himself for
your article?" said Lousteau.

"How should I know?"

"He cried out: 'Pooh! such little articles are soon
forgotten; a great work lives.' But all the same he'll
come to your supper and grovel at your feet, and kiss
your claws, and declare you are a great man."

"That will be queer," said Lucien.

"Queer!" said Blondet, "it is necessary."

" Well, I consent, my friends," said Lucien, who was slightly tipsy ; " but how am I to set about it?"

" Write three fine columns for Merlin's paper and refute yourself," said Lousteau. " We have just told Nathan, after enjoying his wrath, that he 'll soon be thankful to us for stirring up a controversy that will sell his book in a week. Just now he thinks you a spy and a scoundrel ; day after to-morrow he 'll call you a great man, a Plutarch man, a strong mind. He 'll embrace you as a friend. Dauriat has been here, and you have his three thousand francs ; that trick is played and won. Now, then, get back Nathan's respect and friendship. You did not want to injure any one but the publisher. We never attack and immolate any but our enemies. If it concerned a rival, or an inconvenient talent which we wanted to neutralize, that 's another thing ; but Nathan is a friend. Blondet attacked him in the ' Mercure ' for the pleasure of replying in the ' Débats ; ' as a result, the first edition of the book sold rapidly."

" But my friends, on the word of an honest man, I am incapable of writing praise of that book."

" You shall have another hundred francs," said Merlin. " Nathan has already brought you in ten louis, without counting an article you can write for Finot's weekly, for which Dauriat will be glad enough to pay you a hundred francs, — total, twenty louis ! "

" But what am I to say?" persisted Lucien.

" I 'll tell you how to manage it, my boy," said Blondet, reflecting. " Envy, you 'll say, which fastens on all fine works as a worm on the best fruits, has endeavored to undermine this book. In order to find defects the critic was forced to invent theories and set up two lit-

eratures, — the literature of ideas, and the literature of
images. Start from that, and say that the highest reach
of literary art is to infuse ideas into images. In trying
to prove that the visible should be poetical you can regret that our language is so stubborn towards poesy,
and refer to the blame cast by foreigners on the *posi-
tivisim* of our style ; that will give you a chance to
praise M. de Canalis and Nathan for the service they
have done to France in loosening the conventional
bonds of the language. Knock over your other argument by showing the progress of this century as compared with the eighteenth. Invent the word ' progress ' (capital bamboozlement for the bourgeoisie). Our
young literature is done by pictures, — representations,
in which all forms are mingled : comedy, drama, description, character, dialogue, — woven together by some
interesting plot. The novel, which requires sentiment,
style, and reality, is the greatest of all modern literary
creations. It succeeds comedy, which, under our present manners and customs, is no longer possible, the old
laws being so changed. It contains both the fact and
the idea in its presentations, which require the wit of la
Bruyère and his incisive morality, also a treatment of
characters like that of Molière, and the grand machinery
of Shakspeare, with his painting of the most delicate
shades of passion, — that unique treasure left to us by
our forefathers. Thus the novel is far superior to the
cold mathematical discussions and dry analysis of the
eighteenth century. The novel, you can say epigram-
matically, is an entertaining epic. Cite Corinne, and
bolster yourself up with Madame de Staël. The eighteenth century brought forth the problems which the

nineteenth is called upon to solve ; and it solves them
by realities, but realities which live and move and have
their being ; it allows for the play of passion, an element
ignored by Voltaire, — here a tirade against Voltaire.
As for Rousseau, he only dressed up arguments and
doctrines. Julie and Claire are mere lay-figures, without flesh or blood. You can enlarge on this theme and
say that we owe our young and original literatures to
the Peace and to the Bourbons, — for the article is to
go into a Right Centre paper. Ridicule all makers of
systems. Bring in somewhere an indignant flourish.
'Our contemporary,' you can say, 'has put forth many
errors and false arguments ; and with what purpose? to
depreciate a fine work, to deceive the public, and lead to
the conclusion that a book that is selling well has no sale !
Proh pudor !' That honest oath will arouse the reader.
Enlarge here on the decadence of criticism. And then
wind up with a dictum : 'There is but one literature in
the present day, — that of amusing books. Nathan has
struck out a new vein ; he understands his epoch and
supplies its needs. The need of this epoch is dramatic
work. Drama is the longing of a century in which
politics have been a perpetual pantomime. Have n't
we seen in twenty years,' you can say, 'the Revolution,
the Directory, the Empire, the Restoration?' Besides
this article you can put something into Finot's weekly
paper next Saturday, signed DE RUBEMPRÉ in big
letters. Only, in this last article you must say :
'It is the mission of great works to arouse discussion.
This week such a journal has said thus and so about
Monsieur Nathan's book and such another has vigorously refuted its attack.' You criticise both critics, C.

and L., and you give me a little compliment, in passing, on my article in the 'Débats' when the book first came out; after that you end by declaring that Nathan's work is the finest of our epoch. Thus you'll have made four hundred francs out of your week, besides the satisfaction of having written a good deal of truth on both sides. Intelligent readers will agree with C. or with L. or with Rubempré, — perhaps with all three. Mythology, which is certainly one of the greatest of human inventions, puts Truth at the bottom of a well; consequently buckets are necessary to draw it up, and you've provided the public with three! There you are, my boy; now, march!"

Lucien was bewildered. Blondet kissed him on both cheeks, remarking: "Now I must go to my shop."

They all went off to their various "shops." To these *hommes forts* their newspaper was only a shop. They were to meet again that evening in the Galeries de Bois, where Lucien was to sign his agreement with Dauriat. Florine and Lousteau, Lucien and Coralie, Blondet and Finot, were engaged to dine in the Palais-Royal with Du Bruel.

"They are right," cried Lucien, when he was alone with Coralie. "Men ought to be strong enough to use all means to their ends. Four hundred francs for three articles! Doguereau would scarcely give me that for a book which cost me two years of hard work."

"Write criticisms and get your fun out of it," said Coralie, "and never mind the rest. Don't I dress as an Andalusian to-night, and a Bohemian to-morrow, and a man the next day? Do as I do; bow and scrape for their money, and let's live happy."

Lucien, a lover of paradox, set his wit astride of that capricious mule, the son of Pegasus and Balaam's ass. He galloped over the fields of thought as he drove through the Bois with Coralie, and discovered new and original beauties in Blondet's theme. He dined as the happy dine; he signed his treaty with Dauriat, by which he yielded all rights in the "Daisies," and saw no danger in doing so; then he made a trip to the office, scribbled off two columns, and returned to the rue de Vendôme. The next morning he found that the ideas of the night before had germinated in his head, as it always happens with young minds full of sap, when their faculties have been but little used. Lucien enjoyed the pleasure of thinking over his article, and he gave himself up to it with ardor. As he wrote, thoughts arose which gave birth to contradictions. He was witty and satirical; he even rose to some original conceptions about sentiment and reality in literature. In order to praise the book, he called up his earliest impressions of Nathan's work as he had read it in Blosse's reading-room. Ingenious and subtle, he slid from the former savage and bitter criticism of a satirist into the sentiments of a poet, ending his article with a few final phrases swung majestically, like an urn of incense waving its fragrance towards an altar.

"A hundred francs, Coralie!" he cried, showing her the eight sheets of paper written while she was dressing.

Being much in the vein, he wrote with hasty pen the terrible article he had mentioned to Blondet against du Châtelet and Madame de Bargeton. He tasted during this morning one of the keenest personal pleasures of a journalist, — that of pointing an epigram, polishing the cold steel which is to sheath itself in the heart of a victim, and carving the handle to please the readers. The public admires the careful workmanship; it takes no thought of the malice; it is ignorant that the blade of a saying sharpened by vengeance will rankle in the self-love of a mind stabbed knowingly in its tenderest place. That horrible pleasure, essentially solitary and savage, enjoyed without witnesses, is like a duel with an absent adversary, who is killed from a distance by a crow-quill, as if the journalist had really the fantastic power granted to the possessor of a talisman in Eastern tales. Epigram is the essence of hatred, of hatred derived from all the worst passions of mankind, just as love is the concentration of all its virtues. Hence, all writers are witty when they avenge themselves, for the reason that there are none who do not find enjoyment in it. In spite of the facility and commonness of this faculty in France, every exhibition of it is always welcomed. Lucien's article was calculated to put, and did actually put, his reputation for malignant sarcasm high. It went to the depths of two hearts: it grievously wounded Madame de Bargeton, his ex-Laure, and the Baron du Châtelet, his rival.

"Come, let us go and drive in the Bois," said Coralie. "The horses are harnessed; I hear them pawing; you must n't kill yourself."

"Let us take the article on Nathan to Hector's office. I tell you what it is," said Lucien; "a newspaper is like Achilles' lance, which cures the wounds it makes."

The lovers started, and showed themselves in all their splendor to the eyes of that Paris which had so

lately rejected Lucien, who was now beginning to occupy its mind. To occupy the mind of Paris after we
have once understood its vastness and the difficulty of
becoming anything whatever in the great city is enough
to turn the head of any man with intoxicating enjoyment, and it now turned Lucien's.

" Dear," said the actress, " we will drive round to
the tailor's and hurry your clothes ; you might try them
on if they are ready. If you are going among your fine
ladies, I am determined you shall outdo that monster
de Marsay and little Rastignac, and those Ajuda-Pintos
and Maxime de Trailles, and Vandenesses, and all the
other dandies. Remember that Coralie is your mistress ; but you won't play me any tricks, will you?"

XVIII.

POWER AND SERVITUDE OF JOURNALISTS.

Two days later, — that is, on the evening before the supper which Coralie and Lucien were to give to their friends, — the Ambigu-Comique produced a new play, of which it was Lucien's business to render an account. After their dinner, Lucien and Coralie went on foot from the rue de Vendôme to the Panorama-Dramatique by the Boulevard-du-Temple and past the café Turc, which in those days was a favorite promenade. Lucien heard his luck and Coralie's beauty commented on. Some said Coralie was the handsomest woman in Paris; others declared that Lucien was worthy of her. The poet felt in his element. This life was his true life. The brotherhood were far out of sight; those great souls he had so much admired two months earlier now seemed, when he thought of them, to be almost silly, with their notions and their Puritanism. The word " simpleton," so heedlessly uttered by Coralie, had germinated in Lucien's mind, and was already bearing fruit. He put Coralie into her dressing-room, and sauntered with the air of a sultan behind the scenes, where all the actresses welcomed him with ardent glances and flattering words.

" I must go to the Ambigu and attend to my business," he said.

When he reached the Ambigu the house was full; there was not a single place for him. Lucien went behind the scenes and complained bitterly. The sub-manager, who did not yet know him, told him they had sent two boxes to his paper, and that was all they could do.

" I shall speak of the play according to what I see of it," said Lucien, angrily.

" How stupid you are !" said an actress to the sub-manager; " that is Coralie's lover."

The sub-manager at once turned to Lucien and said: " Monsieur, I will speak to the director."

Thus the smallest matters only proved to Lucien the immensity of the power of the newspaper press, and encouraged his vanity. The director came and obtained permission from the Duc de Rhétoré and Tullia, who were in a proscenium box, to put a gentleman with them. The duke readily consented as soon as he knew it was Lucien.

" You have reduced two persons to a state of misery," said the duke. " I mean the Baron du Châtelet and Madame de Bargeton."

" What will become of them to-morrow, then?" said Lucien. "Until now my friends have only skirmished about them, but I, myself, have fired a red-hot cannon-ball to-night. To-morrow you will understand why we have ridiculed Potelet. The article is entitled ' Potelet in 1811 to Potelet in 1821.' Châtelet is the type of men who renounce their benefactors and rally to the Bourbons. After I have made myself more felt I shall go to Madame de Montcornet's."

Lucien then began a lively conversation with the

young duke, brimming over with wit; he was anxious to prove to this great seigneur how grossly Mesdames d'Espard and de Bargeton were mistaken in despising him; but he gave himself away a little by trying to establish his right to the name of de Rubempré when the Duc de Rhétoré maliciously called him Chardon.

"You ought," said the duke, "to become a royalist. You have shown yourself a man of brilliant wit; now be a man of sound good sense. The only way to obtain a decree from the king which will restore to you the name and title of your maternal ancestors is to ask it as a reward for services actually done by you to the Château. The liberals will never make you a count. I assure you the Restoration will end by getting the better of the press, — the only power it has to fear. It ought to have been muzzled earlier; but it will be soon. Make the most of its last days of freedom to get yourself feared. Before long a name and title will have more power and influence in France than talent. If you are wise now, you can have all, — mind, nobility, beauty, and your future secured. Don't remain a liberal one moment longer than is necessary to make good terms with royalism."

The duke asked Lucien to accept an invitation to dinner which the German minister, whom he had met at Florine's, intended to send him. Lucien was instantly won over by the duke's arguments and charmed to perceive that the doors of salons from which he had felt himself forever banished might still open to him. He admired the power of thought. The Press and intellect were really the means which moved society. It dawned on Lucien's mind that Lousteau might some day repent having opened to him the gates of the temple; he himself could see the necessity of opposing barriers to the ambitions which led men from the provinces to Paris. He asked himself what greeting he would now give to a poet who should fling himself into his arms as he had done into Lousteau's.

The young duke watched the signs of Lucien's meditation, and was not mistaken as to the cause of it; he had revealed to that ambitious mind, a mind without fixed will but not without desire, a whole political horizon; just as the journalists, like Satan on the pinnacle of the temple, had shown him the literary world and its riches at his feet. Lucien could not know that a little conspiracy existed against him among those great people whom he was then wounding in the newspapers, and that the Duc de Rhétoré was concerned in it. The young duke had alarmed the society in which Madame de Bargeton moved by an account of Lucien's cleverness and success among journalists. He was asked by Madame de Bargeton to sound Lucien and was hoping to meet him that evening, as he did, at the Ambigu-Comique. Neither society nor journalists were profound; they were not concerned with deep-laid plans; in fact they had no plans at all; their Machiavelianism extended only, so to speak, from day to day, and consisted merely in being ready for anything, ready to profit by evil as well as good. The young duke had perceived at Florine's supper Lucien's main characteristics; he now caught him by his vanities, and made his first essay in diplomacy by tempting him.

When the piece was over Lucien rushed to the rue Saint-Fiacre to write his article upon it. He made it,

intentionally, harsh and cutting; and took pleasure in
thus trying his power. The melodrama was better than
that of the Panorama-Dramatique; but he wanted to
see if he could, as he had been told, kill a good play
and make a poor one successful. The next day, when
breakfasting with Coralie, he unfolded his paper and
was not a little astonished to read, after the article on
Madame de Bargeton and du Châtelet, his criticism on
the Ambigu so softened during the night that although
the witty analysis was retained, a favorable instead of
an unfavorable verdict came out of it. The article would
evidently benefit the receipts of the theatre. His wrath
was indescribable, and he determined, as he said, to say
two words to Lousteau. He felt he was already a
necessary person, and he vowed not to let himself be
ruled and managed like a nobody. To establish his
power once for all, he wrote the article in which he
summed up and balanced all the opinions put forth on
Nathan's book, signed it with his name, and sent it to
Dauriat and Finot's weekly journal. Then, as he felt
his hand was in, he wrote another of his " variety "
articles for Lousteau's paper. During their first effer-
vescence young journalists dash off articles with actual
love for the work, and give away, imprudently, all their
flowers·

The next evening the manager of the Panorama-
Dramatique gave the first representation of a vaudeville,
so as to leave Coralie and Florine free. After supper
cards were to be played. Lousteau came for Lucien's
article on the vaudeville, which was written in advance,
Lucien having seen the rehearsal of it, so that there might
be no anxiety as to the make-up of the next day's paper.

After Lucien had read him his charming little "variety" article on some Parisian peculiarity (such articles made the fortune of the paper), Lousteau kissed him on both eyes, and called him a journalistic providence.

"Then why do you amuse yourself by changing the meaning of my articles?" demanded Lucien, who had written the brilliant article for no other purpose than to give additional force to his complaint.

"I?" exclaimed Lousteau.

"If you did n't, who did change my article?"

"My dear fellow," said Lousteau, laughing, "you are not yet posted in the business! The Ambigu takes twenty subscriptions, of which only nine are served, — to the manager, the leader of the orchestra, the sub-manager, the mistresses of all of them, and the three proprietors of the theatre. In this way each of the three boulevard theatres pays eight hundred francs to the paper. There is as much more to be got out of the boxes they give to Finot, without counting the subscriptions of actors and authors. That scoundrel Finot makes at least eight thousand francs a year out of the boulevard theatres alone. You can judge by the little theatres what he makes out of the great ones. Now, don't you understand? we are expected to be indulgent."

"I understand that I am not free to write what I think."

"Pooh! what matter, if your nest is feathered?" cried Lousteau. "What grievance have you got against the theatre? You must have some reason for murdering that play. Murdering for murder's sake injures the paper. When a journal strikes a blow for justice only it produces no effect. Come, what was it? Did the manager neglect you?"

"He did not keep a seat for me."

"Very good!" said Lousteau. "I'll show him your article, and tell him how I softened it; you'll find yourself better off than if it had appeared as written. Ask him to-morrow for your tickets; he'll sign you forty blanks a month, and I'll take you to a man with whom you can arrange to sell them. He'll buy them all at fifty per cent discount on the theatre price. We do the same trade with tickets that we do with books. The man is another Barbet; he is the head of the *claque*. His house is not far from here; let us go there now; there's time enough."

"But, my dear Lousteau, Finot is doing an infamous business in levying such indirect taxes on thought. Sooner or later —"

"Bless me! where do you come from?" cried Lousteau, interrupting him. "For whom and what do you take Finot? Beneath his false good-humor, beneath that Turcaret air of his, beneath his ignorance and his stolidity, he has all the shrewdness of the hatter from whom he was born. Did n't you see in that office of his an old soldier of the Empire? That's his uncle; and the uncle is not only an honest man, but he has the luck to pass for a fool. He is the scapegoat in all pecuniary transactions. In Paris an ambitious man is rich if he has beside him and devoted to him a henchman who is willing to be a scapegoat. In journalism as well as in politics there are a multitude of cases in which the leaders must never appear. If Finot ever becomes a political personage his uncle will be his secretary, and will receive for him the contributions levied in the public offices on any important matter. Giroudeau, whom you'd take at first sight for a fool, has precisely the sly shrewdness which makes him an unfathomable ally. He is always on duty; he prevents us from being tormented and overwhelmed by clamors, protests, jealousies, appeals. I don't believe there's his like on any other paper."

"He plays his part well," said Lucien; "I've seen him at work."

Étienne and Lucien went to the rue du Faubourg-du-Temple, where the editor-in-chief stopped before a fine-looking house.

"Is Monsieur Braulard at home?" he asked the porter.

"What!" exclaimed Lucien, "do you call the chief of the *claqueurs* monsieur?"

"My dear fellow, Braulard has property worth twenty thousand francs a year; he has all the dramatic authors of the boulevard in his clutches; they have an account with him as if he were a banker. Authors' tickets and complimentary tickets are sold, and Braulard sells them. Try statistics (a very useful science if not abused): fifty complimentary tickets every night from each of the boulevard theatres make two hundred and fifty tickets daily; they are worth, say, forty sous apiece; Braulard pays one hundred and twenty-five francs to the authors, and runs his chance of getting as much more. Thus, you see, authors' tickets alone bring him in four thousand francs a month, — a total of forty-eight thousand a year. But let us suppose a loss of half, for he can't always sell his tickets."

"Why not?"

"Because persons who pay for their seats at the box-offices have as much right as those who hold the complimentary tickets, which are never for reserved places; and the theatre keeps all its choice places. Then there's fine weather and bad weather. But say that Braulard earns about thirty thousand francs under that head. Then he has his *claqueurs;* that's another industry. Florine and Coralie pay tribute to him; if they didn't they wouldn't be applauded at their entrances and exits."

Lousteau gave these explanations in a low voice as they went up the stairs.

"Paris is a queer world," said Lucien, finding greed and self-interest squatting in every corner.

A neat servant-woman ushered the two journalists into Monsieur Braulard's room. The ticket-dealer, who was seated in an office chair before a large roller-desk, rose when he saw Lousteau. He was wrapped in a gray camlet dressing-gown, with trousers *à pied* and red slippers, exactly like a physician or a lawyer. Lucien saw at once that he was a specimen of the rich self-made man of the people, — common in feature, with shrewd gray eyes; the hands of a clapper; a complexion over which debauches had passed like rain on a roof; grizzly hair, and a rather thick voice.

"You have come, of course, for Mademoiselle Florine, and your friend for Mademoiselle Coralie," he said. "I know you very well, monsieur," he went on, addressing Lucien. "Don't be uneasy. I have bought the business at the Gymnase. I'll look after your mistress and warn her if there's any cabal against her."

"That's not to be refused, my dear Braulard," said Lousteau. "But we have come about our newspaper tickets at the boulevard theatres, — I as editor-in-chief, and Monsieur de Rubempré as reporter at each theatre."

"Ah, yes! I heard that Finot had sold the paper. In fact, I knew all about the affair. He's getting on, Finot is. I give a dinner for him at the end of the week, and I shall be very glad if you will do me the honor and pleasure of being present with your spouses. There'll be plenty of fun and racket. We shall have Adèle Dupuis, Ducange, Frédéric Du Petit-Méré, and Mademoiselle Millot, my mistress. We'll laugh much, and drink more."

"I hear Ducange has lost his suit; he must be hard-up."

"I've lent him ten thousand francs; the success of his 'Calas' will pay me back; I'm warming it up! Ducange is a clever fellow; he has got it in him." (Lucien thought he was dreaming when he heard a man of this stamp weighing the talents of authors.) "Coralie has greatly improved," continued Braulard, addressing him with the air of a competent judge. "If she's a good girl I'll support her secretly when they get up their cabal against her, as they are sure to do, on her first appearance at the Gymnase. Listen: I'll put a number of men in the galleries to smile at her and give little murmurs of satisfaction, which always start applause. That's a trick which fixes attention on an actress. I like Coralie; she pleases me; you ought to be satisfied with her; she has feelings. Ha! I can make any one fail I please!"

"But let us settle this business of the tickets first," said Lousteau.

"Very good! I'll go to monsieur's house and get them every month. He is a friend of yours, and I'll treat him as I do you. You say you have five theatres, monsieur; they'll give you thirty tickets; that will be something like seventy-five francs a month. Do you want an advance?" said the ticket-dealer, turning to his desk and taking out a pile of money.

"No, no!" said Lousteau; "we'll keep this resource for a rainy day."

"Monsieur," continued Braulard, addressing Lucien, "I'll go round to Coralie in a day or two and settle about the rest."

Lucien had been looking, not without surprise, at Braulard's office; in it were books, engravings, and suitable furniture. As they passed out through the salon he saw that everything was well chosen, — neither mean nor tawdry nor too luxurious. The dining-room seemed to be the most ornate of the rooms, and he remarked upon it.

"Braulard is gastronomical," said Lousteau, laughing; "his dinners, famous in dramatic literature, are in keeping with his funds."

"I have good wines," said Braulard modestly. "Ah! here are my hands!" he cried, hearing gruff voices and shuffling steps on the staircase.

As Lucien and Lousteau passed out, they met the evil-smelling brigade of *claqueurs* and street ticket-sellers, — fellows in caps, ragged trousers, and threadbare coats; with hangdog faces, bluish, greenish, bloated, wizened, long beards, and eyes both wheedling and savage, — a horrible population which lives and swarms on the boulevards of Paris; selling in the morning trinkets and chains and such things for twenty-five sous apiece, and appearing at night under the chandeliers to ply their other trade of clapping to order, — a population which adapts itself to all the miry needs of Paris.

"These are the Romans who applaud Nero!" said Lousteau, laughing; "they make the fame of dramatic authors and actresses! Seen at close quarters, that fame does n't seem much better than ours, does it?"

"It is difficult to have any illusions about anything in Paris," replied Lucien. "All is taxed, sold, coined, — even success!"

The guests at Lucien's supper were Dauriat, the manager of the Panorama, Matifat and Florine, Camusot, Lousteau, Finot, Nathan, Hector Merlin and Madame du Val-Noble, Félicien Vernou, Blondet, Vignon, Philippe Bridau and Mariette, Giroudeau, Cardot and Florentine, and Bixiou. He had invited his friends of the brotherhood. Tullia, the *danseuse,* who was said to favor Du Bruel, was also of the party, but without her duke; also the proprietors of the newspapers on which Nathan, Vignon, Merlin, and Vernou were employed. Altogether there were thirty guests, Coralie's dining-room not being large enough to hold more.

Towards eight o'clock, when the chandeliers were lighted, and the furniture, hangings, and flowers all wore the festal air which gives to Parisian luxury the atmosphere of a dream, Lucien was conscious of an indefinable sense of happiness, of gratified vanity and hope, as he saw himself master of this dazzling scene;

20

but he never once asked himself by what means nor by whose hand this fairy wand had touched him.   Florine and Coralie, dressed with all the excessive luxury and artistic magnificence of actresses, smiled on the poet of the provinces like two angels sent to open for him the gates of the Paradise of Dreams.   He was dreaming now.   In a few short months his life had so utterly changed, he had passed so rapidly from the extreme of misery to the extreme of opulence that momentary doubts did come to him, as they do to sleepers who while dreaming know themselves asleep.   Nevertheless, his eyes, open to all this beautiful reality, expressed a confidence in his position which envy would have called fatuity.   He himself had changed.   His healthy color had paled ; a look of langour was in the moist expression of his eyes ; but his beauty gained by it.   The consciousness of power and his own strength shone from a face now enlightened by love and experience. He had come front to front with the literary world and society, and he believed he could walk through both a conqueror.   To this poet, who never reflected until the burden of misfortune was upon him, the present seemed to be without a care.   Success had filled the sails of his bark ; at his orders lay the instruments he needed for his projects, — a fine house, a mistress for whom all Paris envied him, a carriage and horses, and an incalculable sum of money in his desk !   His soul, his heart, his mind were, one and all, metamorphosed ; he thought no more of doubting methods in presence of such glorious results.

All this will seem so plainly insecure to persons of experience who know Parisian life that it is only necessary to indicate the fragile basis on which the material happiness of the actress and her poet rested. Without involving himself in any payment, Camusot had requested the tradesmen who supplied Coralie to let her have all she wanted on credit for at least three months. The horses, servants and household went on as if by enchantment for these two children eager for enjoyment, and who did enjoy everything to the full.

Coralie now caught Lucien by the hand and led him, alone, before the company arrived, into the festive scene of the dining-room, set out with a splendid silver service, candelabra bearing forty wax-lights, and the regal delicacies of a dessert arranged by Chevet. Lucien kissed Coralie on the forehead and pressed her to his heart.

"I shall succeed, my child," he cried, "and I will reward you for all your love and all your devotion."

" Pooh ! " she said, " are you satisfied ? "

" I should be hard to please if I were not."

" That smile is all I want," she answered, gliding her lips to his lips with a serpent-like motion.

When they returned to the salon they found Florine, Lousteau, Matifat, and Camusot, arranging the card-tables. Lucien's friends were arriving, — for all these people now styled themselves his friends. They played from nine o'clock till midnight. Happily for him, Lucien did not know how to play any game ; but Lousteau lost a thousand francs and borrowed them of Lucien, who felt himself obliged to oblige his friend. About ten o'clock Michel Chrestien, Fulgence Ridal, and Joseph Bridau arrived. Lucien, who went to talk with them in a corner, thought they looked rather cold and serious,

not to say constrained. D'Arthèz could not come; he
was just finishing his book. Léon Giraud was busy
with the first number of his review. The brotherhood
had sent its three artists, who, they thought, would seem
less out of their element than the rest at a rollicking
supper.

"Well, my friends," said Lucien, assuming a little
tone of superiority, "you'll see now that ' paltry wit'
can prove good policy."

"I don't ask anything better than to be mistaken,"
said Chrestien.

"Are you living with Coralie till you can do better?" asked Fulgence.

"Yes," said Lucien, trying to look unconscious.
"Coralie had a poor old shopkeeper who was fond of
her, but she dismissed him. I'm better off than your
brother Philippe," he added, looking at Joseph Bridau;
"he can't manage Mariette."

"In short," said Fulgence, "you are now a man like
the rest of them, and will make your way."

"A man who will always be the same to you in whatever position he may be," replied Lucien.

Michel and Fulgence looked at each other, exchanging smiles which Lucien saw; and he saw, too, how
ridiculous that speech had made him.

"Coralie is adorably beautiful!" cried Joseph
Bridau. "What a picture could be made of her!"

"And she is good," said Lucien. "I tell you she is
angelic. You shall paint her portrait; take her, if you
like, for the model of your Venetian brought to the
senator by an old woman."

"All women who love are angelic," said Michel.

Just then Raoul Nathan rushed up to Lucien in a frenzy of friendship, caught his hands and wrung them : —

"My good friend," he cried, "not only are you a great man, but you have a heart, which is much more rare in these days than genius. You are faithful to your friends. I am yours for life and death; I shall never forget what you have done for me this week."

Lucien, at the summit of delight in finding himself thus adulated by a man whom Fame was already crowning, looked at his three friends of the brotherhood with a fresh air of superiority. Nathan's effusion was due to the fact that Merlin had shown him a proof of the article on his book which would appear the next day.

" I only consented to write the attack in order that I might reply to it," whispered Lucien in Nathan's ear; "I am with you heartily."

He returned to his friends, delighted with a circumstance which seemed to justify the speech at which they had smiled.

" I am now in a position to be useful to d'Arthèz, when his book comes out," he said. "That alone is enough to keep me in journalism."

" Are you free in it?" asked Michel.

" As free as a man can be when he is indispensable," replied Lucien.

Towards midnight they sat down to table and the actual festivities began. The talk was much freer than it had been at Matifat's, for no one suspected or remembered the opposition of feeling and opinion on the part of the three members of the brotherhood. These young minds, so depraved by the habit of writing for and against both things and men, now came into conflict with each other, flinging to and fro among them the terrible maxims of moral law to which journalism was then giving birth. Claude Vignon, who wished to maintain the august and dignified character of criticism, complained of the tendency of the minor papers towards personalities, and declared that before long writers would bring their own selves into disrepute. Lousteau, Merlin, and Finot, thereupon openly defended the system, called in journalistic slang *blague*, — a word for which there is no equivalent in any other language, meaning a combination of smartness, humbug, satire, vim, gossip, falsehood, invention, and the written " gift of the gab ; " this they maintained was a touchstone by which to recognize real talent.

" Those who come safe out of that trial are strong men," said Lousteau.

" Besides," said Merlin, " ovations to great men need, like the Roman triumphs, a chorus of insults."

" Ha ! " said Lucien, " all those who are attacked will believe in their triumph."

" Are you thinking of number one ? " cried Finot.

" Yes, your sonnets ! " said Michel Chrestien, — " is that how they are to reach the fame of Petrarch ? "

" *Faciamus experimentum in anima vili,*" replied Lucien, smiling.

" I'll-luck to those whom newspapers do not discuss, and on whom journalists cast no garlands at their start. They 'll stay like saints in their niches, where no one pays them the least attention," said Vernou.

" It is success that kills in France," said Finot ; " we

are all so jealous of each other that we try to forget and make the public forget the other man's triumph."

" It is true that contention is the life of literature," said Claude Vignon.

" As in nature, where it results from two principles which contend," cried Fulgence Ridal, " the triumph of the one over the other is death."

" And the same in politics," added Michel Chrestien.

" We have just proved it," said Lousteau. " Dauriat will sell two thousand copies of Nathan's book this week. Why? The book has been attacked, and is well defended."

" An article like this," said Merlin, taking the proof out of his pocket, " is certain to sell a whole edition."

" Read it," said Dauriat. " I'm a publisher wherever I am, even at supper."

Merlin read Lucien's article; every one applauded.

" Could that article have been written without the first?" asked Lousteau.

Dauriat drew from his pocket a proof of Lucien's third article and read it aloud. Finot listened attentively to what was destined for the second number of his weekly paper, and, in his quality as editor-in-chief, he exaggerated his praise.

" If Bossuet had lived in our century," he cried, " could he have written better?"

"No," said Merlin; " but if Bossuet were living now he 'd be a journalist."

" To Bossuet the Second!" said Claude Vignon, lifting his glass and bowing ironically to Lucien.

" To my Christopher Columbus!" said Lucien, bowing to Dauriat.

"Bravo!" cried Nathan.

"Is it a surname?" said Merlin maliciously, with a glance at Finot and Lucien.

"If you go on in this way," said Dauriat, "these gentlemen," with a sign towards Camusot and Matifat, "cannot follow you. Wit is like cotton, — if you spin it too fine it breaks; so said Bonaparte."

"At any rate, gentlemen," said Lousteau, "we ourselves are the witnesses of a truly surprising, unheard-of event in journalism, — I mean the rapidity with which our friend here has been transformed from a provincial to a journalist."

"He was born a newspaper man," said Dauriat.

"My sons," said Finot, rising, with a bottle of champagne in his hand, "we have all promoted and encouraged the start of our young Amphitryon, and he has, I may say, surpassed our expectations. I propose to baptize him journalist in due form."

"Crown him with roses, — the emblem of his double conquest!" said Bixiou, with a bow to Coralie.

Coralie made a sign to Bérénice, who fetched a quantity of old artifical flowers from the actress's bedroom. A wreath of roses was soon made, and the rest of the flowers were seized and grotesquely put on by those who were most drunk, while Finot, the head-priest, poured champagne upon the handsome blond head of the poet, and pronounced the sacramental words : "In the name of Pen, Ink, and Paper, I pronounce thee journalist. May thy articles sit easy on thee!"

"And be paid without deduction of blanks," added Merlin.

At this moment Lucien saw the saddened faces of

Michel Chrestien, Fulgence, and Joseph Bridau, who took their hats and left the room amid a shower of imprecations.

" Queer Christians ! " said Merlin.

" Fulgence used to be a good fellow," said Lousteau, ' but they have perverted his moral sense."

" Who have ? " asked Claude Vignon.

" A lot of serious young men who meet in a philosophical-religious hole in the rue des Quatre-Vents, where they bother themselves about the general meaning of humanity," answered Blondet.

" Oh ! oh ! oh ! "

" They are trying to find out if it turns in a circle or is making progress," went on Blondet. " They have been dreadfully troubled of late about the straight line and the curved line ; they think the Biblical triangle a contradiction, and they have got some new prophet, I don't know who he is, who has pronounced in favor of the spiral."

" Men might invent far more dangerous nonsense," cried Lucien, wishing to defend the brotherhood.

" You think such theories nonsense," said Félicien Vernou, " but there comes a time when they are transmuted into pistol-shots and guillotines."

" They have n't got farther as yet," said Bixiou, " than exploded ideas, and picking up dead men like Vico, Saint-Simon, and Fourier. But I'm terribly afraid they 'll turn my poor Joseph Bridau's head."

" They have led my old college friend and compatriot Horace Bianchon to give me the cold shoulder," said Lousteau.

" Is n't their visible head Daniel d'Arthèz," said

Nathan, "a small young fellow whom they expect to swallow us all up one of these days?"

"He is a man of genius!" cried Lucien.

"Not worth this glass of sherry to me," said Claude Vignon, laughing.

From this point of the feast each man began to unbosom himself to his neighbor. When clever men arrive at this point and give up, so to speak, the key of their hearts, it is very certain that drunkenness has them in hand. An hour later all these guests, who were now the best friends in the world, told each other they were great men, strong men, men to whom the future belonged. Lucien, as master of the revels, had retained a certain amount of lucidity of mind; he listened to all these sophisms, which completed the work of his demoralization.

"My children," said Finot, "the Liberal press must put new life into its onslaughts; nothing can be said just now against the government; and that's a bad look-out for the Opposition. Which of you will undertake to write a pamphlet demanding the re-establishment of the laws of primogeniture? That will give us a chance to declaim against the secret schemes of the court. It shall be well paid."

"I will," said Hector Merlin; "those are my political opinions."

"Your party will say you compromise it. No; do you write the pamphlet, Vernou; Dauriat will publish it; we'll all keep the secret."

"What will you pay for it?" asked Vernou.

"Six hundred francs. Sign it 'Comte C——.'"

"Very good!" said Vernou.

" That's taking the *canard* into politics with a vengeance," said Lousteau.

" It is only attributing intentions to the government, and unchaining public opinion to give it warning," said Finot.

" Well," said Claude Vignon, " I shall never get over my astonishment at a government allowing a parcel of scamps like us to direct public ideas and opinions."

" If the ministry commits the folly of rising to that bait, and comes down into the arena, we can march it round with drums beating ; if it gets angry we can embitter the question and get the populace angry too. A newspaper risks nothing, where the powers that be have everything to lose."

" France is a cipher until the day when journalism is suppressed," continued Claude Vignon. " You are encroaching hour by hour," he added, addressing Finot. " You are Jesuits, without their faith, their fixed purpose, their discipline, and their union."

The party now returned to the card-tables ; the lights of dawn soon paled the candles.

" Your friends from the rue des Quatre-Vents were as gloomy as condemned criminals," said Coralie to her lover the next day.

" They were judges, not criminals," said Lucien.

" Pooh ! judges are much more amusing," responded Coralie.

XIX.

RE-ENTRANCE INTO THE GREAT WORLD.

LUCIEN lived for a month with his time entirely taken
up by suppers, breakfasts, dinners, and other festivities, — carried onward by the resistless current of pleasures and easy employments. He reflected no longer.
The power of reflection in the midst of the complications of life is the unmistakable sign of a strong will,
which poets, or feeble natures, or purely spiritual minds,
cannot counterfeit. Like most journalists, Lucien lived
from day to day, spending his money as he earned it,
paying no heed to the periodic payment of his expenses, — that crushing necessity of these Bohemian
lives. His dress and its accessories rivalled those of
the greatest dandies. Coralie delighted, like all such
fanatics, in adorning her idol. She ruined herself in
giving her dear poet all that elegant outfit of superfluities he had so coveted during his first walk in the Tuileries. Lucien now had wondrous canes, a charming
eyeglass, diamond buttons, clasps for his morning cravats, rings *à la chevalière*, and marvellous waistcoats
in sufficient number to enable him to match his colors
as he pleased. He was a full-blown dandy.

The day on which he accepted an invitation from the
German diplomatist and appeared in the great world,
his transformation excited a sort of envy among the

young men who were present, — men who took the right of the road in the kingdom of fashion; such as de Marsay, Vandenesse, Ajuda-Pinto, Rastignac, Maxime de Trailles, the Duc de Maufrigneuse, Beaudenord, Manerville, etc. Men in fashionable life are jealous of each other with the jealousy of women.

The Comtesse de Montcornet and the Marquise d'Espard, for whom the dinner was given, had Lucien between them, and overwhelmed him with flatteries.

"Why did you abandon society," asked the marquise, "when it was so ready to welcome you? I have a quarrel with you on my own account. You owed me a visit, and I have never yet received it. I saw you the other night at the Opera, but you did not deign to look at me."

"Your cousin, madame, had so positively dismissed me —"

"You don't understand women," said Madame d'Espard, interrupting him. "You have wounded the most angelic heart and the noblest soul I know. You are ignorant of all that Louise was trying to do for you, and how delicately and wisely she was proceeding — Oh, yes, she certainly would have succeeded!" added the marquise, replying to a mute denial from Lucien. "Her husband is now dead, as he was sure to die, of indigestion. You cannot suppose that she would ever have been willing to become Madame Chardon. But the title of Comtesse de Rubempré was well worth obtaining. Love is a great vanity, which needs to be harmonized with all the other vanities, especially in marriage. If I had loved you to extremes, — that is to say, to the length of marrying you, — I confess I should not like to be called Madame Chardon. You must see that. Now that you have learned the difficulties of life in Paris, you know how many turnings and windings we must all make to reach our object. You surely admit that the favor Louise wished to obtain for you — an unknown young man without fortune — was an almost impossible one; she could not, therefore, neglect a single precaution. You men have great intelligence, but we women, when we love, have more than the cleverest man. My cousin intended to employ that ridiculous Châtelet — I can't help laughing over your articles about him," she said, interrupting herself.

Lucien did not know what to think. Initiated into the treachery and trickery of journalism, he was wholly ignorant of the same vices in society; in spite of his native perspicacity he was to be roughly taught them.

"Is it possible, madame," he said, his curiosity keenly excited, "that 'The Heron' is not under your protection?"

"In society we are forced to be polite even to our enemies, and to seem to be amused by bores; and we sometimes appear to sacrifice our friends in order to do them better service. You are still very new to life. How can you, who attempt to write, remain so ignorant of the every-day deceits of the world? If my cousin seemed to sacrifice you to 'The Heron,' it was necessary in order to profit by his influence in your behalf; for the baron stands extremely well with the present ministry. We have tried to show him that up to a certain point your attacks will be useful to him, in order to reconcile him with you hereafter. The ministry console him for your persecutions because, as des Lupeaulx told them, while the liberal press turns du Châtelet to ridicule, it will let the government alone."

" Monsieur Blondet has led me to hope for the pleasure of seeing you at my house," said the Comtesse de Montcornet, when Madame d'Espard left Lucien to his reflections. " You will meet a few artists, a few writers, and a woman who has the strongest desire to meet you, — Mademoiselle des Touches ; a very rare talent among our sex, and one to whose house you ought to go. Mademoiselle des Touches, or Camille Maupin, if you prefer her pseudonym, has one of the most remarkable salons in Paris. She is immensely rich. They have told her you are as handsome as you are witty, and she is dying to see you."

Lucien could only express himself in thanks and look at Blondet with envious eyes. There was as much difference between a woman of the style and quality of the Comtesse de Montcornet and Coralie as between Coralie and a mere girl of the streets. This countess — young, beautiful, and clever — had the peculiar fairness of Northern women for her distinguishing beauty. Her mother was born Princess of Scherbellof; consequently the minister had shown her the most respectful attentions before dinner.

By this time the marquise had finished the disdainful sucking of a chicken-wing.

" My poor Louise," she resumed to Lucien, " had so much regard for you ! I was in her confidence as to the fine future she dreamed of. She would have borne many things, but not the contempt you showed in returning her letters. We women forgive cruelties, — they are often a sign of confidence ; but indifference, no !

Indifference is like polar ice; it stifles everything.
Well, you must admit you lost your future by your own
fault. Why did you break away? Even if you were
rather disdainfully treated, you had your fortune to
make, your name to recover. Louise was thinking of
all that."

"Then why not have told me?" asked Lucien.

"Good heavens! it was I myself who advised her
not to do so. Come, between ourselves, I will tell you
that, seeing you so unused to society, I feared you, —
I feared that your inexperience, your heedless ardor,
might destroy or disarrange her plans. Can you now
remember what you were then? Admit that if your
double of that day were here now you would feel as I
did then; there is no resemblance between him and
you. That was the only wrong we were guilty of; but
there is not one man in a thousand who unites a great
talent with so marvellous an aptitude for social adapta-
tion as you have shown. You are indeed a surprising
exception. You made the transformation so rapidly,
you caught our Parisian air and manner so easily, that
I did not recognize you in the Bois a month ago."

Lucien listened to this great lady with pleasure in-
expressible. She said these flattering words with a
simple, confiding, piquant air; she seemed so interested
in his welfare that he thought it was another phase of
his luck, like that of his first evening at the Panorama-
Dramatique. Ever since that happy evening the world
had smiled upon him; he believed that he possessed, in
virtue of his youth, a talismanic power, and he resolved
to test the marquise, — determined in his own mind not
to let her fool him.

" May I ask, madame, what those plans were that are now chimerical?" he said.

" Louise wished to obtain a decree from the king giving you the right to bear the name and title of de Rubempré. She wished to bury Chardon. That first favor, easily obtainable then, but which your present political opinions have made almost impossible now, would have been a fortune to you. You treat these ideas as flimsy and frivolous; but we know life; we know how solid are the advantages of a title when borne by a handsome and elegant young man. Present to an English beauty, or indeed to any heiress, ' Monsieur Chardon,' or ' Monsieur le Comte de Rubempré,' and you will see the difference in the welcome. The count may be deep in debt, but all hearts are open to him; his beauty, set in the light of his title, is like a diamond well mounted. ' Monsieur Chardon ' would not even be noticed. We have not created these ideas; they reign supreme everywhere, — even among the bourgeoisie. You are turning your back on fortune. Look at that charming young man over there, — the Vicomte Félix de Vandenesse; he is one of the private secretaries of the king. The king is extremely fond of young men of talent, and that particular one was not much better equipped when he came from his province than you were, and you have ten times his mind; but you have no name, — no family! You know des Lupeaulx, don't you? Well, his own name is a good deal like yours; it is Chardin. He would not sell his little farm of des Lupeaulx for a million. He will be Comte des Lupeaulx before long, and his grandson will become a great seigneur. If you continue in your present

21

mistaken course you will certainly fail.   See how much wiser Monsieur Émile Blondet is than you!   He is on a paper which supports power; all the powers of the day look favorably upon him; he can mingle safely among liberals because he is known to have sound views; he deliberately chose his opinions and his protectors.   That pretty young woman on the other side of you was a Demoiselle de Troisville, with two peers of France and two deputies in her family.   She made a rich marriage on account of her name; she receives everybody, has great influence, and will move the whole political world for that little Monsieur Blondet! What can a Coralie do for you?   Help you to make debts, and wear yourself out with pleasures in a few years from now.   You place your affections badly, and you arrange your life ill, — that is what the woman whom you take pleasure in wounding said to me the other night at the Opera.   While deploring the misuse you are making of your talents and your beautiful youth, she was not thinking of herself, but of you."

"Ah! if that were true, madame!" exclaimed Lucien.

"Pray, why should you doubt my word?" said the marquise, casting a cold and haughty look on Lucien, which annihilated him.

He was so confused that he said nothing, and the offended marquise said no more.   This piqued him; but he felt that he had done a clumsy thing, and he resolved to repair it.   He turned to Madame de Montcornet and began to speak of Blondet, praising his merits as a writer.   This was very well received by the countess, who invited him to a small party at her house, asking him if it would give him pleasure to meet Madame de Bargeton, who, in spite of her recent mourning, would be there. It was not a large party; merely the meeting of a few friends.

" Madame la marquise thinks the wrong was all on my side," said Lucien ; " therefore it is her cousin who must say if she will meet me."

" Stop those ridiculous attacks the papers are making on her, which compromise her with a man she despises, and you can soon make your peace with her. I am told you think she cast you off; I can only say I have seen her grieving over your desertion. Is it true that she left the provinces with you, and for you? "

Lucien looked at the countess, not daring to answer.

" How can you distrust a woman who has made such sacrifices for you? " went on Madame de Montcornet. " Besides, beautiful and intelligent as she is, she deserves to be loved under all circumstances. Madame de Bargeton cared less for you than for your talents. Believe me, women love intellect before they love beauty ; " and she glanced at Blondet.

In the house of the ambassador Lucien saw plainly the differences existing between the great world and the questionable world in which he had been living of late. The two aspects of magnificence had no likeness and no point of contact. The loftiness and the arrangement of the rooms of this hôtel, one of the handsomest in the faubourg Saint-Germain ; the ancient gilding and breadth of the decoration, the sober richness of the accessories, all were strange and novel to him ; but the habit he had now acquired of accepting luxury kept him from seeming astonished. His manner was therefore as far removed from assurance and conceit as it

was from obsequiousness or servility. The poet was
good form, and pleased those who had no reason to be
hostile to him; but the fashionable young men, whose
jealousy was roused by his sudden return among them
with his success and his beauty, had such reason. As
the company left the table Lucien offered his arm to
Madame d'Espard, and she accepted it. Eugène de
Rastignac, seeing that the marquise had rather courted
the poet, came up to him on the strength of their being
compatriots, and reminded him of their first meeting at
Madame du Val-Noble's. The young noble seemed in-
clined to ally himself with the great man of the provinces, — inviting him to breakfast some morning, and
offering to introduce him to several of the young men
of fashion. Lucien accepted these proposals.

"The dear Blondet will be there," said Rastignac.

The minister now joined a group composed of the
Marquis de Ronquerolles, the Duc de Rhétoré, de Marsay, General Montriveau, Rastignac, and Lucien.

"Very well done," he said to Lucien, with the German heartiness under which lay a dangerous slyness,
"I am glad you have made peace with Madame
d'Espard. She is delighted with you; and we all know,"
he added, looking at the men around him, "how difficult it is to please her."

"Yes, but she adores intellect," said Rastignac;
"and my compatriot has plenty of that for sale."

"He'll soon find out what a bad traffic he is making
of it," said Blondet, quickly; "then he'll turn and be
one of us."

A chorus began around Lucien on this theme. The
older men threw out a few serious remarks in a despotic

tone ; the younger ones jested frankly about the liberals.

"I am quite sure," said Blondet, "that he tossed up, heads or tails, for Left or Right. But now he must make a deliberate choice."

Lucien began to laugh, remembering his scene in the Luxembourg with Lousteau.

"He chose one Étienne Lousteau for showman," went on Blondet, — "the bully of a petty paper, who sees a five-franc-piece in every column, and whose whole political creed consists in looking for the return of Napoleon and (which strikes me as even more idiotic) for the gratitude and patriotism of the gentlemen of the Left. As a Rubempré, Lucien's sentiments ought to be aristocratic ; as a journalist he ought to be on the side of power, or he will never be a Rubempré nor a secretary-general."

Lucien, who was now invited by the minister to take a hand at whist, excited the utmost astonishment when he declared that he did not know the game.

"My dear friend," whispered Rastignac, "come early on the morning of the day you breakfast with me, and I will teach you the game ; you dishonor our native town of Angoulême, and I assure you, in the words of Monsieur de Talleyrand, that if you don't know whist you are preparing for yourself a miserable old age."

Des Lupeaulx was announced, — a Master of petitions, in favor with the ministry and doing it certain secret services ; a shrewd, ambitious man who quietly pushed himself everywhere. He bowed to Lucien, whom he had already met at Madame du Val-Noble's, with a semblance of friendship which deceived him.

Finding the young journalist in such society, this man, who made friends out of policy, perceived that Lucien was likely to have as much success in society as he had had in literature. He approached the poet through his ambition, overwhelmed him with professions and proofs of interest, in a way to give himself the tone of an old friend, and thus deceived Lucien as to the value of his words and promises. It was one of des Lupeaulx's principles to thoroughly understand the individuals he wanted to get rid of if he found them rivals.

Thus Lucien was outwardly well received by every one. He felt what he owed to the Duc de Rhétoré, to the German minister, to Madame d'Espard, and to Madame de Montcornet. He went up to these ladies and talked to each for a few moments before taking leave, displaying his wit as he did so.

"What conceit!" said des Lupeaulx to the marquise as Lucien left the room.

"He will be rotten before he is ripe," remarked de Marsay, smiling. "You must have some secret reason, madame, for thus turning his head."

Lucien found Coralie in her carriage, which was waiting for him in the courtyard. He was touched by such attention, and told her all about his evening. To his great astonishment, the actress approved of the new ideas that were beginning to amble through his head; she strongly advised him to enroll himself under the ministerial banner.

"You have nothing but hard knocks to get from the liberals," she said; "they are all conspirators, — they killed the Duc de Berry. Can *they* overturn the government? No! You'll never get on through them;

whereas, if you belong to the other side, you will be Comte de Rubempré. You can then do services and be made a peer of France and marry a rich woman. Be an ultra. Besides, it is good style," she added, using the word which to her was the highest of all arguments. "The Val-Noble, with whom I dined to-day, tells me that Théodore Gaillard is really going to start his little royalist paper, called ' Le Réveil,' so as to parry the malice of your paper and the ' Miroir,' and thrust back. According to him, Monsieur de Villèle and his party will be in the ministry before the year is out. Profit by all this, and get in with them now before they come to power. But don't say anything about it to Étienne or to your other friends ; they would very likely play you false about it."

A week later Lucien presented himself in Madame de Montcornet's salon, where he was seized with a violent agitation on seeing once more the woman he had loved sincerely, and whose feelings he had lately lacerated. Louise was metamorphosed. She was now what she would always have been had she never lived in the provinces, — a great lady. Her mourning garments had a choiceness and grace about them which were not those of an unhappy widow. Lucien believed that he counted for something in the coquetry of her appearance, and he was not mistaken. But he had now, like an ogre, tasted young flesh. He remained the whole evening undecided in his feelings, between the beautiful, loving, and seductive Coralie, and the faded, haughty, and exacting Louise. He could not decide on his course. Should he sacrifice the actress to the great lady ? This sacrifice Madame de Bargeton,

who felt her love renewed on again seeing Lucien now
so brilliant and so handsome, expected and awaited
throughout that evening. She had her pains for
naught. Her insinuating words, her coquettish manner, had no result, and she left the salon that night
with an irrevocable desire for vengeance in her heart.

"Well, dear Lucien," she had said when they met,
with a kindliness of manner that was full of Parisian
grace and nobility, "you were to have been my glory,
but you have made me your first victim. I forgive you,
my child, for I know that there is always a remnant of
love in such a vengeance."

By these words, said with an air of regal kindness,
Madame de Bargeton recovered her position. Lucien,
who believed he was absolutely in the right, suddenly
felt that she had put him in the wrong. No mention
was made of the terrible letter in which he had broken
away from her, nor of the causes of the rupture. Women
of the world have a marvellous talent for diminishing
their wrong-doings by pleasant words; they efface them
with a smile, or by a question which pretends surprise.
They remember nothing, they explain all, they question, comment, amplify, play amazement, quarrel, and
end up by getting rid of their evil deeds, as they
wash out spots with soap and water. You know the
spots were there, and very black; but behold! they
are gone, and all is white and innocent. As for you,
you may think yourself lucky if some unpardonable
crime has not been affixed to you. In a moment
Lucien and Louise had returned to their old illusions
about each other; but Lucien, intoxicated with satisfied vanity, intoxicated with Coralie, who made his life

so easy for him, did not reply definitely to a question which Madame de Bargeton put to him with a flicker of hesitation : —

"Are you happy?"

A melancholy "no" would have made his fortune. He thought himself witty and wise in explaining Cora-lie ; he said he was loved for himself, and that ought to make him happy. Madame de Bargeton bit her lips, and the matter ended there. Madame d'Espard pres-ently came up to them with Madame de Montcornet. Lucien felt himself the hero of the evening. He was petted, flattered, and caressed by the three women, who twisted him round their fingers with infinite adroitness. His success in this great and brilliant world was, he felt, nothing short of his former success in journalism. The beautiful Mademoiselle des Touches, so celebrated under the name of Camille Maupin, to whom Mesdames d'Espard and Bargeton presented Lucien, invited him to one of her Wednesday dinners, and seemed much taken by his now famous beauty. Lucien tried to prove to her that he was even more intellectual than hand-some. Mademoiselle des Touches expressed her admi-ration with the naïve rapture and charming affectation of friendship which is so taking to those who do not know the real shallowness of Parisian society, where the habit and the continual need of amusement render novelty the one thing sought for.

"If I pleased her as much as she pleases me," re-marked Lucien to Rastignac and de Marsay, " we could epitomize the novel."

" You both know too well how to write them to wish to act them," replied Rastignac. " Can authors love

authors? There must always come a moment when
they say sharp things to each other."

"It wouldn't be a bad dream," said de Marsay.
"That charming woman is thirty, to be sure, but she
has nearly eighty thousand francs a year. She is adorably capricious, and her style of beauty lasts. Coralie
is a little goose, my dear fellow! only useful to get
your hand in,—for of course a man can't remain without
a mistress ; but if you don't make some distinguished
conquest in society, the actress will be an injury to you
in the long run. I advise you to supplant Conti, who
is just going to sing with Camille Maupin. Ever since
the world began, poetry has had precedence of music."

But as Lucien listened to the singing of Mademoiselle
des Touches and Conti, such schemes flew away.

"Conti sings too well," he said to des Lupeaulx.

Lucien returned to Madame de Bargeton, who took
him into another room, where they found Madame
d'Espard.

"Well, don't you intend to take an interest in him
and assist him?" said Louise to her cousin.

"Monsieur Chardon must first put himself in a position to be assisted without injury to his protectors,"
said the marquise, in a tone that was both gentle and
impertinent. "If he wishes to obtain the letters-patent
which will enable him to resign the unfortunate name
of his father for that of his mother, he certainly ought
to belong to our party."

"In two months' time I shall be able to do so," said
Lucien.

"Very good!" said the marquise, "when that time
comes I will see my father and uncle, who belong to

the king's household; they will speak of you to the chancellor."

The diplomatist and the two women had readily divined Lucien's weakest spot. The poet, enraptured with all these aristocratic splendors, felt unspeakably mortified at the sound of his own name (Chardon), especially as he listened to the sonorous names prefaced by titles with which other men were announced. This pain was renewed wherever he went for the next few days. Moreover, his sensations were equally disagreeable on returning to the scenes of his daily work after spending his evenings in the great world, whither he went in suitable style with Coralie's carriage and servants. He learned to ride on horseback, and galloped beside the equipages of Madame d'Espard, Mademoiselle des Touches, and Madame de Montcornet, in the Bois, — a privilege he had so much coveted on his first arrival in Paris. Finot was enchanted to procure for such a useful reporter a permit to the Opera, where Lucien now spent many of his evenings; for he belonged henceforth to the special world of elegance which frequented it.

The poet returned the attentions of Rastignac and his other fashionable friends by a breakfast; but he committed the blunder of giving it at Coralie's; for he was too young, too much of a poet, too confiding, to suspect the importance of shades of conduct. An actress, kind and good but without education, could not teach him life. The provincial youth proved conclusively to these young men that Coralie was supporting him, — a state of things of which they were jealous, while each condemned it. Rastignac was the one to make the bitterest jokes against it that very evening, and yet he maintained himself in society in precisely the same way; only, he kept up appearances and was able therefore to treat the accusation as calumny.

Lucien had now learned whist; and play speedily became a passion with him. Coralie, eager to avoid all rivalry, was far from disapproving Lucien's course; she encouraged his dissipations with the blindness of a single-minded sentiment, which sees only the present, and sacrifices all, even the future, to the enjoyment of the moment. The characteristics of a true affection are frequently like those of childhood, — absence of reflection, imprudence, heedless improvidence, laughter, and tears.

At this period there flourished a society of young men called *viveurs,* who were rich or poor and all aimless prodigals, — men who lived with extraordinary recklessness; intrepid eaters, but more intrepid drinkers. All were spendthrifts; mingling much wild jesting with an existence which was not so foolish as it was crazy; they recoiled before no impossibility, and gloried in their misdeeds, which were, however, restrained within certain limits. So much originality was developed in their pranks that it was usually impossible not to forgive them. No fact proclaims more distinctly the idleness of mind to which the Restoration had condemned the youth of France. Young men who did not know in what way to expend their vigor, not only flung themselves into journalism, into conspiracies, into literature, into art, but also dissipated in strange excesses the superabounding sap and power of young France. If it toiled, that glorious youth craved pleasure and supremacy; if it followed an art, it wanted treasures; if it were idle, its passions demanded exercise; but whatever path it took it wanted a career, a place, an aim; and the public policy gave it none. These *viveurs* were nearly all endowed with eminent faculties. Some lost those faculties in the aimless life to which they were condemned; others resisted. The most celebrated among them, the most brilliantly capable, Eugène de Rastignac, ended by entering, thanks to de Marsay, a serious career in which he has distinguished himself. The pranks and diversions to which these young men devoted themselves became so famous that many of the vaudevilles of the day were based upon them. Lucien, introduced by Blondet to this dissipated company, sparkled in its midst next after Bixiou, one of the most mischievous minds and inexhaustible satirists of the day.

During the whole of this winter, therefore, Lucien's life was one long inebriation, interrupted only by the sort of journalistic work that was easy to him. He continued the series of his Variety articles, and did at times make strenuous efforts, producing a few fine criticisms carefully thought out. But study was exceptional; the poet never applied himself unless constrained by necessity. Breakfasts, dinners, pleasure-parties of all kinds, evenings in society, and play, took nearly all his time, and Coralie consumed the rest. Lucien never allowed himself to think of the morrow. He saw his so-called friends behaving just as he did, — spending their money as they got it, and careless of the future. Once admitted into journalism and literature on a footing of equality, Lucien perceived the enormous

difficulties he would have to conquer if he endeavored
to rise.   All were willing to have him as an equal; no
one would consent to his becoming their superior.   In-
sensibly, therefore, he renounced the desire for literary
fame, and contented himself with thinking that political
good fortune was easier to acquire.

"Political intrigue rouses fewer opposing passions
than talent; its quiet, concealed proceedings excite no
attention," du Châtelet said to him one day.   (Lucien
and the baron were by this time reconciled.)   "Intrigue
is, in fact, superior to talent, because it makes something out of nothing; whereas the resources of talent are
for the most part spent in making a man unhappy."

Lucien continued his way through this life of ease
and luxury, where the morrow trod upon the heels of
yesterday in the middle of some orgy.   He was still
assiduous in society; he courted Madame de Bargeton,
the Marquise d'Espard, the Comtesse de Montcornet,
and he never missed a single party given by Mademoiselle des Touches.   He went to these parties before
some gay supper or after some dinner of authors or
publishers; the demands of Parisian conversation and
the excitement of play absorbed the remaining ideas
and strength which his excesses left him.   Soon he no
longer had the clear lucidity of mind, the coolness necessary to observe the facts about him and to employ
the tact which those who advance on sufferance must
display at every moment; he was no longer able to
distinguish the moments when Madame de Bargeton's
feelings moved her towards him or withdrew her from
him wounded; he could not see when she pardoned
him, nor when she again condemned him.

Châtelet saw plainly the chances that still remained to his rival, and he became his friend in order to encourage the dissipation which was blunting his energies. Rastignac, who was jealous of his compatriot and found the baron a surer and more useful ally than Lucien, assisted Châtelet. He had reconciled the ex-beau and the poet at a magnificent supper given by him at the Rocher de Cancale. Lucien, who habitually went home in the early morning and did not rise till mid-day, found in Coralie a love that was always the same. Thus the mainspring of his will, weakened by idleness and the failure of resolutions made in moments when he saw his position in its true light, became at last unstrung, responding only to the severest pressure of necessity.

The gentle, tender Coralie, after rejoicing that Lucien was amused, after encouraging his dissipation as a means to the duration of his attachment and the ties that bound him to her, even she had the courage to advise her lover not to neglect his work. Several times she warned him that he had earned almost nothing during his month. Lover and mistress both were frightfully in debt. The fifteen hundred francs received from the sale of the " Daisies " (five hundred having gone to his sister, and a thousand being lent to Lousteau) and the first five hundred which Lucien earned were swallowed up at once. In three months his articles only brought him a thousand francs, though he thought he had been working desperately. But by this time Lucien had adopted the agreeable principles of the *viveurs* as to debts. It is to be remarked that certain truly poetic natures with weak wills, absorbed in sentiment and in rendering their sensations by images, are essentially deficient in the moral sense which ought to accompany all observation. Poets prefer to receive impressions themselves rather than enter into the souls of others and study the mechanism of their feelings. Thus Lucien never asked what became of those *viveurs* who disappeared, nor the cause of their disappearance; he saw nothing of the fate of the so-called friends, some of whom had had property, others positive hopes, others, again, undoubted talent, while many had had intrepid faith in their own destiny, and a fixed determination to take all chances in their favor. Lucien adopted Blondet's axioms as the rule of his future: "All things come out right;" "Nothing can injure those who have nothing;" "We have nothing to lose but what we seek;" "Swim with the current and it must take you somewhere;" "A man of intellect who has a footing in society can make his fortune when he will."

XX.

A FIFTH VARIETY OF PUBLISHER.

This winter, full of pleasures and dissipations, was employed by Théodore Gaillard and Hector Merlin in finding capital with which to start their "Reveil," the first number of which appeared in March, 1822. The affair was managed at the house of Madame du Val-Noble. That witty and elegant courtesan exercised a marked influence over bankers, men of rank, and the writers of the royalist party, who were accustomed to meet in her salon and discuss certain matters which could not be touched on elsewhere. Hector Merlin, to whom the editorship-in-chief of the "Reveil" had been promised, was to have Lucien, now his intimate friend, for his right-hand man, and the latter was also offered the *feuilleton* of one of the ministerial journals.

This change of front in Lucien's position was silently arranged while the pleasures and amusements of his life were going on. This child fancied himself a great politician by concealing for the present his theatrical somersault, and he counted much on obtaining ministerial bounties which would pay his debts and put an end to Coralie's secret anxieties. The actress, always smiling,

22

hid her troubles from him ; but Bérénice boldly warned him that they were heavy. Like all poets, this great man, still in embryo, was extremely pitiful over such distress, and promised to work harder ; but he forgot the promise almost as soon as it was made, and drowned his feelings in a debauch. When Coralie saw the cloud on her lover's brow she scolded Bérénice, and assured Lucien that she could settle all.

Madame d'Espard and Madame de Bargeton were awaiting Lucien's public conversion to ask the ministry, through du Châtelet, for the decree which should grant Lucien the much-desired change of name,—at least they said they were. Lucien had promised to dedicate his " Daisies" to Madame d'Espard, who seemed much flattered by a distinction which authors have since made rare, now that they have come to be a power in the world. When Lucien went to Dauriat and asked why his book did not appear, the publisher gave him several excellent reasons for not as yet putting it in type. He had such and such a work on hand which took all his time. A new volume by Canalis was just coming out, and it was better not to come in contact with it ; Monsieur de Lamartine's second " Meditations" were in press, and two important collections of poems ought not to appear at the same time. . . . Besides, an author ought to trust to the business faculty of his publisher.

Nevertheless, Lucien's needs became so pressing that he was forced to have recourse to Finot, who made him a few advances on his articles. When at night, after supper, the poet-journalist would sometimes explain his situation to his friends the *viveurs*, they drowned his scruples in floods of iced champagne and merriment.

"Debts! was there ever a strong-minded man who had no debts? Debts represented satisfied wants, exacting vices. No man ever forced his way onward until the iron hand of necessity was upon him."

"To great men belongs the gratitude of pawn-shops!" cried Blondet.

"To will all is to owe all," said Bixiou.

"No," said des Lupeaulx, "to owe all is to have all."

The *viveurs* managed to prove to this mere child that his debts would be the golden spur with which to goad the horses that drew the chariot of his fortunes. Look at Cæsar with his forty millions of debt, and Frederick II. receiving a ducat a month from his father! and all the famous and corrupting examples of great men shown in their vices, — never in the omnipotence of their courage and their conceptions!

At last, however, Coralie's furniture and horses and carriage were attached by several creditors, whose bills amounted to four thousand francs. When Lucien went to Lousteau to ask for the thousand francs he had lent him, Lousteau showed him documents which proved that matters were as bad at Florine's as they were at Coralie's; but he offered out of gratitude to put him in the way of finding a publisher for his "Archer of Charles IX."

"How did Florine get into such trouble?" asked Lucien.

"Matifat took fright," replied Lousteau. "We have lost him; but if Florine chooses, he can be made to pay dear for his treachery. I'll tell you about it later."

Three days after Lucien had made this fruitless appeal to Lousteau, the lovers were breakfasting sadly beside the fire in their beautiful bedroom, and Bérénice was cooking eggs on a plate, for the cook and the coachman and the other servants had all departed. They could not sell their furniture, for it was now attached. Not a single article of gold or silver, or of any intrinsic value, remained to them; all were represented by pawn-tickets, forming a small octavo volume that was highly instructive. Bérénice had kept back two forks and two spoons. The little daily journal was of inestimable value to Lucien and Coralie by keeping quiet the tailor, the dressmaker, and milliner, who feared to displease a journalist so long as he was able to write down their establishments.

Lousteau came in as they sat there, crying out, "Hurrah for 'The Archer of Charles IX!' I've just sold off a hundred francs' worth of books; let's divide, my children!"

So saying, he gave fifty francs to Coralie, and sent Bérénice out to get a better breakfast.

"Yesterday Hector Merlin and I dined with some publishers, and we paved the way for your novel with knowing insinuations. It is true you have Dauriat already; but Dauriat is niggardly; he won't give more than four thousand francs for two thousand copies, and you ought to get six thousand. We talked to our new publishers cleverly, and set you above Walter Scott. Yes, you had splendid novels in your pouch. You were not offering a single book, but an enterprise; not one novel, but a series! That word 'series' did the business. So don't forget that you have got in your port-

folio an historical series,—'La Grande Mademoiselle,
or France under Louis XIV.;' 'Cotillon I., or the
First Days of Louis XV.;' 'The Queen and the Car-
dinal, a picture of Paris during the Fronde;' and 'The
Son of Concini, or Richelieu's Intrigue.' All those
novels are to be announced on the cover. We call that
manœuvre striking success in the eye. Keep those fine
titles on the cover and they soon become known, and
you are really more famous for the books you don't
write than for those you have written. The 'In Press'
is another literary dodge. Come, let's be happy! here's
the champagne. I tell you, Lucien, those publishers
opened their eyes as wide as saucers. Why, where are
your saucers?"

"Seized!" said Coralie.

"I see; and I resume," said Lousteau. "Publishers
will believe in all those manuscripts if they see one.
They always want to *see* a manuscript, and pretend to
read it. Let 'em have their fancy. They don't really
read the books, or they would n't publish what they do!
Hector and I gave the impression that you might consider an offer of five thousand francs for three thousand
copies in two editions. Give me the manuscript of 'The
Archer;' and the day after to-morrow we are to breakfast with the publishers, and then we'll get the whip
hand of them."

"Who are they?" asked Lucien.

"Two partners — good fellows, pretty fair in business — named Fendant and Cavalier. One was a clerk
with Vidal and Porchon, the other was the cleverest hand on the Quai des Augustins. They set up in
business about a year ago. After losing a little money

on translations of English novels, they now want to experiment with the indigenous thing. It is said that they are carrying on the business with other people's capital; but it does n't signify to you whom the money belongs to as long as you get some of it."

The next day but one the two journalists went to breakfast in the rue Serpente, Lucien's old quarter, where Lousteau still kept his miserable room in the rue de la Harpe. Lucien, who came to fetch his friend, found that den in precisely the same state as it was on the evening of his first introduction to literary life; but he no longer felt surprised at it; he had been initiated since then into the vicissitudes of a journalist's life, and there was nothing he did not comprehend. The great man of the provinces had received, gambled, and lost the pay of many an article, together with the desire to write them. He had written more than one column by the various tricky processes which Lousteau had described to him as they made their way from the rue de la Harpe to the Palais-Royal on that memorable first evening. Fallen now into the power of Barbet and Braulard, he trafficked in books and theatre tickets; and he was long past recoiling at any praises or any attacks he was ordered to make. Even at this moment he was rejoicing at getting all he could out of Lousteau before it was known that he had turned his back upon the liberals, and would now attack them all the more knowingly because he had studied them in their midst. On the other hand, Lousteau was secretly receiving, to Lucien's disadvantage, a sum of five hundred francs in cash from Fendant and Cavalier, under the name of commission, for having obtained this future Walter

Scott for the publishers who were in quest of a French Scott.

The firm of Fendant and Cavalier was one of those publishing houses which are established without any capital whatever. A great many of that kind existed in those days, and will continue to exist so long as printers and paper-makers consent to give credit to publishers for the length of time required to play seven or eight games of what are called "publications." Then as now, works were bought from authors with notes payable in six, nine, or twelve months. The publishers paid their printers and their paper-makers in the same way; so that they had in their hands for a whole year, gratis, as many, perhaps, as a dozen or twenty works. Supposing two or three of these to be a success, the proceeds of the successful books paid for the unsuccessful ones, and thus they balanced each other, book for book. If the works were all doubtful; or if, by ill luck, the publishers got hold of only good books which could not be sold until they were read and appreciated by the true public; or if their notes falling due were too heavy on them, — they went into voluntary bankruptcy, and sent in their schedules with perfect indifference, being prepared in advance for this result. The chances, however, were in their favor, and they played upon the great green table of speculation with the money of others and not their own.

Fendant and Cavalier were publishers of this description. Cavalier contributed his wits to the business, and Fendant his industry. They possessed a common fund of a few thousand francs, — savings scraped together by their mistresses, — out of which they had given themselves each a salary, which they spent very scrupulously on dinners to journalists and authors, and at theatres, where, as they said, their business was done. This particular pair of semi-swindlers were held to be clever men. Fendant was more tricky than Cavalier. True to his name, Cavalier travelled; Fendant stayed in Paris and managed the business. The partnership was what it usually is between two publishers, — a duel. The firm occupied the ground-floor of one of the old mansions in the rue Serpente, — their office being at the farther end of several large salons converted into warerooms. They had already published a number of novels; such as the "Tour du Nord," the "Marchand de Bénarès," "Takeli," and the novels of Galt, an English author who had no success in France. The fame of Walter Scott attracted the attention of French publishers to English literary products; so much so that they meditated another Norman conquest. They sought for other Walter Scotts, just as, later, the French people looked for asphalts on stony ground, bitumen in marshes, and profits from projected railways. One of the greatest follies of Parisian commerce is to expect the duplication of success, when, in fact, it goes by contraries. Success kills success, — in Paris especially.

So, beneath the title of "Strelitz, or Russia a Hundred Years ago," Fendant and Cavalier bravely added in large letters, " in the style of Walter Scott." They were thirsting for a success; a good book would help to float their stagnant bales; they were, moreover, lured by the hope of getting articles into the papers, which was the grand condition of a good sale in those days; for it is rare that a book is ever bought on its own unassisted merits; it is almost always published and sold for reasons quite foreign to them. Fendant and Cavalier saw in Lucien a journalist, and in his book a manufactured article, the first sale of which would tide them over a period when notes were due.

The two journalists found the partners in their office, the agreement ready, the notes signed. Such promptitude delighted Lucien. Fendant was a small, spare man with a dangerous cast of countenance, — that of a Kalmuck Tartar; small, low forehead, flattened nose, pinched lips, with keen little black eyes, irregular outline of face, a rough skin, and a voice like a cracked bell, — in short, all the outward and visible signs of a consummate rascal; but he compensated for these disadvantages by the honey of his discourse; he reached his ends by talk. Cavalier, a bachelor, a plain-dealing man, and more like the conductor of a diligence than a publisher, had hair of washy fairness, a red face, the heavy build and the eternal gabble of a commercial traveller.

"We shall not have much discussion," said Fendant, addressing Lucien and Lousteau; "I have read the work; it is very literary, and suits us so well that I have already sent the manuscript to the printers. The agreement is drawn up on the stipulated terms, and we always keep strictly to conditions. Our notes are for six, nine, and twelve months; you will have no difficulty in discounting them, and we will refund you the discount. We reserve to ourselves the right to give another title to the book, for we do not like that of

'The Archer of Charles IX. ;' it does not sufficiently excite the curiosity of readers ; there are several kings named Charles ; and in the middle ages there were great numbers of archers. Now, if you had made it 'The Soldier of Napoleon,' well and good ; but 'The Archer of Charles IX !' why, Cavalier would be obliged to give a lecture on the history of France for every copy he sells in the provinces !"

"If you only knew the persons we have to deal with !" cried Cavalier.

"'The Saint Bartholomew' would be a better name," continued Fendant.

"'Catherine de Médicis, or France under Charles IX.,' would be more like Walter Scott," said Cavalier.

"Well, we can make up our minds when the work is printed," said Fendant.

"Whatever you like," said Lucien, "provided the name suits me."

The agreement read, signed, and the duplicates exchanged, Lucien put the notes in his pocket with unalloyed satisfaction.   Then all four went up to Fendant's apartment, where they were regaled on the vulgarest of breakfasts, — oysters, beefsteaks, kidneys stewed in champagne, and cheese ; but these dishes were accompanied with exquisite wines, due to Cavalier, who knew a traveller in the wine trade.   Just as they were sitting down to table, the printer to whom the novel was entrusted astonished Lucien by bringing him the proof of his two first sheets.

"We want to get on fast," said Fendant ; "we expect great things of your book, and we are devilishly in want of a success."

The breakfast, begun at twelve o'clock, was not over till five.

"Where shall I get these notes discounted?" said Lucien to Lousteau as they walked away.

"We had better see Barbet," replied Étienne.

XXI.

JOURNALISTIC BLACKMAILING.

The two friends, rather heated with wine, walked down towards the Quai des Augustins.

"Coralie is immensely surprised at Florine's loss. Florine did not tell her till yesterday, and then she laid it all to you; she seemed bitter enough to wish to leave you," said Lucien to Lousteau.

"That's true," said Lousteau, who suddenly threw away his prudence and unbosomed himself to Lucien. "My friend, — for you are my friend, Lucien; you lent me a thousand francs, and have only asked me for them once, — beware of play. If I had never played I should be prosperous now. I owe every man and God and the devil too. The sheriff is at my heels at this moment. When I go to the Palais-Royal I am forced to double ever so many dangerous capes."

"Doubling a cape" means, in the language of the *viveurs* of Paris, turning out of your way, taking a circuitous path, to avoid either passing the house of a creditor or meeting him. Lucien, who no longer went with absolute indifference through all the streets, knew the manœuvre, but had never before heard its name.

"Do you owe a great deal?"

"No, — a trifle," replied Lousteau; "three thousand francs would clear me. I have tried to pull up; I have stopped playing ; and I have even, in order to pay my debts, done a little *chantage.*"

" What is *chantage?*" asked Lucien, who had never heard the word.

"*Chantage* is an invention of the English press ; they call it · blackmailing.' Those who practise it are so placed that they can influence newspapers. The proprietor of a paper, or an editor-in-chief is supposed to know nothing about it. There is always some one on hand, — a Giroudeau or a Philippe Bridau. Those hirelings find a man who, for some reason or other, wants to escape notice. A great many persons have peccadilloes on their consciences that are very original. There are lots of queer fortunes in Paris obtained in ways that are more or less legal or illegal, — often by criminal manœuvres which furnish uncommonly amusing stories ; such, for instance, as that of Fouché's gendarmerie surrounding the spies of the minister himself and not being in the secret of the forging of the English banknotes, were just on the point of seizing the minister's own clandestine printers ; or the history of Prince Galathione's diamond ; or the Maubreuil affair, and the Pombreton will case, etc. The blackmailer obtains certain evidence, — an important document, perhaps, — and he asks for an interview with the rich man. If the man who is compromised will not pay a certain sum, the blackmailer lets him know that the newspaper press is all ready to divulge his secret. The rich man is frightened ; he negotiates ; and the trick is played. Perhaps you have some risky enterprise on hand which may fail if the newspapers get wind of it. A *chanteur* is sent to you with an offer to buy off the articles.

There are ministers of state to whom *chanteurs* are sent, and who stipulate with them that the paper may attack their political acts, but not their personal doings. There are others who will sometimes give themselves up on condition that their mistresses shall not be attacked. Des Lupeaulx — that fine Master of petitions — is constantly negotiating in this way with journalists. The fellow has made himself a wonderful position in the centre of power by just such relations. He is both an agent of the press and the ambassador of the ministers; he works upon all fears and self-loves; he plays the same game in politics, and buys the silence of the papers as to some loan, or some concession desirable to be made without publicity; here those lynxes, the liberal bankers, get a share of the spoils. You yourself did a little *chantage* with Dauriat; he gave you three thousand francs not to write down Nathan, and called it buying your 'Daisies.' In the eighteenth century, when journalism was in swaddling-clothes, *chantage* was done by means of pamphlets, the destruction of which was bought by favorites and great seigneurs. The inventor of blackmailing was Aretino, a very great Italian of the fifteenth century, who made kings precisely as the journals of the present day make actresses."

"What did you do against Matifat to get your three thousand francs?"

"I had Florine attacked in six papers, and Florine complained to Matifat. Matifat begged Braulard to find out the cause of those attacks. Braulard was fooled by Finot, for I was doing the *chantage*, and he told the druggist that you were demolishing Florine in the interests of Coralie. Giroudeau then told Matifat confidentially that it could all be managed if he would sell his sixth of the weekly paper to Finot for ten thousand francs. Finot was to give me three thousand in case of success. Matifat was just about to conclude the affair, glad enough to recover ten thousand of his thirty thousand, which he thought as good as lost; for Florine had begun to tell him the paper was doing badly. But the manager of the Panorama-Dramatique had some notes he wanted to negotiate, and in order to get Matifat to take them he told him of the trick that Finot was playing him. Matifat, who has a shrewd business head, saw the whole affair. He left Florine, kept his sixth, and is now laughing in his sleeve at us. Finot and I howled in despair. We had had the ill luck to tackle a man who did n't really love his mistress, — a miserable fellow without heart or soul. Unhappily his business is n't one that the press can touch. You can't criticise a druggist as you would bonnets, or fashions, or theatres, or matters of art. Cocoa and pepper and pigments, or tinctures or opium, can't be depreciated in value by a newspaper article. Florine is in a dreadful state. The Panorama-Dramatique closes to-morrow, and she has no engagement."

"Coralie makes her first appearance at the Gymnase in the course of a few days," said Lucien; "perhaps she can help Florine."

"Never!" said Lousteau. "Coralie has n't much mind, but she is not such a fool as to give herself a rival. No; our affairs are well-nigh ruined. But Finot is in such a worry to get back his sixth."

"Why?"

"Because the business is an excellent one. He has a chance to sell out the paper for three hundred thousand francs. Finot would get a third, plus a commission paid by his partners, which latter he will have to share with des Lupeaulx. So I'm going to propose to him a bit of *chantage*."

"*Chantage* seems to be 'Your money or your life!'"

"Better still," said Lousteau; "it is 'Your money or your honor!' Only last week one of the little journals, to whose proprietor a credit had been refused, stated that a watch set in diamonds belonging to a notability of the town had been found in the possession of a soldier of the royal guard, and the facts were promised in another number. The notability hastened to invite the editor-in-chief to dinner. The editor-in-chief certainly gained something, but contemporaneous history has lost a choice anecdote. Whenever you see the press in pursuit of men in power, you may be sure that behind it all there is some discount denied, some service they refuse to render. Blackmailing in relation to private life is what rich Englishmen are most afraid of; it is a large item in the revenues of the British press, which is infinitely more depraved than ours. We are mere children at it. In England they will pay five or six thousand francs for a compromising letter merely to sell it back to the writer."

"How are you going to pinch Matifat?" said Lucien.

"My dear fellow," said Lousteau, "that old villain has written the queerest letters to Florine, — spelling, grammar, thoughts, intensely comic! Matifat is desperately afraid of his wife. We can, without naming him or giving him any chance to lay hold of us, attack him in the very bosom of his lares and penates, where he thinks himself safe. Imagine his fury when he sees the first number of a little tale entitled ' The Loves of a Druggist,' after he has been duly informed that accident had put into the hands of such and such a newspaper a series of his letters, in which he calls ' Cupid ' *Cubid,* and writes ' never ' *nefer.* There 's enough in that eminently funny correspondence to keep subscribers rushing in for a fortnight. He will also be threatened with an anonymous letter to his wife putting her on the scent. The question is, will Florine let herself appear to be persecuting Matifat? She still has principles, — that is, hopes. Perhaps she wants to keep the letters for herself and make her own profit out of them. She is sly ; she 's my pupil. But if Finot makes her a suitable present, or holds out the hope of an engagement, she will give me the letters, which I shall deliver to Finot, — for a consideration. Finot will then deliver the correspondence to his uncle, and Giroudeau will bring Matifat to terms."

This confidence sobered Lucien. His first thought was that he had very dangerous friends ; then he reflected that he had better not break away from them ; because if Madame d'Espard, Madame de Bargeton, and du Châtelet failed him, he might want their terrible assistance. By this time Lucien and Lousteau had reached the miserable shop of Barbet on the quay.

" Barbet," said Étienne, " here are notes of Fendant and Cavalier for five thousand francs, at six, nine, and twelve months ; will you discount them? "

"I'll take them for three thousand!" said Barbet, with imperturbable calmness.

"Three thousand francs!" cried Lucien.

"You won't get as much anywhere else," remarked Barbet. "That firm will fail within three months; but I know they have some good solid works, with a sure but slow sale which they can't wait for. I can buy the whole and pay them in their own notes. In that way I get the books for two thousand francs less than cost."

"Are you willing to lose two thousand francs?" said Étienne to Lucien.

"No!" cried Lucien, horrified at this first rebuff.

"You are wrong," replied Étienne.

"You can't negotiate their paper anywhere," said Barbet. "Your book is Fendant and Cavalier's last throw in the game. They can't print it except by agreeing to leave the copies in the hands of the printers; and a success would only save them for six months; sooner or later, they are bound to burst up. Those men do more tippling than bookselling. As for me, their notes would be a means of doing a stroke of business, and that is why I offer you more than you can get from the regular brokers, who consider only the value of each signature. It is the business of brokers to know if all three signatures would each give thirty per cent in case of failure. Here you have only two signatures, and neither is worth ten per cent."

The two friends looked at each other surprised to hear from the lips of such a cub an analysis which gave in a few words the very essence of discounting.

"Come, no preaching, Barbet," said Lousteau. "To what broker had we better go?"

"Old Chaboisseau, quai Saint-Michel; he does business for Fendant and Cavalier. If you refuse my proposal, you had better see him. But I warn you you'll come back to me, and then I won't give more than two thousand five hundred."

Étienne and Lucien went to the quai Saint-Michel to a small house up an alley, and found Chaboisseau on the second floor, in an apartment most originally furnished. This irregular banker, who was, however, a millionnaire, was fond of the Grecian style. The cornice of the room was Grecian. The bed, standing lengthways against the wall, as in the background of a picture by David, was exquisitely pure in form, and classically draped in purple stuffs of the Empire period, when everything was imitated from Grecian art. The chairs, tables, lamps, candlesticks — in fact, all the accessories — had the delicate, fragile, but elegant grace of the antique. These airy mythological surroundings formed a curious contrast to the habits and ways of the broker. It is observable that the most fantastic of human beings are among the men who are given to the business of handling money. Being able to possess all, and consequently sated and sick of it all, they will take the greatest pains to find some escape from their satiety. Whoever will study this class of men will usually find some mania, some spot in their hearts, about which they are sensitive. Chaboisseau appeared to be intrenched in antiquity as in a fortified camp.

He was a little man with powdered hair, wearing a greenish coat, nut-colored waistcoat, and black breeches terminating in mottled stockings and shoes that creaked.

He took the notes, examined them, and returned them to Lucien, gravely.

"Messrs. Fendant and Cavalier are charming fellows, — young men full of intelligence; but at this moment I have no money," he said in a gentle voice.

"My friend won't make difficulties about the discount," said Étienne.

"I could not take those notes on any terms," said the little old man, whose words cut short Lousteau's suggestion as the knife of a guillotine cuts off the head of a man.

The two friends retired. As they crossed the antechamber, to which point Chaboisseau had prudently conducted them, Lucien suddenly spied among a heap of second-hand books which the broker, once a publisher, had evidently just bought, the great work of the architect Ducerceau on the royal palaces and celebrated châteaus of France, the designs of which are given in this book with extreme care and exactness.

"Will you let me have this book?" asked Lucien.

"Yes," said the broker, becoming a bookseller.

"What price?"

"Fifty francs."

"That is dear, but I want the book; still I can only pay you with these notes which you refuse to take."

"You have one there for five hundred francs at six months; I'll take that," said Chaboisseau, who no doubt owed Fendant and Cavalier some small balance on account.

The two friends returned to the Greek chamber, where Chaboisseau made out a little memorandum of six per cent interest and six per cent commission; in all, a deduction of thirty francs. This he added to the sum of fifty for the Ducerceau, and took from his desk, which was full of coin, four hundred and twenty francs.

"Ah, ça! Monsieur Chaboisseau! those notes are either all good or all bad; why won't you discount the rest?"

"I am not discounting notes; I am paying myself for a sale," said the old man.

Étienne and Lucien were still laughing over Chaboisseau, without understanding him, when they reached Dauriat's, where Lousteau requested Gabusson to tell them of a good broker. The two friends took a cabriolet by the hour and drove to the faubourg Poissonnière, armed with a letter of introduction which Gabusson gave them to what he called "the queerest of human beings."

"If Samanon won't take your notes," added Gabusson, "no one will."

Second-hand dealer in books on the first floor, ditto for coats on the second floor, vendor of prohibited engravings on the third, Samanon was a money-lender on all. None of the personages introduced into Hoffmann's novels, not one of Walter Scott's infernal misers, can compare with what social and Parisian human nature had allowed itself to create in this man, — if, indeed, Samanon is a man. Lucien could not repress a gesture of horror at the aspect of that withered old creature, whose bones seemed trying to pierce through his thoroughly tanned hide, which was blotched with numerous green and yellow spots, like a picture of Titian or Paul Veronese seen near by. One eye was motionless and

stony, the other sharp and shining. The miser, who
appeared to employ the dead eye when discounting, and
the other when selling his obscene pictures, wore a
small, flat wig of a black bordering on rusty, beneath
which his white hair bristled ; his yellow forehead had
a threatening aspect ; his cheeks were sunken squarely
from the line of the jaws ; the teeth, still white, showed
behind his lips, like those of a horse when it yawns. The
contrast between the eyes and the strange grimacing of
that mouth gave him an almost ferocious air ; the hairs
of his beard, hard and sharp, must surely have pricked
like pins. A ragged old coat which had reached the
stage of tinder, a faded black cravat worn to threads by
his beard, and exposing a neck as wrinkled as a turkey's,
showed little desire on the miser's part to modify a sinister countenance by the advantages of dress.

The two journalists found this man seated in a dirty
office employed in gumming labels on the backs of a
pile of old books bought apparently at auction. Lucien
and Lousteau, after exchanging a glance full of questions innumerable excited by the mere existence of such
a being, presented Gabusson's letter and the notes of
Messrs. Fendant and Cavalier. While Samanon was
reading them another person entered the dark and
dingy place. This was a well-known man, of distinguished intellect, dressed in an old frock-coat which
seemed to have been cut out of zinc, so solidified was
it by an accretion of many foreign substances.

"I want my coat, my black trousers, and my satin
waistcoat," he said to Samanon, holding out to him a
numbered card.

As soon as Samanon had pulled the brass handle of

a bell, a woman, who seemed to be Norman by her fresh and rosy complexion, came down the stairs.

"Lend monsieur his clothes," he said, pointing to the distinguished author. "There is some pleasure in dealing with you; but one of your friends brought me a little young man who brutally tricked me."

"Tricked *him!* oh! oh!" said the author to the two journalists, pointing to Samanon with an irresistibly comic gesture.

The great writer gave, like the lazzaroni who redeem their best clothes on feast-days from the pawn-shops, thirty sous into the yellow, wrinkled hand of the broker, who dropped them into the drawer of his desk.

"This is a singular business for you!" said Lousteau to the new-comer, whom he knew, — a victim of opium, who lived absorbed in contemplation in a palace of enchantment, and either would not or could not any longer use his creative powers.

"Samanon lends more on such articles than the pawn-brokers do; and he has, moreover, the awful charity of letting you take out your clothes if there comes a necessity to wear them," was the answer. "I am going to dine at the Kellers' to-night with my mistress. It is easier for me to get thirty sous to borrow my clothes than two hundred francs to redeem them; so I fetch my dress suit, which for the last six months has brought in something like a hundred francs to this charitable usurer. Samanon has already devoured my library, book by book."

"And sou by sou," said Lousteau, laughing.

"I'll give you fifteen hundred francs for those notes!" said Samanon to Lucien.

Lucien gave a jump as if the broker had thrust a red-hot skewer through his head. Samanon looked the notes over carefully and examined the dates.

"And even then," said the usurer, "I must first see Fendant, who ought to secure them with books. You are not worth much," he added, looking at Lucien; "you are living on Coralie, and your furniture is attached."

Lousteau looked at Lucien, who seized his notes and darted from the shop to the boulevard, crying out, "He's the devil!"

There he turned and contemplated that miserable shop, so pitiable and debased with its shelves of shabby, dirty books, and the poet asked himself:—

"What business is done there?"

At that instant the great unknown, who was destined to take part ten years later in the vast but baseless enterprise of the Saint-Simonians, came out of the house extremely well dressed, smiled at the two journalists, and accompanied them as far as the passage des Panoramas, where he stopped to complete his toilet by having his boots blacked.

"When you see Samanon enter the shop of a publisher, a paper-maker, or a printer, you may know they are lost," said the author to the journalists. "Samanon is the undertaker who has come to take a measure for the coffin."

"You won't get your notes discounted now?" said Étienne to Lucien.

"If Samanon refuses," said the stranger, "no one will accept; he is the *ultima ratio.* Gigonnet, de Palma, Werbrust, Gobseck, and other crocodiles who float in the Parisian money market, and with whom,

sooner or later, all men with fortunes to make or unmake have to do, employ him as their scout."

" If you can't discount your notes at fifty per cent,"
said Étienne, " there 's another thing you can do."

" What is that ? " asked Lucien.

" Give them to Coralie, and let her ask Camusot to
cash them. Oh ! you don't like to, hey ? " continued
Lousteau, as Lucien gave a bound. " What childish-
ness ! How can you let such nonsense outweigh your
future ? "

" I shall carry these four hundred francs to Coralie,
at any rate," said Lucien.

" That 's another folly ! " cried Lousteau. " Four
hundred francs will do no good where you want four
thousand. Better keep out enough to get drunk on if
you lose, and play the rest."

" That 's good advice," said the stranger.

They were ten feet from Frascati's, and the words
had a magnetic charm. The two friends went up the
stairs and began to play. At first they won three
thousand francs ; then lost to five hundred ; then went
up to three thousand seven hundred. Here they dropped
again to five francs ; then went up to two thousand ;
risked them, double or quits, on the even number ; the
even number had not passed for five rounds, and they
punted the whole sum ; the uneven came out. Lucien
and Lousteau rushed down the staircase of that famous
resort, having wasted two hours in destructive emotions. They had kept back one hundred francs. On
the steps of that well-known little portico, with its two
columns supporting the tin canopy which many an eye
has contemplated in hope and in despair, Lousteau said,

as he noticed Lucien's burning glance, "Don't let us spend more than fifty francs for supper."

They turned back. In one hour they had three thousand francs. These they punted on the red, which had passed five times, thinking to reverse their former ill luck. Black issued. It was then six o'clock.

"We can dine for twenty-five francs," said Lucien.

This new attempt was a brief one; the twenty-five francs were lost in ten turns. Lucien flung his last twenty-five frantically on the number of his own age and won. Nothing can describe the trembling of his hand as he took the rake and drew in the coins which the banker threw him one by one. He gave ten louis to Lousteau, saying: "Get away to Véry's!"

Lousteau understood him and went to order dinner. Lucien, left alone, placed his thirty remaining louis on the red and won. Emboldened by the secret voice to which all gamblers listen, he left the whole sum on the red and won again. His stomach became like a furnace. Not listening this time to the voice, he put his twelve hundred francs on the black and lost. He then felt within him that delicious sensation which succeeds the dreadful agitations of gamblers when, having nothing more to lose, they leave the flaming palace of their spasmodic dream. He rejoined Lousteau at Véry's, where he hurled himself (to use La Fontaine's expression) into cookery, and drowned his cares in wine. At nine o'clock he was so completely drunk that he could not understand why his porter in the rue de Vendôme told him to go to the rue de la Lune.

"Mademoiselle Coralie has moved to the address written on this paper," explained the porter.

Lucien, too drunk to be surprised by anything, got back into the hackney-coach which had brought him, and ordered the man to drive to the rue de la Lune, making jokes to himself as he went along on that attractive name.

During that morning the failure of the Panorama-Dramatique had become known. Coralie, much frightened, hastened to get permission of her creditors to sell the furniture to old Cardot, who was willing to put Florentine into the apartment. Coralie paid off everything, and satisfied the owner of the house. While this operation, which she called her " grand washing day," went on, Bérénice was furnishing with a few indispensable articles a little apartment of three rooms on the fourth floor of a house in the rue de la Lune, which was close to Coralie's new theatre, the Gymnase. Here she awaited Lucien, having saved from the shipwreck her love and twelve hundred francs in money. Lucien, still intoxicated, related all his troubles to Coralie and Bérénice.

" You did right, my angel," said Coralie. " Bérénice can make Braulard take those notes."

The next day Coralie outdid herself in love and tenderness, as if to compensate her lover with the best treasures of her heart for the indigence of this new home. She glowed with beauty ; her hair escaped from the white silk foulard twisted round it ; her eyes were laughing ; her words as gay as the beams of the rising sun which came through the windows as if to gild their poverty. The room, which was quite decent, had a pale-green paper with a red border ; there were two mirrors, — one over the fireplace, another over the bureau. A cheap carpet, bought by Bérénice with her own savings, hid the bare brick floor. The clothes of the lovers were put away in a wardrobe with a glass door and in the bureau. The mahogany furniture was covered with a blue cotton stuff. Bérénice had saved from the shipwreck a clock and two vases, four pairs of forks and spoons, and six silver teaspoons. The dining-room, which was next to the bedroom, was like that of a clerk living on a salary of twelve hundred francs. The kitchen was on the other side of the landing. Bérénice had a bedroom upstairs in the garret. The rent was only three hundred francs. This miserable house had no porte-cochère; the porter's lodge was in an angle of the entrance, where, through a small sash-window, he kept watch over the seventeen different tenants of the house. This beehive was what notaries call a productive investment. Lucien saw a secretary, an armchair, pens, paper, and ink, all ready for him. The gayety of Bérénice, who counted on the engagement at the Gymnase, that of Coralie, who was studying her part, tied with a light-blue ribbon, drove away the anxiety and the sadness of the now sober poet.

"Provided no one finds out about our fall," he said, "we shall come out of it all right. After all, we have four thousand five hundred francs to the fore! I shall negotiate those notes, and I am going to make the most of my new position on the royalist newspapers. To-morrow we inaugurate the 'Reveil.' I now understand journalism thoroughly. You'll see I shall make my mark!"

Coralie, who saw only love in these words, kissed the lips that said them.

XXII.

CHANGE OF FRONT.

AT this instant, when Bérénice had drawn the table before the fire, and served a modest breakfast consisting of scrambled eggs, two cutlets, and coffee and cream, a knock was heard on the door. Three sincere friends — Daniel d'Arthèz, Léon Giraud, and Michel Chrestien — appeared to the astonished eyes of Lucien, who, deeply touched by their visit, begged them to stay and share his breakfast.

"No," said d'Arthèz, "we have come on a more serious matter than mere consolation. We know all, for we have been to the rue de Vendôme. You know my political opinions, Lucien. Under any other circumstances I should rejoice to see you adopting my convictions; but in the situation where you have placed yourself by writing for the liberal journals, you cannot pass into the ranks of the ultras without injuring your character and perhaps destroying your future. We have come to beg you, in the name of our friendship, weakened though it has been lately, not to sully yourself in this way. You have attacked the Right, the Romanticists, and the government; you cannot now defend either the Romanticists, the government, or the Right."

"The reasons that actuate me are those of a higher

order of thought," said Lucien. "The end will justify all."

"Perhaps you do not fully understand the situation," said Léon Giraud. "The government, the court, the Bourbons, the absolutist party, — call it, if you prefer a comprehensive expression, the system opposed to the constitutional system, — which is divided into many divergent fractions as regards the means of smothering the Revolution, is of one mind as to the necessity of curbing the press. The 'Reveil,' the 'Foudre,' the 'Drapeau Blanc,' were all started for the express purpose of replying to the calumnies, insults, and sarcasms of the liberal press, — which," he added, making a parenthesis, "I do not approve of; and this degradation of our sacred mission is precisely what is leading us to publish a grave and dignified paper, the respectable and worthy influence of which will be felt before long, — well, this ministerialist and royalist artillery in which you are about to enlist is only a first attempt at reprisals, undertaken to give back thrust for thrust and wound for wound. What do you think will be the end of it, Lucien? The majority of subscribers are with the Left. In journalism, as in war, victory is on the side of the big battalions. You will be the scoundrels, the liars, the enemies of the people ; the other side will be the defenders of the nation, honorable men, martyrs ; though more hypocritical, it may be, more treacherous, than you. All this will only increase the pernicious influence of the press, by legitimatizing its already odious methods. Insults and personalities will become its acknowledged right, adopted to swell subscriptions and sanctioned by reciprocal custom. When the evil becomes obvious to its fullest extent, restrictive and prohibitory laws and the censorship — first imposed after the assassination of the Duc de Berry, and withdrawn since the opening of the Chambers — will return. Do you know what the French people will think of all this? They will listen to the insinuations of the liberal press ; they will believe that the Bourbons mean to attack and overthrow the material results of the Revolution, and they will rise in their might some day and overthrow the Bourbons. Not only are you now soiling your name, your life, but you are putting yourself on the losing side. You are too young ; too new to the ways of the press ; you don't know enough of the secret springs and passwords ; you have already excited too much jealousy to stand the hue and cry they'll make against you in the liberal journals. You'll be swept away by the fury of parties, which are still in the paroxysms of fever ; only, their fever has passed from the brutal actions of 1815 and 1816 into the ideas and wordy struggles of the Chambers and the license of the press."

"My friends," said Lucien, "I am not the featherweight, the poet you take me for. Whatever happens politically, I shall have won an advantage which no triumph of the liberal party could ever give me. By the time that triumph is yours," he added to Michel Chrestien, "my future will be secure."

"We shall cut off — your hair," said Chrestien, laughing.

"I shall have children by that time," said Lucien ; "and if you cut off my head, theirs will be on their shoulders."

The three friends did not take his meaning; they had no means of knowing that his intercourse with the great world had developed to the highest degree his pride of birth and all the aristocratic vanities. The poet saw, not without some reason, a great fortune in his beauty and his talents when supported by the name and title of Comte de Rubempré. Madame d'Espard, Madame de Bargeton, and Madame de Montcornet held him by that thread as a child holds a cockchafer. Lucien was flying in a given circle. The words, "He is one of us; he thinks rightly," said three days earlier in the salon of Mademoiselle des Touches, and followed by the congratulations on his conversion of the Ducs de Lenoncourt, de Navarreins, and de Grandlieu, of Rastignac, Blondet, the beautiful Duchesse de Maufrigneuse, the Comte d'Esgrignon, all persons of the highest influence in the royalist party, had completely turned his head.

"Then there's no more to be said," replied D'Arthèz, sadly. "You will find it harder than most men to keep yourself pure and retain your self-respect. I know you, Lucien; you will suffer deeply when you see yourself despised by the very persons to whom you are sacrificing yourself."

The three friends bade him good-by, but they did not offer him their hands. Lucien sat silent and thoughtful for some minutes after their departure.

"Come, don't think of those ninnies any more," said Coralie, springing on his knee, and throwing her beautiful young arms about his neck. "They take life seriously, and life is fun. Besides, you'll soon be Comte Lucien de Rubempré. I'll go and bewitch the

chancellor if you like. I know how to catch that libertine of a des Lupeaulx and make him get your ordinance signed. Did n't I tell you that if you ever wanted
a stepping-stone to reach your ends you should have
my dead body?"

The next day Lucien's name appeared as one of the
contributors to the "Reveil." The name was announced
in the prospectus as a conquest, and scattered broad-
cast in a hundred thousand copies. Lucien went to the
great inaugural banquet, which lasted nine hours, at
Roberts's, next door to Frascati's. The entire chorus of
the royalist press were present, — Martainville, Auger,
Destains, and a crowd of authors still living who in
those days *did* (in the consecrated phrase) "religion
and monarchy."

"We are going to give it to them, those liberals!"
said Hector Merlin.

"Gentlemen," said Nathan, who had enrolled himself under the new banner, thinking that he had better
have the authorities for than against him in a theatrical
enterprise he was then contemplating, "if we do make
war upon them, let us make it seriously; don't fire
powder only! Attack all the classic and liberal writers
without distinction of age or sex; make them all run
the gauntlet of our satire, — and no quarter!"

"But let us be honorable, and turn our backs on
presents, tickets, bribes from publishers. Let us make
a Restoration in journalism."

"Pooh!" said Martainville; "*Justem et tenacem
propositi virum!* Let us be implacable and withering!
I 'll take Lafayette and show him for what he is, —
Harlequin the First!"

"And I," said Lucien, "will take the heroes of the 'Constitutionnel,' Sergent Mercier, the complete works of Monsieur de Jouy, and the illustrious orators of the Left."

War to the death was resolved, and unanimously voted at one o'clock in the morning by editors and staff, whose ideas and divergences were by that time drowned in a bowl of flaming punch.

"Well, we've had a famous religious and monarchical debauch!" said one of the noted writers among the romanticists as the party separated.

This now historic saying, repeated by a publisher who was present at the dinner, appeared the next day in the "Miroir," where the revelation was attributed to Lucien.

This defection was the signal for a terrible uproar in the liberal newspapers. Lucien became their *bête-noire*, and he was inveighed against in the cruelest manner. The misfortunes of his sonnets were brought up, and the public were informed that Dauriat preferred to lose the money he had paid for them rather than risk their publication. Lucien was called "the poet *sans* poems."

One morning, in the very journal in which he had made his brilliant first appearance, the hapless great man read the following lines, written exclusively for him, for the public, of course, could not understand their meaning : —

"If the publisher Dauriat persists in not publishing the sonnets of our French Petrarch, we shall act as generous enemies and open our columns to these poems, which must be piquant, judging by the one we here present."

This was a parody on one of his sonnets, maliciously entitled "The Thistle" (Chardon), and ending with the line : —

"And asses only come to share the feast!"

As he read this terrible attack, the poet wept hot tears.

Vernou, in his paper, talked of Lucien's passion for play, and mentioned "The Archer of Charles IX." as an anti-national work in which the author took the side of the Catholic throat-cutters against the Calvinist victims. In the short course of one week the attack became bitter. Lucien relied on his friend Lousteau, to whom he had lent a thousand francs, and with whom he had certain secret agreements. But Lousteau was now Lucien's sworn enemy; we must here relate why.

For the last three months Nathan had been in love with Florine ; but he did not know how to get her away from Lousteau, who was wholly dependent on her. In the distress and despair to which the actress was reduced by the failure of the Panorama and the loss of her engagement, together with the loss of Matifat, Nathan went to see Coralie, and asked her to get Florine a part in a play of his that was soon to be brought out at the Gymnase. Then he curried favor with Florine on the strength of obtaining for her this engagement. Florine, led by ambition, yielded. She had had sufficient time to fathom Lousteau. Nathan was an ambitious man both in literature and politics, — a man whose energy was equal to his desires ; whereas Lousteau's vices had now destroyed his will. The actress, determined to recover her dashing appearance, gave Nathan Matifat's letters, which the druggist was made to buy for that sixth of the paper which Finot had been so anxious to obtain. Florine then moved into a fine apartment in the rue Hauteville, and took Nathan openly in face of the whole journalistic and theatrical world as her protector. Lousteau was so terribly overcome by this event that he wept at the close of a dinner which his friends had given to console him. They all agreed that Nathan had played his own game. Some of them, like Finot and Vernou, had long known the dramatist's passion for Florine; but every one declared that Lucien had jockeyed the affair at the Gymnase, and in so doing had betrayed Lousteau's confidence and the sacred laws of friendship. The spirit of party, they said, and the desire to serve his new royalist friends, was at the bottom of it.

"Nathan was carried away by the logic of passion; but that 'great man of the provinces,' as Blondet calls him, only thinks of selfish gain," cried Bixiou.

Thus the destruction of Lucien — that intruder, that little scamp who expected to outdo every one — was unanimously resolved upon and carefully planned. Vernou, who hated Lucien, agreed not to let him up. Finot accused Lucien of preventing him from making fifty thousand francs by betraying the secret of Matifat's letters to Nathan. Florine, in order to propitiate Finot, made Nathan sell him the sixth of the paper for fifteen thousand francs; but Lousteau, of course, lost his three thousand, and he never forgave Lucien that blow to his pocket. The wounds of self-love become incurable when the oxide of silver gets into them.

No words can describe, no representations picture,

the rage of writers when their self-love is wounded, nor the energy which takes possession of them when the poisoned arrows of sarcasm pierce their own skins. Those whose spirit of resistance is roused by the attack succumb quickly. Calm men, able to bear in mind that the injurious article is certain to drop into the gulf of oblivion, are those who display true literary courage. So at first sight the weak will seem strong, but their strength is of short duration. During the first fort- night Lucien rained a storm of articles in the royalist papers, where he shared the work of criticism with Hector Merlin. Every day he fired his wit from the ramparts of the "Reveil," aided therein by Martainville, the only one of his new friends who served him without some hidden purpose of his own, and who was not in the secret of agreements between the journalists of both sides, either at Dauriat's in the Galeries de Bois, or behind the scenes of a theatre, after drinking at some revel.

When Lucien went to the foyer of the Vaudeville he was no longer treated as a friend; none but the men of his new party shook hands with him, though Nathan, Hector Merlin, and Théodore Gaillard, fraternized openly with Finot, Vernou, Lousteau, and others of their set who went by the name of "good fellows." At the time of which we write, the foyer of the Vaudeville was the headquarters of literary scandal, — a sort of boudoir frequented by the men of all parties, political magnates, and magistrates. On one occasion the judge of a court, who had reprimanded a colleague for sweeping the green-room with his robe, was seen robe to robe with the rebuked lawyer in the foyer of the Vaudeville. Finot

was there every evening. Lousteau had ended by
shaking hands with Nathan. When Lucien had the
time and the calmness, he studied the behavior of his
enemies, and recognized — unhappy lad ! — their implacable coldness to him.

In those days party spirit engendered hatreds that
were far more bitter, than they are to-day. To-day the
springs of everything are less taut; criticism, after
slashing a man's book, shakes hands with him ; the
victim is forced to embrace his scarifier under fear
of the rod of ridicule. If he refuses, a writer is held to
be poor company, — ungracious, eaten up with vanity,
unapproachable, ill-natured, rancorous. To-day, when
an author gets a stab in the back, when he just escapes
a trap laid for him by a devilish hypocrisy, or becomes
the victim of some treachery, he hears his enemies
wishing him "good-evening," and claiming his respect,
possibly his friendship. All is excusable and justifiable
now that virtue has been transformed into vice, and
certain vices set up as virtues. The leaders of opposite
opinions speak to each other in dulcet tones and courteous phrases. But in these other times of which we
speak it required some courage for certain royalist
writers and some liberal writers to meet in the same
theatre. Hateful provocations were given. Glances
were loaded like pistols ; a single spark was often
enough to produce a quarrel. Imprecations could be
heard on the entrance of men who were particularly
obnoxious to either side ; for there were then but two
parties, — royalists and liberals (romanticists and classicists), — one hatred in two forms ; a hatred which fully
explained the scaffolds of the Convention.

Lucien, now transformed into a royalist and a furious romanticist, from the liberal and violent Voltairean under which guise he had made his first appearance, found himself beneath the weight of all the enmities which hung above the head of the man most abhorred by the liberals of the day, namely, Martainville, the founder of " Le Drapeau Blanc," and the only man who really stood by him and liked him. This support was an injury to Lucien. Parties are ungrateful to their scouts; they willingly abandon their forlorn hopes. In politics above all it is necessary to keep with the rank and file of the army. One of the chief injuries the little journals did to Lucien was the malicious coupling of his name with that of Martainville. It was this that really threw them into each other's arms.

Their friendship, real or artificial, earned them two spiteful articles written by Félicien Vernou, who was bitterly jealous of Lucien's success in the great world, having heard some rumor of his approaching rise in rank, — a rumor which soon spread among his former comrades. The poet's treachery was then still more bitterly denounced, and embellished with aggravating circumstances. Lucien was called the Little Judas, and Martainville the Great Judas; for, as will be remembered, he was accused, rightly or wrongly, of having betrayed the Pont du Pecq to the allied armies. Lucien remarked with a laugh to des Lupeaulx that as for him he had often betrayed the *pons asinorum.* Lucien's luxury, hollow as it was and resting on expectations, was another offence; his enemies could not forgive him his carriage (for to their minds he still rolled in it), nor his splendors of the rue de Vendôme. They all felt instinctively that a man so young, handsome, brilliant, and corrupted by them, must succeed in his new career, and they used all means to overthrow him.

Some days before Coralie was to make her first appearance at the Gymnase, Lucien went arm in arm with Hector Merlin to the foyer of the Vaudeville. Merlin scolded his friend for having helped Nathan in the Florine affair.

"You have made mortal enemies of Lousteau and Nathan both," he said. "I gave you sound advice and you would not profit by it. You have given away praises and done a benefit, and you will be cruelly punished for a kind action. Florine and Coralie can never continue on good terms together after they come on the same stage; one will always be wanting to get the better of the other. You have only our journals to protect Coralie. Nathan, besides his advantage as the writer of plays, can control the liberal papers in theatrical matters; he has been much longer in journalism than you have."

This speech was an echo of certain secret fears which had found their way into Lucien's mind. He did not find either in Nathan or in Théodore Gaillard the frankness and confidence to which he thought he had a right. But how could he complain, being so recently converted? Gaillard alarmed him by hinting that new-comers must give proofs of sincerity for a long time before the party could trust them. The poet became aware of a jealousy within the lines of the ministerial and royalist journals which he had never once thought of, — the jealousy of men when a new-comer appears to share the cake before them; giving them a likeness to dogs over a bone : the same growls, the same attitudes, the same nature. These writers were all pulling secret wires to injure each other's standing with the authorities. Lukewarmness was a common accusation ; to get rid of a competitor there was no perfidy they would not commit. The liberals had not this special cause of intestine struggle, because they were far removed from power and public patronage. The more he saw of this inextricable network of ambitions, the less courage Lucien had to draw his sword and cut the meshes, although he knew very well he had not the patience to disentangle them. He could never have been the Aretino, the Beaumarchais, the Fréron of his day ; he simply clung to his one desire, — to obtain his letters-patent, — feeling well assured that such a restoration of name and title would bring him a good marriage. His future would then depend only on some fortunate chance which his personal gifts would further.

But, unluckily for him, Lousteau knew his secret and how to wound him mortally ; and it happened that on this evening when Merlin and Lucien had come together to the Vaudeville, Étienne had prepared for the latter a fatal trap in which the lad was fated to be caught.

"Here's our handsome Lucien," said Finot, dragging des Lupeaulx, with whom he was talking, up to Lucien, whose hand he took with a specious show of friendship. "I don't know an instance of such success as his. In Paris fortune is of two kinds : material fortune, — money, which all the world can pick up ; and moral fortune, — connections, position, access to a society inapproachable by some, no matter what their material fortune may be. Now, my friend — "

" *Our* friend ! " said des Lupeaulx, with a flattering look at Lucien.

" Our friend," resumed Finot, patting Lucien's hand, " has made a brilliant record in this last respect. Lucien has greater means, more talent, more wit, than all his detractors put together, — and beauty to boot. His old friends can't forgive him his successes ; they ascribe them to luck."

" Such luck," said des Lupeaulx, " does n't come to fools or weaklings. Can Bonaparte's career be called luck? There were twenty generals above him wanting to command the army of Italy, just as there are a hundred young men at this moment who long to visit Mademoiselle des Touches, whom I hear, my dear fellow," — he added, tapping Lucien on the shoulder, — " the world gives you for a wife. Ah ! you are in high favor ! Madame d'Espard, Madame de Bargeton, and Madame de Montcornet are distracted about you. You are going to-night to Madame Firmiani's *soirée*, are you not? and to-morrow to the Duchesse de Grandlieu's rout? "

" Yes," said Lucien.

" Allow me to present to you a young banker, Monsieur du Tillet, a man like yourself, who has made a fine fortune in a short time."

Lucien and du Tillet bowed and entered into conversation ; the banker asked Lucien to dinner. Finot and des Lupeaulx, two men of equal calibre, and who knew each other sufficiently well to always remain friends, walked away, leaving Lucien, Merlin, du Tillet, and Nathan conversing, and seated themselves on one of the sofas of the foyer.

"My dear friend," said Finot to des Lupeaulx, " tell me the truth. Is Lucien really and truly protected by great influence? He has become the *bête-noire* of my staff of writers ; and before I give in to their conspiracies I want to know from you whether I had better stand by him and serve him, or let him go."

Here des Lupeaulx and Finot looked at each other during a momentary pause with significant attention.

" You don't suppose," said des Lupeaulx, " that the Marquise d'Espard, du Châtelet, and Madame de Bargeton have forgiven Lucien's attacks? No ; they have drawn him into the royalist party merely to silence him. They are all trying to find some pretext for getting out of the promises with which they have lured him. If you can find a way you would do them the greatest service, which would not be forgotten. Lucien might have made terms with his worst enemy, Madame de Bargeton, in the beginning, by stopping those attacks on conditions all women like to be forced into. He is young and handsome, and he had it in his power to make her present hatred love. He would then have been Comte de Rubempré ; the ' Cuttle-fish' would have got him an appointment in the Household, or a sinecure of some kind. Lucien would have made a charming reader to Louis XVIII., or librarian somewhere, or Master of petitions. But the little fool missed his chance. Perhaps that is really the thing she won't now forgive. Instead of imposing conditions as he might have done, he has now to submit to them. Coralie has ruined him. If she were not his mistress, he would have wanted Madame de Bargeton again, and he would have had her."

"So we may as well knock him over?" said Finot.

"How will you do it?" asked des Lupeaulx, indifferently, determined to get some credit for this service from the Marquise d'Espard.

"There's a signed agreement which obliges Lucien to write a certain number of articles for my paper. He'll do them all the more readily because he has n't a penny. If the Keeper of the Seals were stung by some sharp article, and made to think that Lucien wrote it, he would declare him unworthy of the king's kindness. There is some such scheme on hand; and in order to make this great man of the provinces lose his head entirely, Coralie is to be attacked. He will see his mistress hissed and left without a part. If the letters-patent are not granted, we can make the most of that, and talk of his aristocratic pretensions and his father the apothecary. Lucien's courage is only skin-deep; he'll give in, and go back whence he came. Nathan has made Florine sell me that sixth of my journal which Matifat owned. I have bought out the paper-maker, so that Dauriat and I are now the sole proprietors. We can manage, you and I, to turn the paper into the service of the court. I protected Nathan and Florine in order to get my sixth; they have let me have it, and I must make them some return. But before deciding on any course, I wanted to know from you exactly what Lucien's chances are."

"Ha, ha!" laughed des Lupeaulx, "I like men of your sort!"

"Well, can you get Florine a permanent situation?" said Finot to the Master of petitions.

"Yes; but you must rid us of Lucien. De Marsay

and Rastignac both declare they cannot stand him any longer."

"Sleep in peace," said Finot; "Lucien won't be able to get an article into any of the papers in defence of himself and Coralie except Martainville's. One paper against all is helpless."

"I will give you a raw spot in the Keeper of the Seals; but be sure you let me see the article before you publish it."

So saying, des Lupeaulx left the theatre. Finot went over to Lucien; and in the good-natured, kindly tone by which so many persons were taken in, he declared that in spite of Lucien's change of opinion he could not give up the articles that were due to him; for his part, he liked a man who was bold enough to make such a change. Lucien and he would continue to meet in the world, and there were always a thousand little services they could do each other. Lucien needed a trusty man in the liberal party to attack the ministerialists or the royalists who gave him trouble.

"If they play you false, what will you do?" said Finot, ending his discourse. "If some minister, thinking he has you by the halter of apostacy, no longer fears you, and sends you to the right-about, you'll want a few dogs to bite his calves. Well, it is war to the knife between you and Lousteau, who demands your head; and you and Vernou don't speak. I am the only real friend left to you. It is a rule with me to live on good terms with men who are really strong-minded. You will be able to do for me in the world you are now entering the equivalent of the services I shall do for you in the press. Meantime, business before all! Send

me the articles agreed upon ; make them purely literary, and then they won't compromise you with your
new friends."

Lucien saw nothing but friendship mingled with
shrewd calculations of self-interest in these proposals
of Finot, whose flattery, together with that of des
Lupeaulx, had put him in high good-humor. He
thanked Finot !

XXIII.

THE FATAL WEEK.

In the lives of ambitious men and all those who can only succeed by the help of men and things, and by a line of conduct carefully planned, followed, and consistently maintained, there comes a cruel moment when some strange power, I know not what, subjects them to harsh trials. All things fail them at once; on all sides the threads of life are broken or suddenly entangled; misfortunes appear at every point. When a man loses his head in the midst of this moral confusion he is lost. Those who are able to resist the first revolt of circumstances, who stiffen themselves to let the whirlwind pass, who by some mighty effort can escape into the safety of a higher sphere, are the really strong-minded of the earth. Every man, unless he is born rich, has what we must call his fatal week. For Napoleon that week was the retreat from Moscow.

This cruel moment now came to Lucien. He had been too lucky; everything had succeeded for him so far, in the world and in literature. Yes, he had been too lucky; he was now to see men and things turning against him.

The first blow was the sharpest and cruellest of all; it struck him where he thought he was invulnerable, — in his heart and in his love. Coralie might not be intelligent; but she was gifted with a noble soul and the faculty of bringing it into view by those inspirational movements which are the sign of a great actress. This strange phenomenon, unless it becomes habitual by long practice, is subject to the caprices of temperament, and often to an innate modesty which controls young actresses. Inwardly ingenuous and timid, outwardly bold and free as a comedian must be, Coralie, full of her love, experienced a reaction of her woman's heart under the mask of her profession. The art of representing feelings — that splendid falsity ! — had not yet triumphed over the nature within her. She felt ashamed of giving to the public that which belonged only to her love. Besides, she had the weakness of all true women; though she felt she had the power of commanding the stage, she wanted the evidence of success. Afraid of facing an audience which might not sympathize with her, she trembled every time she went upon the stage, and the coldness of the public would have paralyzed her. This terrible emotion made every new part as alarming to her as a first appearance. Applause gave her a sort of intoxication, useless to her self love, but absolutely indispensable for her courage. A murmur of disapprobation, or even the silence of an inattentive audience, lessened her faculties. A full and interested house, kindly and admiring glances, electrified them. She then put herself into communication with the best qualities of the souls before her, and felt the power of moving and exciting them. This twofold condition is indicative of the nervous temperament and constitution of genius, and it also plainly shows the delicacy of nature and the tenderness of this poor child.

Lucien had ended by comprehending and appreciating the treasures of that heart; he saw how truly his mistress was still a young girl.

Unfitted for the wiliness of an actress, Coralie was incapable of defending herself against the rivalry and green-room manœuvres of Florine, — a woman as dangerous and depraved as her friend was simple and generous. Parts had to seek Coralie; she was too proud to court authors and submit to their dishonorable conditions, or yield to the first journalist who threatened her with his pen and his love. Talent, already so rare in the amazing art of the comedian, is only one condition of success. Talent is even injurious for a long time unless accompanied by a certain genius for intrigue which was wholly lacking to Coralie. Foreseeing the sufferings his friend must endure on her first appearance at the Gymnase, Lucien desired at any cost to secure her triumph. The money which remained from the sale of their furniture, that which he had earned by his articles, all went in the cost of costumes, the arrangement of her dressing-room, and the many expenses of a first appearance.

A few days before the crucial night, Lucien took a humiliating step, to which his love induced him. He took the notes of Fendant and Cavalier and went to the Cocon-d'Or, in the rue des Bourbonnais, to ask Camusot to cash them. The poet was not yet so corrupted that he could calmly make this appeal. Many an anguish he left upon the way, paving it with dreadful thoughts as he said to himself alternately: "I will!" "I will not!"

Nevertheless, he did enter the little cold, dark office,

25

lighted only from an inner court, where sat, not the
lover of Coralie, the jovial, idle libertine, the easily
fooled Camusot whom he knew, but the grave father
of a family, the wily merchant, powdered with virtue,
and masked by the judicial prudery of a magistrate in
the commercial courts; protected, too, by his dignity as
master of the establishment, and surrounded by clerks,
cashiers, and all the paraphernalia of a great trade.
Lucien trembled from head to foot as he approached
him; for the worthy merchant gave him the insolently
indifferent look he had already seen in the eyes of the
money-changers.

"Here are some notes; and I should be under the
greatest obligations if you would take them from me,
monsieur," he said, standing before the merchant, who
remained seated.

"You have taken something from me, monsieur,"
said Camusot; "I do not forget it."

Lucien explained Coralie's position in a low voice,
stooping close to the merchant, who could hear the
palpitating heart of the humbled poet. It was not
Camusot's intention or desire that Coralie should fail.
While listening he examined the signatures to the
notes and smiled; he was a judge in the commercial
court, and he knew the standing of those publishers.
Nevertheless, he gave Lucien the four thousand five
hundred francs, on condition that he signed a receipt
for "Value received in silks."

Lucien went at once to Braulard, and arranged
matters so carefully with him that Coralie's success
seemed secure. Braulard promised to come, and did
come, to the last rehearsal, to arrange the points at

which his "Romans" should open their batteries and produce a triumph. Lucien carried the rest of his money to Coralie, concealing from her his appeal to Camusot. This relief eased the anxieties of the poor girl and Bérénice, who by this time had no means of supplying the household.

Martainville, one of the men of that day who best understood theatrical matters, had come to the house several times to hear Coralie recite her part. Lucien obtained a promise of favorable articles from several of the dramatic critics of the royalist press, and had no suspicion of danger. But the evening before the one on which Coralie was to make her début at the Gymnase, an event happened that was terrible in its effect on Lucien's mind.

D'Arthèz's book had appeared. The editor-in-chief of Hector Merlin's paper gave it to Lucien to review, considering him the man best fitted for the purpose. He owed his reputation for this class of work to the articles he had written on Nathan. A number of persons were in the office at the time, nearly all the editorial staff were present, and Martainville had come in to settle some point in the general warfare declared by the royalist journals against the liberal journals. Nathan, Merlin, and other contributors to the "Reveil" were talking excitedly of the dangerous influence of Léon Giraud's semi-weekly paper, — an influence all the more pernicious, they said, because its language was prudent, judicious, and moderate. They talked of the brotherhood in the rue des Quatre-Vents, and called it a Convention. The royalist journals had already decided on a systematic war to the death against these dangerous opponents, who became, in fact, the promulgators of " the Doctrine,"— that fatal sect which overthrew the Bourbons after the day when a contemptible vengeance led the most brilliant of the royalist writers to ally himself with it. D'Arthèz, whose absolutist opinions were not known, was included in this anathema against the brotherhood, and the publication of his book afforded the opportunity of making a first victim. It was to be, as the classic saying is, " slashed to bits."

Lucien refused to write the article. This refusal caused a violent commotion among the important men of the royalist party who were present. They declared plainly that Lucien, as a new convert, had no choice ; if it did not suit him to belong to the party of religion and monarchy, he could return to his former camp. Merlin and Martainville took him aside, and pointed out that he would simply deliver over Coralie to the attacks which the liberal journals were sure to make upon her, without the powerful defence of the royalist journals to protect her. As it was, her first appearance at the Gymnase would certainly give rise to a violent discussion, which would give her the notoriety all actresses sigh for.

" You don't understand the matter," said Martainville, " but I do. She will play for the next three months under the cross-fire of our articles, and can then earn thirty thousand francs in the provinces during her holiday. For a scruple — and such scruples will always prevent you from becoming anything in politics — you will destroy Coralie and your own future, and throw away your means of living."

Lucien saw himself forced to choose between Coralie and d'Arthèz; his mistress was lost unless he strangled his friend in the columns of the royalist newspapers.

The poor poet went home with death in his soul. He sat down beside the fire in his bedroom and read the book, one of the finest in modern literature. Tear after tear fell upon the pages. He hesitated long; but at last he wrote a scoffing article, such as he well knew how to write, taking the book as children take a beautiful bird to pluck and martyrize it. His terrible witicisms were of a nature to blast the book. Reading it once more, his better feelings rose again. He rushed through Paris at midnight and reached d'Arthèz's lodgings, saw in the window the chaste and humble light he had so often looked at with an admiration deserved by the noble constancy of that true, great man. He had scarcely strength to go up the stairs, and stood for a few moments motionless on the landing. At last, impelled by his guardian angel, he knocked, entered, and found d'Arthèz reading without a fire.

"Your book is sublime!" cried Lucien, with tears in his eyes, "and I am ordered to attack it."

"Poor child, your bread is bitter," said d'Arthèz.

"I came to ask forgiveness. Keep the secret of this visit; let me go back to hell and to the business of devils. Perhaps we can succeed in nothing until we turn our hearts to stone."

"Always the same!" said d'Arthèz.

"Do you think me base? No, d'Arthèz, I am only a child mad with love;" and he explained his position.

"Let me see the article," said d'Arthèz, moved by all that Lucien told him of Coralie.

Lucien gave him the manuscript. D'Arthèz read it, and could not repress a smile.

" What a fatal use of intellect!" he cried; but he checked himself on seeing Lucien, lying in a chair, overwhelmed with genuine ' sorrow. " Will you let me correct it?" asked d'Arthèz. " I will return it to you to-morrow. Sarcasm dishonors a book, but grave and sober criticism is sometimes a benefit. I will make your article more honorable both to you and to me. Besides, no one knows my faults as well as I do myself."

" In a barren, weary land we sometimes find a fruit to slake our thirst; I have found one," said Lucien weeping, as he threw himself into d'Arthèz's arms and kissed him. " I feel as if I had given you my con- science and should get it back some day."

" I consider periodical repentance a great hypocrisy," said d'Arthèz, solemnly; "repentance then becomes a premium given to wrong-doing. Repentance is a virgin act due from our souls to God; a man who repents again and again becomes a sycophant. I fear that you see only absolutions in your repentance."

The words were like a thunderbolt to Lucien, who walked back slowly to his home.

The next day he took his article (which d'Arthèz had returned to him remodelled) to the paper; but from that day forth he was overcome by a melancholy he could not always conceal.

When the evening of Coralie's début came, and he saw the Gymnase crowded, he went through all the terrible emotions of a first appearance, aggravated in his case by the anxieties of his love. All his vanities

were at stake ; he looked at the faces in the audience as
a prisoner examines those of judge and jury ; a single
murmur made him shudder, a trifling incident on the
stage, Coralie's entrances and exits, the slightest inflections of her voice, agitated him inconceivably. The
piece in which she played was one of those that fall, and
then recover. It fell. When Coralie went on the stage
she was not applauded, and she felt the coldness of the
pit. In the boxes there was no applause except that of
Camusot, which was stopped by persons stationed in the
balcony and galleries calling, " Hush! hush!" The
galleries also stopped the *claqueurs* each time that they
delivered salvos, which were evidently forced. Martainville applauded courageously, and the hypocritical
Florine, Nathan, and Merlin did likewise. But the
play failed. After it was over a crowd pressed into
Coralie's dressing-room ; but the consolations offered
only aggravated her distress. She returned home in
despair ; more for Lucien than for herself.

"We were betrayed by Braulard," he said.

Coralie was struck to the heart and attacked with
fever. The next day it was impossible for her to play ;
she saw herself stopped short in her career. Lucien
hid the newspapers and went into the dining-room to
read them. All the critics attributed the failure of the
piece to Coralie ; she had presumed too much upon her
powers ; she had charmed the Boulevards, it was true,
but she was out of place at the Gymnase ; she had been
led on by a laudable ambition, no doubt, but she had not
rightly estimated her capacity, and had moreover
misunderstood her part. The criticisms Lucien now
read on Coralie were written with the same hypocrisy

as his articles on Nathan. A rage like that of Milo of Cortona, when he felt his hands caught in the oak he had cleft himself, seized upon Lucien; he turned livid; his so-called friends gave Coralie, in the kindest phraseology, the most treacherous advice. They advised her to play certain parts which they knew to be unsuited to her talents. Such were the articles of the royalist press inspired by Nathan. As for the liberal journals, they were full of the scorn and trenchant criticism Lucien himself had practised in their columns.

Coralie heard sobs, and springing from her bed she ran to Lucien, saw the papers, seized them, and read them. After reading them, she went back to her bed and was silent.

Florine was in the conspiracy; she foresaw the result, and had learned Coralie's part, having Nathan for a teacher. The management of the Gymnase was desirous of keeping the play upon the stage, and therefore proposed to give Florine Coralie's part. The director came to see the poor girl, and found her ill and depressed; but when he told her, before Lucien, that Florine knew the part and would play it, for it was impossible, he said, not to give the piece that evening, she sprang up and jumped from her bed, crying out:

"I will play the part myself!"

Then she fainted on the floor. Florine played the part and made her reputation by it, for the piece was redeemed. All the newspapers gave her an ovation, and she became from that day the great actress that we all know her.

Florine's triumph exasperated Lucien to the last degree.

"A miserable creature, whose bread you yourself put into her mouth!" he cried. "If the Gymnase chooses, it may buy back your engagement. I shall be Comte de Rubempré, I shall make a fortune, and I will marry you."

"What nonsense!" said Coralie, with a pallid glance.

"Nonsense?" cried Lucien; "I tell you in a few days you shall live in a fine house, and have your carriage, and I will write you a rôle."

He took two thousand francs and rushed to Frascati's. The unhappy man was there for seven hours, pursued by furies, though calm and cold outwardly. During that day and part of the night he had the most diverse vicissitudes; he won as much as thirty thousand francs, and left the place without a penny. When he reached home he found Finot waiting to speak to him about his "little articles." Lucien committed the great mistake of complaining to him.

"Ah! all is not *couleur de rose!*" said Finot. "You made your right-about-face so abruptly that it is no wonder you lost the support of the liberal press, which is twice as powerful as the ministerial and royalist press. No one ought ever to go from one camp to the other without having made himself a good bed where he can take his comfort for the losses he is sure to meet with. But, in any case, a sensible man goes to see his friends and explain his reasons, and take some advice on his change of front. His friends may pity him, but they will still be comrades (as we are with Nathan and Merlin), and give and take mutual services. Wolves don't eat each other. But instead of that, you have been as innocent as a lamb. You'll be forced to show

your teeth to your new friends if you expect to get bite
or sup out of them. They are sacrificing you now to
Nathan. Besides this, I hear there's a great outcry
and scandal in another quarter about your article against
d'Arthèz. Marat is a saint compared to you. When
your book comes out, it will be attacked and perhaps
destroyed. By the bye, where is that book?"

"Here are the last sheets of it," said Lucien, showing
a packet of proofs.

"All the articles in the ministerial and ultra papers
against that little d'Arthèz that are not signed are
attributed to you. The pin-pricks in the 'Reveil'
against the fraternity in the rue des Quatre-Vents are
very amusing, and all the more so because they bring
blood. But there is a grave and serious political coterie
behind that paper of Léon Giraud's, — a coterie of men
to whom power will belong, sooner or later."

"I have not set foot in the 'Reveil' office for the last
week!" exclaimed Lucien.

"Well, think about my little articles. Write me fifty
at once, and I'll pay for them in a lump; but they must
have the color of my paper."

Finot then went on to tell Lucien in a casual way
about a joke they were getting off on the Keeper of the
Seals, — an anecdote, he said, that was going the rounds
of the salons.

To repair his losses at play, Lucien set to work upon
the articles. In spite of his depression, he recovered
much of the vigor and freshness of his mind, and wrote
thirty of two columns each. After they were finished he
went to Dauriat's, knowing that he should find Finot
there, and wishing to give him the articles privately;

moreover, he wanted to make the publisher explain himself as to the non-publication of the "Daisies." He found the place full of his enemies. Complete silence reigned as soon as he entered ; all conversations ceased. Feeling himself thus shoved back to the lower ranks of journalism, Lucien's courage rose. He said to himself, as he had said to Lousteau in the alley of the Luxembourg, —

" I will succeed! "

Dauriat was neither patronizing nor kind. He was surly, and stood on his rights. He should bring out the " Daisies " when it suited him ; he was waiting till Lucien's position gave them a chance of success ; besides, he had bought the sole right to the poems. When Lucien objected that Dauriat was bound by the nature of the contract to bring out the book, the publisher maintained the contrary, and declared that he could not be held legally to an enterprise he thought a bad one ; he alone was the judge of that. Besides, there was one way of settling the matter which every court would admit : Lucien might, if he liked, return the three thousand francs, take back his book, and sell it to some royalist publisher.

Lucien withdrew, more annoyed by Dauriat's moderate tone than he had been by his pompous impertinence at their first meeting. He saw plainly that the "Daisies" would never be published until he had either the auxiliary force of some powerful connections or had become a power in himself. The poet walked slowly homeward, — a prey to a disheartenment which would have led him to suicide could action have followed thought. He found Coralie in bed pale and suffering.

"Get her a part, or she will die!" said Bérénice, while Lucien was dressing to go to the rue du Mont-Blanc, where Mademoiselle des Touches was to give a great party, at which he was sure to meet des Lupeaulx, Claude Vignon, Blondet, Madame d'Espard, and Madame de Bargeton.

The party was given for Conti, the famous composer, who possessed one of the most beautiful voices ever heard off the stage. Cinti-Damoreau, Pasta, Garcia, Levasseur, and two or three other voices celebrated in the great world, were also present. Lucien slipped round to the side of the room where Madame d'Espard, her cousin, and Madame de Montcornet were seated. The unhappy young man assumed a gay, contented, happy manner; he talked and laughed with all the ease of his splendid days; he was determined not to seem to have need of the world. He dwelt on the services he was now doing to the royalist party,—proved, he said, by the cries of hatred the liberals were sending after him.

"You will be well compensated, my friend," said Madame de Bargeton, with a gracious smile. "Go to the chancellor's office the day after to-morrow with 'The Heron' and des Lupeaulx, and obtain your letters-patent. The Keeper of the Seals is to take the papers to the château; but there is to be a council, and he will not be back till late. Still, if I know the result in the course of the evening, I will send to you. Where do you live?"

"I will go to you," said Lucien, ashamed to say that he lived in the rue de la Lune.

"The Ducs de Lenoncourt and Navarreins spoke of you to the king," said Madame d'Espard. "They

assured him that you were devoting your talents absolutely and unreservedly to the royalist cause, and that
some great reward should be given to compensate you
for the persecutions of the liberal party ; and they represented that the name and title of de Rubempré, to
which you have a right through your mother, would
receive new lustre through you. The king told his
Highness the Keeper of the Seals that he might bring
him the papers authorizing the Sieur Lucien Chardon to
bear the name and title of Comte de Rubempré in his
quality as grandson, through his mother, of the last
count."

Lucien was moved to a gratitude which would have
softened the feelings of a woman less deeply wounded
than Louise de Bargeton. Emboldened by his coming
success, and by the flattering distinctions which Mademoiselle des Touches showed to him, he stayed on till
two o'clock in the morning, in order to speak to his
hostess in private. He had learned in the offices of the
royalist journals that Mademoiselle des Touches was
secretly collaborating in a play about to be produced
for the great marvel of the moment, the little Fay.
When the salons were empty he led Mademoiselle des
Touches to a sofa in the boudoir, and told her in so
touching a manner the misfortunes that had fallen upon
Coralie and himself that she promised to have the
leading part in her play assigned to Coralie.

The morning after this party, while Coralie, made
happy by the promise of a part, was breakfasting with
her poet, Lucien sat reading Lousteau's paper, in which
was an epigrammatic version of the anecdote said to
be current on his Highness the Keeper of the Seals

and his wife. The blackest spite lay hidden beneath its incisive wit. The king was cleverly exhibited and ridiculed in a way that the law could not touch. The following is the tale which the liberal press endeavored to represent as a fact, but which really only swelled the number of its witty calumnies.

The passion of Louis XVIII. for gallant and perfumed correspondence, well spiced with madrigals and epigram, was called the last expression of love, now growing *doctrinaire;* he was passing, they said, from fact to idea. The famous mistress (so cruelly attacked by Béranger under the name of Octavie) was becoming much alarmed. Their correspondence languished. The more wit and brilliancy Octavie displayed, the colder and stiffer grew the king. Octavie at last discovered the cause of her loss of favor ; her power was threatened by the spiciness and muskiness of a new correspondence lately begun with the wife of the Keeper of the Seals. This excellent woman was known to be incapable of writing a note ; she was evidently only the responsible editor of some vaulting ambition. Who, therefore, could it be who was hiding beneath her petticoat? After various secret manœuvres, Octavie discovered that the king was really corresponding with his minister. Her plans were laid at once. By the help of a faithful friend, she contrived that the minister should be detained at the Chambers by a stormy debate, during which time she revealed the deception to the king, and roused his mortified vanity. Louis XVIII. flew into a passion of Bourbonian anger against Octavie, and declared that what she told him was false. Octavie proposed immediate proof, and persuaded him to write a note which required an answer on the spot. The luckless woman, taken by surprise, sent to the Chambers for her husband; but he was then in the middle of a speech; the wife was forced to reply, with much toiling and moiling and all the wit she could muster. "Your Keeper of the Seals can improve it for you," cried Octavie, laughing at the king's discomfiture.

Though a lie from beginning to end, the article was extremely irritating to the Keeper of the Seals, his wife, and the King. Des Lupeaulx (Finot always kept his secret) was said to have invented the story. The spiteful but witty article was a joy to the liberals and also to the partisans of MONSIEUR. Lucien laughed heartily over it, regarding the tale as nothing more than a very amusing *canard*. One of his own articles appeared in the same paper.

The next day he went as directed to join des Lupeaulx and du Châtelet. The Baron was desirous of thanking His Highness on his own account. He had just been named councillor of State on special service, and made count with a promise of the prefecture of the Charente as soon as the present prefect had completed the time necessary to retire on a full pension. The Comte du Châtelet (for the *du* was duly inserted in the ordinance) took Lucien in his carriage and treated him as an equal.

The persecution of the liberals had really been a pedestal for him; without Lucien's articles he might not have been accepted so quickly.

Des Lupeaulx was already at the ministry, in the office of the secretary-general. That functionary no sooner caught sight of Lucien than he gave a start of astonishment.

"I am amazed, monsieur, that you venture to present yourself here," he said to the surprised and stupefied Lucien. "His Highness has torn up your ordinance. He wished to know the author of the shameless article published yesterday; here is a copy of the paper," continued the secretary, holding out the sheet, in which Lucien's own article appeared. "You claim to be a royalist and to be doing services to the royalist cause, and yet you are collaborating with that infamous paper, which insults the ministers, embarrasses the Centres, and is forcing them into an abyss! You breakfast on the 'Corsaire,' 'Miroir,' 'Constitutionnel,' and 'Courrier;' you dine off the 'Quotidienne' and the 'Reveil;' and you sup with Martainville, the most formidable antagonist of the ministry, who is forcing the King into absolutism, which will bring on a revolution just as surely as though he flung himself into the arms of the Left. You may be a very witty journalist, but you will never be anything else. The minister has denounced you to the King, who in his anger blamed the Duc de Navarreins for ever mentioning you to him. You have made yourself powerful enemies, all the more bitter because they were favorable to you. That which is natural in an enemy is shameful in a friend."

"My dear fellow, you have behaved like a child," said des Lupeaulx; "you have compromised Madame d'Espard and Madame de Bargeton, who had answered for your sincerity. They must be furious. The duke of course has blamed the marquise, and the marquise her cousin. You had better not go and see them at present. Wait awhile."

" Here comes His Highness," said the secretary-general ; " I request you to leave the room, monsieur."

Lucien found himself on the place Vendôme, as bewildered as a man who has just been knocked down by a crushing blow on the head. He walked home along the boulevards trying to form a judgment on his life. He saw himself the foot-ball of jealous, grasping, and treacherous men. What was he in this world of ambitions? A child running after pleasures and the enjoyments of vanity ; a poet, without deep reflection, going from light to light like a butterfly, with no fixed plan, the slave of circumstances, thinking well and acting ill. His conscience was a pitiless judge. And now — he had no money ; he felt himself exhausted with life and sorrow ; his articles were set aside for those of Nathan or Merlin. Thus thinking, he walked he knew not whither ; presently his eye caught, in the window of a reading-room, his own name on a poster, " By Monsieur Lucien Chardon de Rubempré " beneath the strange, odd title of a book to him unknown. His book was out, and he knew nothing of it ! — not a paper had mentioned it ! He stood before the window, with hanging arms, quite motionless, not perceiving a group of elegant young men, among them Rastignac, de Marsay, and others of his acquaintance. Neither did he notice Michel Chrestien and Léon Giraud, who came up to him.

" Are you Monsieur Chardon?" said Michel in a tone that made Lucien's very entrails resound like the striking of a chord.

" Do not you know me?" he answered, turning pale.

Michel spat in his face.

" That is your fee for your articles against d'Arthèz. If every man, on his own behalf or on that of his friends, did as I have done, the press would become what it ought to be,— a priesthood, self-respecting and re-spected."

Lucien staggered; he leaned against Rastignac, say-ing to him and to de Marsay : " Gentlemen, you can-not refuse to be my seconds. But first I will make the matter equal."

So saying he struck Michel a blow in the face which took him unawares ; the dandies and Michel's friends threw themselves between the two men, that there might be no public struggle. Rastignac took posses-sion of Lucien and carried him to his own house, rue Taitbout, close to the scene of this affair, which took place on the boulevard de Gand, at the dinner hour. This fortunately prevented the collecting of the usual crowd in such a case. De Marsay followed, and together they forced Lucien to come and dine with them gayly at the Café Anglais, where they drank much.

" Are you good with swords ? " asked de Marsay.

" I never had one in my hands."

" Pistols ? " said Rastignac.

" I never in my life fired a pistol."

" Then you 've luck on your side ; you 'll be a terrible antagonist ; you 'll kill your man," said de Marsay.

Lucien fortunately found Coralie in bed and asleep when he got home. The actress had been called on to play unexpectedly in a little piece, and she had won much genuine applause that was not paid for. This success, which was quite unexpected by her enemies, determined the manager to give Coralie the leading part in Camille Maupin's play. He had ended by discovering the cause of her failure on her first appearance. Provoked by the intrigues of Florine and Nathan against an actress whom he himself thought well of, the manager promised Coralie the protection of the directors.

At five o'clock in the morning Rastignac came to fetch Lucien.

"My good fellow, your rooms are in keeping with your street," he said, by way of greeting. "Let us be first on the ground; it is good style, and we owe those men a good example."

"This is the programme," said de Marsay, as the hackney-coach was rolling along the faubourg Saint-Denis: "You fight with pistols, at twenty-five paces, walking as you please towards each other up to fifteen paces. You have each five steps to take, and three shots to fire, not more. Whatever happens, you are bound to go no farther with the affair. We load your adversary's pistols, and his seconds load yours. The weapons were chosen by all four seconds at a gunsmith's. I promise you we've helped your luck, — they are cavalry pistols."

As for Lucien, life had become to him a bad dream, and he was quite indifferent whether he lived or died. Courage of the sort peculiar to suicide gave him, therefore, a fine appearance of bravery in the eyes of the spectators of this duel. He stood still, without advancing from his place. This indifference was considered a piece of cool calculation. They all thought the poet proved himself "a strong man."

Michel Chrestien advanced to his limit. The two men fired simultaneously, for the insults were regarded as equal. At the first shot, Chrestien's ball grazed Lucien's chin, while Lucien's went ten feet over his adversary's head. At the second shot, Michel's ball went through the collar of Lucien's coat, which was fortunately wadded. At the third, Lucien received a ball in the breast and fell.

"Is he dead?" asked Michel.

"No," said the surgeon; "he'll get over it."

"So much the worse!" replied Michel.

"Oh, yes, so much the worse!" repeated Lucien, bursting into tears.

By mid-day the unhappy lad was in his own bed; it had taken five hours and infinite care to get him there. Though his condition was without immediate danger, it required the utmost precaution; fever might set in, and produce very serious complications. Coralie stifled her own despair and grief. During all the time he was in danger, she nursed by day, and sat up at night with Bérénice studying her parts. Lucien's danger lasted two months. Often the poor girl played some rôle which needed gayety while she was saying in her heart: "Perhaps my dear Lucien is dying at this moment!"

XXIV.

ADIEU!

DURING his illness Lucien was attended by Bianchon. He owed his life to the devotion of that friend, grievously offended, but to whom d'Arthèz had confided the fact of Lucien's visit to him, defending, as far as possible, the unfortunate poet. In a lucid moment, for Lucien had a nervous fever of extreme gravity, Bianchon, who suspected d'Arthèz of some generosity, questioned his patient as to the real facts, and Lucien told him that he had never written any article against d'Arthèz's book except the grave and serious criticism corrected by d'Arthèz himself, and published in Hector Merlin's paper.

At the end of the first month, Fendant and Cavalier went into bankruptcy. Bianchon told Coralie that she must conceal this frightful blow from Lucien. The much-talked-of novel, "The Archer of Charles IX.," published under a sensational name, had no success whatever. To get a little money for himself before their failure, Fendant, unknown to Cavalier, had sold the work in a block to a petty bookseller who had sent it about by peddlers. It was now adorning the parapets of the bridges and quays of Paris. Barbet, on the Quai des Augustins, who had previously taken quite a number of copies, found himself out of pocket to a con-

siderable sum by this sudden abatement of their value.
He had not foreseen it, for he believed in Lucien's talent, and had rashly purchased two hundred copies at
four francs and a half apiece, which would now bring
only half a franc. Alarmed by such a loss, Barbet took
an heroic measure : he put away his copies with the ob-
stinacy of a miser, saw his competitors selling theirs
for almost nothing, and in 1824, when two articles by
Léon Giraud called attention to the real merit of the
book and to d'Arthèz's fine preface, Barbet sold his
two hundred copies for ten francs apiece.

In spite of every endeavor on the part of Coralie and
Bérénice, they were unable to prevent Hector Merlin
from gaining access to Lucien during his illness, and
through him the poor poet was made to drink the bitter
cup to the dregs. Martainville, the only friend now
faithful to Lucien, wrote a fine article in favor of the
book ; but the exasperation of all parties, liberals and
royalists, was such against the editor-in-chief of the
" Drapeau Blanc," the " Oriflamme," and " Aristarque,"
that his efforts did Lucien more harm than good.

After this, Coralie, Bérénice, and Bianchon shut
Lucien's door with a firm hand against all his so-called
friends, but they could not shut it against the sheriff.
The failure of Fendant and Cavalier made the amount
of their notes irrecoverable by a third party, in virtue of
a provision in the commercial code. Lucien was therefore sued by Camusot. When Coralie read that name
attached to the papers, she saw at once the painful and
humiliating step her poet — to her so angelic — had
taken for her sake. Her love was increased tenfold,
and she made no effort to soften Camusot.

When, after the usual legal preliminaries, the sheriff's officers came to arrest Lucien, they found him in bed, and they hesitated to remove so sick a man. Before obtaining an order from the court to place their prisoner in one of the hospitals, they went to see Camusot, in whose suit they were acting. Camusot went instantly to the rue de la Lune. Coralie was called downstairs to see him, and returned bringing papers which released Lucien and declared him solvent. How had she obtained them? What promise had she made? She maintained a gloomy silence, but death was in her face as she came up the stairs.

Coralie played in Camille Maupin's piece, and contributed much to the success of that illustrious woman. The creation of this rôle was the last sparkle of her lamp. At the twentieth representation, just as Lucien, recovering, was beginning to move about and eat, and to talk of working, Coralie fell ill; an inward grief was preying upon her. Bérénice always believed that to save Lucien she had promised to return to Camusot.

The actress had the mortification of seeing her rôle given to Florine. Nathan had declared war against the Gymnase unless Florine succeeded her. By playing her part to the last instant rather than have it taken from it by her rival, Coralie had gone beyond her strength. The Gymnase had made her some advances on her pay during Lucien's illness, and there was nothing more to come to her. Lucien himself, with the best intentions, was still unable to work; moreover, he was forced to nurse Coralie to relieve Bérénice. The poor household was now reduced to dire distress; yet even here they found a friend in Bianchon, — a clever and devoted physician, who gave them a credit at the chemist's.

But soon their situation became known to the owner of the house in which they lived, and to the tradesmen who supplied them. Their furniture was seized. The tailor and the dressmaker, no longer fearing the journalist, sued them. No one would give them credit except the chemist and the *charcutier*, where the cheapest parts of pork are sold. Lucien and Bérénice and the poor sick girl lived for a week solely on scraps of pork cooked in the various ingenious ways known to *charcutiers*. Such food, inflammatory in its nature, aggravated Coralie's illness. Lucien, driven by this misery, went to find Lousteau and ask him for the thousand francs that former friend, that traitor, owed him. In the midst of all his wretchedness, this was the step that cost him most.

Lousteau no longer dared to go to the rue de la Harpe; his creditors pursued him, and he slept about in the rooms of his friends, hunted like a hare. Lucien at last found his fatal sponsor in the literary world at Flicoteaux's. Étienne was dining at the very table where Lucien had met him, to his sorrow, on the day he left d'Arthèz's side. Lousteau offered him some dinner, and Lucien accepted! When, as they left Flicoteaux's, Claude Vignon (who dined there that day), Lousteau, Lucien, and the great writer who had changed his coat at Samanon's, wished to go to the café Voltaire for a cup of coffee, they had not thirty sous among them when they emptied the coppers from their pockets. They walked about the gardens of the Luxem-

bourg hoping to meet some publisher they knew. It
did so happen that a famous printer of that day came
towards them, and of him Lousteau asked and obtained
forty francs. Lousteau divided the sum into four equal
parts, and each took one. Misery had quenched all
pride, all sensitiveness, in Lucien ; he wept before his
three companions as he told them his situation. But
each had a drama of his own as cruelly horrible as his ;
and when their conditions were all made known, Lucien
beheld himself the least unhappy of the four. Thus all
were craving to forget their sorrows, and their thoughts,
which doubled those sorrows. Lousteau rushed to the
Palais-Royal and gambled the nine francs that remained
to him. The illustrious writer went to a vile, contami-
nated house to plunge into pleasures still more dangerous. Vignon turned to the Petit Rocher de Cancale,
meaning to drink two bottles of Bordeaux, and abdicate
both mind and memory. Lucien left him at the door
of that restaurant, refusing to go in. The grasp which
the great man of the provinces gave to the hand of the
only journalist who had not been hostile to him was
accompanied by a spasm of the heart.

"What shall I do?" he cried.

"Ah !" said the great critic, " in this world we must
go with the crowd. Your book is a fine one ; but it has
made men jealous of you. Your struggle will be long
and difficult. Genius is a horrible disease ; every writer
bears in his heart a monster, like a tapeworm in the
stomach, devouring the feelings as soon as they unfold.
Which will conquer, — the disease or the man? Surely
the man must be great indeed to keep his balance between his genius and his nature. Talent grows, the

heart withers. Short of being a colossus, or of having the shoulders of a Hercules, he must end without a heart or without a brain. You are frail and delicate, you will succumb," he added, turning in to the restaurant.

Lucien walked on meditating that dreadful judgment, the truth of which glared like a flame upon his literary life.

"Money! money!" cried a voice within him.

He went home and drew three notes of a thousand francs each to his own order, payable at one, two, and three months' sight, and signed them with a wonderful imitation of David Séchard's signature; then, on the following day, he took them to Métivier, the paper-maker, David's correspondent in the rue Serpente, who discounted them without hesitation. Lucien wrote a few lines to his brother-in-law telling him what he had done, and promising, of course, to obtain the money in time to meet the notes. His debts and Coralie's paid, there remained three hundred francs, which Lucien placed with Bérénice, telling her not to give him a penny if he asked for it; he was afraid the desire to gamble might seize upon him.

The unhappy man, inspired by cold fury, gloomy, taciturn, wrote his wittiest articles by the glimmer of a lamp as he watched by Coralie. Searching for ideas, his eyes rested on that loved creature, white as porcelain, beautiful with the beauty of the dying, smiling with pallid lips to him, gazing upon him with the brilliant eyes of women who die of grief as much as of illness. Lucien sent his articles to the papers; but as he could not go to the offices himself to worry or to entreat the editors-in-chief, they were not inserted. When, at last, he was forced to go, Théodore Gaillard, who had made him some advances, and who, at a later period, profited by the literary diamonds he thus obtained, received him coldly.

"Mind what you are about, my dear fellow," he said to him; "you are losing your wit; don't let yourself down; you want more sparkle and liveliness."

"That little Lucien had nothing but his novel and those first articles in his pouch," cried Vernou, Merlin, and all the others who hated him, when they talked him over at Dauriat's or in the foyer of the Vaudeville; "he sends us wretched stuff!"

To have nothing in his pouch — that hallowed phrase of journalistic slang — is a sovereign judgment, from which it is difficult to appeal when once pronounced. That saying, hawked about everywhere, killed Lucien professionally, though Lucien did not know it, for by that time his troubles were greater than he could bear. In the midst of his crushing toil he was sued by Métivier for David Séchard's notes. He had recourse to Camusot's experience, and Coralie's old lover was generous enough to protect him. This dreadful condition of things lasted two months, — two terrible months crowded with legal forms, notifications, summonses, injunctions; all of which Lucien, by Camusot's advice, referred to Desroches the lawyer, a friend of Bixiou, Blondet, and des Lupeaulx.

At the beginning of the month of August, Bianchon told Lucien that Coralie was doomed, and had but a few days more to live. Bérénice and Lucien spent those fatal days in weeping, unable to conceal their anguish

from that poor girl whose despair at dying was all for
Lucien.   By a strange return upon herself, Coralie requested Lucien to fetch a priest.   She wanted to be
pardoned by the Church and to die in peace.   She made
a Christian end, and her repentance was sincere.

This dying scene, this death, took from Lucien the
last remnants of his strength and courage.   He sat in
utter abandonment at the foot of Coralie's bed, never
ceasing to gaze at her till her eyes were turned by the
hand of death.   It was then five in the morning.   A
bird came and lighted on the flower-pots outside the
window and warbled a few notes.   Bérénice, on her
knees, kissed the dying hand which grew cold beneath
her tears.   Eleven sous were on the chimney-piece.
Lucien went out, driven by despair, which told him
to ask alms in the street to bury his mistress, or fling
himself at the feet of Madame d'Espard, the Comte
du Châtelet, Madame de Bargeton, Mademoiselle des
Touches, or even that terrible man of fashion de Marsay.   No pride, no strength, remained to him.   To get
this money he would even have enlisted.   He walked
along with the sinking, disordered gait of a hopeless
being until he came to the house of Camille Maupin,
which he entered, without the least thought of his disordered clothes, and asked to see her.

"Mademoiselle went to bed at three in the morning,
and no one can disturb her until she rings" said the
footman.

"At what hour does she ring?"

"Never before ten o'clock."

Lucien asked for paper, and then wrote one of those
awful letters in which a beggar of quality shrinks from

nothing. One evening, not so long ago, he had doubted the possibility of such debasement when Lousteau told him of the entreaties made to Finot by young writers; and now his own pen went beyond the limits he had then thought so impossible. Returning, half imbecile, along the boulevard, little knowing what a masterpiece of dreadful power despair had dictated to him, he met Barbet.

"Barbet, five hundred francs!" he said, holding out his hand.

"No, two hundred," replied the publisher.

"Ah! you have a heart!"

"Yes, but I have also a business. You have made me lose a great deal of money," he added, after relating the failure of Fendant and Cavalier; "will you help me earn some?"

Lucien shuddered.

"You are a poet; you ought to know how to make all kinds of verses," continued Barbet. "Just now I am in want of some ribald songs to mix in with other songs taken from different authors, and so escape being sued for piracy. I want to make a pretty little collection and sell it for ten sous. If you will send me to-morrow ten good drinking-songs, or something smutty, you know, I'll pay you two hundred francs on the spot."

Lucien went home. Coralie lay rigid on a flock bed, wrapped in a common sheet which Bérénice was sewing up. The peasant-woman had lighted four candles at the corners of the bed. From Coralie's face shone forth that flower of beauty which speaks in so clear a voice to the living, expressing absolute peace. She was like those innocent young girls who die of anæmic maladies.   It seemed as though her violet lips would part and murmur Lucien's name, — that name which, joined to that of God, had taken her last breath.   Lucien told Bérénice to order from the Pompes Funèbres a funeral costing two hundred francs, including services in the humble church of Bonne-Nouvelle.

As soon as Bérénice had left the house, the poet drew his table beside the body of his love, and wrote the ten songs ordered, with lively thoughts to popular airs.   He went through tortures before he could begin them ; but he ended by coercing his mind to the service of necessity, and wrote as if he were not suffering.   Already he justified Claude Vignon's terrible dictum on the separation of heart and brain.   What a night was this in which the unhappy lad sought poesy to offer it to ribaldry, writing by the light of the tapers, beside the priest who prayed for Coralie !   In the morning he finished his last song, and set it to an air in vogue.   Bérénice and the priest believed him mad as they heard him sing these dreadful verses : —

" Dear comrades, a song with a moral
     Is ever a tiresome thing ;
   For why should we seek after wisdom
     When Folly alone is our king ?
Besides, any chorus will do
When we drink with a vagabond crew ;
Epicurus declares this is true.
   No room for the car of Apollo
   When the chariot of Bacchus we follow.
    For good or for evil
We laugh and we quaff, we quaff and we laugh,
    And let the rest go to the devil !

"Hippocrates promised long living
　　To him who the goblet should drain;
What matter if one leg be striving
　　To follow the other in vain,
Provided the hand can fill up,
And spill not a drop from the cup!
　　Provided good fellows are here
　　Who have drunk with us many a year
　　　Of good and of evil,
Yet still laugh and quaff, and still quaff and laugh,
　　And send all the rest to the devil!

"If any man ask where we come from
　　'T is easy enough to reply,
But clever indeed were the prophet
　　Who could tell where we go when we die.
Light-hearted and gay, let us trust
The powers above, — since we must!
　　It is certain we die;
　　While we live let us fly
　　　From trouble and evil,
By laughing and quaffing, by quaffing and laughing:
　　The rest may all go the devil!"

As the poet was singing this horrible last couplet, Bianchon and d'Arthèz entered. Lucien now fell back into a paroxysm of anguish; he shed torrents of tears, and was quite unable to copy his songs for the printer. When, amid his sobs, he was able to explain his situation to his friends, tears were in the eyes of all who heard him.

"This," said d'Arthèz, "wipes out many a fault."

"Happy those who find hell here below!" said the priest, gravely.

That spectacle of the beautiful dead girl smiling at eternity; her lover earning her funeral with ribaldry; Barbet paying for her grave; the four candles round the actress whose scarlet stockings with their green clocks had lately made a whole house palpitate; the priest who had pardoned her returning to his church to say a mass for one so loved, — ah! these grandeurs, these infamies, these sorrows, crushed by the hand of necessity, overcame the great doctor and the great writer, and they sat down speechless, unable to say a word! Just then a footman came in to announce Mademoiselle des Touches. That noble woman understood the whole scene. She went eagerly to Lucien, grasped his hand, and left two notes of a thousand francs within it.

"Too late!" he said, giving her a look like that of a dying man.

D'Arthèz, Bianchon, and Mademoiselle des Touches left him after soothing his despair with gentle words; but the springs of life seemed broken in him.

At mid-day the brotherhood, all but Michel Chrestien (who, however, had been told that Lucien was not as culpable as he had seemed), were assembled in the little church of Bonne-Nouvelle, together with Bérénice and Mademoiselle des Touches, two supernumeraries from the Gymnase, Coralie's dresser, and the unhappy Camusot. All the men accompanied the coffin to Père-Lachaise. Camusot, who wept bitterly, swore solemnly to Lucien that he would buy the piece of ground in perpetuity, and place a little column on the grave bearing the words, "CORALIE: Died, aged nineteen years, August, 1822."

Lucien remained alone until the sun went down upon that hill from which his eyes could see all Paris.

" By whom shall I now be loved? " he asked himself. " My true friends despise me. Whatever I had done, whatever I was, seemed good and noble to her who is lying there! I have no one left but my sister, and David, and my mother! What are they thinking of me now? "

When he returned to the house in the rue de la Lune his suffering was so great on seeing the empty rooms that he went to live in a wretched furnished lodging in the same street. The two thousand francs of Mademoiselle des Touches, added to the sale of the furniture, paid all debts. Bérénice and Lucien had a hundred francs left on which they lived for two months, — two months which Lucien passed in morbid despair. He could neither write nor think ; he abandoned himself to his sorrow. Bérénice pitied him.

" If you wished to go back to your own town, how could you get there? " she said one day, replying to an exclamation of Lucien's. He was thinking of his sister and mother and David.

" On foot! " he said.

" But you must eat and sleep on the way; you couldn't do with less than twenty francs."

" I will get them," he answered.

He took his coats and his fine linen, keeping only the merest necessaries, and went to Samanon, who gave him fifty francs for his whole wardrobe. He entreated the usurer to give him enough to enable him to take the diligence, but Samanon was inflexible. In his rage and disappointment, Lucien rushed, hot-foot, to Frascati's, risked the whole sum, and left without a penny. When he returned to his miserable chamber he asked Bérénice to give him a shawl of Coralie's. Something in his eyes told the kindly woman, to whom he had admitted his loss at play, the thought that was in his mind, — he meant to hang himself.

"Are you mad, monsieur?" she said. "Go and walk about the streets and come back at midnight; I will earn your money; but don't go near the quays!"

Lucien went, as he was told, and walked about the boulevards, stupid with grief, gazing at the equipages, at the pedestrians, — feeling himself an atom, alone, in that great crowd whirled onward by the lash of a thousand self-interests. His thoughts went back to the shores of the Charente; he felt a thirst for family joys; a flash of strength, such as often deceives these feminine natures, came to him; he would not give up the game without discharging his heart into the heart of David Séchard, and taking counsel with the three angels who remained to him. As he walked idly through the streets he noticed Bérénice, dressed in her best, standing talking to a man at the muddy corner of the Boulevard Bonne-Nouvelle.

"What are you doing?" Lucien said to her, struck by a horrible suspicion.

"There are your twenty francs," she said, putting the money in his hand; "they may cost dear, but they will take you home."

She disappeared before Lucien could see which way she went. It must be said to his credit that the money burned his hand and he wished to return it; but he was forced to keep it as a last stigma of his life in Paris.

On the morrow Lucien obtained his passport, bought a holly stick, and got into a public conveyance on the place de la rue d'Enfer, which took him for ten sous to Lonjumeau. The first night he slept in the stable of a farmhouse six miles beyond Arpajon. When he reached Orléans he was very weary and almost worn-out; but a boatman took him for three francs down the river to Tours, during which trip he spent two francs for food. It took him five days to walk from Tours to Poitiers. Beyond Poitiers he had only five francs left; still, he collected all his strength, and continued his way. Overtaken by night, he resolved to bivouac by the roadside, when he saw a carriage mounting the hill behind him. Unseen by the postilion, the travellers, or the footman, who was sitting on the box, he was able to get on behind between two trunks, which protected him from being jolted off and enabled him to sleep.

Awakened by the sun, which struck his eyes, and by the sound of voices, he recognized Mansle, the little town where, eighteen months earlier, he had gone with David to await Madame de Bargeton, his heart full of love and hope and joy. Seeing himself covered with dust and surrounded by an inquisitive crowd of postilions and others, he was aware that his position was suspicious. He jumped to the ground, and was about to speak when the sight of the travellers getting out of their carriage stopped the words in his throat. They were the new prefect of the Charente, Comte Sixte du Châtelet, and his wife, Louise de Bargeton.

"If we had only known of the companion whom accident has given to us!" said the countess. "Pray get in with us, monsieur!"

Lucien bowed coldly to the couple, with a glance both humble and threatening. He turned abruptly into a cross road, and went to a farmhouse, where he obtained a breakfast of bread and milk, and could rest and deliberate in silence on his future. But not for long. He had only three francs left; and the author of the "Daisies," driven by the fever within him, again pushed on. He walked along the banks of the river, examining the scenery, which grew more and more picturesque. At last, about mid-day, he came upon a sheet of water overhung with willows, and forming a tiny lake. He stopped to contemplate the cool and shady grove and peaceful water, the rural charm of which affected his soul.

A house, close to a mill on an arm of the river, showed its thatched roof covered with sedum among the trees. The simple front of the little building was overrun with jessamine, honeysuckle, and the wild hop; all about it were the brilliant flowers of the phlox, and splendid plants of a succulent nature. Ducks were swimming in a pond of transparent water between two currents which sent the water humming through the sluices. The mill-wheel made a clacking sound. Seated on a rustic bench before the house, Lucien saw a stout and cheery housewife knitting, and watching a child that was teasing the chickens.

"My good woman," said Lucien, coming forward, "I am very tired; I am fevered; I have but three francs; would you feed me on bread and milk and let me sleep in the barn for a week? I want time to write to my friends, and they will send me money, or come and fetch me here."

"To be sure I will," she said, "if my husband will let me. Hey! little man!"

The miller came out, looked at Lucien, and took his pipe out of his mouth to say: "Three francs, one week! we might as well take you for nothing."

"Perhaps I shall end as a miller's drudge!" thought the poet, looking at the exquisite scenery before he lay down on the bed the goodwife made for him, where he slept a sleep that frightened his hosts.

"Courtois, go and see if that young man is dead or living. It is fourteen hours since he went to sleep, and I am afraid to look," said the miller's wife about ten o'clock of the next day.

"I think," said the miller, as he finished spreading his nets to catch some fish, — "I think that pretty fellow is probably some slip of an actor not worth a groat!"

"What makes you think that, little man?" asked his wife.

"Damn it! he isn't a prince, nor a minister, nor a deputy, nor a bishop! then why are his hands as white as those of a man who does nothing?"

"It is very surprising that hunger doesn't wake him up," said the miller's wife, who was getting some breakfast ready for the guest whom chance had sent her. "An actor!" she went on. "Goodness! where can he be going? There is no fair at Angoulême just now."

Neither the miller nor his wife had any notion that besides the actor, prince, and bishop, there is another man, both prince and actor, a man clothed with a glorious priesthood, — a Poet, who seems to have nothing to do, but who reigns above the humanity whom it is his mission to reveal.

"I don't know what else he can be," said Courtois.

"Do you think there is any danger in keeping him?"

"Pooh! thieves don't sleep like that; we should have been robbed hours ago."

"I am neither a prince, nor a thief, nor a bishop, nor an actor," said Lucien sadly, coming into the room, through the window of which he had doubtless heard the colloquy between husband and wife. "I am a poor, weary man; I walked from Paris here. My name is Lucien de Rubempré, the son of Monsieur Chardon, the predecessor of Postel, the apothecary at l'Houmeau. My sister is married to David Séchard, printer, on the place du Mûrier, Angoulême."

"Look here!" said the miller; "isn't that printer the son of the old fox who lives at Marsac?"

"Yes," replied Lucien.

"A queer kind of father he is!" continued Courtois. "He has let his son be ruined, they say, and all his goods sold, when the old wretch has two hundred thousand francs in property, not to speak of the cash he's got hid away somewhere!"

When body and soul have both been broken in a long and painful struggle, the moment when their strength gives way is followed either by death or by a collapse of life resembling death, but from which those natures which are capable of resistance find strength to rise. Lucien, who was in a crisis of this sort, seemed about to succumb altogether when he heard this news, vague as it was, of a catastrophe having happened to David Séchard, his brother-in-law.

" Oh, sister ! " he cried, " what have I done ? My God ! I am a wicked man ! "

He fell upon a wooden bench, pale as death and nerveless. The goodwife brought him a cup of milk, which she forced him to drink ; but he begged the miller to help him to his bed, for he thought his last hour had come. With the phantom of Death before his eyes, his poetic mind was seized with religious thoughts. He asked to see a priest, that he might confess himself and receive the sacraments. Such expressions, uttered in the feeble voice of a handsome youth, touched Madame Courtois deeply.

" Look here, little man ! " she said to her husband, " get on your horse and go and fetch Monsieur Marron, the doctor at Marsac ; he'll find out what's the matter with that young man, who seems to me in a bad way ; and perhaps you can bring back the vicar. I dare say they'll know more than you do about that printer in Angoulême, for you know Postel is Monsieur Marron's son-in-law."

Courtois departed. His wife, imbued, like all country folk, with the idea that sick people must eat, gave Lucien food. He took no notice of her, but abandoned himself wholly to a passionate remorse, which brought him out of his previous depression by the revulsion caused by that moral blister.

The Courtois mill is about three miles from Marsac, which is the market town of the canton, half way between Mansle and Angoulême ; therefore the good miller soon returned with the doctor and the priest. These persons had heard of Lucien's intimacy with Madame de Bargeton ; and as the whole department of the Charente was talking at this moment about the marriage of that lady and her return to Angoulême with her husband, the new prefect, Comte Sixte du Châtelet, when the worthy pair found that Lucien was at the miller's house, they naturally felt inquisitive to discover why the widow of Monsieur de Bargeton had not married the young man she had taken away with her, and whether he had now come back to help his brother-in-law, David Séchard. Curiosity as well as humanity brought them at once to Lucien's assistance. Consequently, two hours after Courtois's departure, the poet heard on the cobblestone pavement round the mill the wheels of the shabby chaise of the country doctor. The two Messieurs Marron came together, — the doctor being the nephew of the priest, and both were well acquainted with the father of David Séchard.

When the doctor had examined his patient, and duly felt his pulse and looked at his tongue, he smiled at the miller's wife to dispel her uneasiness.

"Madame Courtois," he said, " I have no doubt you have some good wine in your cellar, and a good eel in your fish-pond; serve them to your patient; there is nothing the matter with him but exhaustion. When he gets over that, he'll soon be about."

"Ah, monsieur!" said Lucien, " my illness is not of the body, but the mind; and these good people told me a piece of news about the troubles that have come upon my sister, Madame Séchard, that has almost killed me. In God's name, if you know anything about David Séchard's affairs, tell me!"

"I think he is now in prison," replied the doctor. "His father has refused to help him."

"In prison!" cried Lucien. "Why!"

"For notes which he owed in Paris, and had no doubt forgotten; for he seems not to know what he is about," replied Monsieur Marron.

"Leave me, I beg of you, with monsieur le curé," said Lucien, whose face changed visibly.

The doctor, with the miller and his wife, left the room. When Lucien was alone with the old priest, he cried out vehemently: "I deserve the death I feel approaching, monsieur. I am a wretch who can only fling himself into the arms of religion. It is I, monsieur, I, who am the torturer of my sister and brother; for David Séchard has been a brother to me. I drew the notes which David has not been able to pay. I have ruined him. In the horrible distress to which I have been brought, I forgot this crime. When I was sued for the money in Paris by the man who cashed the notes, I thought it was paid by a rich man, a millionnaire, to whom I appealed; but it seems now as if he did nothing about it."

Lucien then related all his troubles. When he had ended his poem, with a feverish apostrophe truly worthy of a poet, he entreated the priest to go to Angoulême and make inquiries of his sister, Eve, and his mother, Madame Chardon, as to the actual state of things, that he might know if there were any possibility of remedying them.

"Until your return, monsieur," he said, weeping hot tears, "I shall live. If my mother, if my sister, if David, do not repulse me, I shall not die."

The eloquence of the youth, the tears of this startling repentance, the sight of that pale and handsome face half-dying with despair, the tale of these misfortunes which were greater than human strength could bear, excited the pity and the interest of the priest.

"In the provinces as in Paris, monsieur," he said, "we must never believe more than half we hear. Do not be too alarmed by news which, at this distance from Angoulême, may be quite erroneous. Old Séchard, our neighbor at Marsac, has lately gone to Angoulême, probably to settle his son's affairs. I will myself go there, and then return here and let you know whether your family, after your confession and repentance, which will help me to plead your cause, will receive you."

The priest did not know that for the last eighteen months Lucien had repented so often that his repentance, violent as it was, had no other value than that of a scene admirably played, and still played in absolute good faith.

[We already know of the return of the prodigal brother, the further injuries he did his family, his effort at suicide, and his meeting with the so-called abbé, Don Carlos Herrera.[1]] The rest of Lucien's history belongs to the domain of the "Scenes from Parisian Life."

[1] Lost Illusions.   Eve and David.

THE END.

www.ingramcontent.com/pod-product-compliance
Lightning Source LLC
Chambersburg PA
CBHW030951110726
47900CB00004B/1222